THE SERPENT SLEEPING

CLASSICS OF ESPIONAGE

General Editor: Wesley K. Wark

Other titles in the Series

EDWARD WEISMILLER

THE SERPENT SLEEPING

With an Introduction by
Timothy Naftali

FRANK CASS
LONDON • PORTLAND, OR.

First Published in 1962 by G.P. Putnam's Sons, New York
This edition first published in 1998 in Great Britain by
FRANK CASS PUBLISHERS
2 Park Square, Milton Park,
Abingdon, Oxon, OX14 4RN

and in the United States of America by
FRANK CASS PUBLISHERS
270 Madison Ave,
New York NY 10016

Transferred to Digital Printing 2005

Website http://www.frankcass.com

Copyright © Edward Weismiller
Introduction Copyright © 1998 Timothy Naftali

British Library Cataloguing in Publication Data
A catalogue record for this book is available
from the British Library

ISBN 0-7146-4729-2 (cloth)
ISBN 0-7146-4279-7 (paper)

Library of Congress Cataloging-in-Publication Data
A catalog record for this book is available
from the Library of Congress

For my children and their children

The original publisher's pagination has been maintained.
Part One therefore begins on page 9.

CONTENTS

INTRODUCTION

THE SERPENT SLEEPING is a profoundly moving account of American innocence coming of age in World War II. Set in the busy channel port of Cherbourg eight weeks after its liberation, *The Serpent Sleeping* follows Johnny Phillips, a callow American counterespionage officer, on a search for a French traitor. This is Phillips's first big investigation and he is beset by doubts about his own abilities and the murky politics of the case. The book's deceptively simple plot eventually confronts the reader with the harsh realities of the world of counterespionage. The uncertainties and moral dilemmas of spycatching come alive as they eat into Phillips's own soul.

Written by a young American who, like Johnny Phillips, faced the unfamiliar task of detecting treason in France in 1944, the novel, though not a roman à clef, is a meticulous evocation of a peculiar time and place. Born in 1915, the author Edward Weismiller grew up on farms in Wisconsin and Vermont. Publishing his first book of poems when he was a junior in college, Weismiller quickly demonstrated a distinctive voice. His *The Deer Come Down*, with a preface by Stephen Vincent Benét, appeared in 1936 in the Yale Series of Younger Poets. An extended stay in Europe soon followed. Elected a Rhodes Scholar in 1938, Weismiller spent a glorious year at Merton College, Oxford. Taking the opportunity to travel extensively in France and Italy, he considered himself 'a young man leading a lucky life'. At that point in his life a quiet future of poetry, scholarship and good conversation seemed his probable destiny.

The Second World War altered the course of Weismiller's life. It interrupted his traditional academic apprenticeship and enrolled him instead in a secret world of spies and counterspies. At Harvard on a graduate fellowship, Weismiller was recruited in the spring of 1943 through his brother-in-law, Westbrook Steele, for the colourful

William J. Donovan's Office of Strategic Services (OSS). Steele was executive director of the Institute of Paper Chemistry in Appleton, Wisconsin, which produced secret inks for the OSS and helped the fledgling US intelligence agency develop the techniques for forging documents. Steele was friendly with the acting chief of the OSS's counterespionage division, who was looking for young men with foreign languages and good brains. Weismiller, whose French was very good, was a suitable candidate.

As one of the first officers of the highly secret counterespionage organization called X-2, Weismiller was brought into the OSS not to forge documents but to learn how to forge other people's lives. By late 1943 Weismiller found himself at the centre of a remarkable experiment in allied cooperation initiated by the British. Ever suspicious of US security, and with the Allied invasion of North Africa looming in 1942, the British had encouraged the formation of a counterespionage unit within OSS. They offered to train its members. More importantly the British at the same time offered to share their most secret information on German espionage with this new group. Since 1940 British code and cipher specialists had been able to read the transmissions of the Abwehr, the German military's intelligence service. More commonly known as ULTRA information, this signals intelligence gave counterespionage services an unprecedented advantage over their adversary. Usually resigned to working with flawed, fragmentary or false information, counterspies found that with ULTRA they could plot the movements and assess the activities of German agents throughout Western Europe.

Having crossed the Atlantic on the *Queen Mary* in late 1943, Weismiller learned the ULTRA secret in London, where he became the first American trained by the British to operate double agents in France. Welcomed into the headquarters of both MI6, the British foreign intelligence service and MI5, the imperial security service, Weismiller spent the spring of 1944 poring over the records of the British double cross system, a network of enemy agents who after their capture had been 'turned' against Berlin by British security.

The British were especially proud of the case of a Spaniard named Juan Pujol, alias GARBO. Since offering himself to the British in 1942, GARBO had created a notional network of twenty-seven agents who regularly fed misinformation to the Abwehr. The genius of GARBO and his British case officer consisted in the intricate and self-contained lives that they created for each of these non-existent agents. Among this cast there was a German-Swiss businessman who lived in the town of Bootle; a Venezuelan who watched marine traffic on the Clyde from a perch in Glasgow; and finally a Communist who thought that his material was being sent to Moscow. All had been invented and, it seemed, the Germans believed what they were getting from all of them. GARBO was so successful that the order of battle figures he presented appeared in the situation reports of the Fremde Heere West, the department of the German General Staff that analyzed the Western armies. At the time that Weismiller was reading his file, GARBO was transmitting five to six messages a day to his control officer in Madrid and was an integral part of the Allied program to deceive the Nazis as to the place and time of the D-Day invasion of the Continent.

Not only did Weismiller see the magnificent British security machine in action, but he was to play a central role in the successful American attempt at emulation. In the summer of 1944 the twenty-nine-year-old Weismiller studied the interrogation report of an enemy agent in Cherbourg. The Americans had captured Juan Frutos, a Spanish national, with his mistress in the first days after the Allied liberation of the port. First recruited by German intelligence in 1940, Frutos was selected, in 1944, to stay behind in Cherbourg in the event the Allies invaded Normandy. Armed with a radio set and some money, Frutos was expected to contact his German control officer in the event the Allied assault forced the Germans to abandon Cherbourg. In the months during which Frutos awaited the start of his mission, Weismiller followed ULTRA descriptions of Frutos and the other hundred German agents left behind at strategic points in France. In these intercepted messages the number and often the code-names of these men were listed; however their real names were hidden. Frutos, for example, appeared in the messages under the pseudonym 'John Eikins'. While Weismiller prepared himself to run his first double agent, other X-2 officers worked with US and French military security to track down these men and give faces to these pseudonyms.

Because Juan Frutos was the first of the German stay-behind agents to be caught in an American sector, the as-yet-untested Weismiller was at the centre of the debate over whether or not to use this man as a double agent. When the first interrogation reports reached

London, Weismiller feared that Frutos was incorrigible. With ULTRA information about 'Eikens' and solid evidence that 'Eikins' was Frutos, Weismiller had an easy time picking out when the agent was lying. And Frutos seemed a congenital liar. Although Frutos admitted his mission to report on the Allies after the Germans left the port, he did not admit to his long relationship with Nazi intelligence, which the Allies already knew about from ULTRA. The Frutos case now required a risky judgement to be made. The case confronted its handlers, as so often in the realm of counter-espionage, with the problem of reading human psychology under stress. Weismiller concluded that if the agent continued to lie, the agent would be untrustworthy and unusable.

The Frutos case put flesh and blood on the aesthetics of double agency. Weismiller's July 1944 recommendation that Allied counter-espionage not risk running Juan Frutos was rejected. A group of X-2 field officers believed the Spaniard could be a useful double agent. Meeting Frutos when he finally crossed over into France later that month, Weismiller understood his mistake, 'he is not an evil man, but he is weak,' Weismiller wrote back to London. 'Like many small men, he lives his life for present benefit, present well-being,' Weismiller explained. With the war nearly won, a man like Frutos, who despite a talent for languages had no trade or profession other than spying, knew which side to back. 'Fortunately for the operation,' Weismiller believed, 'the future of the war is at last crystal clear.'

This Spaniard became Weismiller's first double agent. For the next eight months Weismiller prepared Frutos' messages and managed Frutos' moods. In Weismiller's eyes Frutos, whom he codenamed DRAGOMAN, acquired a certain dignity and became a key player in X-2's double agent network. Later, captured German documents confirmed what Weismiller came to realize once he got to know Frutos: his 'trust' in the man had not been betrayed.

Weismiller developed into one of America's principal experts on running double agents. Between July 1944 and March 1945 X-2 officers established a double cross system of their own in France and Germany. Young Americans, many in their early twenties, found themselves responsible for handling German agents caught with radio sets. Nearly two-dozen such agents operated under US control. Helpless and needy, the German spymasters at headquarters seemed to accept what they received, sending money and supplies to 'their' agents in Normandy, Paris and along the Riviera. After nine months in Cherbourg, Weismiller left for Paris in the spring of 1945 to become X-2's Special Case Officer, with supervisory responsibility for the entire American network. Compiling a weekly report on all of the activities of the network for Washington, Edward Weismiller saw how these double agents could turn a foreign intelligence service inside-out, converting it into an instrument of self-destruction.

The experience of counterespionage was to shape the men and women of X-2 in different ways. Some grew to love the complexity of the game and resolved never to return to the career paths they had been on before the war intervened. One of those was Weismiller's friend in London, James Angleton, who joined X-2 in 1943 and remained in counterespionage until he was forced out of the Central Intelligence Agency in 1975. Angleton served as a perceptive critic of Weismiller's poetry, performing the same role in his development as a writer that the famous John Berryman had played earlier at Harvard. Although Angleton did not transfer to Weismiller his unstinting passion for counterespionage, Weismiller shared his admiration for the revolution in counterespionage accomplished by the British.

Weismiller's first major piece of writing on counterespionage projected this confidence in the value of the endeavour. At the end of World War II, along with a future Yale English Professor Eugene Waith and a future editor at *The New York Times*, John B. Oakes, Weismiller co-authored an extensive two-volume top secret history of the use of double agents by the United States in wartime. Classified until 1991, 'A History of OSS/X-2 Operation of Controlled Enemy Agents' was the most thorough-going assessment of the value of playing agents back against their originating agency ever produced by the US government. The history was intended as a practical textbook. 'It must be remembered,' wrote Weismiller and his co-authors, 'that CEA [Controlled Enemy Agent] operations as they were conducted in France were in the nature of a pioneer experiment, at least as far as United States intelligence services are concerned; and it is the writers's hope that the lessons they learned may serve at least as a guide to the American case officers of the future.' One does not find Therese Bouliard or Estelle de Sombais in the text but there is more than a hint of Johnny Phillips.

Despite the achievements of X-2, Weismiller harboured doubts about the human costs of these games. Unlike Angleton and many others, Weismiller opted not to continue this work in peacetime. He sensed that poetry and counterespionage are incompatible and was eager to return to his first love. The poet uses words to convey a vision of truth; but the counterespionage officer has a different goal. Determined to prevent the enemy from learning the truth, the officer works to obfuscate, discourage and deceive. Words are a weapon in this war as valuable as the M1 rifle that Weismiller had learned to fire.

Besides the discomfort created by the essential dishonesty of double agency, Weismiller was troubled by the basic flaws in counterespionage itself. A decade and a half after completing the secret history, Weismiller finished a public statement on counterespionage. *The Serpent Sleeping* drew upon his less heroic recollections of spycatching. Without ever writing a word about Juan Frutos, Weismiller, subconsciously perhaps, used the novel to contend with the doubts he had as a counterespionage officer. The 600 men and women of X-2 had been told never to keep diaries and it was understood that they would have to take the secrets of ULTRA and double cross to their graves. What moved Weismiller to lift a corner of the blanket over that period of his life was his revulsion at the attitudes of some of the men he had met in wartime counterespionage. Weismiller recoiled at the indifference with which they wielded power over the powerless. The ease with which they tossed around the concepts of treason, spying and deception was deeply troubling. Weismiller left the war with a desire to explain betrayal as he had known it. Spies were not insects, they were human beings; what made them especially human were their manifest weaknesses. These watchers in the shadows were rarely evil. Some had succumbed to the temptation to live double lives, some were moved by ideas, some by money. Others were the prisoners of fear, trapped by the Germans. There was nothing particularly noble about spies, particularly those who had collaborated willingly with the Nazis. But espionage did not inevitably strip them of their humanity.

In *The Serpent Sleeping* the main characters debate the trustworthiness of the French citizens whom they meet. The author of these passages is a Weismiller tempered by the realities of liberated France, not the student of treason in London. The counterintelligence officers who worked in liberated France held two opinions at the same time. France was a virtuous nation for having resisted the Germans;

but suspicion surrounded individual Frenchmen and women who were all guilty of collaboration unless proven innocent. Weismiller implicitly criticizes those around him in X-2 who treated the loyalty or credibility of individual Frenchmen as a bloodless puzzle. Johnny Phillips observes at one point in the novel that counterespionage specialists 'were too used to complexity ... and, inevitably ... they lost the human meaning of every fact they dealt with.'

The Serpent Sleeping, published in 1962, is the most famous of what could be called the X-2 novels. Gordon Merrick's The Strumpet Wind, a more straightforward operational memoir, caused a stir in the old boy network when it appeared in 1951. Nearly twenty years before the British would allow their men to write openly about the wartime practice of turning enemy agents and using them to feed Berlin disinformation, Merrick described his own double agent operation in Southern France, the case of FOREST. Merrick's book was not the first to be written by an X-2 veteran however. That distinction belongs to Ricardo Sicre's A Tap on the Left Shoulder. Sicre's book was primarily a political novel and not a spy thriller. Angered by America's abandonment of the Spanish Republican cause at the end of the Second World War, Sicre spun the story of a young man wrongly accused of Communist sympathies who struggled with French and American ignorance in the borderlands of the Pyrenees to free Spain from Franco's grasp.

Weismiller was the first and only American counterespionage veteran to transform a good spy story into something larger: a meditation on trust and humanity. The result is this classic rendering of the little understood art of counterespionage on a canvas of the frailties of mankind. We are the sleeping serpent that in John Milton's words plays host to the devil. When not vigilant, we lose sight of our own humanity. Years before James Angleton's downfall made the perils of counterespionage the subject of press discussion, a fellow X-2 veteran used a single, fictional case in a French port to make the same point.

MAY 1997   TIMOTHY NAFTALI

Sunday,
August 27, 1944

I.

A faded Calvados sign leaned forward in the blind window of the café. Though the sign might be left over from another time, a world closed like a theatre, *There may be someone there*, Thérèse thought. She leaped from her bicycle, dropped it in a clatter against the wall, ran to the café door and pushed against it with all her strength. It opened easily.

The net curtain at the window puffed like a sail as she passed, and the sign fell. Thérèse did not pick it up. She crossed stumbling to a bare table in the dim far corner of the room and sank into a chair with her back to the door.

The proprietress had stood up as she entered, and now, black-dressed and soundless, was standing beside her. Thérèse clutched at the edge of the table with stiff fingers and closed her eyes. "A Calvados," she said, trying to keep her voice steady. And then, "A—a small glass?"

The old woman stood without moving for what seemed minutes. At last her footsteps creaked away, making more sound now, or was it only that the blood was not pounding so heavily in Thérèse's ears? The woman was gone a long time, and as Thérèse sat there alone she felt less and less upset, more composed, almost calm, though she still trembled.

A glass clinked on the table in front of her, and an opaque purple-red liquid began to pour into it, rising slowly and as though reluctantly, stopping halfway to the brim. Thérèse looked up uncomprehending. The old woman had a smile on her face, a smile impersonal yet kind. "I thought—a little wine," she said. "In that there is quite enough courage. And I have brought bread, and there will be something else in a moment. You are hungry?"

Thérèse thought: To be able to be proud now. Or angry, at

something, at that soldier— Or merely silent, distant. She felt herself beginning to dissolve, and managed to say in an objective voice, only slightly too loudly, "Thank you, madame, but as it happens I have no money with me—only a little—" Why had she not said simply that she wasn't hungry?

The old woman shrugged. "I think you are just returning to Cherbourg. Is it not so? Many come back now. In ones and twos. Eh—" She sighed, and stared out toward the street. "I find it sad."

Unexpectedly a young, deep voice, a man's voice, sounded firmly from a back room. "Tante Hélène, it is *not sad*. It is *good*. Would you prefer them not to come back? It must begin again, must it not? How often . . . ?"

The old woman was smiling once more. "Yes, yes," she said, hardly raising her voice. "You do not know at all what I mean, Jules, and you must not interrupt. It is only"—she turned again to Thérèse—"that this city . . ." She made a vague gesture of the hand. "But they say others are worse. Coutances, did you come through Coutances?"

Thérèse nodded; and there flashed into her mind a single picture, the skeleton of a cow draped high in a tree at a crossroad outside Coutances, like a great torn cloth stretched on a bush to dry, and then forgotten. Of the city itself she remembered nothing. A cathedral? On a steep hill? And around its base perhaps drifts of wreckage. In some meadow there had been burned-out tanks, squatting like huge barnyard fowl. . . . She too sighed, and looked helplessly at the old woman.

"In any case, I was going to say only that one knows the inconvenience of the times," the woman said gently. "All so confused. You will pay me back: there will be plenty of opportunity, and you will not forget the place. Now. A little morsel, after your trip?"

"Thank you, madame," said Thérèse, and felt behind her eyes the tears massing.

It was not strange, she thought, that the woman had guessed her situation. She was grimed with the dust of the road; she had slept in stables for the last two nights, and her dress hung shapeless and soiled. She could feel the deep disarray of her hair. But the odd, wild way she had entered—surely that had not escaped notice? What had the woman thought? She had said something about courage. . . .

Thérèse took a sip of her wine, then shakily brushed a strand of hair back from her eyes. Why had she been so upset? It had been a foolish incident only. She had just reached the top of the hill behind Cherbourg, on the road that leads from Octeville down into the city, and on an impulse had stopped, had wheeled her bicycle up onto the grassy shoulder and let it sprawl there while she looked out through a gap blown in the hedge, over the towers of Notre Dame du Voeu and across the huddled buildings of the town to the harbor and the sea.

In spite of the clearness of the late August sun the view was not beautiful exactly. Nor had familiarity endeared it to Thérèse. She could not even see Equeurdreville, the suburb off to the left where she had lived until just before the invasion a few months ago. There was no reason to stop except—except that the road was all downhill the rest of the way. She stared out over the town and the harbor.

The sea, she thought, the sea is always beautiful.

At the water's edge she saw the Arsenal to the west, and the Gare Maritime to the east, lying in gigantic if expected ruin. Otherwise, except for a single building here and there, the city appeared to stand as before. Only it seemed to have sagged slightly, to have settled a little into the ground, like the leaves in a hollow at the end of winter.

A truck convoy had started to come in behind her; it was not at all the first of her journey, but the pounding of the tires was so close that she could not help turning to watch. All at once a jeep pulled out of the stream of traffic and came to an instantaneous stop in front of her. She remembered once having seen an American Western movie; the horses had stopped like that. She almost smiled as she glanced up. A young—officer?—with a thin, pink face was looking at her with a harassed expression.

"What'cha wanta stop for, Lieutenant?" someone in the back seat asked. "She ain't good-lookin'."

"Shut up," said the lieutenant, and the loud laughter stopped. He twisted around a little in his seat. "Say, doesn't one of you Joes know French, or something?"

There was a silence. "I know something," said the soldier who had spoken first, "but it's the same in any language, and this ain't it."

"God, Peterson, you're wise," said the lieutenant. He looked back at Thérèse. "Damn it," he said, "then I guess it's me that speaks a little French. *Mademoiselle.*" His voice rose.

Was she a commodity, that they talked so? "It is not necessary," Thérèse had said. "I speak English."

There was an outbreak of nudgings in the back seat of the jeep, and someone guffawed.

The lieutenant exploded into anger. "Well, can't you follow signs, then? Or didn't that MP back there tell you to turn off? This road's for military vehicles only. You're liable to get hurt, or cause an accident, the way these boys roll down here."

She had said, "I am sorry. This has been the way we take. No one showed me any other."

"I oughta look at your papers," the lieutenant said sourly.

Automatically she had reached out toward the bundle that was strapped onto the handlebars of her bicycle.

"Ah, nuts," said the lieutenant. "I wouldn't know if they were any good if you did show 'em to me."

There was a loud blaring of horns. The Negro driver of a six-by-six had swung in behind the lieutenant's jeep; traffic had tied up behind him. "Listen," the lieutenant said quickly to Thérèse, "you going down into town?"

She had nodded reluctantly.

"O.K.," he said. "Go ahead of me, and I'll see you're all right. Don't turn off until I say you can. Hear? Traffic in town's routed too. I'll sound my horn twice. Will you get going now, please?" He made an imperious gesture with his hand; the driver gunned the motor of the jeep.

Thérèse had looked at him evenly. Then she had said "I am sorry" again, turned and picked up her bicycle, steadied it and mounted. In a moment, without a backward glance, she had turned out into the road and was coasting with increasing speed downhill. She could hear the jeep following her, close behind.

And in a moment more, the ugly wall of the cemetery had risen to her left.

Had she forgotten that this way would take her . . . ? No.

Only, she had refused to remember. Now she had cried out silently *I am not ready.* . . . The wall dipped inexorably to reveal the ranks of gravestones on the hill behind; curved; rose again (but it was too late); ran on and on. The graveyard. Sacred land. The sacred land of France. . . . At last a street opened to the left, and in wild escape she had swung across in front of the jeep, into the narrow entry, bumping up onto the sidewalk to avoid the barrier that blocked the street off to traffic.

Someone was shouting behind her, and the jeep's horn brayed loudly, but she would not look back. Would they follow, those men? She had seen the café; she had needed it to afford her safety, a few moments' rest. Now in her ears a voice said, "Don't turn off until I say you can. Hear?" Gravestones gave her their false, their paradisal smile. And to her shame the stones, the lieutenant's voice, were in spite of all she could do shouldered out of the way by another voice jeering "What'cha wanta stop for? She ain't good-lookin'."

Her new life.

She was in Cherbourg. Now she would have to decide.

Decide what? She took another sip of the wine, and felt it blur and shiver in her veins. She was too tired, almost, to remember.

The old woman came back with a plate of some kind of stew; Thérèse smiled humbly at her and ate, hardly knowing what the tastes were. But they were good. The woman sat down in the opposite corner again and picked up her work—a black sweater that she was raveling, rolling the crimped yarn into a ball.

Suddenly the scraping of a chair sounded from the back room of the café, and footsteps moved, half dragged, across the floor. Thérèse looked up. A young man was standing in the archway between the rooms, smiling down at her.

"So," he said. "I have fixed it, Tante Hélène. Now bring me a Calvados, will you? And more—wine for the girl here." He sank down into the nearest chair, across the table from Thérèse. "You will permit me?" he asked.

"Jules." The old woman's voice was heavy. "Let her alone. She has enough to trouble her."

"But I am not going to trouble her! I am her friend!—a friend of all young ladies. Young ladies know this, and so, I am sure, does she." He grinned cheerfully at Thérèse. "Is it not so? You must tell my aunt. She is so kind of heart that it makes her foolish."

Thérèse felt an impulse to respond, but no words came. She managed a quick, crumbling smile, and then dropped her eyes away, to the bare wood floor.

The old woman brought a small tumbler of a yellowish liquid to her nephew, who sipped and swore. "Agh! it will take years . . . ! Mademoiselle?"

Thérèse looked up again.

"Is it true, what Tante Hélène supposed? You are just returning to Cherbourg?"

With difficulty she said, "Yes."

In her ears there sounded a harsh voice she would have forgotten if she could: the voice of Mme. Corrail. *So—they permit one to travel, the magnanimous Americans! Now every day that you do not return to Cherbourg is a day you must expect part of the little that remains to you to be stolen. . . .*

The young man was looking at her with a direct, approving expression on his face. "I too have just returned," he said. "I have been away for a long time." He raised his glass. "To—our coming back."

Tears blinded her, but tears of weakness, of weariness, surely; tears that had to do perhaps with the few sips of wine she had drunk before she had eaten. For she had ceased days, weeks ago, to shed tears over her father, and what else was there to weep for? The dog, the mean-faced, suffering little dog? No.

"Jules!" the old woman exclaimed indignantly. "Now see. Be glad you are back, yes, every moment, as I am; but how do you know what *she* comes back to? Have the grace to be silent."

The young man's voice, when it resumed, was incorrigibly tranquil. "She comes back to marry a miserly old farmer who owns all the butter in Normandy, but now she sees how handsome I am, in spite of the limp, and she will marry me instead. Is it not so, mademoiselle?"

"*Jules!*"

Thérèse would have laughed if she had not been involved

16

still with the tears. But in a moment she had forced them back. She wished she too could make a joke, or simply say something matter-of-fact, think something matter-of-fact. After a silence during which the young man regarded her with friendly calm, she brought out, "I come back—mostly, I suppose, to work. To attend to a house."

"Your own? You are not a servant."

"No, I—" she said. "Or yes. I do not—know what I am."

"Ah, that is so with me also," he said quickly. "But there is the work." For a moment his eyes searched her face. Then he went on. "Think how it would be if you had nothing to do."

"Will I be stronger, m'sieur," she said quietly, "if you can make me say that I agree? In fact, some tasks are not so pleasant as others. All the same I will not complain."

He gave her a wry smile. "Mademoiselle, I do not mean to make great speeches. Nor play the hero. Work is I suppose needful to me, because it exacts my attention. It helps me not to think. And when I do not use my mind, then it heals. . . ."

She had been looking at him, but now she turned her head away.

He said hastily, "Though if the work were upon the edges of the wound . . ."

Grief pressed toward her again, and she stared at the tables of the café, all empty: if there were others here, this one young man and what he said would not seem so—fateful. But she could turn the conversation. With effort. Have many come back? she could ask, or Were you a prisoner? . . . His voice said in her mind, *You are not a servant. I was not a prisoner.*

Unreasonably, she felt something like anger.

"Mademoiselle, forgive me." His face was, she saw, gentle, and recovering its smile. "Truly the solution is that you must marry; do you not see? Not, of course, the miserly old farmer. But if you choose the right man, then he will do easily such things as might be painful for you to do; and you—here in Cherbourg you too will have work enough, I assure you!"

You will marry? Mme. Corrail had asked. *You are not too fine? Too fine!*

All at once she wished to hear no more, to talk no more, well-intentioned as the young man was, or seemed. She was at the end of her strength; and thinking made it worse, talking or trying to respond when she had talked so little for so many weeks was impossible.

"I shall think about what you say," she said, in a voice she could not make light. She rose. "Now it is time for me to go on."

The old woman burst out, "You drive her away, Jules. With your moralizing, and your foolish jokes."

"No, no." Thérèse turned toward her benefactress. "But it is getting later. . . ."

"Yes. Why do you not stay the night, mademoiselle? I shall make Jules be silent. There is"—her voice took on a heavy dryness—"more work, for example."

How without being rude . . . ? She walked to the window, looked out, and to her relief saw that there was still much light left in the sky. "Perhaps in an hour or so I will come again," she said. And then, feelingly, "You are very kind."

As she walked back toward the tables the young man rose awkwardly to his feet and stretched his hand out to her, his expression abashed. "Let me say one more thing."

The old woman said, in a rising tone, "Jules, I tell you, you talk too much."

He hesitated. "You do not give me time to talk only a little! Either of you! Mademoiselle . . ."

"Yes."

"You spoke of a house, but—not of any person. If this means that you are alone; forgive me, I know I am clumsy; and—if later you think that you need help, or would like it; I should be glad if I could be of use to you." He regarded Thérèse with a gaze that was honest and warm. "Now goodbye. And—thank you for coming back."

"It is I who—must thank you." She shook her head. It should have ended by now. "I do not understand."

The young man cast a quick glance at the old woman, who stood there with her hands folded, disapproval on her face. "Tante Hélène will say I am sermonizing again. At least I am not making foolish jokes!"

Indeed, though he spoke hurriedly, his voice had become deeply serious. "I mean only—well, that a city is a kind of— agreement, is it not? Even a kind of faith. And to come back is then to keep faith. I knew men who would say, I shall not go back to such and such a place, there is nothing for me there. Or: I shall not go back, it would only be painful. . . . I could not understand them. Cherbourg is my city, and I want to spend the rest of my life here. This I can do because—people come back—to do I do not know what, but what must be done."

He shrugged, and looked at her almost obstinately. "Do you see? I mean my thanks. And maybe, yes I hope, that my return helps you too."

Unable to speak Thérèse nodded, and turned to the old woman. "I thank you both—more than I can say, madame," she brought out. "And I will come to pay you as soon as—" She stopped. "I have a few francs now . . ."

The old woman made a decisive gesture of refusal. "But tonight?" she asked. "You have not said you have other—"

"Thank you. I shall see, madame. And now *au revoir*."

The old woman reached out a staying hand. "Listen," she said, "you must not— Agh, I do not talk well. But when you come back I will tell you what was done to help me during the Occupation, with my husband dead, and Jules gone. By friends, and neighbors, and sometimes by people I did not even—"

Thérèse closed her eyes, and again nodded.

"Child, you worry me," the old woman said. "But *au revoir*. Jules and I are here."

Wordlessly Thérèse smiled, turned, and walked out the door, reaching the sidewalk and sustaining the bright sidelong blow of the narrow sky before she began, a second time, to weep.

She would of course go back only when she could discharge her indebtedness; not before, to become further indebted.

Yet now Cherbourg seemed changed to her. She would have to think how, and what it meant; but in spite of her tears it had to do with courage, or the possibility of it. She had lived such a strange life in this city, she saw: five years, and she knew no one—no one at all, really, but her teacher, her beloved Mlle. Vaugiron, who had been away so long now; and a dear, majestic, silent, bitter man dead in a bombed house. Yet it was a city of thousands—many of them, certainly, good people. People in whose midst she could make some kind of life. Without help, if need be. But she could have help—would be offered it perhaps freely, on all sides. That was the revelation. Not that she needed help, or would accept it: she would earn her way.

And now what should she do? Go at once to the bombed house?

And begin, as the Corrails had so severely instructed her (knowing her, as they said) to pick through the stones for sodden, torn, but usable clothing, bits of furniture, utensils that could be salvaged, however bent and rusted they were. . . .

No, no, she thought, stopping dead in the street. Why had she come back, at all?

Because she would stay no longer with the Corrails. And granting that, what else could she have done but come back here?

She walked on, wheeling her bicycle. It was the difficulty with the past, she saw. Even if it seemed to destroy itself, it did not. What had once seemed a protecting wall, or a window, or a door, were no longer that; but still they waited, stone, splintered wood, broken glass, to be picked up. And then you had to do something with them, you could not stand holding them in your hands, in your arms.

It was more like that than an agreement, or a matter of faith.

The sharp blaring of a horn sounded almost in her ears, and there was a huge rush of metal in front of her, so close that she was forced to leap back for safety. The bicycle swerved away from her hands and nearly fell. Without noticing it she had passed another crude barrier and entered a cross street where there was traffic; she had narrowly missed being hit by a jeep. Soldiers going by stared at her; one whistled piercingly. She looked stiffly out at the street, and when it was clear for the moment, crossed. But her reverie was broken. Where was she, where was she going?

The street she had crossed had been the Rue Asselin; if she had turned left on it, that would have been her quickest way out to Equeurdreville. To the stone, the splintered wood, the broken glass that were hers.

No, she had to have a plan.

Will you get going now, please? the lieutenant said.

All the days of her journey, all the weeks before it, she had managed not to think of the actual moment when she would first touch with her hands the rubble of the house in Equeurdreville; or of the later moment when, sorting through, she would find perhaps a shoe of her father's, and would set to work, thriftily, to find its mate. . . . *No, no,* she cried in soundless outrage. *No, I do not want—*

There were men and women of the city in the street now, not only soldiers. She stopped as though to seek the gaze of her fellow townsfolk, to ask them a question she could not phrase.

I do not want my home.

Could one simply abandon a house, and everything in it?

Why not? she thought. After all, what if she too had been killed?

But then she would have to go away, surely. Otherwise one day the gendarmes would come to her, and say, "Thérèse Bouliard? What are you going to do about the house on the Rue Pasteur?" and lead her back by the hand. . . .

Let the Corrails come themselves, and take everything, even the husks of my father's life. . . .

So long as she herself had gone away.

Odd, she thought, to learn that she could live in this city, and then to learn that she would go, all in a single minute.

But she would not go without seeing her friend, her one beloved friend.

She turned north into the Rue Emmanuel Liais and stopped once more. Now it was clear to her where she must be going. From here she could be, almost without delay, at the park. She had been, sometimes, at peace in the park. . . .

No, there was nothing to be done there.

But why not? she asked herself. She could think there, and she must think. . . .

She wheeled her bicycle along slowly. And I could rest in the park, she thought. Indeed she was too near exhaustion to cycle now all across the city, across or around the Avant Port and the Bassin du Commerce, on east to the Avenue Carnot and down the Rue du Champs-de-Mars to Mlle. Vaugiron's house; even if to go there were the right thing. While after a half hour of rest, of sitting among the great, still trees . . .

She could see so well that walled, that secret haven, and at its center the quiet pond where the goldfish passed back and forth like plump waves of light beneath the shadows of the lily pads. *She must think.* Decisively, she turned her bicycle into the Rue de l'Ancien Hôtel-Dieu.

Mlle. Vaugiron had left Cherbourg, with the other teachers, sixteen months before. And though the house in the Rue du Champs-de-Mars belonged to her, there was nothing to indicate that she would already have returned to it. After all, Thérèse thought, I, with nowhere else to go, am only now returning; from less far away. And if I should go to find her, all that distance, and she were not there . . .

She was trembling with fatigue.

Precisely so: Mlle. Vaugiron must not in any event see her as she looked now, Thérèse realized. Crumpled; abject; a thing to be pitied. An object of charity. For she knew her friend. At once, selfless and loving as always, Mlle. Vaugiron would seek to give her—too much. Even if she had not enough for herself. Shelter; food; clothing; money. . . .

No. Whatever Thérèse's life was to be, she must make her own way. It was one thing to be moved because people were kind, were willing to help, and another to accept important gifts, or even invite them. When she saw her friend (she closed her eyes and bit her lip—please let it be soon!) she would have to be rested, clean, in easy command of herself. They would talk together about their experiences for precious, casual hours, as they had talked for precious, relaxed hours of the past. And then, with no dramatic goodbyes, but because she did not know what else to do, Thérèse would go away.

Meantime there was no longer anything to think about, anything to decide, for the decision had been made. Instead of turning in at the entrance of the park, Thérèse mounted her bicycle and began to cycle on out the Rue de la Bucaille toward Equeur-dreville. For if she were not to go to her friend, nor back to the café, she must go to the house on the Rue Pasteur, the bombed house. There was no way on she could accept that did not, after all, lead through it.

She would sleep there only; some one of the rooms away from

the street would, in the heat of summer, at least afford her privacy, and shelter enough.

And perhaps even, once she was there, being there would not seem so terrible. Perhaps after some days she could in spite of everything begin again. . . .

So, M'sieur Jules, she said to herself, and smiled only a little ironically. It may be that I will keep the faith after all. Perhaps that is the joke: that life makes one keep faith, whether one had felt able to or not. And no matter for the pain. Because in the end there is no other place to begin than the place where one left off.

She cycled carefully among the speeding jeeps and trucks; but soon the traffic was left behind and within a few blocks she was almost alone on the street. *My new life,* she said to herself, *I am going toward my new life.* . . . She noticed, without wishing to, a tremendous hole in the sidewalk here, an entire building empty and seized by the light there, a row of houses boarded up and sagging against improvised wooden supports. *I am not ready,* she thought, but knew she would never be ready, and tried a smile of courage, aware in spite of herself of how it felt upon her face. Perhaps, after all, a little help . . . From the young man Jules; someone. . . . *And why not? Why not accept kindness?*

It seemed that no time at all had passed before she rounded the corner and coasted down the familiar street, the empty Sunday evening street, to come to rest before what had been her house. It looked— Her eyes widened.

The remembered cascade of rubble had been cleared away, the unbroken stones piled neatly at the edge of the street. The breached wall of the neighboring house had been repaired. In her own house the furniture stood in a kind of grotesque museum orderliness, as though this were the model for a life deeply broken into, but preserving appearances before the world. And yet there was an obvious musty smell in the air, of desertion, of desolation.

Had the neighbors done this? To be of help?

Faced with those rooms she saw nothing she had expected, no scene of her past life, and all at once for that very reason she could not bear it. Tears came to her eyes and quickly she shielded her brow with her hand, though no one was watching. *I am so tired of weeping!* she thought.

At that moment a voice said gruffly, "Ma'm'selle?"

She started violently. It would be a priest; as on that evening it would be—

But it was not the priest. It was—she should have known it —an American soldier. Standing there. He should have been in a jeep, she thought, blowing the horn at her.

Only this one, she said to herself bitterly, *cannot say I do not belong here.*

He was a man older than most, middle-aged nearly; he stood silent, grinning deprecatingly, one gold tooth showing. He wore a white helmet and white puttees. She recognized him for a military policeman.

Sharply she said, "What is it?"

"Ah, hell," he said, "don't get mad. I just have to ask you if you're Thérèse Bouliard."

"I am."

Sudden shock leaped to his eyes and his mouth sagged open. He seized her arm.

She thought, *Why it—hurts,* and looked up at him. "Let go of me," she said in a dry, faint voice, and when the clutch of his fingers only tightened, "Must—must I call . . . ?"

"Say, that's a *good* idea," the MP said. "Call somebody."

She could only stare at him. Finally, in a voice breaking with humiliation and weariness, she said, "I have no—time—"

Pride and importance grew in his eyes as he returned her stare. "Miss, you got all the time in the world. You're under arrest."

Monday,
August 28, 1944

II.

The street emptied, a narrow tributary, into a square the north side of which lay open like the mouth of a stone river. Johnny Phillips consulted his map. The Place de la République. He said the words over silently to himself, shivering a little and smiling. Then he angled up toward the waterfront, where an equestrian statue—again the map came out—a statue of Napoleon rose black and glittering in the early morning sun. Most of the pavement intervening was still in shadow, and beads of water furred its stones. In contrast, the light that cut across the corner of the buildings ahead and splashed against the side of the Hôtel de Ville looked dry and garish.

In spite of the map, Johnny wasn't going anywhere in particular. It wouldn't do any harm for him to start getting his bearings, of course; they'd flown him over from England only the day before, so this was his first morning in Cherbourg. But what he really wanted was just the walk, by himself. He wanted to feel the excitement of being in France. At last he was close to the enemy, or in a place, at least, where only a little while ago the enemy had been; and he wanted—proof, almost, or a physical sign—something to confirm to him that he was going to have a job to do. A real job: not later, and somewhere else, and alone, but here in the midst of the war, and now.

He tried to brush from his mind the thought that things were not beginning well here. He had not expected to be welcomed with open arms; but yesterday it had seemed almost as though his arrival, his very presence, were an inconvenience. No one had been at the airfield waiting for him to get in; at last a driver had showed up, but had jolted him back to town with no more than a sulky word or two in answer to his questions. At Johnny's new headquarters, a narrow and dingy building that had once

27

been a hotel, the young captain in charge had given him a phony grin, squashed his hand in a split-second grip, shouted, "I'll want to talk to you later," and disappeared; Johnny had seen him thereafter only at chow, muttering in a low voice to one of the men at the other end of the table. The place had seemed generally in a state of turmoil, yet no one had taken the time to tell him what, if anything, was going on.

At last the boy they called Carl had popped out of a doorway and shoved this map into Johnny's hand, and he'd trailed off up to his room to study it. He had a room to himself; that was something.

And the map— Well, maybe things weren't so bad. Johnny whacked the paper in his hand against his leg and looked up, looked around him. A map could mean action. A busy headquarters meant, or ought to mean, something to do, sooner or later. In London they had given him reports, analyses, folders. Day after long day he had read, had read until he had ceased utterly to understand why he was reading. Everyone had read. The Rumpelstiltskins of army intelligence had spun whole suites of rooms full of paper, and still the probationers waited, as if they had always expected to wait forever. Johnny grinned. He at least had got loose. He was in France.

The statue loomed gigantic before him now, and firmly he walked over to see if there were anything carved on the plinth —to see what Napoleon had to do with Cherbourg.

J'AVAIS RESOLU

(*Have resolved? Had resolved?* Johnny asked himself. *I ought to know that. . . .*)

DE RENOUVELER
A CHERBOURG
LES MERVEILLES
DE L'EGYPTE

Oh, great, Johnny thought. And also my name is Ozymandias, King of Kings, and here I come, ready or not.

But where's the war? This one, I mean.

One or two French workmen in dark blue untidy clothing were ambling along the sidewalks or crossing the streets, and down a side alley Johnny saw a bunch of GI's burst from a doorway, swinging their mess gear and talking loudly. They turned in his direction. He stopped for a moment, involuntarily. But in a moment they had disappeared into another building and he started walking again.

A French laborer was striding jauntily toward him along the harbor front. The man half paused as Johnny approached, and smiled a tentative and ingratiating smile. Johnny glanced at him in surprise, then nodded. The laborer pulled at his beret several times, rapidly—as if he were pulling at his forelock, Johnny thought—and cleared his throat and spat daintily to one side as Johnny came abreast. Then, wiping his mouth with the back of his hand, the laborer inclined his head and said in tones at once cheerful and confiding, *"Un soldat américain. Qu'aura une cigarette pour moi?"* He peered up into Johnny's face. His breath was acid.

Delighted, Johnny laughed out loud. The old fraud, he thought—and he's had a drink already, too, early as it is. Johnny was low on cigarettes; in fact he didn't smoke much, and he wasn't sure he'd brought any with him at all.

The workman leaned forward and said a little more loudly, pointing to himself, *"Cigarette? Pour moi?"*

Johnny patted his pockets and located a flattened pack. "Sure, sure," he said. He offered the cigarettes, then took one himself. With a flourish the man drew from his pocket a box of matches —they were American, Johnny noted with increasing amusement—and lit Johnny's cigarette and then his own.

"Thank you," said Johnny. *"Merci."*

The workman nodded his head vigorously, many times, and fluttered his hands. Still nodding and bowing and puffing, he edged off, and with a last wave turned and sauntered away down the sidewalk.

They like us, Johnny thought contentedly to himself, resuming his walk. Who'd just come up to you like that in England, and . . . ? Well, of course the situation was different, people were different. But still . . .

He wished he'd been here weeks before. This was good, but it must have been really fine to ride through a newly liberated city, and be lost for awhile in that wild excitement which, all the papers said, had accompanied the first arrival of the American troops. You couldn't expect it to be the same now. The invasion had been—how many weeks before? Eleven, almost twelve. And the breakthrough a month before almost to the day. Already Paris was back in the hands of the French.

Well, the liberation wasn't over yet. The Germans were still in France, were in a sense still here in Cherbourg, or why would Johnny be here, why would the Americans be here at all?

Massive as a fortress, row after row, tier upon tier of wooden boxes stood piled high on the Place Napoléon. K RATIONS, they were marked. . . . Johnny's vision was blocked. He crossed over and walked along beside the food dump. Where at last it came to an end he found himself gazing curiously into a couple of empty drydocks that lay like huge sunken bathtubs, half filled with the pale morning light. Unsatisfied, restless, he turned again toward the water, and after a moment came to a stop at the barricade that closed off the shore area to civilians.

At once a vast, shadowy, greenish hulk, half in and half out of the water, caught his eye. Within the flat circle of the inner harbor there were three sunken ships. The biggest lay on its side like a dead waste of the sea, an island of rust and slime, blocking the entrance to the commercial port at the right.

Beyond this, across the corner of the harbor, lay the transatlantic docks, and from behind their dark mass streamed the cold early sun. Johnny's eyes, lifting, could not pick out details at once, but when they adjusted he caught his breath sharply. The docks were nothing now but mountainous ruin, cliffs and crags of desolation. Torn blocks of concrete perched on the slopes like the boulders of a shattering rock slide. Rusted iron bars as thick as a man's arm bristled everywhere from the rubble, bent crazily or snapped off.

Well, there was the war.

Johnny had seen little of what they said had happened to London, but he had fire-watched once during an air raid. That had seemed, somehow, a dream, a distorted and misplaced Fourth of July. Here the Germans had actually walked where now he was walking, had worked this monstrous destruction almost with their own hands, and left it behind as an earnest of what they meant to do to those who touched them too closely. For a moment Johnny was aware of a tightening of his breathing, of an excited, violent pulse in his chest that was almost like fear.

His gaze swung back the width of the harbor. Away to the left, on—he looked at his map—the seaplane base, the skeleton of a giant hangar stood in clear view, sagging on its buckled girders, its corrugated metal roof cocked at a frivolous angle, like a drunkard's hat. Beyond, the walls of the Arsenal enclosed what seemed no more than hills of scrap, of filthy slag. And though Johnny could see from where he stood a few American tankers and cargo vessels at anchor in the harbor, and though there were signs here and there of the repair work of American engineers, the legacy of the battle seemed overpowering and final.

He had wanted to see this. But that it had actually happened —that was something else.

Yet as he stood there leaning against the barricade, Johnny became, little by little, aware of the firmness of the stone underneath his elbows and of the sounds at his back of the purposeful awakening of a great military port in a country at war. Already jeeps and trucks crowded the streets that paralleled the waterfront; now, as he turned to look, the Negro drivers of some Ducks sauntered down past the barrier, and the first of the clumsy vehicles was soon waddling down the cement strand into the water. Over on the Quai Longlet, a crane was working.

Johnny straightened and brushed a spot of dried mud off the front of his uniform. One of the Duck drivers was singing loudly, another was cursing the singer with querulous and inventive thoroughness. Low, mysterious, a boat whistle sounded. Suddenly, just below the barrier, an army private walked past Johnny and made his way over to a half-stripped engine that stood up on blocks off the cement apron. The private grunted, got down on his back, inched his way under the engine and began to hammer lightly at some recalcitrant part.

Johnny watched him for a moment. All at once he had to say something, he didn't quite know why. He called out softly, in a friendly voice, "Hi. What're you doing?"

There was a brief silence. The private inched out from under the machine again. He sat up and looked at Johnny without smiling. "What'd you say?"

"What're you doing?" Johnny repeated.

"What I'm told," the boy said shortly, and lay down and got back under the engine.

Johnny dropped his eyes and looked with absorption at his watch, then turned and started walking, slowly, back toward headquarters. Funny. But the kid was probably just generally sore at something.

Johnny remembered the affability of the French workman and thought, That was an act.

He shook himself a little. What was he getting worked up about? The Frenchman had wanted a cigarette. All right, what the hell, Johnny thought, I'd rather look like someone who'd give a man a cigarette than someone who wouldn't. And as for the GI back there—the guy hadn't said anything so terrible, after all. He'd said only what was in fact the literal truth: he was doing what he was told. Doubtless Johnny too would, at first anyway, be doing what he was told. You couldn't fight a war any other way. You didn't say: Get the port in working order. You said to one man: Fix that engine; to another: Handle that crane; and so on. You didn't say: Destroy the German Intelligence Service; you said— Johnny grinned. He didn't know what you said. Not yet.

Suddenly there was a muffled explosion behind him, and he jumped and looked around; a geyser of black earth and debris was boiling up from some point behind the transatlantic docks. Johnny looked questioningly at the people going past in the street, but no one, soldier or civilian, seemed alarmed, or even much interested. Routine, thought Johnny; routine. All at once his spirits lifted immeasurably and he took a deep breath of the damp salt air. It was good just being here, being a part of the real war at last.

A row of naval officers in summer khaki approached along the sidewalk, and at the proper interval Johnny saluted, smartly and with pleasure. The officers were visibly startled, and the salutes he got in return were nondescript. He had to laugh, though he hadn't done it as a gag. But he was glad this wasn't a saluting town. It seemed you could always tell where the real work was being done.

Johnny was almost back at headquarters. He looked at his watch again. By now surely, he thought eagerly, things would have begun to move. Now he would find out about the work. He would find out what you did, in counterespionage, when you did what you were told.

Johnny walked briskly into the lobby of the hotel. There was no one behind the desk. Papers lay everywhere. What if someone who didn't belong there should come in and start thumbing through them?

But of course no one would. It was only in the movies that the shadowy figure slipped in the minute everyone's back was turned, and found within thirty seconds the one document he wanted, on which all the crucial information was recorded clearly, concisely, and completely.

Who was supposed to be on the desk, anyway?

The frosted glass door that led into what had been the hotel manager's apartment swung open, and Carl, a short, muscular youth with pitted skin and dark hair that stood on end like the tip of a fine watercolor brush, hurried into the room. His face was as red as its habitual mustard tint would permit it to be; he was scowling. Behind him a voice boomed out, and he compressed his lips angrily and stopped, holding the door open, listening without turning his head.

"When you get those goddam reports *done,* Dolin, we'll talk about it again. Not before then. Now. Find Phillips, and then by God you get down to work. Hear me?"

Carl looked grimly at Johnny and called back, "Phillips just blew in, Captain."

There was a silence. Johnny said nervously, "I guess—should I go right on in?"

"Yeah," Carl said. "I would."

Johnny caught the door as it swung toward him, walked through and found himself in a chilly, unfurnished room. A second door stood partly open in the far wall. Johnny crossed, transferred his overseas cap into his left hand and knocked.

"Yes!" a voice shouted.

Johnny slipped through and paused just inside the corner room where Captain Weiller sat at an enormous leather-covered desk. Weiller was not dwarfed by the desk. He was a solid young man, with thick, dry red hair and a heavy, rather handsome face; he was surveying Johnny carefully now, and his lips, in the tight repose of his features, looked ragged, as though he chewed them. Johnny stood silent for a moment; then he said, "Am I—are you ready to see me, Captain?"

"Mm." Weiller pointed at a chair alongside the desk and unexpectedly smiled. "I am, I really am." The smile left his face.

Uneasily Johnny crossed the room and sat down.

"Let's get the unpleasantness out of the way first, Phillips," Weiller said. "You're to be on deck here. I know I haven't been able to talk to you so far. There's a good reason for that. But you can assume that you wouldn't be here if I didn't need you, and that means that I need to know where you are. Every minute. Got that straight?"

"Yes, sir," Johnny said. He leaned forward in his chair; in spite of the brusqueness of the captain's tone he felt a surge of pleasure, of excitement. *You wouldn't be here if I didn't need you.* "I'm sorry, honestly. You can count on me. It was just— no one was around when I—"

Weiller lifted his hand. "Believe me, I know where everyone was. The lecture's over." His lips parted once more in a brief grin. "Now. You all set? Stuff moved in? You had anything to eat this morning?"

Johnny nodded. "I raided the kitchen." For some reason he found himself blushing.

"Carl will give you the dope on meals and so forth."

All at once Weiller seemed to be studying his hands; in a moment he took a jackknife out of his pocket and started paring his thick, ridged nails with the heavy blade. "Mr. Phillips, I certainly am glad you speak French," he said at last in an off-hand voice. "What else can you do?"

Johnny's heart sank. "I don't speak French, sir," he said. "I can just read it. And understand a little bit." He looked away apologetically. "I never told anyone I spoke it."

Captain Weiller regarded him steadily. Then he shrugged.

"Can you *really* read French, well enough to do some good with it?"

"Yes, sir. I've had four years of it, two in high school and two in college. I need a dictionary sometimes, but not too often."

"You've been to college. Where? Did you finish?"

"Columbia. No, sir, I joined up after my sophomore year."

"Not drafted?"

"No," Johnny answered shortly.

"How come?"

Johnny stirred restively in his chair. "Well, I was a pre-med, sort of. I could have got deferred, I guess. But I didn't want to."

Again Weiller asked, in a decided voice, "How come?"

Johnny looked at him with the beginnings of annoyance, but he was answered only by a bland and intent stare. What's he trying to make me do, he wondered—tell him how patriotic I am?

"I don't know. I guess I didn't want to be a doctor. I didn't really have much of a start."

"A pre-med with two years of college French," said Captain Weiller. His eyes fell closed; suddenly his mouth gaped in a tiny yawn which grew and grew till it seemed to take possession of his entire body, contorting and shaking him in his chair. "'Scuse me," he mumbled thickly. "Tired." He straightened up and smiled at Johnny. "Fair enough. I was in business, myself. How long you been with the organization? Did you get in back in the States?"

"No," Johnny said. "The London office got me out of the replacement depot at Lichfield. I was in London—oh, a little over three weeks, I guess."

Weiller put his elbows on the desk and leaned his head forward against his hands. "Well," he said after a moment, "they can teach you a lot in three weeks. Did you get to work out on any of their cases?"

"Their cases?" Johnny said doubtfully.

Weiller's face went blank and tight.

Hastily Johnny said, "All I meant was, what . . . ?"

There was a knock at the door. Behind Johnny Carl's voice said, "Captain? Murch is back."

"Fine," Weiller said. "Tell him just to wait for me. I'll be as quick as I can."

"Yes, sir," said Carl. The door jarred shut.

Weiller looked at his watch. "Phillips," he said abruptly, "I should be out of here. What I'm getting at is, did you ever take part in an interrogation?"

Johnny's heart began to beat suffocatingly. He knew he'd have to say no, but before he could bring himself to, the captain went on, "How much *did* they teach you before they sent you over?"

"Not very much, sir," Johnny answered reluctantly. "I read a—a lot of case folders in London, with interrogation reports in them, but—Colonel Blake said we'd all of us mostly have to get our training in the field."

The captain said bitterly, "That's dandy for him."

Johnny had stopped being annoyed; he could see that, unhappily, he did not meet the captain's needs. But he had stopped feeling cheerful, too. Of what use could he be, after all? Not much, it appeared—a clerk-driver, maybe, slightly glorified. Even that might have seemed good to him awhile before; but the knowledge that Captain Weiller had wanted him to be something else, something better, depressed him. "I'm sorry," he offered vaguely.

Captain Weiller turned and stared at him. "Let's not be too god damned sensitive, Mr. Phillips," he said evenly. "Let me tell you what I'm up against. I lost two of my best men a couple of days ago—transferred to Le Mans. They're needed more there than here, I'm told—that place is still to be cleaned up, whereas here the work is mostly all done. Mostly all done, my ass!" he exploded violently.

Again Johnny could feel his heart pumping. "I'd certainly—" He had to clear his throat and start again. "I'd certainly be glad to try an interrogation, Captain," he said. "The trouble is —as I told you, I don't speak French."

Weiller had taken up a pencil and was making a deep graphitic trench in the handsome inlaid leather surface of the desk. "This girl speaks English," he answered curtly. "I don't know how well, and she'd be bound to pretend her English was worse than it really is, to give herself time to think when you've got her on the run. But now you've been warned about that, at least." He stared hard at Johnny. "For Christ's sake you must have learned *something* over there," he said. "Didn't you? About the Abwehr and so on?"

"Well, sure." Johnny sat up straight in his chair. "I—I didn't mean to sound stupid, Captain. It's just—this sounds like a pretty big job. But you do learn a lot about interrogations from reading those case folders, sure." He leaned forward. "I don't see why I couldn't do this if I knew what I was looking for."

"Look, kid," said Weiller, and to Johnny there seemed almost to be dislike in his voice. "If you knew what you were looking for you wouldn't have to interrogate, would you?"

"I meant—"

"This is a serious business," the captain went on quietly. "It ought to be handled by someone a lot more experienced than you, God knows. But if we haven't got the personnel, I don't see what we can do about it. We don't know how much this girl has got up her sleeve; she may be dangerous, and she's certainly important. I just can't let her cool any longer— she's already had too damned long to cook up a cover story in. Overnight without anyone to talk to was well and good; it might have scared a confession out of her. But it didn't. She isn't the kind that gets scared. Says she has nothing to confess. That means there's work to be done, and the sooner we get at it, the better."

"Who is the girl, Captain?"

"Name's Bouliard, Thérèse Bouliard. About your age, little older maybe."

"Oh," said Johnny. He smiled at Captain Weiller uncertainly. "I'll—do my best with her, Captain."

Captain Weiller's own expression faded; he looked despondent. Then he said, "Sure, sure. Send me in, Coach, and all that." For a moment he buried his head in his hands. When he looked up he had achieved a bright and glassy smile. "O.K., Mr. Phillips," he said. "That's the spirit. You've got a job. It *is* a big job, but as a matter of fact you're right, you ought to be able to do it." His voice became soft and cold. "I'll sure as hell snatch you off it if you can't. And I'd rather not do that, once you've taken it on."

Johnny reddened swiftly, more with embarrassment than with anger, though he resented the sudden change in the captain's tone. Weiller half rose from his seat and was staring at him sharply, as though he were watching for the slightest emotion that might show in Johnny's face. It was a horrible trick, Johnny thought, so—so open, without any civilized pretenses about it at all. Like a grade-school bully kneeling on his victim's arms, trying to make him admit that it hurt. "Would you—I mean—give me whatever background you think I ought to have, please?" he asked. But he could not keep the stiffness out of his voice.

Slowly Captain Weiller leaned back in his chair, and smiled. "Remember what I said to you awhile back?" he asked. "Let's not be so sensitive. That's the first thing you've got to learn in this business, and the last thing you must ever forget. You've got no personal stake in any of this; you've got no personal feelings. Understand?"

Johnny kept on looking at the floor. "No, sir," he said finally. "Why?"

Captain Weiller snorted. "For Christ's sake. Because everybody you'll be working against will have his emotions completely under control," he said. "And if they discover you haven't, they'll tie you up in knots, and you'll be no good to anybody. And a danger to the Allied armies as well."

He stopped, and his voice became kind. "I'm not attacking you, Phillips. After all, I'm about to trust you pretty far, don't you think? All I'm saying is this—Americans are the biggest suckers in the world, for an honest face, or a hard-luck story, or a plausible lie. We're taught to be sincere, and we don't know, most of us, when someone else isn't being sincere. We prefer to be good, and we can't imagine that someone else may prefer to be bad, and may really know how." He paused and there was a dead silence in the room. "The way you learned it, a prisoner was innocent until he was proved guilty. I'm telling you, from now on until you're through with this game—they're guilty until they're proved innocent, and even then you can't afford to be so god damned sure. Got it?"

There was an odd sinking feeling at the pit of Johnny's stomach. "Yes, sir," he answered quietly.

Captain Weiller continued to stare at him for a moment. Then, finally, his gaze relaxed. "Good," he said softly. "Fortunately, if you have any sense at all, you won't have to worry about that in this first case of yours, for there just isn't any doubt about what's been going on. The girl's only a little thing, it's true. And she has big, brown, frightened eyes. And if you didn't have the story you might think there was never anyone so foully wronged. But the evidence exists. However innocent she looks, Phillips, she's guilty. She's a German spy."

III.

CAPTAIN WEILLER'S office was the one room on the ground floor of the hotel that ever got any sun; and even now, in full summer, there was only a small slant-lidded box of light that shifted around almost imperceptibly in the corner by the desk and then, abruptly, was gone. Johnny sat watching the rays dwindle and disappear while the captain was out of the room. As the last of the light evaporated, leaving a gray emptiness, cold seemed to strike from the inner walls of the building, and Johnny shivered.

He was torn by conflicting senses of pleasure and apprehension. It was hard for him to sit still, and yet almost painful to move. It had occurred to him just after the captain had left that if he got up and walked around, the captain might return to find him someplace where for some reason he shouldn't be, and think he was snooping; Johnny had stayed in his chair by the desk for a good many minutes because of that. But the desk top was absolutely bare, the drawers pushed shut, all the other surfaces around the room—steel cabinets, safe, typewriter table—empty. Indeed the office seemed deserted, as though it were a place to which no one ever came.

Johnny got up and walked over to the window from which the sunlight had just disappeared. The blue of the sky he had seen earlier that morning had retreated to a queer-shaped geometric figure up beyond the looming buildings. Suspended in it as though in an uncertain magnetic field, a sea gull rocked and teetered in the wind, slipped precipitately out of the frame as though it could not withstand the pressures, and then beat its way laboriously back, to hang awkwardly centered once more upon the depthless blue-gold screen.

He had never known anyone like Captain Weiller before, Johnny thought. The situation too was extraordinary, somehow beyond anything he had imagined. And uninitiated as he was, it would seem that he must be guided through it with the utmost care; yet here he was being thrown into it, with a few words of introduction, by a man who apparently did not like him—or like certain things about him, at least.

Of course Weiller must be hard pressed, working with so few men. But what about this unlived-in office? Well, obviously other people would handle the desk work. But then why didn't Weiller interrogate this girl himself? If, as he said, she was so important. It didn't seem to make much sense.

But there must be reasons, a lot of them, and perfectly good. Doubtless he'd understand everything in due time.

And for the present—as he thought of what he was about to do, he felt excitement spreading through him like a cold fire. There was this case, this girl with the big brown eyes, who was certainly a spy, and who might be dangerous. Suddenly Johnny felt throughout his body the icy tingling of fright. He had never thought he was a coward, but nothing had ever happened that he need have been much afraid of, either, he recognized. A spy—almost for the first time he registered what the word meant, and it whispered evilly in his head. *Dangerous.* Obviously she wouldn't be armed any longer, for after all she'd been captured, and presumably searched. But what insubstantial weapons, what powers might she not still have . . . ?

Yet there she was, and he was to interrogate her. In a moment his excitement had soared again to pleasure and pride. It was a real job, at last, and somehow—he didn't know how—he would do it well.

The gull jerked out of sight like a lantern slide that has been put in the projector upside down and now must be transposed. From the empty room between the entrance hall and the office Johnny heard the heavy, decided sound of the captain's footsteps. As Johnny turned, the door opened and Weiller said wryly, "Nice view, huh? I see the sun's gone down for the day." He glanced at his watch. "O.K. We've got a few minutes; I've sent Murchison ahead. But let's get on it, shall we?" He was carrying in his right hand a white card and a few

41

sheets of paper; with them he motioned Johnny to take the seat by the desk.

"Carl's mislaid the file," he said. "He's looking for it now, and you can glance over it after I've left. For now, let me give you a fill-in on the story, and a general idea of how to go about this. You'll have to concentrate. Ready?"

"Yes, sir," said Johnny.

Walking over by the window, Weiller clasped his hands behind his back and cleared his throat. "In the first place," he said, "this girl would probably only be a side issue if we could get hold of her father, but we can't, for the simple reason that he's dead. Both her parents are; the mother seems to have been dead for a long time. And the house the old man and his daughter lived in is all smashed to hell, hit by a stray bomb —late in May, according to one of the neighbors. He actually saw Bouliard's body. If he's not lying, and there's no reason to think he is.

"It was the father who was supposed to be the chief spy for the Nazis in Cherbourg, and he was the one we knew about before we got to France. So as soon as my men and I arrived, we went to work to round him up. The reports said he was a schoolteacher. But they didn't give his name right, it turned out, and our investigations had just about drawn a final blank when, nearly three weeks ago now, a linecrosser named Korvac turned himself in to our people down at La Haye-du-Puits. And he cleared up the Cherbourg case, at least as far as identifying who we were after."

"Linecrosser?" asked Johnny confusedly. It was not that he did not know the phrase; but the details were coming pretty fast.

"Remember those famous case folders of yours?" said the captain irritably, looking at his watch again. "A linecrosser is someone sent through your lines by the enemy, of course, to get information, or commit sabotage, or make contact with existing agents, or something of the sort. This man had been a radio instructor and technician at a spy school in Paris, and now he had a mission, or several missions, connected with the Cherbourg agent—whose real name he said he had not been

42

told, but there was a cover name, Ansel, and an address which turned out to be Bouliard's.

"So that ended the search—or almost. Korvac's principal job was to find out why 'Ansel' wasn't working, and help him get started if the trouble was technical—something wrong with the transmitter. He had an extra transmitter with him, and some spare parts besides. He also had ten thousand francs, to pay Ansel two months' advance salary if the agent's story was O.K. In case it wasn't"—here Weiller looked sardonically at Johnny—"he was carrying a pistol."

Johnny shivered slightly. He wished he could take all this as a matter of course, but he could not. "Uh—where does the girl come in?" he asked.

The captain smiled at him, a tight-lipped smile. "Believe me," he said, "I'm in just as much of a hurry as you are, Phillips. Maybe more."

Johnny looked down at his hands, which lay folded in his lap.

"Well," said the captain, "finally, Korvac was carrying a note. And it was addressed, not to Bouliard himself, but to Bouliard's daughter Thérèse. Considering the fact that it was to be used only if Korvac had just had occasion to rub out Thérèse's father, you might find it a little grim; but there it is. I don't of course recall the exact wording, but you'll find it in the file, when Carl turns it up.

"The meaning of it was something like this. The writer was sorry that Bouliard had seen fit not to go on working; and he was sure that Thérèse would share that regret. Korvac—only he had a cover name too; Émile, I think it was—was going to take over the job in Cherbourg. If she would consent to assist him in his work as freely as she had already engaged to assist her father—that was the implication, the note didn't actually say that—she would *continue* to be amply rewarded. The note was signed 'Bloch.' "

Johnny stirred in his chair. This time he was not going to be trapped. "Well," he remarked composedly, "that doesn't seem to leave much doubt, does it?" He gazed at the blank view out of the window, then looked uncertainly up at Weiller. "I should think all you'd have to do would be to show her that note, and she'd be bound to confess."

"Sure," said Weiller. He pursed his lips. "But look at it this way. You want the truth, as fully as you can get it. You want all the details of this girl's contact with German Intelligence; everything she knows about her father's contacts; the complete story of their training, payment, projected plans, everything. This case might lead us to a whole lot of others, you know. Now. The more papers you show the girl—the more exact details you admit to her that you know about her career—the easier it is for her, in a way. Because she can build her story around those details, narrow it down to cover them and nothing else. Do you see?"

Johnny nodded doubtfully.

"We could break her on the basis of that note, of course," Weiller said. "And maybe we'll have to, if she turns out to be really stubborn. But if we can get the story out of her without tipping our hand at all, it'll eventually be more use. Naturally you've got to make her think you know everything to begin with, and that if her story deviates a hair's breadth from the already established truth, why—sssst!" He made a throat-slitting gesture. "To do that you can use names; Ansel, Bloch—perhaps Korvac and Émile, only—no, I don't know, skip those, because there's every evidence that she doesn't know Korvac, and the more you ask her about things she genuinely doesn't know about, the more she's likely to try to hold out on you."

Johnny was laboriously cataloguing facts in his head, trying to pick up significances that had escaped him, or parts of the story that had been missed. Finally he said, "How come the girl's only been arrested just now? I mean, if Korvac turned himself in as long ago as you say?"

The captain smiled grimly, his face turning a little red. "Because she wasn't in town," he said. "Remember?"

"Well, sure, but—you must have—"

"Go ahead. How would you suggest we should have gone about finding the girl and catching her?" the captain asked. "I'm interested."

Johnny flushed. "I didn't mean that everything wasn't done the way it should have been," he said.

"No. All right," said Weiller. "Answer my question."

"Well, I—would have—I mean, it sounds silly," said Johnny

uneasily. "You said you'd found out that her father and mother were both dead, and you'd talked to the neighbors. If the girl wasn't staying with any of them, why maybe at least they'd have known where she was. With relatives, perhaps. Or if not, maybe you could've found out who the girl's special friends were? I don't know."

Weiller stared at him, the heavy lines of his face relaxing slowly in an expression of guarded approval. "You know," he said, "you've got some sense. I wish to Christ you were trained, of course, but common sense helps."

Johnny moved his features around in a conscious attempt to acknowledge the praise, but the results felt peculiar and he gave it up.

"Anyway," the captain said. "You're right. We did ask the neighbors. But actually there weren't so many to ask as you might suppose. You see, there've been two evacuations of this city. First, in the spring of 1943 the Germans kicked out what you might call the superfluous population—everybody who wasn't needed to keep Cherbourg going as a key station in the coastal defense network. That still left a lot of people here, though. Right after the invasion the Germans drove out everybody they couldn't count on actually to fight on their side. Both times, a lot of those who had to leave just went out into the country; they slipped back into town as soon as the fighting was over this June. But others had to go farther to find a place to roost, and it's taken them longer to get back. Like Thérèse herself."

Johnny thought a moment. "Is there anything to show—why she wasn't killed along with her father, by the way?"

"No. But it seems the raid the bomb was dropped in was an early one, before curfew. Obviously the girl's escape was an accident; she just happened to be somewhere else."

There was a silence, and Weiller looked at his watch. "Jesus Christ," he said. He began to pace to and fro, forcefully, behind his desk. As swiftly he stopped, and looked intently at Johnny beneath lowered brows.

"Uh—can Carl or somebody tell me the rest of it, sir?" asked Johnny. "I don't want to hold you up."

Weiller sat down and drummed his fingers on the desk top.

45

"Thury can just play hopscotch with Murchison for awhile," he said finally. "God knows I've waited often enough for him, and anyway, we're almost through."

"Thury," Johnny said. If the name had appeared in the story before, he could not remember it.

Weiller made an abrupt gesture with his hand. "Nothing to do with this case. French counterintelligence. My opposite number." He leaned back in his chair. "The rest of the story is this. When we learned finally that Bouliard had been our man and that his daughter was involved, of course we had to get onto that tack. Sure enough, the father had once taught English at the Lycée des Jeunes Filles, and we found out that Thérèse spoke English; so—through another office that was cooperating with us—we let it be known that we needed the girl badly as an interpreter. That gave us a chance to ask after her generally in the neighborhood. No one knew exactly where she'd gone. A friend of Rameau's, the neighbor who'd actually seen Bouliard's body, said he'd talked to the girl, and she'd told him she might go to the farm of her father's brother-in-law; he didn't know, but he thought it was down somewhere between Granville and Avranches. She didn't tell him either the brother-in-law's name or the exact place. All he knew was that the father and the daughter had both gone down to visit sometime during May; they'd only been back about ten days when the bomb fell. And no one else knew any more."

"That's strange," Johnny hazarded.

"Not so strange, when you consider how mixed up everything's been here. Anyway, the Bouliards had lived in Cherbourg only for about five years. And they were closemouthed people; the neighbors felt friendly enough toward them, but didn't actually know much. Especially that was true because socially the Bouliards were a cut above most of the neighbors: he was an intellectual, a professional, a traveled man, and they're mostly shopkeepers and so on."

"Still, the Bouliards must have had friends somewhere in town," said Johnny.

"You try to find out who they were," said Weiller sourly. "It turned out that Bouliard hadn't taught for several years—I don't know why, unless maybe the Germans weren't interested in the youth of Cherbourg learning English. Anyway, what Bouliard did do—that, curiously enough, we couldn't find out. Of course we know what he did *really;* but most spies have a cover employment of some kind. As you know. So the neighbors won't get suspicious." He slouched down into his chair. "The whole story's pretty much up to you to get out of the girl."

Johnny nodded. He wished he had a comment to make, a question to ask. . . . He did have. "Sir . . . ?"

Weiller looked up. "What is it?"

"The transmitter Bouliard was supposed to have. I—I can't imagine that the girl was traveling with it. Anyway, if she had been, there'd be no question of *breaking* her now, would there?"

"Good for you," Weiller said quietly. "And what else?"

Johnny became excited. "Well, if it was somewhere in the house that got bombed, that ought to settle things too. Except— no, I suppose she could pretend *she* didn't know anything about it."

"We searched the house," Weiller said. "Thoroughly. Late one night. But—the neighbors had cleaned the place up, weeks before. We didn't find a thing."

Johnny looked at the captain in sudden alarm. "But then somebody else may have found the transmitter. And might even be working with it right now."

"Not working with it, I don't think. We checked with Army Signals, and they said there wasn't anything on the air they didn't know about. Anyway, remember that Korvac was supposed to find out why Bouliard wasn't transmitting—and was supposed to take over if he wasn't *going* to transmit. So that doesn't sound as if anyone else, except Thérèse herself, would be in on the deal."

"I—I guess not. Still—"

"I know. That transmitter."

"What did the neighbors say? About the house, I mean."

"They said the cleanup had been done just as a kindness to the girl."

"Whose idea was it?"

"Rameau's. And we'd investigated him pretty thoroughly before we'd dared ask him questions, so I *think* it's probably the truth." Weiller paused for a moment, then unstrapped his watch and laid it on the desk in front of him. "Look. I've *got* to get going. We can't be *sure* that one of the neighbors didn't take the set. If they did, we may well be in for trouble. Except that the girl likely wouldn't *know* she was safe on that particular score—we picked her up the minute she got in. Unless Tochyk flubbed it, of course. But he told me—"

Johnny shook his head. "Sir. Who is. . . ?"

"One of my men. We had him out there dressed in MP uniform. Carl can tell you. Anyway, back to Bouliard's radio set and espionage instructions, just possibly they got blown up, completely destroyed—though it's funny in that case that we wouldn't have found a shred of anything incriminating. Maybe the girl hid the stuff; if so, you'll have to find out where. Maybe it's buried. Or Bouliard might not have worked from his own home—the setup might be somewhere else."

Johnny said, "Could I have a sheet of paper?"

The captain shrugged slightly and gave him a pad and pencil from a desk drawer. "This is all right for now," he said. "But before you go in for the interrogation, you'd better have your questions thoroughly in mind. Doesn't do to let the subject see you're at all unfamiliar with the case."

Johnny nodded and wrote a couple of sentences rapidly on the pad. Then he looked up. "That's—is that about it, Captain?"

"Except for the papers, yes. I've got our file card on Bouliard alias Ansel here, and the rundown on the network he was supposed to be a member of. You may find you're already familiar with that. Carl ought to have found the folder on Thérèse Bouliard by now; that's where we keep Korvac's interrogation report at the moment, and you can't of course get by without reading *it*." He rang the bell on his desk decisively. "Now. Do any last points occur to you?"

Johnny felt stupid. Certainly not all the questions had been cleared up. But he felt the need of thinking the story out by himself. Dumbly he shook his head.

"Remember that trip to the brother-in-law's farm in May? That's one place you've obviously got to find out about, that farm. Maybe the set was moved in May, and if it was, it's probably there; if Thérèse did something with it later, it may or may not be there. But you can see you've got to find out, can't you?"

Johnny sighed. "I certainly can," he said.

"As a matter of fact, you've *got* to find where that set is, and Bouliard's instructions, because—so far we don't have any physical evidence against either the father or the daughter. With the original lead to Bouliard, and Korvac in our hands, I don't think we'll need it; but still, it would cinch things if we could locate the real, concrete evidence."

Johnny nodded. "But if she had the set with her, wherever she was, why would she have had to come back here at all? Just to risk getting picked up, I mean," he said.

"She and her father were supposed to work in Cherbourg, remember?" Weiller said in a flat voice. "This is obviously an important observation point. A lot of military equipment is brought in here, and later on presumably troops will be landed." He paused. "Anyway, don't you think it's kind of suggestive that as soon as the whole peninsula was open for civilian travel again—as it has been only for the last few days—why, up she pops in Cherbourg?"

"I guess so," said Johnny.

"Oh, you've got a swell chance to break her," the captain said more cheerfully. "She's got too damned much to explain; I don't see how she can hold out, if you don't let her get the upper hand, and from the looks of things you aren't going to." He grinned encouragingly. "Now, when I've left, you look over the files, and when you're ready go on up to the girl's room."

"Is she here in this building?" Johnny asked, startled.

"Of course—where else?"

Johnny shook his head.

"We've got a kind of cell block upstairs for interrogation cases. You'll get the hang of things soon. Ask Carl about anything that puzzles you. If—" His tone grew heavier. "If he hasn't gone to take a god damned *walk*." He stared angrily at the door for a moment; then he pursed his lips and looked back down at the desk. "Now, for the interrogation." He put his watch back on, took the pad from Johnny and began scribbling on it.

While he was writing, Carl knocked lightly at the door and entered. Weiller looked up, scowling. Carl walked across the room and put a folder on the desk. Then he said in a hesitant voice, "Sir, Captain Thury . . ."

Gruffly the captain said, "What about him?"

"He's on the telephone."

"What the hell, is he bored with Murchison?"

"Murchison isn't there, sir."

The captain crashed to his feet, his face turning red. "Oh for God's *sake*," he said. "Not Murchison *too*—" Suddenly he became very still. He turned to Johnny. "You wait here." To Carl he said, "You kept him on the wire?"

"Uh—yes, sir."

"*Great.*"

Weiller was almost running as he left the room.

Carl looked serenely at Johnny. "That's the Bouliard file, there on the desk," he said. "Happy reading."

"Thanks," Johnny said.

IV.

ACROSS the city at this very moment Cécile Aubanne would be sitting in a back room of Thury's "little inn," as he called it, and in another part of the building Thury himself would be preparing to entertain his American confreres; not with fat geese and ale, but with expostulations and wine.

For surely he must guess that they were not coming to decorate him.

Murchison smiled, almost affectionately. He understood Thury, or half-understood him; and the funny thing was that he liked him, too, even admired him in a way. The man was wildly energetic and unsystematic; but he was also cheerful, warmhearted, and sensitive. More than anything else he was enamored of a France which he would, if he could, simply will into existence, though how it could in fact come to exist he did not seriously think. . . . But perhaps that was wrong; perhaps he merely assumed that for all practical purposes, he was France. Once Murchison had heard him say to Weiller, with ecstatic calm, "I am a Frenchman, you see. I live here. I shall be here long after you are gone."

But who would be here or would not be here in five or ten or twenty years didn't a great deal matter at the moment. In fact Weiller might be gone from Cherbourg far sooner than Thury could even imagine, if Weiller was slated, as he seemed fairly certain that he was, to be moved on up to Paris after SHAEF moved up, to be put in charge of all secret counter-intelligence operations in the American zone in France. But if Thury was now playing with matches in the TNT shed, the explosion that could follow might scatter his own mangled limbs, and Weiller's, halfway across the ETO, and neither one would in any effective sense be staying or going anywhere.

The thought made Murchison automatically lengthen his stride, and when he realized what he was doing he grinned wryly to himself and slowed down. He was not their savior, his role was not that crucial. He had, now, merely to hold Thury till Weiller arrived for their awkward conference. And though the job was not an especially easy one, though it had to be done smoothly—for he intended to justify the captain's confidence in him—

Already Weiller was giving him more responsible jobs.

Into his mind there intruded, as it did every day now whether he wished it or not, the faint sense of this new difference in himself. And the difference was not even real, he told himself, it meant nothing, yet—

Sergeant Murchison. Lieutenant Murchison.

Lieutenant.

If the commission came through, could he simply be happy with it, take satisfaction in what it would let him accomplish, without being proud? Was he up to that? Was anybody?

The others, Carl especially, would imagine that he *was* proud. Murchison wondered whether Carl had been told what was in the works. The transfer of Rhodes and Bailey was the first sign of a shift forward, a shift which acknowledged the rapidity with which the armies were moving, and it could not be long before Weiller himself was involved in the shift. Then who would be left in charge of the Cherbourg team?

He would be. He, Murchison.

That is, if the captain's recommendations carried weight.

Weiller had big ideas, but he was responsible, he was no fool; and he knew a lot about the long-range plans of the outfit.

Waiting at a corner to cross the street, looking at the heavy traffic, Murchison thought: As long as the war goes on, this will never be an unimportant place.

It was a good thing he hadn't taken a jeep; he'd get to Thury's faster on foot.

But there'd be such a thing as getting there too fast.

Suddenly Murchison's ears started ringing, the sound coming up swiftly, as though from deep down or far away, and who would that be, thinking about him? Thury? Weiller? His own parents? It came to Murchison that *they* probably thought about him simultaneously, in a kind of chorus—his father down at the paper, his mother at home. More because they plain had the same feelings and ideas about everything than because they were so crazy about him; though they were that. Murchison smiled sadly. Far more, even, than they loved Jim, their son, they had loved Jim-and-Louise; and still, when Louise had left him, they hadn't changed toward him.

His father had said only one thing, in a voice so gentle that it had almost broken him down, him, the polished, I'll-handle-my-own-affairs young man of the world: "Always tell yourself the truth, Jim. If you do that, you'll know who you are when you're with—other people."

He was walking at an even pace through the shadowed, unshadowed morning, along streets he knew without knowing anything about them. Now, outside the long window of a closed furniture store, a window that was as empty as once he had made his life, he glanced at his watch and speeded up a little. He ought not be late enough so that Thury would really notice or be offended. But could he think of something so natural to talk about, so appropriate for him—still after all a minor member of the American team—to bring up, that Thury would be reassured: would misunderstand the reason for the meeting's having been called, and even find it matter-of-course that Weiller was not at first there?

No. Because it didn't make sense.

He could think up a name and ask to look for it in the Gestapo files, certainly; but there was nothing in that to require Thury's own presence. He could bring up one of the closed cases—but Thury was touchy, and all too likely to think that something new had come up, something important, that was being kept from him. They could talk about Thérèse Bouliard— No again. There had not so far been an interrogation, which Thury was going to have difficulty enough in believing, since he would not have handled it that way; but in any case, this meeting had been arranged before the Bouliard girl's arrest, and so had obviously been intended to concern something else. There was in fact nothing to talk about but Cécile Aubanne. And about her Murchison was not to inquire before the arrival of the captain.

"Don't do anything but—keep him busy till I get there, Murch," Weiller had said. "Talk about anything. The New York Stock Exchange, how to grow sunflowers, sow gunflowers, *I* don't care." It hadn't been remarkably helpful.

No, Murchison admonished himself firmly, it hadn't, because Weiller was on the spot—and a bad spot at that. In a way, of course, Thérèse Bouliard's arrest was wonderfully promising; or Weiller thought it was, hoped it might be. What he hoped, obviously, was that Thérèse would turn out to be a full-fledged spy—or rather not turn out to be but admit being, admit it right away, so that Weiller could get a fast and detailed report out of her interrogation, carry it over to Thury, give it to him —and use it, in whatever way worked best, to control this Aubanne business. . . .

But I don't think it's going to work out that way, Murchison thought, and stopped still on the sidewalk. He tried, carefully, to erase the thought from his mind. Weiller knew more about the Bouliard case than he did; Weiller knew more about spies generally than he did; Weiller was intelligent. But to suppose that the world would give you exactly what you needed, exactly when you needed it . . .

Well. A man could be lucky. Weiller could be. And Thérèse's father, no doubt about it, had been set up as the chief Wehrmacht spy for the Cherbourg area.

Only it was Murchison's hunch, from what little he had seen of Thérèse, that she was not likely— Again he closed the thought out of his mind.

He ought to be interrogating Thérèse Bouliard himself, and it was really unlucky that things had taken such a turn that he couldn't. On the very day that Rhodes and Bailey had left, Murchison had bumped into Cécile Aubanne on the streets of Cherbourg. He'd nearly jumped out of his skin. She hadn't seen him, so far as he could tell; he'd tried to follow her, but she'd simply melted away into thin air, and that was suspicious too. What was she doing wandering around loose? For she'd been picked up at night in the port area weeks before, arrested, interrogated; Rhodes and he had both taken a crack at her, but hadn't turned up anything of likely interest except that her character was an absolute cipher, and that she'd had no good reason for being where they'd picked her up. Finally she'd been turned over to Thury for further questioning and for whatever disposition he should see fit to make of her. Everyone had expected he'd put her in the hands of the civil authorities. But he'd kept temporizing; he was awaiting certain reports from the Résistance, he'd said; she'd had a few questionable contacts, of no importance, but every small bit of information was of use; she was trying to remember; there was no hurry. . . . Of course, when she was completely cleared, she would be released, presumably, and after that could within limits go where she liked; but the point was she hadn't *been* cleared so far as anyone knew, and until she was, she should remain a prisoner. No one else Thury had got his hands on had been let out in this way. So what was he up to?

Murchison had reported to Weiller, who'd been angry and upset, and properly so: it was damned poor security, if nothing else. The scheduled weekly meeting between Weiller and Thury wasn't due to take place until the following Thursday. Weiller had figured that the activities of Aubanne, if that was the right word for them, couldn't wait. So he'd called Thury and made this Monday morning appointment with him—without telling Thury what it was he wanted to talk about. Thury had been anything but anxious to grant the interview. Something was up, all right.

And then, on Sunday, Thérèse Bouliard had been arrested. Weiller had telephoned Thury, had asked him and his secretary to come over to help in her search—as much as anything, Murchison thought, to show Thury that the American team was now in triumphant possession of a really important body, a spy who presumably held the key to the entire espionage situation in Cherbourg. But to Weiller's astonishment, only the secretary, Estelle de Sombais, had showed up; her captain, she had explained caressingly, regretted, but he was so terribly busy. . . . *Busy doing what?* The appointment set for this morning was all the more urgent now; Weiller had to talk to Thury quickly even though in the circumstances he might have preferred to wait—had, somehow, to get him onto the subject of Cécile Aubanne, get him if possible into a corner. And Murchison had to be there, since if Thury admitted nothing, and if Weiller was correct about what was in the cards otherwise, Murchison—*Lieutenant James Murchison*—might, in a matter of a month or less, be up to his ears in whatever little mess Thury had cooked up.

Hopefully this new man, Phillips, was a quick study. Phillips who, new to Cherbourg as he was, would almost any hour now begin the interrogation of Thérèse Bouliard.

Carl could have done it.

But Weiller would not use Carl.

Murchison sighed. It was easy to criticize Weiller, and seldom altogether right to. If only, he found himself thinking, it were not necessary to work with the French, the whole thing would after all be so easy. . . .

But doubtless the French felt the same way. Whose country was it, anyway? For the time being, of course, a German spy working behind Allied lines would be working against—the Americans, the English. Numerically the French army didn't amount to a hell of a lot. So far as the French themselves were concerned, however, it amounted to a great deal; and they were right to take pride in it, right not to let themselves lose their pride.

Quite naturally the French army had an intelligence section, and within that section, counterintelligence units; quite naturally the heads of these, of whom Thury was one, worked—with a status only theoretically equal—in liaison with their American or British opposite numbers, under general Allied command. But one day, as Thury said, the Americans and the British would be gone. And then what were the French to have —the files on a lot of dead cases? Or continuing cases, agents they had developed and were running themselves, whether the Americans and the British had sanctioned their activities or not?

Thury did not trust the Americans; or rather he felt wounded by them, felt that they looked upon France slightingly and kept from him information the French were entitled to have. In addition he had become, it seemed, disappointed in Weiller, had come to think him a glorified policeman, overcautious, dependent on authority, conservative, slow. He himself, Thury had made it clear from the beginning, was a man of ideas; rather than allow the security of Cherbourg and of all the Allied armies to depend on the laborious rounding up of a series of nobodies, of stupid collaborators, he would in Weiller's position have done something bold, have gone out magnificently to meet the German espionage threat. As it was, with his limited authority, his limited resources . . .

It was lucky, Murchison thought soberly, that Thury was not in Weiller's position. Weiller was not the most inventive man in the world, true enough; but he was at least thorough, and careful. He was sound.

For days after Korvac's arrest Thury had urged emphatically that Korvac be brought up to Cherbourg and put into radio contact with his German spymasters—he had had with him, after all, a transmitter, a cipher, instructions that could have been adapted to his personal use. But no one on the American team would have thought for a moment of trusting Korvac.

"So you do not trust him," Thury had said. *"Nom de dieu.* I trust nobody: but this man would not betray *me,* I assure you, for he knows what France intends."

And when Weiller had (tactfully, after a few days) informed him that Allied Headquarters would not permit Korvac to be run as a controlled agent with Thérèse Bouliard still unaccounted for, Thury had said darkly, *"Écoutez.* The Germans propose to have a spy working in Cherbourg: that is obvious. If you and your headquarters do not avail yourselves of the spies you know, spies whom the *Germans* after all think good enough —" He had shrugged and thrown up his hands. "The girl might of course appear, inconveniently; but she could—is it not obvious?—be got out of the way." And finally he had said, with an odd smile, "They are, you know, very stubborn, very persistent. The Germans."

Weiller had not pointed out, and it had not been Murchison's place to point out, that "the girl" might return to Cherbourg without "appearing," without that is being arrested; and if she were a fully trained and active spy, she might start working, might even make radio contact with the Germans on her father's set, using his wavelength and his instructions. And what would the Germans think if their one Cherbourg case suddenly became two unrelated cases? Especially if the messages sent began to contradict one another? No, the risk was *not* worth taking.

Would Thury now propose, Murchison wondered suddenly, that—now Thérèse Bouliard was safely under arrest—Korvac might after all be put on the air? *Why hadn't he showed up the evening before?* Had he simply lost interest, given up trying? *Or did he no longer want Korvac on the air, having, perhaps, plans of his own now?*

No, surely— Murchison's thoughts had brought him back, as he had counted on their doing, to the important point. Surely Thury's own prisoner, Cécile Aubanne, was not a German spy. And if she was not a spy, nothing Thury could do could make her into one. She was a minor informer, at most; with no one, now, to inform. Her name was not in the central files, it was mentioned in none of the reports; nor was any name like hers. Weiller had as usual been meticulous about having a check made. London had no description available, even, that could possibly fit her.

Could the French conceivably be setting up an organization to work against their own allies, to gather information about American and British order of battle and so on—in the interests of, say, the future, of the completeness of their own files? . . . If they were, they must have much higher sources of information, perfectly legitimate ones. The thing need not and so would not be done through locally recruited and poorly placed civilian agents. And Thury, a counterintelligence officer, would in any case have nothing to do with such matters. Unless he had decided that it was his patriotic duty to free-lance. . . .

What had Cécile Aubanne been doing on the streets of Cherbourg? Was it simply that Thury was by nature casual, took chances, was not security conscious? There had been right along, after all, that business of Estelle de Sombais. . . .

Or faced with Weiller's methodical, intelligent, slow maneuvering, had he been driven into rebellion?

The way Murchison had taken had brought him to within a couple of blocks of the rear entrance to Thury's headquarters. He looked once more at his watch. He was—a little late, a little later than he had meant to be; and though he had been letting his thoughts work, he had, still, no plan.

Once more he stopped on the sidewalk. Yes he had!

Whatever Weiller was planning to say later on, he, Murchi-

son, would ask Thury whether—no matter how Thérèse Bouliard's interrogation turned out—he would still advise Korvac's
being brought up to Cherbourg and put on the air. That would
be taking a chance, but it wouldn't commit them, not in the
least. And Thury, if he weren't playing secret games, would be
gratified to be asked. *If he got flustered, however—advised, now,
against the use of Korvac . . .*

It would be easy for Murchison to explain to Weiller what
he'd had in mind.

He began walking again, swiftly, conscious that a relaxed
smile was growing on his face. He didn't like playing tricks on
Thury, but—

Across the intersection ahead of him, looking neither to left
nor to right, walked Cécile Aubanne. She was wearing dark
glasses, but it could be no one else. She moved like an apologetic
tank. It took her a long moment to disappear, walking at her
slow, hopeless gait in a direction away from Thury's "little inn."

This was rapidly becoming, Murchison thought with a dry
nervousness, a greater test of his ingenuity than it had been
intended to be. For what was he to do now? He had, literally,
only seconds in which to decide.

Thury was waiting.

Had Aubanne been given instructions to go out at this hour
because Thury had supposed that Weiller and at least one other
member of the reduced American team would be tied up safely
with him?

Or had Aubanne been waiting for the Americans to come?
Were they intended to see her and to follow her?

No, that was—that made no sense. Unless Thury were deliberately trying to frighten Weiller into working more with him,
more independently of conservative Allied direction.

But if that were Thury's motive, it would show up pretty
quickly.

Thury could wait. Presumably, under any explanation of
this, he would wait. And Weiller would get there eventually,
and would have to make what sense he could of Murchison's
absence. If Thury became alarmed when he discovered that
Murchison was supposed to have arrived earlier, that would be

very revealing, and besides it might give Weiller a way into the tricky subject of the conference, and all the advantage he needed.

It was a pity that before Weiller started in on Thury, the question about Korvac could not be asked.

Murchison rounded the corner. Cécile Aubanne was still in sight, a block farther on, walking in the general direction of the port. He had to find out, if he could, what she was doing.

This time it was easy to follow her, for she did not walk swiftly and she did not turn around. For a moment, once, she stopped altogether while a butterfly described off-balance circles in the air around her; at another time she speeded up, almost lumbered into a run as a dirty, starved-looking dog rose up from beside the wall, sniffed at her ankles and then took a few tentative steps along beside her. Crouched back on its haunches, the dog looked up with smeary, listless eyes as Murchison passed a few moments later.

Suddenly, with as much passion as he ever allowed himself now, Murchison wished that they had more time—not time to meet crises or to avoid crises, but time really to find out about the men and women they dealt with, time to find out who these people were as human beings instead of as bundles of data destined to be sorted out into a card file. For too much was always missing from the data. It mattered of course whether a person had done something hostile to the Allies, had had dealings with the enemy, were engaged in treason; but the fact that Cécile Aubanne must try to run from a sick dog all at once meant more, it seemed, than anything Murchison had learned from asking her questions. And if he could be around her, study her long enough, he might come to know—what, indeed, he had to know; what drove her; what she was.

But was it Cécile Aubanne he was thinking of now? Without saying the words he knew that it was not. He had catalogued Louise, even before their marriage. With her marvelous young figure, her vivid, dusky coloring, she was extraordinarily beautiful, desirable; all men looked at her, all men must want her. He had distrusted everyone. She had liked being with people. He had watched with a fanatic severity every man who ap-

proached them, the friends who came to their apartment. But
—he had not realized it till much later—Louise herself he had
hardly looked at, after the first. At least he had seen no more
than the thing he expected others to see.

They had not talked, not spent those quiet, exploratory hours
together of which, surely, a marriage must be made. They had
not even quarreled; when his fits of jealousy came upon him he
had become icy, controlled, withdrawn. Once or twice she had
tried to protest her devotion to him: suggestive, since he had
accused her of nothing. They had left abruptly a party given in
her honor; she had smiled at many men. Days, almost weeks,
they had spent in which, if he had looked at her at all, he had
withered her beauty with his eyes. *Had she watched him, seen
in him any gentleness of gesture, anything she could hold . . . ?*
For it was he who had been the betrayer, not she.

And when he had started having an affair, a punitive and
therefore rather public affair with the homely fiancée of one of
his old college acquaintances who was in an army camp somewhere, Louise had left him. Not at once; but when at last she
went, it was without a word. More terrible than that, she had
disappeared. She had no family. She had—disappeared. She had
become a real statistic at last, a missing person.

But she had loved his parents as they had loved her. . . .

I am doing the only thing I can do, Louise, he said to himself
for the thousandth time. However slowly, I am making myself,
remaking myself, into a decent, honorable, responsible person.
And when I can show you that that is what I am, I will begin
to look for you again.

Inside him there was the old feeling of something tearing, the
vacant knocking that would not end until he could turn his
whole mind, forcibly, to something else.

If Cécile Aubanne had vanished he would not have been surprised, but he had in fact been following her with some automatic part of his attention, his senses recording the pale color of
her dress in the sun, her characteristic uncertain movement
among the figures, civilian and military, that now populated the
sidewalks. There she was, still the same distance ahead of him,
but no longer, in this busier part of the city, the sole grotesque. . . . Bitterly he remonstrated with himself: must she be

a grotesque, and the ill-clothed, the ill-fed of this country with her? And the fat—*sergeants,* the sloppy GI's—

But you do not get there all at once, he told himself, not patiently but with a still resignation. You do and think what you know how to do and think; and try neither to congratulate yourself upon, nor to ignore, the fact that you have got that far.

With more people on the streets now he could afford to move closer, and so speeded his pace a little. Just then Cécile Aubanne stopped before a narrow shop window and held out her hand softly to touch the glass; he turned away until out of the corner of his eye he saw that she was walking on again. They crossed the street on which his headquarters lay, too near it almost for him to credit that she would dare let herself come so near, and walked on down toward the harbor. What did she expect to see, or to do?

A breeze off the water struck them as they rounded the corner onto the wide harbor front, and all at once he felt sweaty, wished he could abandon this task and stand in the live air watching the water, looking at the great ships massed beyond the inner breakwater and at the smaller boats shimmering toward them and away from them, listening to the sound of machinery and to the cry of gulls. But now he must follow Cécile Aubanne with special care.

She was hugging the buildings, walking very slowly, peering into every doorway. Before the massive building which contained the chief American naval offices she stopped. She stood for minutes, it seemed, staring alternately at the heavy doors and at the column of plaques which, affixed to the stone to right and left of the doorway, identified cryptically the offices within. Suddenly the doors opened to release a cluster of young naval officers, chattering gaily amongst themselves; they ambled off without paying any attention to her, and as the tall doors began their movement back toward rest, Cécile Aubanne slipped through.

Murchison had been in the building only once or twice, and it was an effort for him to recall what it was like inside. There was a wide corridor, not brightly lit, with office entries on either side—but few, for the ground-floor rooms, he remembered, were most of them gigantic. There was no place in the corridor that would afford even partial cover. On the other hand there would likely be several people walking in and out and through, men in army uniform as well as men in the garb of the Navy. He must find out where she went. He opened the door a crack in time to see her standing graceless in the middle of the corridor, her feet not quite far enough apart, her hands hanging like lumps at her sides. Then abruptly she lurched toward the first doorway on her left and walked through.

Murchison let the outer door slip closed again. There was nothing to do now but wait. He walked a few steps down the sidewalk and stood negligently turned away, looking out once more toward the water but this time seeing nothing, or recording nothing he saw, his senses narrowed down to register, when it came, the sound of a heavy door grinding faintly on its hinges. Gulls creaked high above him; footsteps scuffed or slapped, near or distant. There was a throb in the air of a heavy motor running perfectly. Two seamen passed him, one of them saying in a whining voice ". . . tried to get sent back to be there when the kid was born, but shit, you know him . . ."

When after many minutes the sound he was listening for came, he silently counted to ten, then turned as little as would suffice to let him catch a glimpse of the area around the entrance to the building. Cécile Aubanne, her head lowered, was trudging away in the direction from which she had come. She might be going back now where she belonged, or she might not; he would have to let that happen as it happened. Suddenly he realized that he could have telephoned Carl from one of the other offices in these few minutes he had had, and got Tochyk sent down here to follow the woman away while he tried to find out what she'd been doing inside; but it was too late for that now. She turned for a moment at the corner, but not to look back: she had never once looked back, he realized, in all the time he had been following her. Her turning face scanned the harbor as with a kind of weak radar; a white bat, he thought for no reason, clumsy in the daylight, reduced to its automatic functioning. When she was gone he walked rapidly back to the building she had just left, and hurried in.

In the reduced bloom of artificial light he saw, when his eyes had adjusted, a naval commander in summer tans standing in the doorway of the room Cécile Aubanne had entered. Commander—the name escaped Murchison, though he had met the man, he thought, or had him pointed out. The commander's face was annoyed and puzzled; he was looking back down the corridor toward a room from which loud laughter issued. Murchison walked up to him respectfully.

"Sir," he said, "excuse me. But—did a Frenchwoman come in here a moment ago? May I ask?"

"Huh?" The commander turned toward him. "Oh. Sure, you can ask. Walked in, gave me the fisheye, and walked right out again. If you're looking for her"—he pointed down the hall— "you might try back there. Something's stirred those idiots up, anyway."

"Thank you, sir," Murchison said.

"If you go in there, tell 'em from me to pipe down, will you?" the commander said. "I'm trying to think." He turned and disappeared into his office.

Somewhere behind the suspended focus of his thoughts Murchison found himself wondering, as he walked back along the glowing floor of the corridor, what this building had been before the war. Even the occasional crack in the plaster of its walls could not lessen the air of grandeur about it, the promise of sumptuousness in its waste space. Maybe a naval headquarters. He could have been on an errand to the Navy anywhere, London, Washington— He entered the room from which the laughter had come, a high, vast room white and gold and heavy rose floating above the foreign, matter-of-fact desks and office chairs. Silence fell as he stood there; faces turned, lifted toward him, an occasional bubble of soundless mirth still escaping.

Before he had thought how to begin, one of the two chief yeomen in the room said, "You, uh, lost too?" Uncertainly a new ripple of laughter commenced.

"Can it," someone said.

Murchison smiled. "I didn't mean to butt in," he said. "But I've been—" He reconsidered. "Tell me, did a Frenchwoman . . . ?"

The boy in whites sitting closest to him bounced back from his desk. "Not a *woman*," he said. "A real *zombie*." He paused

64

as if struck by something. "Excuse me. She ain't your girl, is she?"

"No." Murchison smiled again, then took the plunge. "But she had no business coming here. I've got to find out what she was doing. If you can tell me."

The chief who had spoken first said, "Uh, I don't know why not. She said she wanted a job. She had a grubby piece of paper she kept, uh, waving at us, like a recommendation or something; I couldn't make head or tail."

A job! A recommendation! He tried not to show his surprise. "What—kind of job?"

The boy in whites exploded into laughter again and pointed helplessly at one of his fellows, a tall blond youth who was sitting at a typewriter desk across the room. On his lap was a brass cuspidor, which he began polishing assiduously with a white cloth held in his left hand. With the index finger of his right hand he typed, hunt and peck, with exaggerated and painful slowness. His brow was furrowed, yet his face wore a bashful and provocative expression. His right leg he had hauled up precariously onto the table beside the typewriter; the trouser leg was pulled up above the knee, exposing a thick calf matted with golden hair. He smiled sweetly at Murchison. "Claimed she'd do anything," he said.

Once more the room rocked with laughter. "The Wave of the future," someone moaned.

"Goddam *tidal* wave!"

A steely voice spoke from behind them. "Almost through with your romp, you men? Because I believe there's work to do."

There was a scurry and a clatter and the room was quiet, heads bent over desks, over papers, hands fumbling in wire baskets. Murchison half turned. The commander nodded at him coldly and left.

Quickly, embarrassed, Murchison said to the chief, "That all there was to it?"

"That's all. We don't hire, you know that. She left her name. Said we could run it through a security check, and then if we ever changed our minds . . ."

"What name did she give you?"

65

The chief fished a piece of paper out of his pocket and handed it over. On it was written, in stiff pencil strokes, *Marie Clair*.

"Any address?"

"I didn't ask, uh—"

"Thanks," Murchison said, and nodded, and left.

It was unbearably clumsy, he thought in bewilderment as he walked on back to the hotel. Thury couldn't be behind it. Was she, after all, simply on the point of being cleared and released, and trying to find a way of getting started over?

But that phony name— And there would be a lot of secret information going through the naval headquarters. . . .

If she was being released wouldn't Thury have told them?

Was Cécile Aubanne, in spite of every likelihood to the contrary, an enemy agent, albeit a stupid one—an agent of whose activities Thury himself, somehow, might not know?

Or was this all a gag, a device of Thury's to get them worked up, to manipulate them, to interfere . . . ?

He liked it less and less.

We all have a talent for betrayal, Murchison thought.

He too. He hadn't changed. For he'd been ready enough to trick Thury. He'd make a first-class officer, a fine chief of mission. Weiller at least was direct. Weiller would do well to stay, whether Paris needed him or not.

As for himself, there were worse things than being a non-com. How had he got into this business?

Perhaps because it was after all worthwhile countering, as far as one could, the out-and-out treasons of which human beings were capable.

But he was not so messianic.

Louise he thought. I will not say your name again today. I've got to find Weiller, he'll have to figure out what has to be done. Maybe, by now, he knows all about it, knows exactly, has everything under control.

But I have nothing under control.

You do not get there all at once.

66

V.

THAT Weiller had failed to return was not surprising to Johnny. But it did nothing to increase his confidence, either.

By the time he had finished reading through the scattered papers on the Bouliard case it was eleven o'clock—too late, he found himself hoping, to start Thérèse's interrogation before lunch. But he did not know when the captain might turn up again; and though Weiller had told him to wait, he could not have meant him to wait forever.

The interrogation had not been formally planned, it was true. But they'd discussed most of the important points. Or he guessed they had. Nothing about what *order* to bring them up in; that must be a part of what you had to figure out ahead of time. . . . Johnny's weary mind refused for the moment the rush of new ideas, the awareness of ways to go wrong, that accompanied this thought. Stiffly he leaned back in the captain's chair and let his gaze wander around the empty office.

He felt very much alone, very much in a foreign land. And it was not only the strangeness of the—the lives, the happenings he had been studying, he told himself. Never in America had he been in a building that smelled like this, that had this damp, raw, fungus odor. Nor had he ever before seen such furniture, furniture that seemed unmeant to be used, or even touched by the hand.

All at once, without having intended it almost, he pushed his papers together and carried them out to where Carl Dolin would be sitting. Carl was talking over the telephone, his feet up on the desk in the middle of a rat's nest of classified documents. His ferocious expression did not alter when Johnny walked in. "Yas —yas—" he was saying. "Well in Christ's name how should I know? I suppose he'll do it when he gets around to it. *I* can't tell him to get the hell on with it, can I? Yas, sure, he knows about it." With apparent unwillingness, he paused to listen again. "Ah, tell the colonel to go back to sleep, and you'll wake him up when the report comes in. Maybe next Tuesday." He hung up, righted his precarious balance, and set the telephone down heavily on the oak desk.

"Oh, it's you, is it?" he said. "Well, whattaya know? Everything?" His tone was sarcastic, but a sour smile seemed to deny that there was any personal malice in what he said.

"Oh, sure," said Johnny glumly. "Or anyway enough to know I'm in about ten feet over my head." He sank down on a bench that was standing against the wall of the narrow entryway-lobby. "God, I wish I knew more about this stuff."

"That's the spirit," Carl said. "And oh-by-the-way—here to tell you is the latest installment of the Counterespionage News." He leaned across his desk and handed Johnny a piece of paper. "Papal bull I mean. Captain scribbled this out and told me to give it to you. I typed it; you couldn't have read his lousy handwriting."

"Thanks," Johnny muttered, and turned his face away and began reading.

PHILLIPS:

Sorry to have to pull out.

Naturally, if the girl's decided to talk by the time you get up there, there won't be any problem. Otherwise I'd simply announce to her that the facts of her case are well known to us, and that you're there to take down her story. Point out that it will be well for her if what she says conforms to what we already know.

If she still plays dumb, just start interrogating, organizing your questions under headings something like these: Life before contact with German Intelligence Service, full details of first and subsequent contacts, and so on, and so on.

If she keeps denying contact, say O.K., you'll take her story as she wishes it to be known; but warn her she's making a great mistake, and *make her account for every minute*

68

of the Occupation years, both for herself and for her father. You'll have seen a dozen ways to trip her up by the time she's through. Then you can pour it on, all at once.

About the Bloch note—remember what I said; let her tell her own story in her own way as much as you can. If nothing works, then finally I'd just hand that note to her quietly. After that it'll only be a matter of taking dictation. Good luck. I'll want a report this evening.

BW

"Yes, sir," said Johnny shakily to the blank wall. "No trouble at all, just come back in fifteen minutes and I'll have it for you." He sat down on the bench again and plucked at the papers of the Bouliard folder. He had been so grateful to be given a responsible job, and he was still grateful. But as he tried to remember—any detail of the thousands he was now supposed to know, the thought came to him of the girl somewhere upstairs, waiting, waiting for him, certainly by this time ready for him. He knew nothing. He could feel the blood pounding in his ears, in his throat, in his stomach, and suddenly he wondered whether like a child he was going to be sick.

Carl coughed. As Johnny looked up wanly the boy at the desk smiled an exaggerated smile. "Do you wish to be quoted as saying that you liked it better back in the minors?"

"That's where I belong, I guess," Johnny said. "Anyone could do this interrogation better than I can. *You'd* certainly—" He blushed. "I mean—"

"Don't give it a second thought," said Carl wryly. And then, "Weiller'd have put the scrubwoman onto the job before he'd have given it to me, so you might as well go ahead with it."

Johnny looked questioningly at him.

"Hadn't you caught on? Little Caesar and me, we don't get along so good." Carl leaned back in his chair and clasped his hands behind his head. "I was a sucker to let him know I hadn't finished typing those reports, of course; that took care of me, right there."

"Oh," said Johnny. "Well, he kind of beat up on me, too, so I don't know why he didn't give me the typing job and—"

Carl's good humor seemed completely restored. "Wouldn't

69

have been moral. He's got to improve my character. Anyway, there'd be no sense in your being put on the desk yet. It's not the big job, I don't mean that, but you won't be able to do anything with it until you've been around awhile. That creep from G-2 that just called up for instance—what would you have said if somebody'd asked *you* where the Schmidt report was? See, I been typing it on and off for the last week, but just in my spare time. It's not important. I'll get it to 'em when I get damn good and ready. The thing is, if the colonel doesn't have something to push around on top of his desk he feels left out of things. Well, it'd be a lot better for the Army if he had been left out. Screw him."

Johnny started involuntarily. "Colonel who?" he said. "What colonel?"

"Engstrom." The corners of Carl's mouth pulled down derisively. "He's the guy we work to in G-2—if you don't care what you say. I bet I've been into his office five times with reports or something, and found him balanced on two legs of his chair, snoring. He's bald as a coot, and he sits with his back to a window; I always figure if I see him with a big adhesive plaster all over his head, I'll know what's happened."

Johnny smiled; then, as he thought of the possibilities, he grew more sober. "Isn't that kind of a bad setup?" he said.

"Why?" Carl's voice sounded surprised.

"What about the work . . . ?"

"What about it? You don't think the officers do it, do you? Anywhere in the Army?"

Johnny did not answer; there seemed no point. But he said after a moment, "As a matter of fact I wondered, and maybe you can tell me. I mean—why the captain didn't take on this interrogation."

Carl looked at him keenly. "You're sure trying to get rid of it, aren't you?"

"Not exactly." Johnny flushed. "It just seems so damned important—I don't know. And he knows I haven't had much of any experience."

"That suits him down to the ground," Carl said. "Right now he isn't especially interested in sticking his neck out, see?" He leaned forward. "I'll give you the low-down on something. Weiller's playing footie with the top brass of this outfit. There's going to be a spot in Paris for an earnest young officer, it seems, and he figures he's in line for that spot *and* for a majority if he doesn't foul up out here. They knocked his props partway out from under him by carting off Rhodes and Bailey, but all is not lost, maybe, if everything just moves fast enough. So he's playing it cool. Stalling. Get it?"

"I— No," said Johnny.

"Well, look. He went up to talk to the Bouliard dame for a few minutes this morning. But he didn't really buckle down to the job. Too busy. Too much else to do. Busy busy. You get the picture now."

Johnny shook his head.

"Hell. Supposing this girl doesn't break the first time round—" Carl interrupted himself hastily. "Don't worry about it, I don't mean that, she's practically bound to—but just supposing she didn't? Well, my God, the way things are he couldn't afford to have her crossing *him* up, could he? If *we* fail, then—well, *he* didn't recruit us. He can't make too much of being shorthanded, because he's still supposed to run a tight show. But he can fill the pouch with paper—any sort of junk, the Schmidt report—to show that Thérèse Bouliard is only one of many cases he's got to cope with; he can act noble but uncomplaining; and finally he can send the girl herself on up the line, if he has to, saying 'Importance of subject indicates that she should be interrogated at the highest echelon' or some damn thing. He'd likely get away with it."

Johnny looked at Carl incredulously.

"You think I'm kidding?" Carl said. "Hah. But of course if you break her—which you will—he can pat you on the head, not too hard, and go on upstairs and get a little extra stuff out of her, and go on being the big guy who's way ahead of the game."

"He's not as bad as all that, is he?" Johnny protested. "In there I thought he was pretty impressive—obviously he knew the whole thing by heart. I won't say I didn't get griped at him once or twice—"

Carl just looked at him.

"But anyway, what I meant back there was," Johnny said, "he told me Thérèse Bouliard was really important. He said she couldn't wait. And surely he wouldn't risk the case just to be in the clear himself, would he?"

"Why not?" Carl put his feet up on the desk again. "But hell, Phillips, I'm not trying to pull you over on my side of the fence, especially. Matter of fact, Weiller had a couple of other reasons for going off to see Thury this morning. He goes over there once a week—oftener, of course, if there's something special doing; but they have a regular time when they keep check on how things are going generally. Like you were probably told, the French army has a counterespionage setup same as we have. But two heads are no better than one, and Frogs are Frogs, and Weiller's always scared they'll hold something out on him if he doesn't keep a close check." He shrugged. "Myself, I don't know. Only I do know that Thury gives the captain lunch after these meetings, and breaks out the wine, and the captain has a ve-ry good time. Keeping in touch with the French may not be too easy, but it's got its rewards."

Suddenly Johnny felt irritated and depressed. Why did everything have to be spoiled by people? This morning, walking back from the waterfront, he'd felt pretty good; now he was scared, and dispirited too. Listlessly he got to his feet. "Guess I might as well go on up," he said. "If you can take me now."

Carl looked at him sharply, then dropped his eyes. "Say, Phillips—or what do they call you, John? Jack?"

"Johnny." It was the name he had always had.

"Well. I didn't mean to make you feel lousy about all this. It's a pretty good job—interesting, and I guess the captain isn't too bad, for a captain. Anyway, he's going to get out of here, remember? If we're lucky. They're going to waft him up to heaven on angel wings. And then we can all settle down."

"Who's—who's going to take over here?" Johnny asked. He did not really care.

"Why, God's only grandson, of course. Murchison. He's already a mainstay in the lunch-with-Thury routine. And Weiller's just put in for a commission for him."

Johnny burst out sharply, miserably, "Carl, don't you like *anybody?*"

After a moment's silence Carl said quietly, "Don't mind the way I talk." He paused. "You're damn right I like Murchison.

He's worth two of—well, me, for instance. And when he's in charge he'll anyway give me a *chance*."

Johnny made a defeated gesture.

"No, not this interrogation, I didn't mean that," Carl said. "Take it easy, will you? If Murchison can't do it, and Weiller won't, you're the right man for it. I'd bank on that."

Johnny sighed, shook his head and gave Carl a wraithlike smile.

Carl grinned back. "Let's cut it, huh? I'll take you on up now if you want. Got enough paper and pencils and so on?"

"I guess so." He had the pad the captain had given him; from the Bouliard folder he extracted the note signed "Bloch," and tucked it in firmly among the clean back pages. "Maybe I should have some extra pencils." He picked up the folder and cards from the bench, took a last, lingering look at them, and gave them to Carl. Silently the boy at the desk put them down, then handed him three sharpened pencils from a drawer.

"Mademoiselle Bouliard," Johnny said in a clear voice, "let me say at once . . ."

"Right," Carl said. "Let's go." He walked over and snapped the lock on the front door.

"Carl—before we go up—you've done things like this before, haven't you? Have you got any advice for me? Have I looked over everything I should have?"

Carl thought for a moment. "Weiller showed you Bouliard's stuff, I suppose."

"I—what do you mean, her stuff?"

"Well, we searched her, of course, when Tochyk brought her in. Matter of fact it was funny—I don't suppose you ever thought how you'd go about searching a dame?" Carl giggled reminiscently.

Oddly enough there was something remotely consoling to Johnny in all this—the instant suggestion of vulgarity, the reminder that others had been in routine contact with the prisoner. Dangerous. . . . She might have been dangerous, he thought, but surely the very indignity of submitting to search had made her a little less so. "What—did you do?" he asked.

Carl led the way to a tiny room at the rear of the ground

floor, whose door he unlocked with difficulty and pushed open. It was so dark inside that he had to press the light switch when he entered. The room lighted up. "That's lucky," he said seriously. "For you too. Sometimes the juice is off in the daytime."

Johnny looked around him questioningly. There were boxes of papers piled all over the floor, and in the corner a worn old bicycle, with what looked like a bundle of rags strapped around the handlebars. The room smelled musty and unused.

"Wish the goddam Navy would come and get this stuff," Carl said sourly. "The papers. This hotel was occupied by a minor naval command under the Krauts, and for some reason or other they didn't destroy their records. No interest to them, for us anyway. But the Port Commander's office seems to want them, and we said we'd hold them."

He was making his way toward the bicycle through the piles of papers; halfway across the room he paused and looked back at Johnny. "Oh, I was telling you about searching Bouliard. Well, first we called up the colonel, but he didn't have any ideas; just sat at the other end of the phone squeaking. Wanted to know when we were going to interrogate her, and was she pretty."

"Oh, of course," Johnny said. "He'd be in on this case too, wouldn't he?"

"Sure, but hell—" Carl looked at him firmly. "Anyway, like I say, the colonel didn't have anything to offer, so we were still up a stump. Finally someone thought of calling Thury. And you know what he did?"

"What?"

"Sent over his secretary!"

Carl paused for effect, but Johnny could only stare back at him.

"O.K., that may not surprise you first off. The thing is, this girl—her name's de Sombais—was the *Gestapo* secretary here all through the Occupation! Can you beat it? Of course she was denounced right and left when the Germans got kicked out, but Thury got his hands on her—he was going to put her in the jug, everybody thought—and the first thing you know she winds up being his secretary! He says she saved all the

74

Gestapo records for the Allies, and maybe she did, I don't know; but by God if she did I'll bet it was strictly to save her neck. Of course, Thury swears she's pure as the driven snow; but I guess it's all in how you look at it. Everyone knows she's sleeping with him. As apparently she did with many a good German before him. Jeez—what a country! Wouldn't it give you the shakes to think of that dame handling all the secret French documents, and some of ours too—after what she's been up to?"

Johnny nodded absently. As he talked, Carl had unstrapped the little bundle of clothing from the handlebars of the bicycle and had passed it over; now Johnny squatted down in the middle of the floor to see what there was. It wasn't much—a heavy dark blue dress of some sleazy cotton material, with two paper-wrapped packages inside.

Carl kept on talking. "Well, this de Sombais, she was more than happy to be of any help, of course. We didn't like the idea a bit, but we'd bought it, and that was that. And she may be all right, as Thury says; if she's smart, she probably knows the Germans aren't coming back, and she'd *better* be all right. But anyway. When she saw Bouliard her whole face lit up. 'Why, Thérèse,' she says, in a voice like ice cream, 'imagine our meeting like this!' Then she whips Bouliard into the undressing room, or whatever you want to call it, so fast you can't see straight.

"Bouliard yells once, and then de Sombais comes out with the clothes, and we all go through them. Nothing there—just like there isn't anything in that stuff you've got. And according to de Sombais, who you could see was real disappointed about it, nothing hidden on the girl herself, either. Finally we went all over the bicycle; no concealed papers, not a damned thing. Pretty smart girl. But that de Sombais—Jesus, am I glad I'm not French. They're going to spend years now chopping each other up into mincemeat."

Johnny was looking soberly at the contents of the paper-wrapped bundles. One of them contained a dry, hard roll, broken in pieces now, its exposed surfaces a heavy unpalatable-looking gray under the gray-brown crust. The other package contained a pair of white underpants, thin and perfectly clean, the elastic at the waist broken and frayed in several places. He stared at them for a moment. "Isn't there anything else?" he asked abruptly.

"Not a thing. Traveled light, didn't she?" Carl looked thoughtful. "Wait." He rummaged through his pockets and drew out a white envelope. "I got this out of the safe for you. It's her *permis de circuler.*"

Johnny drew the paper out of the envelope and read it through. Then he handed it back and looked questioningly at Carl.

"Seems to be all in order. But you realize it doesn't prove much one way or the other; no reason why they shouldn't let her come back to Cherbourg, if this is—or was—her home."

Johnny nodded; he did not feel like speaking. He could see, now, why the captain had kept on insisting "You've got no personal feelings," and "Let's not be sensitive." It was fatally easy to dream up a pathetic story to go with all this; and if it was easy for him, he could imagine how much easier it would be for the girl. Well, now at least he was prepared.

"O.K., Carl," he said. "Thanks a lot; that does it, I guess. I better get to work."

Carl put the girl's possessions together again, in the far corner where they had stood before; then the two left the room, turning off the light and locking the door behind them. Carl led the way up the narrow stairway, of which flight after flight climbed toward a small, dingy skylight in the roof. Yet in spite of the many turnings to the stairs, the many landings, there were not so many floors to the hotel, it seemed. The offices were on the ground floor, the men's quarters on the second; then there was a floor that was, so far as Johnny could tell, untenanted, and on the fourth floor, just under the skylight, they stopped. A boy whom Johnny recognized as Glid Barker, the driver who had brought him in from the airfield, sat listlessly against the corridor wall; he was tapping the holster of his forty-five and whistling softly something that might have been "Alexander's Ragtime Band."

"That's the room over there." Carl pointed down the corridor to the left of the stairwell. "Number forty-seven." He grinned. "I wouldn't bother to knock. Just walk right in and make yourself at home. Here's the key."

Johnny stared at him, agonizingly aware of his ease, his jocularity, his matter-of-course air. He himself had felt confident once or twice during the morning; now suddenly he felt as though he could do nothing—as though he could not even begin. "Honest, hadn't you better tackle this?" he whispered to Carl.

"Nuts," said Carl. "Go on in there, fella. Hit 'em hard."

Slowly Johnny turned and walked down the corridor to the blank door. The paint was ugly, he noticed, mottled and marbled and cracked; the doorknob was of cheap carved wood. He could feel Carl's and Barker's eyes boring through his back. The silence was like a deafening sound. Quickly he inserted the key in the lock, turned it, and threw open the door upon absolute darkness.

VI.

AFTERWARD Johnny wondered why he had not asked Carl how the room was laid out, or why Carl had not told him without being asked. But now as he stood there in the doorway he was conscious of nothing but shock. The darkness of the room seemed to pour out over him, to inundate him like a giant wave; and in another, greater wave, gathering behind the first, it was as though something evil were gliding toward him, towering over him.

Almost he took a step backward; but somehow, just in time, he regained control of himself and reached out to grope for a light fixture on the wall inside the door. There was one there; with relief he flicked the switch. Instantly an almost blinding glare, coming from a table to his right, slashed through the half of the room away from the corridor.

It was not a large room; with the light on, Johnny felt almost as though he could touch both side walls if he stretched out his arms. In the far wall there was a window whose glass appeared to have been painted black. And on the floor below it, as at the end of the room's brief avenue, lay a straw mattress covered with gray and white striped ticking. There was no bedstead, and no other bedding. Curled up on the mattress in the angle of the wall was the figure of a girl, slight, thinly clothed against the damp air of the stone building. The girl's hands were over her face, but not as though she were weeping; her body was taut, pressed back defensively against the wood and plaster.

Johnny walked into the room, and shut the door behind him, silently. It was easy to see why the girl had not had the light on before; there was not a single chair in the room, no place

78

she could sit down or lie down but the mattress, and there the light transfixed her brutally.

Suddenly Johnny was angry. He recalled how he had felt once at school when some malignant brat had unexpectedly struck a match and thrust it, blazing, close up to his eyes. He had struck out in fury, astonishing himself and his tormentor. The fact that the girl's gesture, now, was wholly defensive made him strangely uncomfortable. He hated the position he had been forced into, the method which had already been dictated to him as clearly as though the captain had shouted it at him; somehow he wanted the girl too to hate it and resist it.

But then he had to remind himself that she was evil: not even "guilty until proved innocent," since there seemed no question of that, but simply guilty. And guilt meant that her casual choice would have butchered thousands of American soldiers in raw blood, and still would do so if it could.

A glance told him that the whole room was arranged to tyrannize over its occupant. Unless she had stood at the table by the door waiting for him—suddenly he realized how startled he would have been if she had done so, since she would have been almost upon him as he entered—she must cower beneath the glaring light. There was a reflector behind the bulb to reinforce its brilliance; this shaded the corner of the room behind it. And since the light fixture was clamped to the fore edge of the table, a little space was in fact left behind it, on the side toward the wall, where it would be possible to sit unblinded by the light. Obviously this place was meant for the interrogator, who, in comfortable shadow, could see almost without being seen. But even where he stood, by the door, Johnny realized, the girl could hardly see him, so there was no particular point in her uncovering her eyes.

This tableau could not endure forever. He was choosing what he would say when a knock came at the door behind him. He opened; it was Barker, with a chair.

"Carl said you'd want this," the boy said sulkily.

Johnny thanked him and closed the door again. Carl, too, he thought. In a moment he might himself have seen that he could not do without a chair; but he would have asked for two.

And yet—there was no fundamental, irretrievable cruelty

here, only a deliberate use of humiliation, of exasperation, as a method of keeping the prisoner off balance. But surely, he thought, the ends of justice could be achieved through more dignified and worthy means. . . . Perhaps so; but it was also true that he himself understood such means no better than he understood this. He could hear Weiller saying coldly, "Let's not be too god damned sensitive, Mr. Phillips." There was so much he had to learn; perhaps when he had learned it this philosophical struggling would seem ridiculous to him. Confused and depressed by his own indecision, he dragged the chair over to the relative shadow of the table, put down his paper and pencils, and sat down. The sound of wood scraping on wood seemed to hang in the air, like a mutter of thunder.

When Johnny looked up again, the girl's hands lay inert at her sides; she was staring. It was almost, he thought, like the stare of a blind person—the eyes exceptionally light, and wide, yet clearly unseeing. The hollows beneath the eyes were nearly black, even in the glare of the unshielded lamp; they looked in a way as though they had been put on with makeup, staged by her for effect, therefore, as the rest of this curious scene had been staged by Weiller.

The girl's skin looked yellow in the strong light; probably she was rather brown, Johnny thought. Her features were not regular, but the skin stretched so tautly and smoothly over the high cheekbones, over the unassuming lines of forehead and nose, that a look of tensity and focus was achieved far stronger than the harmonies that produce beauty. Some people might even have called this girl ugly, Johnny saw; her face was certainly too narrow and pointed. But there was so much bewilderment in the expression, so insistent and sorrowful a question, that it was hard to judge how the face would look in tranquillity, or under the changing impress of happiness.

Suddenly Johnny realized that he had already made a judgment: the girl was bewildered and unhappy. Unhappy she had every reason to be, but for the rest— He shivered. I am not competent to do this, he said to himself again. If the acting has begun, I'm damned lucky to have this light out in front of me; and if it hasn't . . . Oh, God. Well, he told himself—at Lichfield, too, I asked myself, What am I doing here?

Shielding her eyes once more with her hands, the girl rose to her feet and took a few tentative steps toward him. The movement disconcerted Johnny. "Please—go back and sit down," he said.

Slowly the girl complied, but as she sank to the mattress again with unexpected dignity, she said fiercely, "It is not justice! You do not tell me, any of you, why I am here."

She was not going to confess, then.

"Mademoiselle Bouliard," Johnny said in a thin, dry voice which he could barely keep steady, "let me say at once that there is no doubt—can be none—either as to what you have done or what you were prepared to do." It was his rehearsed speech; it sounded like one. But perhaps she would not notice. "Most of the details we already know; for we have talked with one of your—employers. And he was less loyal to you and to your father than you would have been, perhaps, to him."

The girl's eyes were wide; she was staring at a point somewhere at his feet with an expression of dismay on her face. Johnny cleared his throat and his voice grew stronger.

"It is obvious," he said, "that there must be some unimportant details which we do not as yet have. Be sure that we shall get them, either from you or from others. In all fairness, however, we intend to give you an opportunity to tell your own story fully. You would have done better to give us that story voluntarily; but you did not give yourself up, nor have you offered since your arrest to tell us what you know. I am here to give you your last chance. I am speaking to you in English; you are to answer me in English. Start from the beginning and tell me the full story of your father's work, and your own work, for the Nazis."

"For the Nazis!" The words were a cry, so startling, so full of horror that Johnny jumped in his chair. He had felt more and more sure of himself as he spoke; it had seemed that any reasonable human being must respond. Now, staring at the girl's face, in which shocked emotion, or a vivid semblance of it, covered any other thought she might have, he could find no words.

Thérèse Bouliard waited for none. "M'sieur—for God's sake," she said in a shaking voice. "I plead with you. I do not know what enemy we could have had, to tell you such things, such lies about us. But they *were* lies! You must believe! There was no one in France who did not have to—deal with the Nazis in one way or another, since that they forced us to do. And spiteful people could always look on, and say it was too much. Or too little. But I—" Her voice quieted. "M'sieur, was it that Estelle de Sombais? She, you must know, worked for the Gestapo for many years! She is not to be believed! I—I have never worked for the Nazis, at all, in any way, I swear it!"

Johnny's heart felt like a lump of stone. He had lost completely; he had won nothing. Even his conviction was assailed—wary as he had tried to be of emotion, her voice was deeply moving.

Yet he distrusted the readiness with which she had sought to shift the blame. And after all, the stakes here were very high. Perhaps she could sense his inexperience and was willing to pit her acting talents against it. Well; he would not be put off. He said firmly, "And your father—you wish me to believe that he did not work for the Germans either?"

The girl hung her head. When she raised it again there was a dazed, frightened expression on her face. She said, "I—believe that he did. But as I have said, many did so. Surely you understand this? You would have to arrest, oh, a quarter of the people in Cherbourg, perhaps more, and the same all over France, if to have worked for the Germans during the Occupation were to be counted a crime. Let me tell you, my father did not like to do that; he was very proud. And he was without work a very long time before he consented. But our savings were not great, and—" There was a hard, growing indignation in the look she turned toward the shadows where Johnny sat. "Even the French, m'sieur, must eat. And France, though captive, was not dead; she had to go on. It is no shame to us that that is so."

"Perhaps I have not made myself clear," Johnny said huskily. "I know, of course, that during the Occupation some of your countrymen were forced to go on with their regular work under orders from the Germans. Or take other jobs in which their position was similar. But—" He paused. "For those who were willing to take advantage of them, we know that entirely new opportunities arose as well—opportunities that most people

82

might have frowned at, perhaps, so that usually they have remained secret." Johnny leaned forward in his chair and said in as cold a voice as he could command, "Not always. I should like an account now, please, in full detail, of your father's *secret* work for the Germans. And your own."

The light was so strong that he could not tell, but he thought that the girl turned even paler than she had been. "Secret?" she said in a trembling voice. "I—my father was a teacher, you do not understand. Not a scientist. He taught languages. And I am not trained at all. What could we do that would be secret?"

It was very hard, thought Johnny wearily. He wondered what a trained interrogator would do in a case like this—what Captain Weiller would do. There must be some way of tripping the girl up at once, making her betray herself, so that she could not go on with these protestations of ignorance. But what would it be?

He could produce the Bloch note. Should he? In a way it would be a great relief. But Weiller had said he should save it; and he could see that now, with nothing admitted, nothing established, the note too could be treated as part of the whole horrifying, bewildering attempt to get her into trouble. After all, he had not failed yet. The thing was not to get rattled. If she was playing for time, so might he. No matter what was happening, she was still worse off than he was.

"Mademoiselle," he said, "you are wasting much time. Not mine; I have only this to do. But your own, for—perhaps there is not so much time for you as you think. And unless you tell me your story, you have not even the smallest hope. I repeat that we know a great deal about you." He gazed at her seriously, and realized suddenly that she could not see the impressive gravity of the expression he had assumed. He went on hastily, "You admitted that your father worked for the Germans during the Occupation. Let us start there. What work was it? When did it begin? Everything, please."

Slowly her wide-eyed stare toward the shadows where he sat dulled and dropped. In a muffled voice she said, "There is not much I can tell you."

Johnny sighed heavily. "I warn you not to be unwise."

"It is not unwisdom! I will tell you what I can, it is only not very much. While my father taught, I of course knew these things, but afterwards—only that what he did was not wrong."

"And how did you know that?"

She straightened up jerkily; when she spoke there was in her voice a tremendous pride. "Because he was good. Good men do not do bad things."

Johnny pulled the pad and pencil toward him. He would have to begin sometime to take notes. "When did your father stop teaching?"

"In the autumn of 1940. The head of the Lycée told him he could not go back. It was the Germans; they said they had proof that he had been a Freemason, and though he had not, in the end there was nothing he could do." She paused. "We thought—perhaps—that they had learned instead that he had lived in England, and loved the English civilization; it might have been that they were—afraid of what he might say in his classes."

"Your father loved the English?"

"Yes, m'sieur."

Johnny smiled sardonically to himself. "And the Americans too, I suppose."

She said in a hardly audible voice, "Not so much, m'sieur."

At the sound of the obvious truth, he sat bolt upright in his chair. "Why—not?"

"You must not be angered," she said hurriedly. "It was an old affair with him, I think; he had a brother once who went to America—my father even helped him to go—and he did well there, Uncle Charles, but his success did not make him—generous. Or so my father said; and he thought it was America that had done this, and the way Americans were. Even the money my father had lent was not returned, though soon he had great need of it. And when France was defeated, and England very nearly, and still America did nothing, then he was very bitter—in a general way, you understand."

"And when America did enter the war?" Johnny had a sheepish feeling, now, that he was exploring a very unimportant side issue, but after all he could not be sure.

The girl was looking more and more embarrassed. "It was

84

the Germans who—declared war on America," she answered. "My father thought that otherwise nothing would have been done. But this is not wrong, surely? I mean, against the law? He had many thoughts, as people do, and perhaps not always just thoughts, but—" She shook her head. "If you knew only this about him you would not know what was important."

Johnny persisted. "You think these opinions of your father's were not in every way just?"

The girl hesitated. Then she said proudly, "What do you wish me to say, m'sieur? I studied much in school. I did not think they were just. At that time I did not think even Germany was entirely to be disliked, though we were not taught, you understand, to be friendly. But I suppose this is a crime now, too."

Johnny wondered how the girl dared talk like this, since after all she did not know him. Perhaps she was trying to give the impression of scrupulous honesty. But with most interrogators, surely, it would have done her little good. Could it be real, after all, a real honesty that would hide nothing? But then why would she not admit the connection with the Germans? The consistent answer, that no such connection existed, was denied by the paper evidence, which could scarcely be coincidental, or entirely mistaken. She seemed so young; and was obviously harder, more complex, than any other girl he had ever known. He had better start over again.

"What was your father's full name?" he asked coldly. The name was in the file.

"Pierre Paul Bouliard."

And your mother's name?"

"Anna. Anna Plonwy, before she was married. She was Polish."

"Polish? But your father was French?"

"Yes, m'sieur. Born in Paris. He was the son of a bookseller."

"How did he happen to learn so many languages?"

"He had traveled, m'sieur. His father did fairly well in business; he wished the two sons to see something of other countries. After the first war my father spent a year in Spain, and then a year in Germany, and then two years in England. And then he came back to Paris and met my mother, whose family had taken refuge there. From some trouble; I do not know exactly."

Johnny was scribbling rapid notes; it was a moment before he could go on to the next question.

"Your father had a brother Charles, you say. Any other brothers or sisters?"

"No, m'sieur."

"And your grandparents?"

"What do you mean?"

"Are they still alive?"

"No; they died many, many years ago."

That was a very lucky thing, thought Johnny, for them. "Now your mother's family."

The girl said reluctantly, "We did not know much about them, after the first. I, never, of course. My mother died when I was born, and the families were not much connected afterward. My father told me once that his parents had thought it— not a good marriage."

"Why?"

"My mother's family had no money. And they were not established; no one knew about them. The parents could not read or write, I do not think even in Polish—he was—" She looked at him with a troubled brow. "An *égoutier;* do you know that? As in *Les Misérables.*"

Johnny nodded without speaking and wrote the word down in French. He did not know what it meant; but she was not to learn that. In a moment he said, "Were there other children in the family besides your mother?"

"Oh, yes. I think many. Some in Poland still, and several with the parents—besides my mother, two sons and a daughter, at least."

"And you do not know what became of them?"

"Only my mother's sister. Rose. She lives not so far from here —Sartilly. Between Granville and Avranches. On a farm; her husband's name is Corrail, and they have quite a big farm. It is nice."

The farm. He was beginning to get somewhere, he thought.

86

When he spoke, he tried to keep his voice casual. "You and your father kept in touch with them, then?"

The girl looked a little perplexed. "In touch?"

"You saw the Corrails often, or got letters from them?"

"Since we have come to Cherbourg, we saw them—oh, once or twice. Not much. My father more than I." She looked toward him uncertainly. "For me, they are not very—good. We do not—did not like them."

"Why not?"

She shrugged. "Oh—it is all money with them. What things cost, what they are worth. That place is beautiful, where they live, but they will never know it. And their friends—are the friends of money too. All cold." Her brow creased. "You can understand what I mean?"

"Yes," Johnny said. The girl was wandering, though it did not perhaps matter; and he had found out enough about the farm for the present. Still he would have to organize his questions better.

The story was a simple one so far, and rather likable. But after all, it was silly to think of people as all bad, or all good; and the virtues, the fine and sensitive characteristics of an evil person might make him all the more dangerous, even sinister, in the end.

"Now, mademoiselle," he said, "I should like to go back to your father. Was he always a teacher, and if so where? You have said that he went from England to Paris, where he married your mother. When was that? And recently you have lived, it seems, in Cherbourg. Please tell me what happened in between, and exactly when it happened. When were you born, for example? And have you, or had you, any brothers or sisters? If you tell the entire story just as it happened, from the beginning, it will be easier for us both."

The girl passed her hand before her eyes in a soft, lingering gesture. At length she said, "You will tell me if I do not say— enough? For I am not sure what interests you. I do not know what you are trying to find out."

Johnny answered dryly, "I'll interrupt if I need to."

"Thank you," she said seriously. "Well, then, my father returned to Paris in—the spring of 1923, it would have been. He was the elder son, and he was to carry on the book business. He was not, however, I think good at affairs. He helped in the shop, and it was there he met my mother, who was learning French and read a great deal. You understand, she was trying to better herself. She was very intelligent, my father says; and he was having trouble with his family, and he found her very pleasant and understanding. He did not like her family, after he knew them, either, and he saw they were not suitable; but then they did not seem to look upon things as the French do, and he did not think he would have trouble with them. Besides, he was very stubborn, and when his parents said he should stop seeing my mother, then especially he would not do so." She looked up, her expression sad. "It can be like this, do you know? At the time it seems very difficult. But many years later we— shrug our shoulders, you say?—and cannot so much regret, because things happen as they happen." She looked toward him, then away, and said in a tentative voice, "One day I—think I shall tell also the tale of how the Americans arrested me."

He said gruffly, "Your story, mademoiselle."

"Yes, m'sieur. . . . They were married then, my father and mother, late in 1923, and I was born the next year, and it was then my mother died. At this my father was reconciled with his parents. He had tried to make his own way with what he knew of languages, but he had not done well alone; and the father— my grandfather—still needed him in the shop, since the brother Charles was not interested in books, not in the least. We lived in Paris for about ten years, I recall. At first there was a wet nurse for me; it was planned that my grandmother would bring me up. But she was already old, and died I think when I was four; and Grandfather after that had little interest in anything, even the shop, and soon he too died."

Johnny had thought of something. "What had been your grandparents' political and religious beliefs?" he asked. "I mean, what was your father brought up to believe?"

The girl looked alarmed. "Why—I do not know," she said. "Ordinary things. They were Protestant; they believed in the government. My father too, except—" Her eyes were downcast. "He was not religious. It was because so many things went wrong for him, I think—he could not believe there was a good God in heaven. But," she said hastily, "he always said he would not stop me from believing, if I could."

"And do you believe?"

There was a pause. Finally she answered sadly, "Sometimes."

Johnny said, "All right. Go on with the story."

By now she seemed unaware of the brightness of the light, or almost so. Her eyes stared, as though through the light into darkness.

"I told you my father was not—clever at affairs," she said. "Soon after the death of my grandparents my Uncle Charles demanded to go to America, though it would take more than his share of the money there was to do so. Of course I do not know this myself; it is what my father has told me. The money was found, but—it was too much, or not wisely arranged, I do not know, and within a year the old business failed. Already my Uncle Charles had written that he was doing well, and had asked for more money still to be sent so that he might take advantage of the wonderful opportunities. He was I think interested in mechanical things. My father answered that he was himself in serious troubles, and had to have back the earlier loan; but it did not come. Uncle Charles wrote that my father was improvident, and should not be permitted to ruin them both—I have seen that letter. My father wrote again, but after that there was no more word, and as I have told, the bookstore failed. After the stocks were sold, and what properties there were, a little money was left. My father then decided to be a teacher of languages, and began the studies necessary in that regard—I do not know exactly what. This was in Paris still—continuing up to—1933, I think. There should be records, is that not so? If the Germans have not destroyed them."

"It doesn't matter," Johnny said. "So your father started teaching in 1933?"

"Not regularly, m'sieur. The times were not the best; he could not at once find a place. It was then we left Paris. My father thought that in the south, where there were many villas owned by the English, he might find some English children to teach. But this was not so. After a time he found a place at a lycée in Arles; this was in 1934. In 1936 we moved to Montargis, south of Paris. And in the summer of 1939 to Cherbourg. We have been here since. This is all, m'sieur." It was a statement, but her voice rose on the concluding words.

"Well," said Johnny. "No, I don't think it is all, quite." They had come around, again, to the difficult part. "Your father taught here, you've told me, at the Lycée des Jeunes Filles, only for a year. And you've lived here five years. I ask you once more. What did he do after the Germans arrived in 1940?"

She looked at him, not defiantly but with an unhappy dignity. "I have told you, m'sieur. I do not know."

Johnny was still taking notes from the earlier testimony; now he bent closer to the table and prolonged the task as he tried to figure out what to say. It was hopeless, he supposed. He had avoided the conflict for a time only; now he was no better off than before. Yet somehow he felt easier about it—perhaps more accustomed to his role. He turned back to the girl. "You wish me to believe this, mademoiselle?"

"Oh, yes, m'sieur," she said eagerly, her pale eyes wide. "Because it is true, it is honestly true."

"You lived alone with your father?" he asked gently.

"Yes."

"So that you had only each other to talk to."

She hesitated. "For the most part, yes."

"And you wish me to believe that for the last nearly four years before his death your father was working, working perhaps as hard as before, leaving the house in the morning, coming back in the evening, with no one else but you, his own daughter, to hear what he had been thinking and doing during the day, and yet he said nothing, and you asked no questions, and never learned a single thing about how he occupied himself?"

She was sitting bowed over the mattress as though by a heavy weight; her fingers plucked at the coarse, striped ticking. As Johnny finished speaking she looked up miserably.

"No," she said in a low voice. "It is not exactly like that. But a little."

Johnny sat back in his chair. "You'd better explain," he said.

"M'sieur," she broke out, "do you not see that this is very difficult for me? I must tell you that my father was in some ways

90

a strange man, though I understood him and loved him; but where I understood, had of necessity to understand, you will only doubt because you do not know him. And m'sieur—perhaps you are not so—cruel as all this seems; once or twice since we began I have thought that. Yet I do not understand what you are trying to do, and I must defend myself—I must defend my father!"

Her voice through this had grown more and more agitated; now slowly her eyes brimmed with tears, and the tears spilled over. Johnny was aghast—not so much at the tears as at the thought of what they meant. The girl was no longer in control of herself; and he had reason to be glad of this. It was not a pleasant business.

In a voice that was painfully unsteady, the girl went on, "It is not that I would hide the truth, but the truth is that I do not know the truth, though not for the reasons I fear you will imagine, and since you—attack, and attack, I—find it difficult to present to you the knife."

Johnny said, "Mademoiselle Bouliard—you must recall that I represent the American armed forces. The security of the American armed forces is my only interest. If your father did not threaten that security, if you do not do so, I assure you that you have nothing to fear. Only you *must* tell me everything you know—can't you see that? How can I—" His tone also was growing emotional; he paused to steady himself. "*We* have evidence to prove you are guilty; unless *you* give evidence of your innocence—even though you fear how some of it may be interpreted, but you must trust us for that—how do you imagine that you can be cleared of the charges against you?"

It was as though she had not heard past the first few words. "I—threaten the American Army? My father do so? M'sieur—in what way? How can you think this?"

Johnny said urgently, "Tell me fully what your father did after he lost his job as a teacher. Or as much as you know."

She answered in a subdued voice, "Very well, m'sieur. At first of course he did nothing; that you will understand. Except look for work. But there was no longer any teaching open to him. We had not much money put by, since it was only a few years that my father had worked regularly. And then, too, when we had come to Cherbourg he had bought the house in which we lived. It was—I think a kind of—magic, m'sieur," she said unsteadily. "He thought that then we would stay." She looked vacantly at the wall. "As we did."

"You owned the house?" Johnny asked hastily.

She shrugged. "There was a large debt upon it. But we owned it, yes."

"How long did your father look for work before he found something?"

"I do not know exactly, m'sieur. A very long time. It was a —a dreadful time. My father was very proud, you see; when he could not find work it was very terrible for him. And of course there were certain things that he did not at first think of doing —it was not that he was not strong enough, but he was a traveled man, you understand, an educated man, and it was hard for him to think of becoming a laborer. But everything else was closed. Before the war he might have found something in the port, where in several kinds of work it was necessary to speak English; but now this was all gone. There was no use for languages."

"Except German," said Johnny thoughtfully.

The girl on the mattress shivered. "Yes, German," she said. "But he did everything he could think of before he went to the Germans. He tried working as an untrained laborer, in private trades; I remember how it horrified him, he would go out in the morning dressed in his ordinary clothes so that the neighbors would not see, and then change to work clothes in the church, or in a urinal somewhere. He told me that once. When he was explaining that he could not do more. I of course," she said proudly, "did not question this. But he could not make enough money that way, being untrained; he was not, you see, a—a craftsman. And it tired him too much. At last he told me that he would register for work at the Kommandantur, where he could use his knowledge of German. He was ashamed; he felt as though he were selling his soul to the devil." She tossed her head and looked defiantly toward Johnny through the blaze of light. "It was not so, of course. Many things were controlled by the Germans, directly or—in hidden ways, and if the French had not worked on, as best they could, soon they would have had no country."

"Did he get work at once, then?" asked Johnny.

Once more the girl lowered her gaze. "I do not know, m'sieur," she said. "I know only that he left the house every day, as you said, in the morning, and late in the afternoon returned very tired. Once I asked him whether he was working, or merely looking for work, and he said that I must not ask him again. He said that I must trust him to do the best he could. It was very difficult for him, he said, and that of course I knew; he was restless and very gloomy, and sometimes angry, at nothing. He told me that because of his knowledge of languages, the Germans had occasionally small tasks for him, but that there was nothing certain, so that he had to go to see every day, and be ready, whether or no; he had refused some tasks, he said, because he had not felt them to be honorable, and this he would always do. I could be sure, he said, that whatever he was doing, he had thought about it deeply and had decided that it was not wrong. And unless he himself wished to speak to me of the matter again, it was not to be discussed. Naturally I said no more. And he said no more. This continued until my father's death." She fell silent. Then, "M'sieur, I swear it," she said in a trembling voice. "Never in his life did my father do anything dishonorable. And that is all, all, I can say."

Suddenly Johnny realized that he believed her. Not that her father was innocent—after all, Korvac had had the address. And if Bouliard would not tell his daughter what he was doing during those doubtful years, there must have been some very grave reason. But everything about Thérèse herself attested her sincerity; even the grief, the uncertainty in her voice as she spoke of the last years of her father's life, were in her favor. For if she knew her father to be guilty, she would not now be trying to preserve her own faith in his innocence—only to convince her questioners. Her whole attitude would be different. If she were acting, surely she would act some other part; surely she would have thought up some better story.

Unless, now that her father was in any case dead, she thought it no harm to indicate his guilt (but subtly, subtly), knowing that she could not save everything, but planning, at least, to save herself? It was possible. But so involved; if she could do this, he, at least, could not touch her. But he did not believe it. He did not believe that she was acting at all. Nor that she was lying.

The only evidence against her, the only reason to connect her with her father's crime, was the note. He took it out of the back pages of the pad and looked at it again. It was written in indelible pencil, on graph paper; it had been folded in quarters, and the paper was almost worn through along the creases, so that the note was not easy to read:

CHÈRE THÉRÈSE,

Je me demande pourquoi ton père ne travaille plus. Est-ce qu'il doute que nous n'ayons la victoire? C'est à regretter. Mais ne revenons pas au passé. Toi, je me dis chaque heure que tu restes fidèle, ce n'est pas possible que tu m'as abandonné, ton Rudolph. Rapelle-toi que tes amis d'autrefois sont toujours tes amis. Et tu sais, le nouvel ordre est très fort, il va rester.

Celui qui porte cette lettre, Émile, c'est un ami sûr et très habile, qui pense tout à fait comme nous. Tu peux avoir confiance en lui. Il aura dès maintenant le poste de Cherbourg. Travailler pour lui, c'est travailler pour nous. Tu pourras avoir sans doute des informations très intéressantes; donne-les-lui, à Émile, et les récompenses que tu a reçues auparavant ne seront rien, crois-moi, à celles que le futur t'apportera. Au revoir, ma petite, ma chère Thérèse, et mille remerciements de notre Grand Chef, comme toujours de moi.

BLOCH

Well; if the letter was to be believed, he was quite, quite wrong. But as he looked at the girl and then back again at the sheet of paper in front of him, it did not seem possible that there was any connection:

DEAR THÉRÈSE,

I wonder why your father is no longer working. Does he doubt that we shall be victorious? Too bad. But let us not look back. I tell myself hourly that you have remained

94

faithful, it is not possible that you have abandoned me, your Rudolph. Remember that your friends of times past are still your friends. And you know that the new order is strong, it is going to survive.

The man who brings this letter, Émile, is a trustworthy friend and a very clever man, who thinks just as we do. You may have confidence in him. He will have the Cherbourg post from now on. To work for him is to work for us. Doubtless you will be able to get some very interesting information; give it to him, and the rewards you have had in the past will be, believe me, nothing to those the future will bring you. Goodbye for now, my little one, my dear Thérèse, and a thousand thanks from our Great Chief, as always from me.

BLOCH

Really, it was ridiculous—"It is not possible that you have abandoned me, your Rudolph." How did these people expect to be taken seriously?

But it was not the Americans, of course, by whom they wished to be taken seriously. Well; something would have to be done about this.

"Mademoiselle," he said, and saw her start violently. "One or two more questions," he went on quietly. "You had, I suppose, friends, you and your father?"

"A few," she answered, in a puzzled voice.

"But some who were invited to your house occasionally, to spend the evening perhaps—or whom you visited?"

"These were not many," she said. "My father—I have told you that he had a difficult life, m'sieur. He did not easily trust people, and almost never—admitted them to his affections. Especially here; at first he thought to enjoy the company of his fellow teachers, but after he lost his position, it seemed to him that they—were scornful of him." She added hastily, "I do not know if that was so."

"And you? You had schoolgirl friends, no doubt."

She shrugged bitterly. "I am no longer a schoolgirl, m'sieur. Though it will doubtless amuse you that at one time I thought Estelle de Sombais a friend."

95

Johnny wrote the name down without comment, though his imagination seized on the possibilities. What would the captain say to that? Perhaps Mlle. de Sombais would have to be asked for evidence, but could what she said be believed at all?

"No," said Thérèse Bouliard in a low voice, "there is only one person I count my friend now. You understand, my father would not have liked young persons always to be running through the house. But in any case it seemed more natural to me to be with older persons. When I was at the Lycée I had a most excellent teacher, Mademoiselle Vaugiron; and we have been very close for years. I do not think—there is a finer person in the world."

"Is she in Cherbourg now?" asked Johnny.

"I do not know. It may be. A year ago in April the Lycée in which she taught was evacuated far to the south; but she had a sister at Les Pieux who needed her help, and whether she has managed to return—you would have to find out for yourself. She lives in a house on the Rue du Champs-de-Mars, a—detached house, you say? The only such in the street. And of the blue-green stone. I would have gone to see whether she had come back, but then I was arrested."

"We can ask her to confirm some of the things you have said—"

"Oh, yes!" she broke in. "Oh, yes!"

"But for now," Johnny went on firmly, "I am more interested in some others. Friends not of you alone, nor of your father alone, but of you both. I am interested for example in Rudolph Bloch."

"Rudolph Bloch!" She looked aghast. "But you must be—making a joke! Rudolph Bloch is a German!"

"Yes," said Johnny. "You did know him, it seems."

She reddened violently. "Yes. I knew him. But he was not our friend, m'sieur; he was a very disgusting—" She looked up, terror in her eyes. "You said at the beginning that you had talked with—one of our employers, and I did not know what you meant. Was it this man you spoke of?"

Johnny went on staring at her, without answering. He was himself almost frightened; he had been close to concluding the

96

girl utterly innocent, and now that he had no more than half revealed his trump card, it seemed that she might be after all on the verge of breaking, of admitting the guilt she had up to now concealed. He was a poor excuse for an interrogator, all right.

"M'sieur," she said, "when I told you before that I did not know what my father was doing, that was true. But it seems that he was connected with this Rudolph Bloch, you are right, and I had forgotten. I was only—acquainted with him for a very short time."

"From when to when?"

"It was—in April of this year, I think." She considered, then shook her head. "I do not remember exactly. But yes, it was in late April." She paused again, then said timidly, "I suppose—you wish to know how it was?"

"Please," said Johnny in an expressionless voice.

"The thing is," said Thérèse, "how can I prove to you that he was not our friend, but our enemy? As it turned out. And if you have an accusation from him, it will be, I am sure, only his word against—against mine. M'sieur, would you believe the word of a German against that of a Frenchman?"

Johnny answered, "I do not yet have your—word. Your story."

"Yes," she said dazedly. "Well, then, one day my father brought home this man, and when later in private I asked who he was, my father said that it was someone with whom he worked. I wondered very much, since my father was cold to him; it did not seem that he wished to entertain him. But the man came a number of times, and was always very friendly. He spoke French with a curious accent, but quite well—at first he spoke of Alsace, and I presumed he was Alsatian, but my father told me that he was a German, and this surprised me most of all, since I knew how my father felt." The girl began once more, suddenly, to look embarrassed.

"Perhaps I should not especially have disliked this man if I could not see how my father felt about him—as I have said, he did his best to be gay and—and kind, and why should he not have been better than the others? Though sometimes—he looked strangely." She glanced up at Johnny as though with apprehension. "And then one day he came to call alone, before my father had returned from work, and this made me—very uncomfortable, because I had not thought about this at all."

"What did he say to you?" asked Johnny.

"Nothing especially; he told great bragging stories about himself, I do not remember them, except you would have thought there was nothing he could not do, in all of France. And he said he hoped I was a dutiful daughter and helped my father in every way I could, and I said that, of course, I did. And he patted me.

"I told my father about all this when he came home, and he was very angry. Nevertheless the next day M'sieur Bloch came back, and he told me that he had a very great influence at the place where my father worked and could do my father much harm, or much good, and then he tried to—make love to me, m'sieur." Her voice had become jerky and there was an expression of hard dislike on her face. "I did not want to hurt my father, you understand, but this was very terrible, and I—I could not endure it. I fought him, and—and he became furiously angry, like a mad pig, and I cannot tell you how frightened I was. But he went away, saying threatening things about my father, so that I was forced to tell my father what had happened when he came home. And then it was all right, because my father said the man had no power, after all, and he would see that I was not disturbed again. And I was not."

"You never saw Bloch again?"

"No." She closed her eyes. "But immediately after, my father took me on a visit to Tante Rose, to the farm at Sartilly, and this he said was so that Bloch should not make any more trouble. For me, you understand. And not long after we returned—" Her eyes opened very wide; once more they looked like the eyes of the blind. "My father was killed."

Suddenly a great many things seemed to Johnny to fall together. Leaning back from the table, he said gently, with a relief which he hoped was not obvious, "Can you remember the dates of that visit in May—exactly?"

Her expression showed the effort to recall. Finally she said, "It was—the end of April or the beginning of May when we left, I do not know exactly. We arrived back in Cherbourg on —the eighteenth of May, or the nineteenth."

"Your father thought that by then there would be no more trouble with Bloch?"

She stirred restlessly. "Oh—I do not think that this stayed in his mind. He wanted me to remain in Sartilly for awhile, it is true; the farm life, you know, is very healthy. But I wished to be with him." Her eyes began to fill with tears and her voice became unsteady. "Sometimes I wish—that I had remained with him—very much more."

Johnny got to his feet and pushed his papers together. "Remember, mademoiselle," he said, and realized that his words were almost inaudible. He cleared his throat. "Remember that if you are innocent it will soon be found out, and you will not be held."

She looked up swiftly. "I may not go now? You have seen, it is all a mistake; if it was that Bloch who accused us, it was for revenge because—I would not do as he wished. You may believe me, m'sieur, I have no reason to lie!"

Johnny said, "Whether I believe you or not doesn't matter. I will tell your story to—my commanding officer, and he will decide what is to be done. Is there anything else you wish to say?"

Wordlessly she shook her head. Then she almost whispered, "But, m'sieur—if this is over, please, is there a place where—I could wash? It is not very clean, this mattress, and—when I came, also, I was soiled, from my journey. I have some clean clothes—" She began to clamber to her feet.

He said, "I don't know. I'll ask. You'll have to stay here for the time being."

A look of disappointment came to her face, but she remained standing.

"It's late," said Johnny, "and I expect they'll be bringing you something to eat too. I'll do the best I can for you."

There was a moment's silence, and then she smiled for the first time since he had entered the room—a wan, uncertain smile, which touched her lips only, not the pale open wells of her eyes. "Thank you," she said.

Suddenly he was horrified; he started nervously and almost looked around to see whether anyone had heard her. "Do you want the light off?" he asked abruptly.

"Please," she said.

He strode to the door, opened it, and with a flick of his finger plunged the room into darkness.

There was no one in the hall. How long ago had he himself last stood here? From the outside he closed the door, locked it, and with the steadiest of gestures put the key in his pocket.

VII.

"INNOCENT?" asked Carl, incredulously. "Jesus! Mister, I want to be around when you tell the captain that."

"Well," Johnny said, suddenly annoyed, "I guess you can make it. If you try hard."

"Keep your shirt on," said Carl. "It's the captain's face I want to watch, not yours. You got to remember, not confessing's one thing, innocent's another. Bouliard's his prize, so far."

Johnny shrugged. "Yeah. Well, he could have had her right from the word go if all he wanted was to pin something on her."

"You really think she's O.K.? In spite of—"

"Say, Carl," Johnny interrupted, "when will the captain get back? I'd better get these notes of mine written up, hadn't I? And what about chow? Have you guys eaten?"

"I had 'em save a plate for you back in the kitchen. Thought you wouldn't want to be interrupted, probably."

"Thanks; that's fine. Gosh, I'm hungry." Suddenly Johnny thought of something. "What about her?" He jerked his head toward the upstairs. "When does she eat?"

"Oh, Barker takes care of her. You don't have to worry. He says she hasn't touched anything so far except water, but you can bet she'll come around."

The poor kid, Johnny thought. If he was hungry, what must she be? But after all—his mouth pulled down wryly at the corners—he guessed these people weren't as dependent as he was on eating regularly. "Oh, by the way," he said, "she asked if she could wash, and get her clean clothes back. I told her I'd see."

"We-ell—" Carl hesitated. "That depends on the captain, of course. But I wouldn't bother about it. It won't hurt her any to stay dirty awhile. Give her something to think about."

Johnny stared at him in disbelief. "But—honest to God, Carl, didn't you hear what I said? She's probably innocent! And even if she weren't, what's the point of treating her like a—like an animal?" He recalled his first emotions upstairs. "That whole setup—the lights and all. What good can you do that way? It would just make me mad. Anyway it certainly wouldn't make me any more cooperative."

"Are you sure?" asked Carl ironically. "You haven't seen so many of these characters, you know, and—" Apparently he thought better of what he was going to say. "But hell, don't look at me. It isn't my show. You might think of it this way, though —they're brought in because it's pretty certain they're guilty of something, and something pretty damn bad, at that. So what's the point of treating 'em like they were made out of whipped cream? You know how little most of the French have got now —and how they're starving in Paris, the good ones along with the bad ones. Why give the bad ones a better break than the rest?"

"Ah, skip it," said Johnny. It was no time for a demonstration of logic, or humanitarian principles either, apparently. He felt bad-tempered; maybe eating something would help. He went on back to the kitchen, found his plate in the warming oven of the gigantic iron range, and sat down with it at the oilcloth-covered table nearby. He had plenty of paper still. As he ate—Spam, dehydrated potatoes, canned spinach—he considered how he would begin. "Thérèse Bouliard was born—" He had never written an interrogation report before. But you couldn't go far wrong like that.

Three quarters of an hour later the last paragraphs were falling into shape.

It is the opinion of the interrogator, therefore, that while Pierre Bouliard was no doubt guilty, his daughter Thérèse was genuinely ignorant of his true relationship with the Germans, and was not implicated in it. It may be imagined that Rudolph Bloch would have recruited her for the German service if his plans had gone well; but they did not. This, as has been remarked, developed from Mlle. Bouliard's testimony *even though she never saw, or even learned of the existence of, the Bloch note;* there is, therefore, no reason to doubt what she says. She must have remained in the clear until the end.

Bloch's letter, addressed to her, was presumably written out of a desire for vengeance, after it had become clear to the Germans that Bouliard was not going to maintain radio contact with them after the invasion. If Korvac had managed to reach Bouliard, his own evidence shows that, if necessary, he would have executed that vengeance himself. The alternative was that Korvac might fall into the hands of the Allies—as in fact ultimately he did. In the event of this, the vengeance could still be taken care of, by the letter which Korvac carried.

Johnny read over what he had written. It sounded good to him, but not, somehow, final. He added two more sentences. "The plan was most ingenious. Fortunately, it has failed."

Carl was still at his desk when Johnny came back out, the marked-up and interlined pages of his report in his hand. Tochyk, his face as somber as a bloodhound's, was sitting on the bench against the wall, reading his mail. Johnny laid the report on the desk and walked over to the file to put away the Bloch letter.

"You done writing this?" asked Carl. "O.K. if I look at it?"

"Why—sure, I guess so," Johnny said. "But I'd better type it, hadn't I? Won't the captain be back pretty soon?"

"He might be, or he might not. Why don't I do the typing for you? I got nothing better to do, and that way I'll get to read it at the same time. Besides, I know the form the captain likes." He considered. "I could show you, of course."

"Go right ahead and type it," Johnny said. "And thanks." The report was pretty fair, he thought; he did not mind having Carl see it. Particularly when he himself had acted so foolish about starting in on the interrogation; this would show Carl that he'd pulled himself together, at least. And suddenly he realized that he was tired, nervously more than in any other way, and would be glad to get away from this and stop thinking about it altogether. There was a garden out in back of the hotel, and some lawn furniture that looked as though it had been left out in the rain for years. He'd go out there and relax for awhile. "If the captain comes in," he said, putting a hand on Carl's shoulder to show there were no hard feelings about the difference of opinion they'd had earlier, "I'll be out back."

"O.K.," said Carl. "You better be getting your strength back, robbing the tiger of his prey the way you plan to."

Johnny grinned and went on out.

It wouldn't be so easy to stop thinking about Thérèse Bouliard, he realized as he settled a chair in a pleasant corner under the faint blue of the afternoon sky and sat down. Even in his own mind, though, he didn't want to review the arguments in favor of her guilt or innocence. What had convinced him finally that she was not guilty was not just a list of arguments; it was the way she'd reacted to questions; the expressions on her face; the attitudes of her body. And it didn't matter to him what the damaging appearances were, particularly since those were so easily explained. He was, simply, convinced of the girl's honesty.

It was something else which nagged at his mind now—Thérèse's complete, and apparently unfounded, faith in her father.

Of course, if she had her doubts, or had ever had them, this was not from her point of view the time to say so. Not unless she thought some admission of guilt was inescapable, and she was trying to shift blame. But she wasn't. Perhaps she knew in her inmost heart that her father might be guilty? Johnny didn't think so, though the girl recognized that her father had had weaknesses—that he was a proud man, somewhat impractical, and hard to get along with.

Obviously she had understood him, and had loved him as he was; had even, at times, stood as a buffer between him and the rest of the world. And yet—she had not understood him, for he'd been capable of committing treason, and she had not known that. She'd lived with him alone for many years, and had not noticed the inescapable flaw in his nature that would have to destroy them both at last, and might have destroyed, or helped destroy, part of the world at the same time.

Treason. You could say the word, Johnny thought, but how could you really take in what it meant? It was like trying to imagine the face of another planet, the continents of stone, the depthless fissures, the corroded air. And a man at home there, a man who, impossibly, looked from the outside exactly like other men. How could Pierre Bouliard, a dweller in those frightening wastes, have convinced his daughter Thérèse that he was her father, a father, a man enough like other men so that one had only a little left to explain? *He had had bad luck, life had taught him distrust of others*—and for years he had been able to live two lives simultaneously, one whose barren principle was betrayal, and one whose rich principle was faith. It was perfectly impossible, Johnny thought; and it had happened.

Were Europe and America in fact different planets? The strangeness Johnny felt here . . .

No, of course not.

What did he actually know about America? His own town in New York, his own kind of small town, yes, perhaps; but if he thought, he knew enough to realize that his life had been an island only, in bays, vast riding seas, thundering oceans entirely strange to him. Seattle, New Orleans, Minneapolis—he had assumed them to be within his world, but it was an empty assumption. What part of the human soul could you buy or sell in St. Louis, what need would always break a certain kind of man in Tucson? What granddaughter of the Mediterranean sun slouched in pulled rayon where against a sooty American pane, with thoughts in her mind for which he would not even have language? *Treason*, all right, men were various, and capable of strange things.

But how could Thérèse have believed, how could she still believe, in Pierre Bouliard? Because she was weak?

Or because she was strong? Was it a victory to love so, not to admit doubt, not to judge or agree to the right of others to judge?

Well, most people loved the members of their own families. Faithfully or—selfishly, or stupidly, however you wanted to look at it.

What a hell of a thing to think. What was wrong with him, anyway? He sounded like Weiller.

And *that* wasn't fair, either. What was he trying to talk himself into?

Couldn't he just do a job without setting himself up as God and deciding who was right and what was wrong and what everybody ought to have done instead of what they did?

Well, you couldn't help wondering about certain things. It was no crime. He didn't have to sail into himself this way, either.

Sometimes he didn't understand himself. . . .

He got up restlessly from the plaited metal chair and began to pace the walled-in square of untended lawn. He had tried of late not to remember his mother's voice, though it was not an unpleasant voice—quite the contrary—dry, matter-of-fact, often amused, even when she was saying something that hurt more than she intended it to. But now the voice came to him quite clearly, as it had come downstairs in the library on the evening when he'd announced that he was not going on with his pre-med course, not going to take advantage of the immunity to the draft which that course had afforded him: "My dear, I'm sure that at your age I knew more about my own motives than you seem to."

His father had said, "Maude."

"Don't interrupt, Robert. No—if I were the usual kind of mother I suppose I'd say, 'Go, my son, and God bless you.' I'm sorry, Johnny, but I can't say that. Don't you see that in your position it's easier to go than to stay, and that that's the long and the short of it?"

He had not thought it easy to be in his position at all, but he had not been able to say that.

"If you do go," his mother had continued, "you'll be wasting all the training your father and I have tried so hard to get for you. When you come back you'll feel you're too old to pick it up, so it's like sentencing yourself to a lifetime of mediocrity. When you could accomplish so much, and when—don't deceive yourself—the government would even very much prefer you to go on as you're going. What reason can you possibly have left?"

What reason, indeed?

It was strange how clearly the words remained with him. "I can't stop you from going, of course—as I haven't been able to keep you from doing other things. But at least admit to yourself that the real trouble is you're unwilling to do the work that going on at Columbia would mean. Oh, and unwilling to face other boys of your generation, and so on. Even though you'd be in the right. If you *can* admit those facts, I think—perhaps you'll reconsider."

106

"Really, Maude," his father had said quietly. "You sound as though the boy were planning to commit a crime."

"Do I?" She had laughed. "Well, in a way of course I happen to think it would be a crime of a kind—a small crime, perhaps, but against—the future of society. Of course I'm a woman; I don't have a man's ideas about—heroism. I'm sure Johnny's telling himself that it's a deep feeling for humanity that's sending him forth—sympathy for the oppressed, and all that. Whereas I should say it was a complete failure of understanding, and therefore a *failure* of sympathy. You have to have—some realistic sense of what the world is, and what the world needs, before the idea of sympathy takes on any meaning, Johnny."

He had not been able to say anything, for he could see that in most ways she was right, as she was so often right. He'd been too restless to go on studying, and that was the truth. It wasn't that he'd felt he'd have much chance of accomplishing anything in particular if he were to join the Army. But a student was always busy preparing *himself*, thinking about *himself*; and what he would do for others was always going to be some other time. Suddenly, with talk of the war all around him, Johnny had felt cut off, left out; that others were enlisting had seemed enough reason for him to enlist. It wasn't even that he'd felt he hadn't the right to exempt himself when others could not exempt themselves. He'd wanted, simply, and perhaps selfishly, the kinship of joining up with others, of working with them, taking the same kind of punishment they took, helping them and being helped.

But there had doubtless been another reason, after all—a final reason. He hadn't been strong enough to bear the burden of his mother's rightness, of her understanding, which had seemed on that evening to leave him naked and bowed in the middle of the big room. He *had* wanted, he realized suddenly, to be thought a fine person; and instead he had had to hear the truth and feel the humiliation he had so often felt, hearing the truth about himself from his mother's lips.

"I don't like to bring myself into it," she had said at last, "for it's not a personal matter, don't misunderstand me. But—you mustn't suppose it's been easy to arrange college for you. I've sat up a good many nights wondering how it was to be managed. Neither the time nor the money was wasted, and I'd never mention it if this hadn't come up. But—if it *is* to be wasted now, I'll feel—well, rather deflated, to say the least."

"I'm sure your mother doesn't mean to give the impression that that's all she would feel if you went off to the wars," his father had said in the silence that had followed.

"No," she had said, her voice unnaturally bright. Johnny had listened with all his being for the sound of affection in her voice; and it had been there, or its equivalent had been, a severe control which must after all have had something to hide. "But I do think, Robert—Johnny—we mustn't bring our emotions into it. Our hearts could break for the world, so easily, if we let them. But this is for—reason to decide, surely?"

It had been, and yet he had decided by emotion; an emotion of whose existence she could not have guessed. He dreaded and resented her dissatisfactions with him; often he felt that they could not be just. Yet it was curious how much he loved her and how involved with her he felt. He had got out at last for the most ignominious reason, just to be getting out—just because, restlessly and thoughtlessly, he had begun the breach, and somehow he could not remain to face the inescapable fact of the thoughtlessness. A failure of understanding. A failure of sympathy, in the greatest sense of the word. . . .

This wasn't getting him very far, he thought, shivering; and all at once he felt lonely, and the walled square, like the captain's office earlier, said to him that it was foreign, a place that was not his home. Thérèse Bouliard's emotion, her faith in her father—unrealistic they might be in one sense, but in another they were very realistic, because they arose directly from a human need, a need of society. Doubtless, too, Bouliard had had qualities that inspired faith. And the girl's ability to give that faith seemed to Johnny suddenly a very wonderful thing—a sign of maturity, everything. He himself, merely separated from his family, which it seemed likely was in every way more worthy of admiration than Thérèse's father, could only pick restlessly and rather meanly at his memories of them. Across the gulf of death Thérèse brought her father much more.

And yet, if he knew himself, he had a good chance of being

108

wrong even in making these judgments. He had hated the replacement depot; but now he wondered whether it would not have been better all around if he had stayed back there, since if he was so capable of misunderstanding, he was almost bound to do more harm than good in this world of incredible complications and subtleties.

His own reactions, it seemed, were as direct and simple as a savage's. He recalled the thrill of fear, the sense of the Enemy, he had had that morning when he had first seen the gigantic wreckage around the harbor. He recalled how emotionally he had reacted to the situation of the girl in her makeshift cell. Was all this, too, a failure of understanding—ultimately a failure of sympathy? The captain obviously thought he was naïve; and as obviously, the captain was right.

Depression settled in upon him. And suddenly he thought of the report which he had just finished writing. Without really revising his opinion, he could see that he had made a lot of sweeping statements, a lot of remarks that might sound pompous or foolish. It was the kind of thing that happened all too easily when you were writing, because you were working toward a conclusion, and things got shaped to fit that conclusion and blown up somehow to make it sound really conclusive. He could think of half a dozen sentences he would like to change; he wondered if there would be time before the captain got back. He stopped his pacing and headed back into the building.

In the front office Carl was finishing typing. Captain Weiller was standing beside him, ready to take the last sheet from the typewriter. In his hand were a half-dozen partly crumpled sheets, evidently the first pages of Johnny's report. The captain looked up silently as Johnny entered; then he looked down again, snatched the last sheet from Carl's hands and read it through steadily. Even in the poorly lighted room it was apparent that his color deepened as he read; his lips tightened and the cords in his neck swelled. Finally, and slowly, he straightened the pages together in his hands and looked up.

"Well, Phillips?" he roared. "Do you want to go upstairs and play pat-a-cake with this woman, or could I perhaps have a word with you in my office?"

VIII.

"I COULD, of course, say it's my own damn fault," said the captain, staring at Johnny with a glittering intensity across the broad leather-covered desk. "Would that help?"

For a moment, in the outer office, Johnny had felt frightened; now suddenly he was almost calm. He could have got some unimportant things mixed up. In places perhaps he'd written badly. But about the interrogation itself he could not believe that he was fundamentally wrong. And he could not let the captain bully him.

"I don't know what you mean, sir," he said firmly.

"He doesn't know what I mean." Heavily the captain drummed his fingers on the desk. "Very well, Mr. Phillips, I'll tell you. I mean that for a man with a college education you don't seem to me to have gone about this very intelligently. I mean that if I sent that report of yours up the line, everybody'd have hysterics or heart failure, one of the two. I mean that you seem to have handed Bouliard her alibi on a silver platter. And finally I mean sure, I know you haven't had much experience in this work, so you can blame it all on me if you want to. But you wanted the job, remember. And I wouldn't have thought that being inexperienced would have excused you from paying attention."

Damn it, Johnny thought, if he'd done a lousy job it had at least been better than there'd been any reason to suppose he could do. The captain knew perfectly well— Why *hadn't* Weiller done this job himself? Carl's explanation—blame it on someone else—

Carl was unfair.

It depressed Johnny to remember that he had indeed been eager to be trusted, eager to do something important—had wanted, the part of the time he wasn't scared, to take on this interrogation. But that had been before he had seen the girl and heard the sound of her grief. That had been when the problem had seemed—he was forced to admit it—like a strange puzzle or an exciting, half-terrifying story in a book, not like an exercise in compounding human sorrow. He saw, now, how greatly relieved he had been when he had been able to believe the girl innocent; it had meant that he would not long have to intrude upon her. Now the captain was trying to reopen the matter, to reintroduce the doubts he himself had managed to expel. And Weiller was the commanding officer here; his rights in the matter were not to be denied, however much one might object to his tactics. One could not, as one could not in a scene with one's parents, simply walk out.

"I—don't think I gave her an alibi, Captain," he said tonelessly. "How did I?"

"I think I'd better start asking *you* some questions," said the captain brusquely. "If you don't mind. It may not be entirely too late yet. Is this all the information you got from the girl?"

"Yes, sir."

"Does it seem to you enough?"

"Well—yes, sir, I thought it pretty much accounted for everything."

"I see," said the captain gently. "You were trying to account for things, then? You were trying to prove a theory?"

Johnny saw the pitfall. "Not at first, no, sir. Only toward the end it all seemed to me to fit."

"And you didn't try to get any information that might not have fit."

"Well—sir, if you think you've got everything explained, you don't go out of your way to—mix yourself up, do you?" He shouldn't have said that, he saw; the captain was beginning to smile, without humor. "I mean—it isn't—natural. It just wouldn't occur to you."

Weiller said, "I can see your trouble, Phillips. It *wouldn't* occur to you—if you were trying to make the evidence mean a certain thing. But if you're just trying to get all the evidence together, to be puzzled over and thought out later, why then you don't stop until you've asked *all* the questions. You don't by any chance think you did ask all the questions, do you?"

"Why—I suppose not. Honestly, though, sir, I asked all I thought of. I did the best I could. I can go back and ask anything more you want me to."

"Why do you suppose," the captain said musingly, "you didn't think of any more questions to ask? After all, I'd even given you some more, and those you forgot completely."

It was as though some old wound that had never healed properly were suddenly exposed and probed. Johnny burst out, "Look, Captain—I'm sorry I did it wrong." Humiliation and bitterness were in his voice. "But—I could have been up there all day, and all night, and all tomorrow, couldn't I, if I were to have asked her every question I could possibly have thought of? You ask what you think's important; you've got to stop somewhere."

"Do you?" said the captain. "Yes, I suppose you had a constitutional to take, or something." He stared at Johnny, a cold watchfulness in his eyes. "You must forgive me if I'm stepping on your toes, by the way; you *are* so sensitive, you know. Actually I was just trying to make you see something."

Johnny waited, his face flushed, his eyes downcast.

"What's the conclusion of your report?" asked the captain.

"That—Thérèse Bouliard is innocent," Johnny answered defiantly.

"Who would like us to believe that she is innocent?"

"Why—anyone who's interested in seeing justice done, I should think." Johnny's voice was stormy. It was a dangerous thing to say, he knew; but the captain's measured calm, his appearance of patient detachment, were beyond words annoying.

"Justice," breathed the captain. "But supposing she were guilty? You haven't *proved* that she isn't, you know; you've just worked up a set of arguments—that don't hang together too badly, I'll admit—that show she *may* not be. But supposing she *is* guilty, then does 'anyone who's interested in seeing justice done' want her to appear innocent?"

"Well—no, of course not."

"Then who does?"

"She does, I guess."

"Doesn't it seem a little strange to you, Mr. Phillips, that you

112

got such a neat set of indications that Thérèse Bouliard is innocent—when you got so little else?"

Johnny had been sitting in the chair he had occupied during his interview with the captain that morning; now he got up and walked over to the window. "I didn't—realize I'd got so little else," he answered, his voice deeply troubled in spite of all he could do. "I got the story of their earlier lives, for example."

The captain spread his big hands out on the desk and stared at them for a moment before replying. "In a sketchy sort of way, yes. Of course you found out almost nothing about the people with whom Bouliard and his daughter had contact, in the various places they'd lived. Even here in Cherbourg. And supposing the girl is innocent—you yourself accept that her father was not, and yet you're not going to find out much about him unless you find out what he did in the world of men—and find out the names of men who can be asked about him."

"Well," said Johnny, "I mean after all, he's dead; does it matter so much?"

"Matter," the captain roared, "of course it matters! I've told you. We need every scrap of information about the enemy service, and its personnel, and how it operates, that we can lay our hands on. And like I say, even supposing Thérèse Bouliard is innocent—which I don't believe—she may have a lot of information, a lot more than she realizes. A complete story of her life, and her father's life, during the Occupation is absolutely necessary! Hell, even Bloch, whom she admits she knows, she 'can't remember what he said.' Well, she'll damned well have to remember. That, and a lot more."

"O.K.," said Johnny wearily. "I'll get back on it right away."

"No you won't," said the captain grimly. "We're not through here yet. If you believe that Bouliard was guilty but his daughter isn't, what do you suppose his relationship with Bloch was?"

"Why—I thought Bloch was his boss. His German chief."

"Local, or not?"

"What do you mean?"

"Well, Bloch was here in Cherbourg in late April or early May; or so the girl says. But he was in Paris when he gave Korvac the letter to take to Thérèse. Well, now, where did he belong? Was he a real big shot, from headquarters, with a good many minor spymasters and their spies on his string, or was he an unimportant character, with just Bouliard and maybe one or two others to take care of?"

"Why—I don't know. I should think you'd have to ask Korvac."

"Maybe. But Korvac was small fry himself; he can be asked again, but you must see that Thérèse too has to be made to recall everything the man said to her."

"Of course," said Johnny. He added, "Everything she can remember."

The captain bared his teeth in a grin, and reddened, and shook his head.

Johnny said abruptly, "Captain, I've got a question. If you're so—sure this girl did work for Bloch, herself, why would she have admitted that her father worked for the Germans at all? That sounds pretty damaging, especially if she couldn't go, or wasn't going to go, any further. Why didn't she cover up completely?"

"How could she cover up?" the captain asked softly. "If her father hadn't had some kind of job, in fact a job with the Germans, or a job that was pretty useful to the Germans, he'd have been kicked out of town last year. Obviously he wasn't, and everybody knew it." Weiller glared at Johnny. "Besides, look. Thérèse Bouliard just got back to town. *You* know that we haven't been able to find anyone in Cherbourg who knew anything *about* Bouliard's work for the Germans, because I told you so. But she doesn't know that. So why run the risk? After all, someone must have known something—particularly if some of the work the father did was more or less legitimate. And the girl could hope that that work was all we'd ever hear about—and if it wasn't, she'd at least register the idea that it was all *she* knew about."

Johnny was silent.

"Phillips," said the captain. "I don't want to get sore about this again, but look at the whole thing this way. You thought, when you talked to her, that she was innocent—"

"I didn't to begin with," said Johnny quickly. "Honestly I didn't."

"O.K., O.K. But she had a story that fitted in with innocence, and—though maybe she's just a good actress, or a mediocre actress with a hell of a strong reason to make it good this time —she *seemed* to you innocent. So you're convinced, and you can't understand why I'm raising so much hell. Is that it?"

"Sort of, yes," said Johnny.

"All right. I'm not blaming you too much. But now let's look at it this way. The only real evidence we have one way or the other is that note; and *it* says she's guilty as hell. Let's start all over again, from there. She's guilty, and she's picked up and searched and thrown in a locked room overnight. Luckily for her she has nothing incriminating on her, so she isn't a goner from the beginning; she still thinks she's got a chance to make it through. But she knows she wasn't picked up for nothing. Somewhere along the line the beans have been spilled, and her only chance is to pretend that a terrible mistake has been made.

"Well, there aren't very many things that could have gone wrong, after all. Her father's dead; he isn't talking. No one else in Cherbourg, so far as she knows, has anything on her—though one or two people, like Estelle de Sombais, may have their suspicions. But de Sombais worked for the Gestapo—which would mean that her hands wouldn't be so clean either. More important, though, the Gestapo presumably wasn't in on the show Thérèse and her father were connected with; so if de Sombais or someone like that has put in a denunciation, there's probably nothing there she can't handle with a simple denial."

"But I—" said Johnny.

The captain held up a hand. "Wait till I finish. What I was going to say was that if that was her reasoning, she'd have been right about it: the Gestapo didn't handle this particular kind of military espionage, and Estelle de Sombais *doesn't* have any real evidence against the Bouliards—she just suspects they were German spies."

Johnny felt his face tightening. "You mean she was asked about it?" He looked away resentfully. "I wish I'd known that."

The captain colored slightly. "You should have known. I mean, it should be in the file somewhere, if it isn't. The thing was—after something that happened here when the Bouliard girl was first brought in—"

"I know, sir," said Johnny. "Carl told me that much."

"Well, afterward we asked Estelle de Sombais about the Bouliards, but she didn't have any actual facts. Just—woman's intuition, you might say. I suppose that's why Carl didn't put a note in the file. You'd better take care of it, though, later on."

"Yes, sir," said Johnny.

"Well, then. Bouliard's sure she can handle a mere denunciation. But she doesn't dare take anything for granted. What else might have happened to get her in trouble? Something connected with their German employers—with Bloch. He might have been captured, might have given her away. Or someone unknown, connected with him, might have been. So that's what she's got to take care of. And if she can provide a story that will take care of it in advance, without seeming to, she's better off than if she can't. Doesn't that make sense?"

Johnny said, "I guess so."

"All right. Now what has she got to cover up? First is the fact that she and her father have been working for the Germans for a good many years—three, or three and a half; at least her father has. And the time has got to be accounted for, because everyone in town knows that Bouliard hasn't taught since 1940. At the same time it can be proved that he wasn't wealthy; the explanation, whatever it was, would have to account somehow for the fact that money went on coming in. Fortunately her father was a very silent man, who didn't make friends easily but didn't make real enemies, either—not the best type for a spy, incidentally, but not the worst, either. She could spin a yarn about his having been driven into some vague—but perfectly honorable—work for the Germans, and be pretty sure that no one in Cherbourg would have had any more exact information from Bouliard himself. And she could say that her father never said much to her, either, and that would cover her —not very well, but well enough, perhaps."

The captain's voice took on a slight edge. "Actually, she doesn't seem to have figured out any cover for her own activities, but then she didn't have to, because you didn't ask her for any." The captain looked searchingly at Johnny. Acidly he went on, "Are we assuming that she just sat home cooking bacon for four years, the bacon Daddy was busy bringing home?"

Johnny did not reply.

"Well, anyway. If she's lucky, that does the job, and the money. Now, unless I miss my guess, there's one more item along in here that you didn't think of, in spite of all that folder reading you did in London. A spy has to be trained. When was Pierre Bouliard trained, and where? Did he, for example, always know how to handle a radio transmitter and receiver? Of course not. All right. Listen carefully. Bloch, or anyone else, might have given him and Thérèse lessons in Allied order of battle and military equipment and signs, here in Cherbourg, but the radio training—which maybe both of them got, maybe only the father—would likely have been given somewhere else. Therefore it's my hunch that you'll find, if we ever get a more complete story of Bouliard's activities during these years, that he made at least one, and perhaps several, longish trips out of town; and on these Thérèse may or may not have accompanied him. O.K. Does anything occur to you right off?"

"N-no," said Johnny.

"You said yourself, in that fancy report, that since they'd lived in Cherbourg the girl's father had made more trips down to the farm at Sartilly than Thérèse herself had made. Well, that's her story: all set up, as you see. What can we do about it?"

"Go to Sartilly, I suppose."

"Well of course."

"I should think we'd better go pretty quickly, too, hadn't we?" asked Johnny after a pause. "I mean, they're probably expecting Thérèse back, and if she doesn't come pretty soon they'll begin to think something's up. I—I didn't ask her when she'd planned to go back down; I guess I should have."

Weiller said, "When Auntie and Uncle see the nice Americans drive up, whether it's today or next week, they're going to know that something's in the wind, don't you suppose? But we've got a lot of reasons to go down, and we'll go soon, don't worry."

Johnny said sadly, "I can see how that about the trips to Sartilly *might* have been a setup. But I don't see why it need have been. Again, why wouldn't she just skip it—if she were guilty, I mean? It only brings up an awkward subject. But if she's innocent, why then of course she doesn't know what her father's absences meant, and has no reason to hide them."

"If she's guilty, on the other hand," said Weiller, "she knows very well what we're looking for; and if she can give it to us without involving herself, why then she will. I'm afraid this doesn't paint a very pretty picture of the dear little thing—it means she's throwing her father's carcass to the wolves, if you see what I mean. But as you yourself remarked, after all, he's dead; what difference does it make?"

Johnny had a faint, unhappy recollection that even he had wondered at one point whether the girl was suggesting her father's guilt in order to underline her own innocence. But much more recently he had reflected, and reflected with humility, on the remarkable faith in her father which the girl showed. It seemed to him that the Thérèse Bouliard the captain was talking about and the one he had interrogated upstairs were two completely different people, unconnected in time or space. And he had no conviction, now, that one was more real than the other; if the Thérèse he had spoken to had chosen some facts and rejected others in order to simplify her role, certainly the captain had a similar talent.

Weiller was watching him keenly. "Are you beginning to see it?" he asked. "Now for the last points. I noticed that in your conclusion you made a lot of the fact that Thérèse accounted for Bloch without ever having been told there was a note written by him and implicating her. Well; you can see now how worthless that argument is, can't you? Remember *she* didn't bring up Bloch; you did, and she nearly jumped out of her skin when you did it, too. But once the name was out, all she had to do really was trot out the Bloch story she'd prepared in advance. It made her nervous, of course; it was getting pretty close to the mark. But ultimately, wherever it left her father, it left her in the clear—or she thought it did."

"I just—it doesn't seem real," said Johnny, shaking his head dazedly. "Two complete stories, both of them apparently airtight. I don't know. I *was* sure of mine, or I wouldn't have written like that—and I can see now that I didn't really prove anything, but—sir, I don't think you have either, if you don't mind my saying so. And I don't—see why you're so unwilling to believe that she may be innocent. *You* must have heard someone telling a story at some time or other and been absolutely certain he was telling the truth. Haven't you?"

"Yes," said the captain grimly. "I've been wrong, sometimes, too."

"Yes, sir," said Johnny. "Do you want me to start in all over again?"

"Mr. Phillips," said the captain, "you said you didn't think I'd proved anything. As a matter of fact I don't think I have either; I was just trying to point out to you that a reasonable doubt of the girl's innocence exists—and that the facts you interpreted to mean innocence could as well be arranged to read guilt. As long as guilt remains possible we're not through. You should understand that. But I'll tell you why I really believe that she was mixed up with her father in this, if you want to know."

"Yes, sir. I do."

"This doesn't *prove* anything either; it's just one of the things that experience makes you sure of. I really don't think Bouliard's very likely to have been able to keep what he was doing from his daughter—especially when they were so close, and lived alone together, and when so far as we know Bouliard didn't have anyone else to confide in. Spies are weaklings, Phillips—almost without exception. Oh, if they go over to the enemy out of political conviction, then maybe there'll be a certain strength to them. But few of them do; and certainly there's no reason to suppose Bouliard did. No. I've seen, or read the case histories of, a lot of them. Usually they don't mean to involve their families in the beginning. But either they get too lonely and blurt the whole thing out—because being a spy, you can see, would be the loneliest work in the world—or their spymasters move in on their families, and get them thoroughly involved—on purpose, to keep pressure on their spies, so they won't desert. Even the story you got from the girl corroborates that. You can bet that in fact Bloch moved in on Thérèse far earlier than she says he did; and that in one way or another— maybe both ways—he did enlist her support. Because what else could she have done? Denounced her own father, or walked out on him? The Germans wouldn't have let her do either. And she would have been useful, if she were trained to gather information for her father to transmit to the Germans. That's what Bloch's note shows did happen. It's just too likely, Phillips—it's exactly the sort of thing that would happen—must happen—whether we like to think about it or not."

Johnny did not like to think about it. He said stubbornly, "You admitted yourself, though, that it—it isn't certain. It isn't proof. What if Bouliard did have the guts to keep his daughter out of it?" His voice began to shake. "All I mean is, you—you can't crucify her. You've got to be sure."

"I'm going to be sure," said Weiller. "I'm going to be a lot surer than you are now, Phillips. Let me give you one more thing to think about, before you get too god damned worried about me. According to your way of looking at the story, I gather, Bloch made a couple of passes at the girl, and she got very indignant and told her father, and he got very indignant and maybe did or maybe did not have a fight with Bloch, but anyway didn't want his daughter either working for the Germans or laying for them, so he took Thérèse to Sartilly while things cooled off. Is that right?"

Johnny felt himself reddening. "More or less."

"So," Weiller went on, "they whiled away many a long hour down on the farm—really *many* a long hour—and then at last, on about the eighteenth of May, Bouliard came back to Cherbourg—and Thérèse came with him. Now, doesn't that strike you as odd?"

"Why no," Johnny said. "It doesn't."

"It does me," Weiller said. "Why was Bloch supposed to be any less lecherous on the eighteenth of May than he'd been three weeks earlier?"

Johnny could only look bewildered.

"To translate," Weiller said sarcastically, "*if* the visit to Sartilly was just to get Thérèse away from Bloch, why didn't Bouliard come back up by himself and make sure there'd be no further danger before he let Thérèse come back?"

"I don't know," Johnny said. "Maybe something happened down there that made them want to leave. Or have to."

"Maybe," said the captain dryly. "It would be worth finding out about. For now let's just say they threw caution to the winds, came back together, and by an extraordinary coincidence had no more trouble with Bloch, though the father wasn't killed until ten days later, and the invasion wasn't until—roughly—ten days after that." Weiller shook his head. "Maybe you don't think *that* requires explanation, either; but I certainly do."

"Why—" Johnny considered. "Maybe Bloch *was* a headquarters man. And maybe Bouliard knew it, knew that Bloch was only in Cherbourg at certain times of the month, so they'd be safe after the eighteenth of May. Isn't that possible?" He stared questioningly at the captain. "Because Bloch *must* have been gone by the time Bouliard was killed. Or he would have known, and he would never have sent that note by Korvac."

"We-e-ell," said Weiller. He sounded, Johnny thought, a little disconcerted. "It can't have been a matter of certain times of the month, because Bouliard was killed on a day when, in the preceding month, Bloch *had* been in Cherbourg. But you're right, maybe Bouliard knew somehow that Bloch wouldn't be in Cherbourg around May eighteenth." He paused. "Of course he must have expected he'd come back *sometime,* and what was supposed to happen then?"

"I just—don't know, Captain," Johnny said.

"Well, let's skip it for now," said Weiller. "Instead, since you brought it up, let's take a look at that note of Korvac's. According to Korvac himself, he was coming to help Bouliard out, *if* Bouliard had stopped working simply because he was having technical trouble. In that case, when he was fixed up, Korvac would presumably have gone along, leaving Bouliard and Thérèse to do their work; and the note from Bloch would never have been produced. Right?"

"I guess so," said Johnny uneasily. He didn't much like to have the captain working out his own theory for him. It was like a chess game; he feared a trap, just from the way his opponent was acting, but so far he could not tell where it would lie.

"If Bouliard's reasons for not working were less creditable, then Korvac was to execute him; and he was to set himself up in Cherbourg instead of Bouliard. But he was to use Thérèse as a leg woman, I suppose you'd call her, persuading her to work with him by presenting to her Bloch's note."

"No, no," Johnny broke in excitedly, "that's exactly what I *don't* think. It just wouldn't make sense, even if she were the most rabid pro-Nazi in the world—and you've talked to her a little, whatever she is you know she couldn't be *that*. But I mean, that plan would have been too dangerous—she'd have some feeling for her father, after all, probably a lot, and according to my theory, remember, she certainly had no reason to love Bloch. So why wouldn't she get revenge on Korvac right away by turning him over to the Allies? And that certainly wouldn't do Bloch any good."

Johnny looked urgently at Captain Weiller, trying to find some sign of assent, or of uncertainty, in the captain's face; but Weiller's expression did not alter. After a moment Johnny said, a little crestfallen, "Maybe if Korvac had had to shoot Bouliard, he'd have had to shoot Thérèse too. Or if not, then he'd have had to handle the father quickly and in secret, without ever getting in touch with the daughter—that is, if he expected to work himself. In that case—I guess Bloch would have given him instructions to call it quits right there, and let the revenge against Thérèse go."

Captain Weiller smiled benignly. "But then what was the note for?"

"Why—" Johnny stared at him in perplexity. "As I said. For revenge against Thérèse *and* her father in case Korvac should happen to fall into the hands of the Allies."

"How do you suppose Bloch handled that in his instructions to Korvac? Wouldn't it have been a little tactless to say, 'Here's a note to give the Allies in case you fall into their hands, poor boy'?"

"Why—"

"You yourself just got through saying that it wouldn't do Bloch any *good* if Korvac fell into the hands of the Allies. Just think, from the Germans' point of view, what would have happened if Bouliard had still been alive—as so far as we know they presumed him to be—and had been trying to come up on the air. Even if Thérèse weren't involved with him, and had, as you say, spurned Bloch's advances, and all that. Then if Korvac fell into the hands of the Allies before reaching Bouliard, wouldn't the note blow up the whole scheme and sacrifice not only Korvac, but also another perfectly good agent whose existence could otherwise have been kept secret—just to get a foolish revenge on a girl?"

"I—I guess so," said Johnny. "I guess that wouldn't be so good. But—it's awfully queer. How *can* you explain the note?"

"There's only one way to, that I can see," said Weiller softly. "And that's to take it at its face value. To look at it as a note from Bloch to Thérèse that was meant to reach Thérèse, and that meant what it said. And *that* means that unless Bloch was the worst damn fool the world has ever seen, the relationship between him and Thérèse must have been what the note implies —that is, he must have known Thérèse well enough to be certain that she would *not* turn Korvac over to the Allies for having murdered her father, provided it was done on orders from Bloch." Captain Weiller stood up indolently behind the desk. "And *that*, Mr. Phillips, means that the girl upstairs is not quite such a bundle of charm as you've been thinking." He lowered his voice solemnly. " 'The plan was most ingenious,' " he intoned. " 'Fortunately, it has failed.' "

Johnny was perspiring; he felt almost sick. "I—O.K.," he burst out. "If I did as badly as that, there's no use my going up there again. I don't know. I'll do whatever you want, but—"

"Don't worry," said the captain. His tone was cold, but he was smiling. "You're not going up there again, not just now anyway. But I trust you'll be thinking about this."

Johnny nodded miserably. "Who're you going to put on it?" he asked.

"I'm going up myself," said the captain. He stared thoughtfully at Johnny. "Maybe you'd like to look at this?" He tossed the pages of the report over so that the individual sheets fluttered apart and sailed to the floor around the chair where Johnny was sitting. "Oh, sorry," he said. Then he turned and walked out of the room.

For a time Johnny sat alone in the office, turning over and over in his mind the arguments which the captain had forced him to accept. And forced was the right word, too, he thought resentfully. He could find no flaw in the captain's reasoning; obviously he himself had been very hasty in his interpretation

123

of the Bloch note, just because there was something he'd wanted to believe. But what, he asked himself, did the captain want? Had he figured all this out a long time ago, and if so why hadn't he interpreted the note for Johnny before he had sent him up to interrogate? That he had been in a hurry was no excuse, when something so important was involved.

Of course, Johnny reminded himself, the captain *had* said flatly that the girl was guilty; his explanation of the note was simple and literal, and considering his instructions, he might not have expected Johnny to go beyond that simple and literal surface meaning. But at least he might have said that no other interpretation would stand up. . . . Oh, well, thought Johnny. He was angry at having been caught out in so stupid a mistake, and that was the size of it. But he *was* angry, and couldn't seem to help being.

For there was something else: why, if Weiller had not intended to put him back on the case, had he spent so much time explaining to Johnny exactly how wrong he had been? Had it been, perhaps, just to humiliate him? There seemed no other very likely reason. Why hadn't Weiller gone upstairs as soon as he'd read the ill-fated report and started reinterrogating at once, if that was what he intended doing? He was just rubbing my nose in it, Johnny thought bitterly. He's a bully; he's been bullying me all along; he enjoys doing it. And the way he stalked off there at the end, like God or God knows who, leaving me to pick up the papers he'd scattered all over the floor.

It was by this time late afternoon, and the room, cut off so long from the direct light of day, was becoming shadowy in the corners, and indistinct. Damp breathed from the inner walls. Johnny thought vaguely of turning on the lights; but he did not belong here, nor did he wish to stay until the captain should return with further evidence of his own superiority and Johnny's mismanagement. The only reason he did not leave at once, Johnny realized, was that he was reluctant to face Carl and the others in the outer office. They knew the captain as well as he, or better, and they would perhaps be sympathetic; but he did not want sympathy. He did not know what he did want—not to be involved at all, perhaps, but there was no magic that could rescue him.

He looked at the papers. He ought to leave them where they were, for the captain to pick up himself. But however resentful he might for the moment be, there was in him a deep acceptance of his failure. In the dim light he got down on his hands and knees and gathered the papers together, then rose, sorted them out and arranged them on the captain's desk, put the report under his arm and walked out through the dark, empty rooms into the lighted main office, the old lobby of the hotel.

Carl, as the door closed behind Johnny, looked up and acknowledged his arrival with a grin and a curious little shake of the head. Johnny gave him an abashed smile and, walking over, tossed the report onto the desk. "Do you want to make a bonfire of this?" he asked. "The captain tells me it isn't the last word on the subject."

"Nuts," said Carl, getting up to take the report over to the file. "Who knows, maybe this'll be the way it'll end up. Anyway," he said reassuringly, "even if Old Ironsides does get something more out of her, there's a lot of good stuff here that won't have to be done again."

"Thanks, Carl," said Johnny, in a voice so small that he wondered afterward if Carl had heard him. He looked around the room. Tochyk was still, or again, sitting on the bench against the wall, this time shuffling a pack of dirty cards and dealing them with absorption onto a series of piles arranged in a long oval on the bench beside him. The one who must be Murchison was sitting on a hard chair by the window that looked out on the narrow street, his back to the room, a magazine unopened on his lap. As though he had felt the searching quality of Johnny's glance, he looked around after a moment and smiled quietly. "Hi," he said.

There was a pleasant definiteness to his face, Johnny thought as he nodded shyly in response. He had seen Murchison only distantly, at the table, the night before; now his eyes took in with involuntary care the young man's neatness, the smoothness of his brown hair, brushed straight back, the softness of his eyes and of his clear skin, the exact tidiness of his uniform. Everything about him, even his voice, was soft and smooth, yet he did not give the least impression of effeminacy.

Under Johnny's unintentionally prolonged gaze Murchison smiled again. "I hear the captain's giving you a rough time," he said.

Johnny looked away, embarrassed, mumbling assent.

"Don't let it get you down," Murchison advised quietly. "It's hard to take sometimes if you don't understand him, but he isn't so bad really—and he isn't as mad at you as he lets on, either."

"Ah, don't hand him that," said Carl bitterly. "Weiller's just a loud noise that isn't hooked up to his brains, and you know it." He stared at Murchison belligerently. "Sure, he's got brains, I know he has, I always said so, didn't I? Trouble is how he uses 'em."

Murchison returned his gaze amiably. "Did I tell you what we were doing today, Carl?" he asked. "Or rather what we weren't doing. We weren't getting anywhere—all that time. Thury's having secrets."

"Oh!" Carl said. "So that's why the old boy is so sore!" He turned to Johnny. "You're just out of luck, I guess. Until this other thing blows over, whatever it is. That Thury." He glanced back at Murchison. "What's it about? Can you say?"

"Sure, I don't see why not," Murchison answered. "Something has gone fishy with Cécile Aubanne. You know, the captain thought—we all thought—she didn't amount to anything; in fact we were assuming that she'd be released before now. Well—in a funny way she has been, because I bumped into her on the street last week. Did I tell you?"

"No," Carl said. "I didn't hear that."

"But Thury's still holding her, if that's the right word," Murchison said. "And the captain set this conference for today to try to find out what's going on."

"Say, that's right," Carl said. "This isn't the regular day they get together, is it?"

Murchison looked at him. "You know it isn't, Carl," he said.

"Tut, tut." Carl's voice was airy. "Am I supposed to keep track of the old man's timetable? He wants to let me in on what he's doing, he always can."

126

Johnny saw that Murchison was giving him a covert look.

"Anyway. You remember he sent me on ahead this morning. And when I'd almost got to Thury's, darned if I didn't run into Cécile Aubanne *again*. This time I followed her, down to the port offices, where—of all things—she applied for a job. Don't ask me what's behind it, because I don't know."

Carl whistled. "Did *Thury . . . ?*"

"I told you, Carl. I don't know. I came back here for a minute, you remember, but Weiller wasn't here, so I went on over to Thury's headquarters again. And everybody pretended it wasn't funny at all that I hadn't got there before, and we all had lunch."

"What'd you have?" Tochyk broke in, his voice longing.

Murchison grinned. "Oh—food, Antie. While it was being put on I got the captain aside for a couple of minutes and told him what had happened. He about blew his stack. And then we all sat down—"

"De Sombais too?" Carl asked.

"De Sombais too. She was very lively. All *she* wanted to talk about was Thérèse Bouliard. So Weiller said her interrogation was just being prepared, and you could see Thury didn't think the captain was leveling with him. He kept giving us both dark looks, and Weiller kept giving him dark looks, and Estelle de Sombais kept talking about how untrustworthy innocent-looking girls like Thérèse Bouliard are, and after a few glasses of wine Thury began to make remarks about how cumbersome Weiller must find it to work for so many bosses and how he didn't think anything was going to get accomplished if we in Cherbourg didn't show a little initiative, and I could see Weiller's face was getting redder and redder, and if Estelle de Sombais hadn't been there he'd have blown up. But"—here Johnny saw that Murchison was talking directly to him; why was that?—"the captain wouldn't ever take the risk of humiliating Thury before his secretary; that would be—" He paused. "At least Weiller can treat you like one of the family."

"Big deal," Carl said heavily. "Get on with the story, huh?"

For a moment Murchison looked away out of the window again. "Sure," he said. "Well. I could tell Weiller didn't want to bring up the Aubanne business with de Sombais around, though I'm not certain *I* wouldn't have, it might have been interesting to watch her face. But however much she obviously knows, Weiller won't admit as a matter of principle that she's a member of the French team, exactly, or has a right to be in on everything, so he hung on, and my God, I've *never* seen a lunch last so long. Thury drank more and more, and once predicted somberly, apropos of absolutely nothing, that the Powers would not sanction his being shown the true version of Thérèse Bouliard's interrogation report, because he would have ideas about what might be done with Thérèse; and of course Weiller denied this hotly; and then Thury said in a secretive voice that even somebody as unimportant as Cécile Aubanne might be used with very interesting effect . . ."

"Jesus," Carl said. "*That* was a slip."

"Maybe." Murchison paused. "The thing is, you can't really tell with Thury what he means to let slip and what he doesn't. Sometimes I think he loves getting into a tangle of intrigue for the pure hell of it. But the captain thinks he's got something dirty up his sleeve; and he could be right. And Thury's planning being what it is, he's afraid that whatever's going on will blow up in all our faces, and he'll catch hell from the colonel for not having found out about the deal and prevented it. After all, keeping in close touch with the French is one of his jobs, isn't it?"

Carl shook his head, as though with reluctant admiration. "The goddam French."

A heavy sound of protest came from the bench where Tochyk sat. Carl grinned, and winked elaborately at Johnny. "Take it easy, old man," he said. "Nobody's complaining about that witch you're shacked up with." He turned back to Murchison. "What's the captain gonna do?"

Murchison said gravely, "What can he do? You know Thury; occasionally he gives, but he still thinks it's more blessed to receive. As for instance, finally Estelle de Sombais pulled out and Weiller told Thury point-blank that we'd been seeing Cécile Aubanne around Cherbourg. And do you know what Thury said?"

"No, what?"

"He said—very drunken-delicately—that she was having serious female complaints, and that he had to let her out practically every day to go see her doctor!"

Carl burst into a guffaw of laughter.

After a moment Johnny said, "Did you—did Captain Weiller say anything, then, about your following this woman today? And about her applying for that job?"

Slowly Murchison shook his head. "It's pretty complicated, you know," he said at last. "It'll take a lot of figuring out, and we could get into a very unfortunate position if we jumped the gun. Maybe, after all, the job thing is nothing but Aubanne wishing that she were really free at last—"

"You don't believe that, do you?" Carl asked.

"Carl, I don't know what to believe. And maybe Thury's hinting that he *might* do something with Aubanne just to be sure of getting the straight goods on Thérèse Bouliard. Anyway I think we got as far with him today as we were going to get. Which is not very far, I grant you. Except—"

He turned to Johnny once more. "This may explain why the captain was so—upset about your report, Phillips. He says he *thinks* Thury's pretty honest on a trade, and he *thinks* now that's the only way he can be handled. He'd hoped to be able to send over a good, solid confession from Thérèse Bouliard in the morning, and he thought the implication of the conference today was—maybe—that Thury would then give him the real dope on how, or whether, he's using Cécile Aubanne. If there's real information to be got there, and Weiller can get it quickly, he can perhaps stop the deal from going too far. But if there's a delay—" He shrugged significantly. "This padding around town, if it means anything, could become—very serious."

"Well, damn it," said Johnny, "I couldn't give Weiller what I didn't think was there, could I?" He looked at Murchison defensively. "I expect any of you could have got a confession out of her—"

"No, no," said Murchison quickly. "Don't think that. The advantage is all with them, you know, unless they're really caught with the goods." His eyes held Johnny's for a moment. "And besides," he added in a lower voice, "maybe Thérèse Bouliard *is* innocent, just as you thought. If she is, obviously we don't want to sell her out just to have trade goods for

Thury. Naturally the captain's disappointed. But even he isn't so bloodthirsty that he'd want to sacrifice this girl if it should really turn out that she was innocent."

Doubtfully Johnny shook his head.

Carl had gone back to his typing; Tochyk was staring in bafflement at a card which he had drawn from the pack in his hand. In a moment Murchison picked up the magazine in his lap and began to read. Johnny put his head in his hands, and sat without moving. Complication upon complication—he had never felt so confused. The one thing that was clear was that Thérèse Bouliard's interrogation had mattered even more than he had known.

It could not have been very long before he heard the heavy footsteps of the captain crashing down the stairs. In a moment Weiller strode through, his lips compressed in a thin, angry line, his expression set and wooden. He looked neither to right nor to left; but just before he passed through the door into his outer office, he said in a flat voice, "Mr. Phillips." Apprehensively Johnny got up and followed him.

Back in his own office, seated behind the broad expanse of his desk, the captain appeared to be staring through Johnny, who remained standing uneasily just inside the door.

"Mr. Phillips," said Weiller at last, in a voice from which the last trace of warmth had been eradicated, "I had a lot to think of this morning, and now I've got still more to think of. Your ruinous performance today. The girl's closed up completely; all she'll say is she's innocent, and she's told you everything she knows. Perhaps there's more than you put in your report?"

"Oh, no, sir," Johnny protested.

"In that case," said the captain, "I'm afraid we've a lot of work to do still." He paused, and then went on in a cold, silky voice, "It's going to be just as hard on you as on anybody, Phillips. Naturally I'd like to—spare your sensibilities, but it happens I've no men to use even in such a good cause as that." His voice was rising angrily. "I've explained to you about the Bloch note. Thérèse Bouliard is guilty, and I know she's guilty, and you're going to help me prove she's guilty!"

"Did you—show her the Bloch note?" Johnny asked haltingly.

"Yes," the captain said.

There was a tart silence. But when Weiller spoke again, it was in the same smooth, cold tone as before. "For reasons which I need not explain to you, there's no time to be lost. You haven't been very useful so far; but you will be useful before we're through. As our friends in London said, you will get your training in the field. You've closed one avenue to us, for the time being; others must be opened. You're excused now, Phillips. But you're to report back here immediately after chow. That's all." Weiller gave the bell on his desk an insistent ring.

Johnny continued to stand uncertainly by the door. "I— could you tell me what we're going to do tonight, sir?" he asked. "I'd like to be thinking about it, getting ready any way I could."

Weiller stared at him coldly. "Why, yes," he said. "That's not a bad idea. Do you remember that you got from the Bouliard girl the name of a friend of hers here in Cherbourg, a Mademoiselle Vaugiron?" His lips tightened again into a hard line. "We're going to find her, by God I don't care where she is, if she's down a well, or up a tree, or somewhere the other side of Paris, and we're going to interrogate her until she tells us something that makes sense."

Johnny stared at him in vague alarm. "But, sir—I mean, whatever the girl may have done, surely her friend at least isn't —I mean you can't—"

"I am of course notoriously brutal," said Captain Weiller, "but this once I think perhaps you may trust me. Is there anything else you must say, right at this moment?"

"No, sir," said Johnny.

"Then if you'll excuse me, I have a great deal to do." Weiller nodded meaningfully at the door.

Johnny turned and walked out in silence.

IX.

MLLE. CAMILLE VAUGIRON dismounted a little stiffly from her bicycle and leaned it against the wall of her garden shed. Then she untied the paper-wrapped vegetables from the rack and carried them toward the house. It was getting dark, and she was very tired indeed; she had had to go to a good many farms to get enough food for the next few days. But in the end she had been especially lucky. The parents of a former student of hers, who lived out between Saint-Pierre-Église and Barfleur, had just killed a fowl, and she had been able to buy the giblets from them, and even the neck. She would have broth; it had been a long time since she had had a chicken broth.

The path to her back door led through what should have been her garden, and she surveyed it sadly as she passed between the desolate rows of weeds. Once she had had flowers here, a true English garden, with primroses and verbena and stock. But the last years of the Occupation had brought a scarcity of food for city dwellers even here in Normandy; and the year before she had ruefully torn up her flower beds. It had made her feel for the first time older than her years. But still in the cold spring, in the midst of her teaching, she had managed to get the soil spaded up and a few vegetables planted. Thérèse had helped her.

And then almost at once orders had been issued for the Lycée to be moved, to Vire, far to the south, and she had had to leave Cherbourg. In the summer she had tried to return, but had not been permitted to do so. She had thought it best then to go to Les Pieux, to stay with her sister Marie, who was in any case to have a baby in July—and René, the child's father, in Germany, sent away to work there only a few months before.

They had discovered him doing something suspect in the *police auxiliaire des voies*. Sabotage? Marie had not known, but it had seemed unlikely; René attended to his land and his family and did not think beyond them, or so one could have sworn.

Shortly after Camille Vaugiron had arrived in Les Pieux the baby had been born—prematurely—and had died. Marie had had to do too much heavy work in the late months of her pregnancy. Was that it? One said so. Whose fault was it, then? The Germans', of course—everything in the world was the Germans' fault. And the fault of the Italians, and the French, and the Americans, and the English—it was hardly possible to complete the list.

Or useful. If one knew what omission, what seizure of anger, what indifference, what hatred, what greed, what cunning, what subtle act of betrayal had been ultimately to blame—but oh, far, far back—for cooling the blood in that tiny, unfinished body, one would know so much—so much, and so little. Mlle. Vaugiron had in the course of her studies read much philosophy. But it was curious, she thought, how nearly useless a philosophical point of view could be. For all the perspective it should have given her, she had wept quite as long as her sister had over the dead child.

That was emotion, certainly. But common sense could also nullify one's perspective. It was, for example, for all practical purposes useless and indeed stupid to remind oneself that events were complex, that the enemy had some virtues, or one's allies some faults. So philosophy, like a stepchild, had to wait; and one lived by common sense when he could, and emotion when he could not.

But the garden. She was staring at the weeds, and not seeing them at all. She dismissed from her mind almost as soon as it occurred to her an uncomfortable realization—that in the last year her thoughts had wandered more than ever before. But she was a vigorous woman still, not really old, she told herself, and both physically and mentally unusually sound, unusually well coordinated, for the sixties. When one was alone the thoughts always wandered. There was nothing to be feared in it.

Seeing her ruined garden now in all its luxuriance reminded her again of something that had been puzzling her ever since she had returned to Cherbourg a few days before. What was strange was not that there were weeds, but that there would have been something to weed: dried pea vines, a few spindling carrots and turnips showed here and there in the jungle growth. Unless such things reseeded themselves, the garden must have been planted again this spring. And I do not, Mlle. Vaugiron said to herself, know very much about vegetables, but surely they do *not* reseed themselves? At least not in rows.

Thérèse. It could only have been Thérèse.

But already the garden was impossible to salvage. Which meant that Thérèse had not yet come back, she and her father. They would have been sent away before the fighting for Cherbourg began; all Mlle. Vaugiron's neighbors who had been in the city at the time of the invasion had been sent away. And if Thérèse had already returned, she would certainly have come here to save what she could for her friend, to pull the weeds, to set things in some kind of order. . . . Tomorrow, Mlle. Vaugiron thought, I will bicycle over and leave a note, against the day they come back. I trust that M'sieur Bouliard will not object to that.

She sighed, and smiled, and pulled a huge ragweed that stood by the path. It hurt her hands and arms, and she stood a moment until the ache subsided. God willing, she thought, next summer I shall have flowers again. It was the stock she had loved most of all. As she walked toward her back door now she advanced into its remembered aroma, a spicy fragrance still hot with departed suns, like a thick and tangible suspension in the air, recalling peace, and assurance, and a world not broken, not even badly made.

There was so much to do. And it was amazing how much time one lost, these days, just in the foolish business of staying alive. Such a simple affair it had been once: a few hours' shopping a week had been enough, and beyond that one had been able to spend time enriching one's life, or sharing in the lives of others. Teaching, and talking. Listening to music. Gathering together with love the beautiful objects—pieces of furniture, books, paintings—that made the difference between a raw, unmeaning world and a world where the soul and the senses could alight together and find equal rest, equally find the mirrored chambers that content them. The world in which she lived now was absurdly simplified; it was as she had always thought of life in a primitive society, especially since so many of those fortunate ones in France who still had possessions, something they owned, had become as savage and sullen as so many clouted tribesmen.

Perhaps this was natural. During the Occupation the wants she herself had felt most keenly had been abstract; but with the liberation—not by it, she thought—had returned the insistent demands of the physical world. Now one could speak of anything, and spoke of food. Now one could move freely, and went in search of firewood. Now one could praise, or blame, at will, and had largely lost the power of judgment, had largely forgotten the profound significance of the earlier predicament in the petty irritations and perplexities of the current one. It was as though certain values, denied, had maintained themselves in all purity in some secret well of the spirit; and now, granted currency once more, had flowed forth to lose not only their uncommon value, but almost their identity.

At any rate, one was concerned now perhaps more than ever before with possessions. And in respect to them, Mlle. Vaugiron was she knew fortunate, at least in the long run: her house was still standing, and was in need not even of the smallest repairs. Yet she had sustained some loss, enough so that in a real sense she shared the experience of her countrymen.

One did not know quite how to feel about it. A Nazi officer —he had in the beginning lodged next door and had, in spite of all her coldness to him, visited her often while she remained in Cherbourg, commenting ecstatically upon the good taste she had shown in assembling her furnishings—had moved into her house when she had left it and, according to the neighbors, had lived there until after the invasion. Admiring to the last, he had loaded most of her possessions into a truck and taken them with him when he had left Cherbourg. And now Mlle. Vaugiron was finding life in an almost empty house more awkward, more seriously distasteful, than she would have thought possible—especially since many others had fared, she knew, so much worse than she.

It was not the discomfort exactly, though that was not without its importance. But in a subtle way, the things which the Nazi officer had left behind constituted a direct—and unerring —judgment upon her for her few compromises in taste. And this was the more deeply galling because it was genuinely difficult for her to grant the enemy a true appreciation of the things of the spirit, an appreciation even more accurate perhaps than her own. For she could not, try as she would, altogether disentangle the aesthetic from the moral. And the implications were troublesome, they nagged at her, puzzled her, when for example she looked at the earth-touched lines of the cabinet that had been left (so really good; and at that price . . . !) and recalled the delicate, soaring grace of the cabinet that had been taken.

Of course one could say that the aesthetic standard was valueless, or irrelevant, or even dangerous; but who had most recently tried to teach the world to say just that? No, it was a disquieting thing, no matter how one attempted to dismiss it. And the man was a good Nazi, too, she could have sworn it.

Fortunately he had made the whole thing ridiculous by an almost comforting piece of German arrogance. He had left in the house a note addressed not to her but to the American Army authorities, apologizing punctiliously for leaving the house unfurnished ("if it should cause them any inconvenience"), and assuring them that he would bring the furnishings back when he returned with the victorious German armies, which would of course in their good time dispose of this invasion nonsense. A man with a head like that— Well, doubtless the world had to show some incomprehensible mixtures.

Nevertheless she was relieved in a way to be forced to spend a good deal of time in her kitchen, whose amenities, being strictly utilitarian, had not attracted Oberstleutnant Schwendt at all, and were therefore intact.

As she entered the back door she tried the lights, and found them working. It was good; her supply of candles was not imposing, and that little sergeant from the office where she had gone to report her missing furniture had not brought her any for a long time. Quickly she walked through the rooms of the little house, closing shutters, adjusting the blackout at the unshielded windows.

For awhile her sergeant had been superb: he had even brought her a few tins of milk, and naturally chocolate. It was a pity that he had nothing to recommend him but these things, and the obvious fact that he was far from home and needed someone to be kind to him. She had been very kind, she thought; and if in the end she had realized that he could not be interesting, she had done her best to think nothing of that fact. But she had not been sure herself what she should do—in the circumstances (since he had kept bringing her little, useful gifts) it had seemed dishonest to pretend more friendship, or sympathy, than she felt.

And somehow he must have sensed her discomfort; she had never been good at dissimulation, and in any case the perplexity she had felt had been quite real. With a mixture of dismay and amusement she realized that he could hardly have avoided mis-understanding her true feelings: he must precisely have reversed them, and have concluded that she was playing a kind of callous, precarious and worldly game—for candles. And—oh, the poor boy!—chocolate. She hoped he had found a more worthy re-cipient of these benefactions than she.

And perhaps the electricity would soon be restored altogether. It was coming now, she had heard, from the power plant of a disabled ship in the harbor, but the city's own power plant must, surely, be put in order soon.

She laid her parcels on the kitchen table and sat down for a moment on the bench alongside to rest. Almost at once there echoed sharply through the small house the sound of a firm knocking at the front door. She lifted her head. Who could it be? There was a bell, as her friends knew.

For an instant she wondered whether her blackout could have come unfixed somewhere. But a quick glance at the kitchen windows showed her that it was all right there. And in the front rooms of the old house, the heavy shutters were more than ade-quate to this modern assignment.

The knocking came again, more decisive than before. She sighed, rose, made her way through the dark house to the front door, and opened it upon the dim half-light of the August evening.

Two American soldiers stood on her doorstep; she had seen

neither of them before, she was sure. The larger of the two, red-haired, heavy-faced, wore captain's bars. The other was nothing —a—private, was it? Such an odd term, she had always thought, for any army. But the boy had a pleasant face, thin, with large eyes and a sensitive mouth. The captain's mouth, his whole expression, seemed unnaturally stiff, as though he were merely illustrating an anger, or an importance, of which he was not himself fully convinced.

"*Messieurs?*" she said. She held the door almost closed behind her, blocking off with her body the light from within.

"*Bonsoir, mademoiselle,*" said the captain, as if he were stating a necessary fact. "*Vous vous appelez . . . ?*"

He waited, stony of visage, while she regarded him with an even gaze. Another of those Americans, she was thinking, whose accents were half instruction, half determination.

"I am Miss Vaugiron, Camille Vaugiron," she said at length. "You may speak to me in English; I understand well." She was proud of her own accent—only with the short "i" did she have a little difficulty, so that unless she were thinking about it she said "thees," and "Mees." It was faintly annoying.

She saw the captain give his companion a quick glance; then he turned to her again and said, "May we come in? You could help us a great deal by answering some questions. If you would be so kind."

Now what was this about? She was hungry and tired, and the tone of the man's voice belied the courtesy of his words. "I am about to prepare my supper," she said indecisively. She ought perhaps to ask them to come back later in the evening. But she needed rest; if they returned late they would stay even later; it would be better to satisfy them now, however much she might wish to go on about her work.

The matter was decided for her. "We shan't take much of your time," said the captain firmly.

A considerate young man, evidently, she thought ironically. "*Entrez donc,*" she said, in a cool voice. "Come in."

They followed her through the dark front rooms into the kitchen. "I do not have many chairs," she said. "You will not mind sitting out here?" Without waiting for an answer she took the newspaper-wrapped parcel from the table, carried it over to the drainboard, extracted a small potato and two turnips, and began preparing them for the pot. Under the circumstances perhaps there was no need for her to be overcourteous, herself.

"There has been a denunciation," said the captain's voice in a tone that suggested affability, "and we've learned that you would be in a position to help us get at the truth of the matter. I'm sure you would wish to do so."

Ben, of course, she thought; I should have known it. Having been away, she had managed so far to avoid getting involved in the throat cutting. But it was not to be hoped that she could avoid it altogether. She turned toward her visitors. "Who is denounced?" she asked impersonally. "What is the accusation?"

The captain had spread his squat fingers on the table before him, and appeared to be examining them with care. The man chooses his words, she thought; she became suddenly watchful. "M'sieur?"

He looked up tranquilly. "I was thinking," he said, "that perhaps there would be no need to trouble you, after all. The American Army, as you may suppose, has to have a great many interpreters. There was a girl we were thinking of using, until she was accused of collaboration with the Germans; but it's occurred to me that I wouldn't have to bother with her if—" He stopped, and produced a smile in which she did not believe. "You speak English so well. Would you consider employment with the Army as an interpreter?"

Mlle. Vaugiron replied brusquely, "I am a teacher. My work will soon I trust begin again. About whom did you wish to ask me?"

"A pity," said the captain. He paused, then went on in an offhand voice, "The girl's name is Thérèse Bouliard."

She felt a painful pressure in her chest, as though rough fingers had closed around her heart. She walked as casually as she could, and she hoped without faltering, from the sideboard to the table, and sat down facing the captain. She often grew fond of her students, and some of her colleagues she respected and valued; but Thérèse was the only person in Cherbourg for whom she really cared deeply. It would have to be Thérèse.

And yet, how could it be? When had she returned? Why had she not come to see her old friend?

"I—I am surprised," she said in a faint voice. "I know this girl well; if she is criticized I think there must be malice at work. Who accuses her?" She directed a grave and level glance at the captain. "And of collaboration—for Thérèse, what would that mean? You must know, she is a girl of the highest moral character." In spite of all she could do, her voice grew anxious. "M'sieur—where is she? She has not been harmed?"

"No, no; of course not." The captain was, she thought, looking at her sardonically. "Mademoiselle, you must not be concerned; we are here to clear up a very trifling matter. If you grow too agitated"—he spoke deliberately now, and there was a questioning note in his voice—"we must fear that there is more in the accusation than we had at first supposed."

She could feel the color beating in her cheeks. Her first instinct, to treat this as though it were nothing, had been correct; not for worlds would she do Thérèse harm. Recovering, she said steadily, "These are times, as you know, in which many are accused. And one does not like to see a fine person befouled with slander, especially when it may have serious consequences. But if you say the matter is trifling, I am of course reassured. Ask me any questions you have. I will do my best to answer."

The captain said swiftly, "What relations did Thérèse Bouliard have with the Germans?"

"None," she replied with rigid control. "And of all people— aside from the girl herself, that is; and her father—I am the one who should know best." She paused in perplexity. "That is why I say the charge of collaboration cannot be—honest, m'sieur. All of us had to pass the Germans in the streets; many did a little more, and some did much. But for Thérèse there was no occasion to—have a relationship. And I assure you, no inclination. She disliked the Germans. When her father went to work for them—"

"Yes?" breathed the captain.

She looked at him, startled. He was leaning forward over the table, a curiously intent expression on his face.

"Do not misunderstand, m'sieur," she said quickly. She felt a little at a loss; it was so laborious, all this, since one could not, apparently, assume the sincere desire to understand. Well, she too could choose her words, if she must. "You recall that you just now offered me a post with the American Army, because I have the use of English as well as of French. Yet I assume you are proposing nothing dishonorable? Just so the Germans made use of the services of linguists, in their—offices, their administrative offices. The employment cannot have appealed to all those who were forced to accept it, but—you must see that it was not necessarily wrong to accept."

"I thought," said Captain Weiller, "that Bouliard was a teacher, like yourself."

"Yes." She did not know what to say or how quite to explain, for she was not herself perfectly clear about what had happened. "But I have lived here for many years, and he—he came in 1939, just before the war began. After the Germans arrived he lost his teaching position, did you know that? There was some charge—which M'sieur Durand could not oppose, he knew Bouliard so little."

"Durand?"

"The head of the Lycée."

"Were there charges against you also?" asked Captain Weiller. "Did you and Bouliard teach the same subject? Did you also teach English?"

"No, no. I am a teacher of history, m'sieur. Thérèse was my student. No, there were no—"

"One moment," said the captain. He took a small pad of paper and a pencil from the breast pocket of his uniform jacket and began writing swiftly. "When was Thérèse Bouliard your student? For how long?"

"From 1939 to 1941. I taught her in both my courses, ancient and modern history."

"You found her a good student? She had a clever mind?"

"She has a good enough mind, m'sieur. I am sure you will find her—alert, able to serve you."

The captain did not reply at once. "We find her already—very intelligent, I think," he said. "I am surprised that you speak no more highly of her abilities than you do." He was silent for a moment. "She mentioned you as her particular friend. Was this —presumption on her part? If she was not one of your best students . . ."

141

Camille Vaugiron said, "Presumption, no. And she was, assuredly, *one* of my best students. Only . . ."

Her thoughts drifted back toward those early years; one dealt so much with the present, or the immediate past, that it was difficult to recall one's first impressions of a person whom one had known for many years. Thérèse as a student. . . . Gradually the girl's figure as she had first seen it became clear before her eyes—tiny, dark, quick and yet somehow clumsy, touchingly so, like a young animal that has not yet learned how its legs and body, and mind, work together. Thérèse had been silent for weeks in class, yet there was an intensity to her silence that had been more arresting than the speech of most of the girls.

And Mlle. Vaugiron had soon learned that the girl was the only child of the new language man, the widower Bouliard, a strange, haughty, distrustful creature who would not be happy it seemed until all of his new colleagues had become impatient with him, or indifferent to him, or downright angry. And yet (one heard these things quickly) his students actually liked him, admired him. His teaching was without warmth; but they learned. Many, indeed, learned who had not troubled to do so before. All this had surprised her: Monsieur Bouliard was by no means the prototype of the man who loves to teach, or teaches well. But then why was he a teacher? What ambition would he have preferred to satisfy?

The captain was looking at her impatiently, and she tried to recall his question. Ah, yes: why had she from the beginning thought so highly of Thérèse? She sighed. They will not look upon the teacher as a human being, she thought. In fact she had seldom been most fond of the students who had done most creditably in their work.

Poor Thérèse, poor motherless child, and with such a father, whom she adored fiercely, Mlle. Vaugiron had learned, quite without knowing ultimately what his emotions toward her were —though it was obvious that he depended on her. The girl had needed reassurance; she had needed to be advised; she had needed to be relieved of worries which she could not bear; she had needed to be taken by the hand and led kindly and casually into adulthood. . . . And she herself, thought Mlle. Vaugiron, what had she needed? A daughter. Again she felt the painful pressure on her heart. It was not the sort of thing one told an unknown American officer.

"I am a teacher, yes, m'sieur," she said, looking quickly at the captain and then looking away again, "but I know that there is more to a person than his need to learn. In the end, one values others for—reasons one cannot explain."

The captain sighed. He was exasperated with her, she could tell, but she cared very little. Of course, the sooner she gave him what he wanted the sooner he would go. But what could that be, in heaven's name? She put on an expression of candor and looked at the captain directly once again. "In many respects we are doubtless similar, Thérèse and I; is that what you wish me to say? There are ways of thinking, and feeling. A sympathy. I do not mean that I felt sorry for her: it would be unnecessary, she has strength and—I think I have said—fine moral qualities. But one thinks a person good, and interesting, and one feels an affection."

When his expression did not change, she drew her brows together. "Still perhaps I do not understand your questions? You know that I am the girl's friend; you cannot expect that I will tell you she is bad. To me, if I understand goodness, she is good. As far as the Germans are concerned, I am sure she had nothing to do with them; I should have known if she had during the time I was myself in Cherbourg, for she spent much time with me then, and we spoke of day-to-day happenings, and all our intimate thoughts. But to you this is of course not proof. I do not know what you will accept as proof."

The captain leaned back in his chair and surveyed her without expression. "I do not necessarily depend upon you for proof of anything, mademoiselle," he said. "For information, yes. If you have any that is of value. What do you mean when you speak of 'the time when you were yourself in Cherbourg'?"

"The Lycée was moved away in April, 1943, m'sieur. I accompanied it."

"So you saw Thérèse Bouliard last—when?"

"At that time. In April of last year."

"Yet you say that you of all people know best that Mademoiselle Bouliard could not have been guilty of collaboration."

"Yes, m'sieur. Because I know her—best. The year I have been away does not matter."

"It's mattered a lot to the Germans," Captain Weiller said. "But all right." He sighed. "You say that Thérèse Bouliard has not been your student since 1941; did she leave school in that year?"

"No, in 1942. She has not told you?"

The captain ignored the question. "What do you know about her employment afterward? Since you know her so very intimately."

"Her employment?"

"Yes; what did she do?"

"Of course, I know what the word means." Camille Vaugiron felt an irritation which she managed with difficulty not to show. "Thérèse has had the managing of her father's house—a great responsibility for a girl of her age, I assure you. Though in the ordinary family the girls are of course trained for this by the mother. But Thérèse has no mother." She paused. "The child has not worked for wages, if that is what you mean."

The captain was watching her with an intentness which made her slightly uncomfortable. "I wonder why not."

"Please?"

"I gather that there were some difficulties, financially, after the father lost his teaching position. Didn't the girl even try to find a job then?"

Mlle. Vaugiron looked at him curiously. "It is clear that you are not well acquainted with Pierre Bouliard, m'sieur."

She saw the young soldier glance at her swiftly, as though startled. She must seem to him—disrespectful, was that it?

The captain barked, "Go on, please."

The rudeness of his tone angered her momentarily, but she said, "M'sieur Bouliard is not the kind of man to permit his daughter to work when he is not working." She regarded the captain steadily. "I would be sure that he has found employment now, for example, with one of the American offices; or that he has seen M'sieur Durand, and will resume teaching; or you would not be permitted even to consider employing Thérèse."

"Time must have hung rather heavy on the girl's hands," the

captain said, "if she was around the house all the time after she left school in 1942."

"I believe that it did, m'sieur," Mlle. Vaugiron said. "Or rather on her mind. It is not easy to run a house, and buy when there is nothing to buy, and do well, all without means. Of work she had enough to do. The father did a great deal for them both, of course, while she was still in school. And he insisted that she complete her studies. But when she had done so, then she assumed the—keeping of the house?—and it was I believe at some time after that that he began to work for the Germans."

"Was she contented with the arrangement? Didn't she think of marriage, or a career of her own?"

Mlle. Vaugiron said quietly, "In France, you understand, it is not usual even now for a woman to have a career. And as for marriage—there has been no question of this that I know of. Her father has needed her, you see." She looked away.

"I do see," the captain said. "And if *he* needed *her*, and the Germans needed *him,* that must be why the Bouliards, both of them, were allowed to stay in Cherbourg when last year so many others, like yourself, were forced to leave."

Mlle. Vaugiron brought her eyes slowly back to meet the captain's direct, ironic gaze. "I do not know what M'sieur Bouliard did for the Germans," she said. "I repeat, however, that linguists must have been useful to them in many ways essentially innocent. And I think that he had a right to fend off starvation, and Thérèse to care for him in Cherbourg or wherever she was permitted to do so." She concluded, a little stiffly, "But I am sure this does not matter to you, what I think?"

"On the contrary," he said urbanely. "I'm very much interested in your impressions of the situation. Indeed, I'm very much interested in you yourself, as Mademoiselle Bouliard's—teacher. I've been thinking. It was the Germans, you say, who caused her father to lose his teaching position." He leaned forward in his chair, staring at her with a bright, friendly smile. "How is it that they permitted you—or anyone—to go on teaching modern history?"

She made an involuntary gesture with her hands. "They had their own ideas, of course."

"And you—"

"I had mine. Naturally."

"It must have been very difficult. When one had—so much responsibility for the formation of the ideas of the young."

There was an indefinable quality in his voice, a seriousness that seemed too close to solemnity to be real, and she felt, suddenly, an astonishing discomfort. Yet how could he be mocking her? Why should he be? Had the accusation against Thérèse been sufficient already to condemn the girl in his eyes? Was he trying now to extract a confession—or was he trying to convince himself—that she, Camille Vaugiron, had corrupted Thérèse's mind? But why should he go to such lengths, when after all he was not required to employ the girl, if he could not forget his suspicions? She said abruptly, "One had to be careful. But it was not—an impossible situation."

"I'm sure it was not."

Suddenly she was angry, and she did not wish to show it— indeed, did not wish to be angry at all, for it was foolishness, she knew. But this man, this American officer—she was no heroine, of course she was not, but she deeply resented the implication with which he was obviously baiting her that she had not resisted the pressures that had been brought to bear on her, or had not altogether resisted.

And in a way she *had* compromised, in the sense that she had thought it worthwhile to teach all the truth possible, instead of giving up her work and seeing it done by someone who might see an advantage in teaching whatever lies the Germans might desire. This man, and all the rest, all the Americans she had met, seemed to have a fantastic double opinion—that the French people in the abstract, or at any rate that part of the French people that one meant when one spoke approvingly of "the French," had performed marvels of resistance, had been utterly incorruptible; but that any actual French people one met must naturally have been corrupted.

Well, and perhaps they had been, she thought wearily—the absence of truth was corrupting, the absence of information. And the full truth had not been in France for many years. Lies were like drugs; their poisonous effects upon the body, their dulling, distorting effects upon the mind, did not cease with the administration of the last dose.

146

Still she could not say to this man, who had doubtless withstood nothing more difficult than the rigors and the boredom of military training, that she was at fault. And she would not protest her innocence. It was all too complex; it wearied her even to think of it. He had no right to come here. . . . She shook herself a little. It was not her guilt or innocence that were questioned, but Thérèse's.

The eyes of the young soldier were shifting back and forth from the captain to her, she noticed; the captain was merely staring at her, waiting. For what? Suddenly she leaned forward across the table. "Listen to me," she said in a low voice. "I do not know what you wish me to say, but I shall tell you the truth about what I know, quickly, and then hope that you will leave me to my supper, because I am an old woman, and hungry, and tired. It is with Thérèse Bouliard as I have told you: I myself cannot believe that she has at any time done wrong. It remains then to ask why she is accused. M'sieur—I am sure you know better than I do what is involved. But I should inquire into the motives of the accuser. I had not thought the girl had enemies —though—" Mlle. Vaugiron had an instinct for telling the truth, a preference for it, which even the years of the Occupation had not eradicated. She finished anxiously, "It is true she has few friends."

The captain looked at her sharply. "Why would you say that was?"

She was committed. "I should say it is the father's fault, m'sieur. He—objects, somehow, to ordinary human contact, or so I have always considered. And he objects for his daughter as for himself. I think he feels—an enmity in the world; and an enemy—may pretend to be a friend, in order to betray." Was she right to say all this? Was it true even? "Through his daughter also he is vulnerable; and so he discourages her from extending her friendship to others. Certainly very few guests come to that house."

The captain's voice was bland. "He finds you, however, a suitable friend for his daughter."

If it had not been so strange a performance, she thought, she might have been amused. "I think, m'sieur, he has recognized a little that Thérèse might need some things which he could not supply. I never heard that he objected to our friendship. On the other hand he has not, himself, become a friend of mine; indeed I think he has treated me all the more distantly because his daughter spent so much time with me. Here, you understand, in this house—I did not visit there." She paused. "And I remind you that I have not been in Cherbourg now since the removal of the Lycée, so that recently the question has not arisen."

The captain frowned. "Are there any other close friends at all, either of the father or of the daughter?" he asked.

She considered. Then she said unwillingly, "It must seem strange. But there are none that I know of. Unless they have been made in the last year. But—I would think not."

She fell silent for a moment. Then she went on. "I used to feel sorry for Thérèse: when she did not think how it sounded, she spoke sometimes of other people almost as—a stranger to the world. At first I used to try to find friends for her; to bring them here. But this frightened her, and she withdrew." She looked up. "I do not think this will have changed. You see, even for me it was difficult to make friends with her, though she wanted my friendship very much."

The captain was smiling.

She sighed. "I soon saw what part the father played in her life. She understood him as you would have supposed only a much older person could have done. But she would not question, and she would not criticize. She knew that he had no one but her, and from her earliest childhood she had apparently determined that he should not be disappointed in her. If among other things his distrust of the world meant that he wished the strictest—separateness, she would see that nothing she did impaired it." She smiled bitterly. "After I learned this, he was hardly mentioned between us. And she was grateful, and was much more at ease with me than ever before."

The captain said, "This is a curious story, mademoiselle."

"It is," she said defiantly.

"I presume then that she did not speak to you of her father's employment with the Germans. How was it that you learned of this?"

"*Mon capitaine,*" she said, "*c'est une bataille entre nous?* You

148

seek always to surprise me. If you do not think I speak the truth it is always your privilege—"

He broke in, "I am trying to *discover* the truth."

She sighed again. "Thérèse did, of course, tell me that her father was working for the Germans. I do not know how else I should have discovered it. I offered once—" She looked through the archway behind the captain into the darkness of the front rooms, the darkness of past years. "It was when I did not know that M'sieur Bouliard had found work. And I feared for them, for Thérèse of course particularly—I feared they might be in straits, and too proud to tell anyone. Thérèse was so thin-looking, always more weary; as people grow when they have not enough to eat. And at last I told Thérèse that if she needed money she must accept it from me. Because I myself had no one but her. She told me then that her father was working in the German offices. She did not know in what capacity, and I saw that it frightened her. So I explained to her what I have told you: that of course a linguist would have many uses to an occupying army; honorable uses as well as others."

The captain said, "You recognize at least that there might be others. Do you have any slightest inkling of what function Monsieur Bouliard performed for the Germans?"

"Naturally not, m'sieur. I know only what Thérèse herself was able to tell me, and this was in fact nothing."

"Could you tell us the name of anyone who might know?"

"No, m'sieur."

The captain's fingers drummed like metal on the bare wooden table top. "You have, in fact, nothing more to say about this?"

Mlle. Vaugiron stared at him in perplexity and distaste. "You said once you wished information. If I tell you more it is opinion, and that is not the same thing."

The captain said wearily, "Your opinion might provide me with ways of getting further information elsewhere. If however you do not wish this—"

"Listen," she said. "I wish—to help the child, and in this to be honest. But I wish also to eat my supper. I have thought one thing. You do not say from where the accusation against Thérèse has come; but it may be—do you not think?—in reality an accusation against her father. From someone who thinks he did wrong, and presumes that she must also have done wrong. But—" She slumped wearily in her chair. "For you Americans, surely it is not impossible to find out what he did? If you do not trust what he says himself? Cannot others from this city be found who worked with him? And then you would know, and would not need to seek for information of this kind from me, when I know so little."

For a moment nothing more was said. Then the captain replied, "We do not expect you to tell us more than you can. And we shall soon be through. It is, you must see, not easy for us to understand the Bouliards; and yet it is of some importance that we do so." He leaned toward her over the table and said slowly, "You've helped us a great deal already—to understand the father, and the girl. But—I am not yet quite content. You were a colleague of Monsieur Bouliard's at the Lycée. You have told us that it was on account of the Germans that he lost his job. You must see that under the circumstances, every known relationship of this family with the Germans must be explored."

"Under the circumstances!" Camille Vaugiron could no longer disguise the anxiety that had been growing in her as the captain spoke. "M'sieur, what *are* the circumstances? At the beginning you said that this was a trifling matter, but—"

"Perhaps," the captain intervened smoothly, " 'trifling' was not quite the right word; but I did not wish you to be needlessly alarmed. The concerns of my organization are secret and are not, of course, trifling to us; nor could we admit anyone to our premises—where this important work of ours is done—without the most thorough investigation. I'm sure you understand. Now. Would you tell me, as far as you can, how it happened that Monsieur Bouliard lost his position in 1940?"

Mlle. Vaugiron said weakly, "M'sieur Durand could tell you this better than I. Or M'sieur Bouliard himself."

"I daresay. But here we are now; and what you tell me may be of use."

"Well, then—as far as I can. But I fear there is no connection whatever here with Thérèse."

She looked up questioningly, but when the captain made no sign she went on, "In fact, m'sieur, it is not a story which—is easy to understand. For I have been told that even here in northern France there were some cities where the Germans appeared to take no interest in what was taught in the schools; and others where they were somehow kept from interfering. Except that the Jews, of course, could teach nowhere. In some places there was a degree of further regulation, but it came slowly. In Cherbourg—" Mlle. Vaugiron cast about helplessly. "I do not know. The Germans came to us almost at once."

"To Monsieur Durand?" the captain asked.

"To him, yes. They made it clear to him that if the schools were to continue at all as we would wish, he would have to cooperate with them fully. In these circumstances, I think he— did his best."

"To cooperate?"

Mlle. Vaugiron gazed at him in silence.

"Well. What happened?" The captain's voice was impatient.

Mlle. Vaugiron shook her head wearily. "Of those whose subjects were of interest to them they made full examination; and M'sieur Bouliard, like myself—and there were a few others —M'sieur Bouliard, I say, was the object of one such examination. But—" Again she shook her head. "I do not know why. He alone, of us all, was not permitted to go on teaching."

"Sir—there's something about that in my report." The boy was speaking, for the first time. "Mademoiselle Bouliard said—"

Camille Vaugiron saw the captain turn toward his companion and give him a sharp repressive glance. Then, "What do you *think* the explanation is, Mademoiselle Vaugiron?" he asked insistently.

Abruptly she got to her feet. "I have told you that I do not know!" she said. "How could I know? Except that he was not —one of us. Not thoroughly known to us, to M'sieur Durand. But surely it is not to M'sieur Bouliard's discredit that the Germans did not trust him to . . ." She felt her voice trailing away. The captain was staring at her. She finished, stubbornly, "To serve their—purposes?"

A direct, mocking smile appeared on the captain's face. After a moment he said, "Yet they trusted even him enough to employ him themselves, later."

"Please!" Mlle. Vaugiron burst out. "M'sieur Bouliard is—

was at that time—an unfortunate. But I do not think he has ever been a bad man. You said you wished to understand."

"I do," said the captain.

"And I wish you to understand, though I know so little. At least I wish you to see what a difficult life Thérèse has had—and to believe that it has developed in her nothing but loyalty and integrity. Perhaps—there are people who hate her father, or doubt him. Who wonder as you did at his remaining in Cherbourg during the last year of the Occupation. If so I think that is why you now have a denunciation of Thérèse. But, m'sieur—you must see that there is no possibility of *her* being guilty of wrong! Why—what could she have done? What is the charge? 'Collaboration.' What—"

The captain got to his feet. "I fear we have tired you," he said, in a tone she could not read. The boy rose also and stood awkwardly waiting, his eyes downcast. Then the captain said, "You can recall no other connections the Bouliards had with the Germans?"

"None, m'sieur. I am sure there were none, except—the innocent, the necessary."

"And one final question. Do you remember the name of the German who interviewed you and Bouliard and the others at the Lycée in 1940?"

She closed her eyes and was silent, trying to force her mind, her memory, to obey her. "No," she replied at last, opening her eyes again wearily. "No."

"It's all right," said the captain. "Thank you very much indeed for all the help you've given us."

She stood unsteadily, brushing a thin lock of hair back from her forehead. "M'sieur," she said. "If I may ask you. Is Thérèse at her home?"

There was no reply.

"But you said it is all right!" she cried. "I wish to see her! Where . . . ?"

"Good night," the captain said.

The two turned, walked through the dark front rooms and out into the night. The closing of the front door was merely a sound that said nothing.

Outside in the street, the two men walked in silence toward the jeep, which had been left around a corner, some blocks back toward the main part of Cherbourg.

Finally Johnny said, "She didn't know that Bouliard is dead."

"No." The captain's tone was light. "And I didn't think it was our business to tell her."

There was another silence. "Well," Johnny said, and sighed. "Anyway she wasn't much help, was she?"

"I suppose I'd better point something out to you, before you start drawing conclusions again," the captain said in a hard voice. "This woman's situation isn't the same as Thérèse Bouliard's, obviously; therefore I couldn't *interrogate* her, I could only put some questions to her. Especially since I had to be careful not to scare her too much, at first anyway. Do you understand?"

"Yes, sir," said Johnny.

But he did not understand; and he remembered, as Weiller apparently did not, the words that had been said at the end of the afternoon: "We're going to interrogate her until she tells us something that makes sense."

Perhaps, of course, the captain, in cooling off, had recognized that he would have to be a little circumspect with Mlle. Vaugiron. But even in view of this his questioning had not seemed so very expert to Johnny. The story was a strange one, it was true. And a pathetic one.

Again doubt assailed Johnny. Perhaps nothing would be found out because there was nothing to find out; there were only private areas of pain and wretchedness to be invaded and exposed. And because he must do something, the captain would invade them and expose them; and come out with nothing but the pain made worse. Poor Thérèse, Johnny thought—even if she were in some unknown way guilty, it hadn't been much of a life she'd had. At least she'd been lucky to have a friend like Mlle. Vaugiron. Thérèse's teacher had seemed to him a fine person; he had been embarrassed and ashamed at the thoughtless way in which they had treated her.

The captain said, "I suppose you realize that almost no one in the world is indifferent to the people he knows. And therefore you can't expect disinterested information from anybody. The result is that you've got to ask enough questions of a leading kind to be sure of the bias that goes with the information you're getting." He stared over at Johnny. "Obviously this poor, infatuated, childless female wasn't going to tell me anything that would incriminate her young friend, if she could help it. All we could hope to do was get some facts that meant perhaps more than she thought they did. And get her mad, and then smooth her down, and finally tire her out, so that somewhere, some way, she'd spill something she didn't mean to, if there was anything she could spill."

So he'd done it all on purpose. Johnny was again bitterly resentful of the captain's methods, which arose, if not out of simple inhumanity, then out of an astoundingly rigid conviction that the girl must be guilty. "What did you find out?" he asked brusquely.

"Oh, not as much as I'd hoped; but as much as I'd expected." Weiller's voice was matter-of-fact. "You didn't think Vaugiron's evidence was all straight sailing, did you?"

"Why—I don't know. It seemed to me she really believed what she was saying, but"—he spoke carefully—"that doesn't make it necessarily true, of course. I don't think I noticed anything out of line, though."

"It didn't strike you as odd that Mademoiselle Vaugiron said she'd know about any connection of the girl's with the Germans, up to the time she left anyway, because Thérèse and she told each other everything that happened to them, all their 'intimate thoughts'—and I quote—yet Bouliard himself was off limits as a subject of conversation, and Vaugiron represents Bouliard as ninety-nine percent of his daughter's life?"

"Well—all right, sir, yes, that's *odd*, but—"

"But what? Add it up. Thérèse told her dear friend and teacher all her intimate thoughts except ninety-nine percent. On the basis of the one percent, Vaugiron is sure Thérèse had no truck with the Germans. Well, I'm not. And if Vaugiron has any brains, which she has, I'll bet she isn't either. It's clear that Thérèse kept her off the subject of Poppa—Poppa who worked for the Germans—except that *once* she let her explain that it was O.K. to work for the Germans, it might happen to anybody.

The rest of the time they must have talked about the price of lamb chops, or maybe the price of lamb chops in ancient Assyria." Weiller looked at Johnny savagely. "Hogwash. I'm not saying Thérèse *did* tell her secrets to Vaugiron, though obviously Vaugiron knows more than she's told us, and suspects more than that. I *am* saying that it's clearer than ever that Thérèse Bouliard has *got* secrets. And it's my job to see to it that she doesn't keep them. Does that make any sense to you? Because if it does, maybe I can expect a little help from you from now on."

"I don't know," said Johnny rebelliously. "I mean—excuse me, sir, honestly. But I don't know if it does make so much sense to me. Do secrets have to be bad? But anyway, Miss Vaugiron hasn't been in Cherbourg since—when was it she said, sir?"

"April, 1943," Weiller said softly.

"And she thinks Bouliard didn't start working for the Germans until some time after his daughter finished school, which was in '42. So maybe there're only a few months between the time Bouliard began with the Germans—and who knows, maybe he *didn't* start right away as a real full-fledged spy—and the time Miss Vaugiron left Cherbourg."

"All right. What are you getting at?"

"Just that—well, why do we have to *assume* that something went wrong, so wrong that even Miss Vaugiron found out about it, just in that short time? After all, Thérèse Bouliard said that Bloch didn't—"

"Now this is very hard," the captain said, stopping for a moment on the sidewalk to stare at Johnny and then walking on more slowly. "You needn't tell me what Thérèse Bouliard said. Nor how Vaugiron's remarks *could* be O.K., and *could* fit in with a theory of the girl's innocence. Phillips, *for God's sake.*" Here he stopped again. "We don't *assume* anything. On the other hand, what I've been trying to show you is that *it isn't our business to be reassured.* Can't you get that through your head?"

"Yes, sir," Johnny said. "I—I wasn't trying to prove anything."

"I won't comment on that," the captain rejoined. He walked on once more. "Anyway—let's say you've stopped trying to prove something. Now. What comes next, would you say?"

Johnny fell into step, a little behind him. "I—I don't think I know enough to say, sir," he said unhappily. "I'll just—wait and see what happens."

"You mean," said Weiller in a soft voice, "that you're not collaborating with me on this case any more?"

"Of course I'll do anything I can, sir!" Johnny answered desperately. "It's just—you said yourself, after I'd interrogated Thérèse Bouliard, that—I should have just interrogated her, not tried to prove anything." As if you yourself haven't been trying to prove something from the very beginning, he thought bitterly. But if it's *your* theory, of course it's O.K.

"What a good idea," said the captain placidly. "Who shall we interrogate next?"

They were within sight of the jeep now; in a moment or two, Johnny thought, he'd be unlocking the ignition and starting the motor, and the captain would let him go. "Shouldn't we see the head of the Lycée, sir?" he asked. "Durand?"

"I might put somebody on that tomorrow or the next day," said the captain lazily. "There's not much to be done there. No, we've got other things to do, you and I. Is this jeep in good order?"

"Barker said it was, sir."

"See that it's gassed up, and ready for a good long trip, before chow in the morning, will you? We'll start right afterward."

"Yes, sir." Johnny did not know whether he was expected to ask more, or not. Finally he said cautiously, "Should we carry extra gas, sir? I mean—how far are we going?"

The captain smiled gently. "Not far tomorrow. Just to La Haye-du-Puits. Your girl friend seems to have trouble talking to us; I thought maybe she'd like it better talking to Korvac. And we could listen."

"But," Johnny protested, "you said yourself she isn't likely to have known Korvac. So what will you gain by their seeing each other?"

"Think about it," said Weiller softly. "That's what I'm doing."

They drove back to the hotel in silence.

Tuesday,
August 29, 1944

X.

Bruce Weiller, his uniform in perfect press, his overseas cap adjusted to the precise angle, his captain's bars shining, sat stiffly in the back seat of the jeep as it jolted along through the uninteresting countryside. The extraordinary discomfort of the vehicle made him, as always, sharply aware of his military bearing; but in any case he had not yet relaxed from all that saluting he'd had to do before they'd left Cherbourg. It had been partly on account of the girl, he supposed; he'd had to show his permit to a succession of MP's, and even the GI's along the sidewalks, sensing something unusual in the situation, had mostly saluted instead of looking deliberately away as they would have ordinarily.

But often soldiers saluted Captain Weiller under any circumstances—even when they could not see his bars; he looked like an officer, he knew, and apparently like the kind of officer who insists on the letter of military courtesy. So far as this affected him at all, he was amused by it, in a wry sort of way. In his own conduct, and in matters that concerned himself alone, he chose to abide by the army forms as he would have chosen to abide by the terms of any contract to which he had made himself a party, whether or not he fully believed in them; whether others did so or not concerned him little. He was, he thought, neither an undisciplined sloven, as some officers were, nor an officious prig; he was merely a man with a job, a man in charge of important work, and he proposed to see that the work got done as efficiently as possible in these circumstances just as he would have in any other.

Phillips wasn't making good enough time; of course he'd never been over the road before. And apparently the potholes, the generally gone-to-hell surface, astounded and appalled him.

It oughtn't have been too hard to figure out what would happen to a road over which a war had traveled. The boy kept craning his neck out the side or peering over the windshield in a timid, ridiculous kind of way, as though he could see any better for all that stretching; and still he did not pass other vehicles when he could have done so, and outside of Cherbourg had got interminably stuck behind a convoy of trucks, a port battalion moving out, God only knew where to. Not that it mattered; Captain Weiller did not waste his time thinking about what did not concern him. But they had hovered behind that long, ungainly column for an exasperating length of time.

Still, he wanted, if possible, not to get angry at Phillips today. It wasn't altogether the boy's fault if he was inexperienced. And it was lack of experience that made him naïve and trusting, too; he was used to thinking well of people, and to accepting as true what they merely wished, or hoped, was true. But it complicated the job, and God knew the captain was having a bad enough time as it was.

Quite without his volition, there stole into his mind the thought that he could have put either Murchison or Carl Dolin on the job now, and should have done so; but he swept the idea away stubbornly. Somebody had to be left in charge of the Cherbourg station, and in the circumstances, who better than Murchison? It would be good experience for him. Anyway he had to go see the colonel about Cécile Aubanne, about Thury. Have a kind of preliminary talk, you might say. And Carl had his own work, work that had to be done.

Phillips had to be broken in as quickly as possible, after all. He was bright enough; sometime he'd be of real use, perhaps. And for the present—well, it was irritating to have to lead him along by the hand, yet the duty was clear. All that high-school freshness— The captain's lips tightened bitterly. The world at large had no more use for it than this particular corner of the Army. It would be well lost.

Of course he *should* keep from getting angry, and he knew that. But he himself was assailed on all sides, he was weary and overworked, there was no respite in sight, and he had not always lately been able to keep emotion out of what he was doing. If you always expected the worst of people and of situations you were never taken by surprise, you were never disappointed, you could always see clearly and quickly what your possibilities and your alternatives were. But however well prepared a man might be to have the worst happen, he might still deserve not to have it always happen, every time. Sure, it's nice to get the breaks, thought Weiller; I'd like it, who wouldn't? Right now, for example; on this case. But I'm not getting them; I'll have to fight it through, every inch of the way, without much of any help, and then I'll have to start in all over again on Thury.

It was no special pleasure, he thought, to have to prove to Phillips that the world wasn't so very fine a place. And doubtless the boy would damn him for it forever. It was irritating to think that one would be blamed for demonstrating the world's evil, as though one had purveyed that evil himself—and especially when someone like this was involved, a boy whose stubborn misreading of the world had so much vitality and so little foundation, and whose good fortune—rather than desert—it had been that life had thus far seemed to corroborate his misconceptions.

Well; maybe it wasn't such good fortune. And even if it was, of course the boy wasn't to blame for that, either. Captain Weiller forced himself to survey with tolerance, almost with kindness, the back of Phillips' head, the slight shoulders hunched a little forward toward the wheel. It was hard to find the right tone—incisive but without emotion, leaving no room for emotion. An excess of sternness, and the boy would think himself persecuted; an excess of patience, of kindness, and the lesson would not sink in, the necessary attitude would not be produced.

As if I didn't have enough on my hands, thought Weiller. That was what angered him really, not the boy's softness at all —it was those sons of bitches back in London, yanking his best men and then sending this kid out, telling him he'd get his training in the field. Sure. And whose skin did it come out of? Not theirs. But he had the problem now; and it was a matter of principle with him that he would not let it lick him, or even, as far as he could help, let it get him down, even for a minute.

Fortunately the girl did not bother him; the problem as it touched her was an abstraction, a puzzle merely, which he must and would solve. Of course she was a human being; but the things that made her so were not a part of the problem, and therefore no concern of his. If Phillips could only learn that, he'd be a lot better off. The job was not to sit in judgment; it was to determine guilt or innocence as a matter of fact rather than as a matter of emotion, or as a basis for moral reflection. The job was the protection of the Allied armies, and nothing must stand in the way of the job's being done—too much depended on its being done perfectly and absolutely.

If this girl was at all guilty, then, she must be put away; and the French themselves could weigh greater and lesser guilts when they would, temper justice with mercy, and all the rest of the rigmarole. The French could consider her as a human being: he must, and Phillips must, consider her as a wooden figure possibly employed (and whether voluntarily employed or not made, for the present, no difference) in the struggle between the Allies and Nazi Germany.

The girl herself, of course, kept bidding—and quite naturally so, if inconveniently—to be considered as a human being. And her friend, Mlle. what's-her-name—same thing. That was the real reason why the interview of the previous evening had been a failure; it had led, perhaps inevitably, to much "understanding," but little enough establishment of fact. Still, the facts would emerge; and if he had anything to say about it, they would emerge in time to be of some use. Phillips might think him hardhearted if he wished. But in truth he had nothing against the girl—not even the fact that she was French and not American. To most Americans, he knew, this was the ultimate, the unforgivable breach of taste. But if Thérèse Bouliard was innocent of espionage, then she could be anything else she pleased—frail or strong, hysterical or calm, French or German or Hindu. It merely didn't stand to reason that she was innocent; and therefore the case would have to be continued until the real facts appeared.

He wished he could explain all this to Phillips. But it wasn't easy, it wasn't perfectly straightforward. For one did, occasionally, treat these people, these suspects, as human beings, and had to do so. One had only their human qualities to get hold of, for example, in an interrogation. Perhaps the best way to say it was that you manipulated them, but had yourself to be proof against manipulation. He recalled for example the trick he had pulled that morning, just before they'd begun the drive. Phillips had brought the girl down to the jeep. In her presence he, Captain Weiller, had presently—and as a casual part of the routine—taken his forty-five from the holster and tested it, ejecting a cartridge which fell gleaming at the girl's feet, its blunt, ugly nose communicating to her its unmistakable message. Then he had put the pistol back in its holster and strapped it on, climbed into the back of the jeep and waved the girl into the seat beside the driver. Her face had told him that the charade had worked; he need hardly watch her now, sitting bound by her own terror beside Phillips, but could send his thoughts ahead to plan the interview that was to come.

They were entering Valognes at last; again an MP stopped them, and after looking briefly at their papers, asked Phillips to name, at once, five brands of American cigarettes. Good enough gag, thought Weiller as Phillips stuttered through the list, but what was the deal? Were there some parachutists landed that he hadn't heard about, or some German prisoners escaped, or something? He'd have to inquire, though of course he would not do so in front of the girl. He directed Johnny to turn right from the great, gashed, open square before the ruined church, and put him on the back road that led to Saint-Sauveur before he went back to his own thoughts.

Phillips, it occurred to Weiller in passing, had seemed completely flabbergasted at the sight of Valognes; and the captain realized that this was the first of the really wrecked towns the boy could have seen. It was quite a sight, the first time. Curious, though, how quickly one got used to such sights—how quickly a smashed building came to seem as natural as a whole one, and how soon the human significance of the destruction evaporated. Again it was not a matter of hardheartedness, for no one welcomed the destruction; and it had meant American deaths too. But it was the way of war, and sooner or later one lost the ability to react. Not to lose it, indeed, might be looked on as a kind of sentimentality, an excess of sensibility, a useless denial of the present and of the future, since one could not forever, except in the unreal struggles of the mind, go on bleeding the same blood from the same wounds.

Troubled, the captain turned his thoughts back to the girl. It must seem to her that she was doing very well—or might seem so to her, but of course she was scared stiff, she hadn't the guts to stand the consequences of what she'd done any more than any of them had. And if she hadn't yet been forced to admit anything, at least she'd succeeded in proving nothing in her own defense, either. When they had left Cherbourg she had asked, fearfully, where they were going; Phillips had begun to answer and then, recalling his instructions, had said nothing. She was obviously off balance, wondering what was going to be done with her. And that was the way it ought to be; her uncertainty was all to the good.

Captain Weiller sighed. He could not pretend that things were going well. He had never seen a case begin so promisingly and then disappear into thin air as this had done. The undoubted guilt of Bouliard, the undoubted guilt of Korvac, the entire espionage situation that was to have covered the Cherbourg peninsula for the Germans laid out before him—and he had nothing in his hands, nothing. Bouliard dead. Korvac—Korvac was captured, it was true, but ironically he belonged to the La Haye-du-Puits team, and La Haye-du-Puits hadn't even been the place he'd been intended to work. The girl would damned well have to be made to talk, Weiller thought grimly. He could not and would not be hung up like this. That fool Thury—had he taken the transfer of Rhodes and Bailey as a sign that Weiller was losing power? If Thury broke away, at any rate—God forbid—the colonel would land on Weiller like a ton of bricks. He'd be tippity enough when Murchison told him even a little of what was going on now. Thank God Murchison was shaping up reasonably well; he would know what *not* to say, could probably be trusted not to let the colonel see that there was at this very moment a crisis in military security in Cherbourg. The time to make that admission was not yet, though the groundwork had to be laid. With luck, the time would never come. . . .

The good old colonel, who had no more brains than he knew

what to do with, and that was for sure. The colonel, whose real understanding of military security was limited to a perception that he could do worse than stay in the regular Army after the war. The colonel, who kept wanting Weiller to get him a French floozy to sleep with, but didn't dare come right out and say so, and was sore at him because he wouldn't take the hint. Weiller snorted; de Sombais would jump into bed with the colonel as soon as eat, he knew—maybe sooner. She had a real talent, that girl; of a rather unpleasant kind, it was true. She was dead to find out what was going on in American intelligence. It would serve everybody right if he got those two shacked up together— the colonel, who would be the last to know what was going on in American intelligence, and de Sombais, who would either think him tremendously closemouthed (which would be quite a joke) or would realize that he was a dope and give Thury the signal to go ahead on his own, thereby producing a situation that would certainly blast the colonel loose from his moorings. Unfortunately it would also blast Weiller loose, probably. A pity that one could not play such games. He'd have to remember to warn Carl Dolin and Tochyk that Estelle de Sombais was and would remain a strictly hands-off proposition; he'd seen her look speculatively at Carl, who doubtless would not feel like turning anything down, and considering that Carl knew the files pretty thoroughly, all parts of the files, that wouldn't be such a hot combination.

The surface on this minor crossroad was in pretty good shape and the jeep was bowling along smoothly, making fair time at last. Weiller looked at his watch; they wouldn't be so late after all. At least they'd make it in time for chow, and Korvac and Thérèse could be put on the mat afterward—the afternoon would afford plenty of time, and according to the plans he'd made there was no question of their driving back up tonight anyway. He didn't like Starr, the head of the La Haye-du-Puits team, but the fellow had a comfortable setup and would prob- ably be cooperative. What, he wondered suddenly, would he do with the girl? Well, obviously Starr would be able to make some sort of arrangement.

Reluctantly, almost with despair, Weiller turned his mind back toward the central problem: what a confrontation with

165

Korvac would do to break down Thérèse Bouliard's story. He had been avoiding thinking about it really, for he had grave doubts that it would work; he'd hit on the plan in the first place because it was dramatic, and he thought both Thérèse Bouliard and Phillips needed a good jolt. With Thérèse, the shock of the confrontation might be enough, he hoped, properly handled, to produce a confession. But what did proper handling mean in this case?

It was baffling; he'd never been in a situation where he'd had to make so much from so little. He'd never had a case where so few leads presented themselves. Possible lines of investigation sank into the ground like trickles of water in a desert, and an interview like last night's which should have opened up a dozen avenues made it clear instead that the ground one was exploring was a virtual waste which no one had learned, and where no one could serve as guide.

If only the confrontation could be with Bloch; then things would certainly happen, and fast. But Korvac, according to his own testimony, had never had any contact with the Bouliards, so there would be no real value to that first instant in which he was shown into the room where Thérèse was sitting. She would doubtless be frightened, just in general, but she was frightened now and yet not convinced that the jig was up. It was discouraging; and there just wasn't much time.

Further, it was clear enough that every time a plan was tried unsuccessfully, he lost ground; already there had been two failures, and he could afford no more. Damn the girl. He stared at her angrily. She sat hunched and silent, lost in what private triumph, he wondered, or what private fear? She was clever at masking her thoughts, he'd have to hand it to her. If only, now, there were some way of reading what was going on in her mind, the rest of the story would be short. . . . Though no one could see him, he flushed in vexation. He did not usually ask for advantages, even in fantasy; he did not usually need to.

He could, of course, have the girl sent to England. But he hated the idea. He told himself that quite apart from anything else there was no time; not with Thury acting the way he was. Weiller knew that he still had enough of a hold to get the truth from Thury if he had something to exchange for it. But he had nothing except this Bouliard case, and it had therefore to be broken quickly. He set his jaw. Everything conspired to make the job difficult. But he would do it, because it must be done, and there was no one else capable of handling it at all. Or capable, for that matter, of taking the responsibility.

It was damned unfair, he thought furiously, that it was this very determination of his to do a job that had put him on the spot. For obviously, after Phillips had first muffed the case, the best thing to have done would have been to send the girl back up the line for interrogation by an entirely new group of people, by—well, sure, experts, if you wanted to put it that way. But because of his local responsibilities, he was not able to take that proper and plausible way; instead he was now committed before his men to seeing that the Bouliard affair was itself settled, and settled quickly. He could not fail. It was not, he told himself, a matter of personal pride. But a commanding officer had to *be* in command of the job he was responsible for; his prestige did not matter in itself, but it did matter to the soundness of the team relationship, and therefore to the accomplishment of future work.

Future work. . . . All of France opening up, and he perhaps— God, he wanted to do a big job, the biggest job he could.

But he could not waste time thinking about that now. For one thing, on the most practical level, he could not leave Cherbourg in a mess. *And if Cherbourg were in a mess he might not be chosen to—* How much time did he have? God damn it, that was not the point.

Shorthanded as he was, he'd been helpless to get this Bouliard case properly started. But now the case was damaged, he had no alternative but to straighten it out, however difficult that might be. . . . He sighed again. It was hard to be alone, but then people were always alone. It was merely necessary to avoid getting emotional about it. The boy at the wheel doubtless felt himself thoroughly friendless and far from home; and doubtless he would be amazed to learn how nearly impossible he in turn had made the captain's position.

Of course everything might turn out perfectly well. After all, Korvac had apparently been pretty close to Bloch, and since the mission Bloch had given him had, unquestionably, been to Thérèse and her father, a detailed discussion of that mission by the other spy involved, and a spy who had furthermore admitted his guilt, might well unnerve the girl and make it impossible for her to hold out any longer. In the little room in the Cherbourg hotel, the most vivid thing before the girl's eyes had obviously been the future—what would happen to her if the charge against her were proved. Confronted with Korvac and the past he could evoke, she would perhaps be overwhelmed by that past and forced into a confession.

If only the Bouliard house had not been so thoroughly damaged, they could have miked it, and then after the girl's return sent Korvac in to make contact with her as if he had never been arrested. That would have tied the case up quickly enough; in her conversation with Korvac Thérèse would have convicted herself. But he had not dared depend on the girl's staying at the house for any length of time at all, it was in such bad shape, and so that plan had not been feasible.

But—his mind darted ahead quickly. Korvac had turned himself in, and had given his story willingly. Perhaps he would not be unwilling to lend himself to some scheme or other down here that would be as certain to trip the girl up. Could a room be miked now, so that Korvac and Thérèse Bouliard might converse there ostensibly in private? No, no, that would be senseless and transparent, things had gone too far for that. But something might be managed. The captain struck his forehead with his clenched fist, as though by so doing he might jar an idea to the surface of his mind. All this damnable, tortuous maneuvering, when the case should have been such a simple one to break.

Sullenly the captain looked around him, and after a moment realized that they had got off the road. Abruptly his anger exploded. Damn Phillips! Now, how in the hell had he managed that? Weiller barked an order to stop and got them turned around, and with some difficulty and some hard words, back on the right road again. It was too much. He didn't like to bawl the kid out in front of a prisoner, but for Christ's sake! If Phillips couldn't use his head—and apparently he couldn't—he might at least use his eyes!

XI.

THE man who entered the room had a face like a wound. His cheeks were extravagantly red, and his skin seemed hardly strong enough to contain the blood that coursed behind it, as if a mere touch of fingers to cheeks must tear them and loose the flow, and the fingers come away dripping. He looked as though it must be agony for him even to speak.

The heat in the unventilated room was a physical burden, the air an almost solid medium to which the glaring light bulb in the ceiling contributed what seemed a natural property. Korvac advanced slowly against the light and the heat, staring with wide eyes at the occupants of the room, smiling a glazed and twitching smile. He had a high, round, pallid forehead, sparse hair, and a small, pointed chin; he carried his head tipped slightly forward, as though the weight of his brain pulled his whole head out of balance on the short, tremulous neck. His body, though thin, looked oversized and ungainly, his limbs poorly knit together; he appeared to conquer his tendency to awkwardness by making only the smallest, most deliberate of movements. And always he stared, the blood striking at his cheeks; and continually he smiled, the same fixed, confessional smile.

He turned first to Captain Weiller and made him an uncertain little bow, like a maimed bird pecking at something; Johnny saw that Weiller, whose face was shining with sweat, flushed and looked angry. It was certainly too hot in the room. But Korvac appeared not to notice. His eyes traveled attentively, and yet abstractedly, over the others—Lieutenant Starr, the interpreter Hudson, Johnny himself—until they came to rest on Thérèse Bouliard. She was sitting on a hard chair against the wall of the room, trying to shield her eyes, which Johnny knew were red with crying; she had wept silently, to herself, almost all the way down. Knowing he should feel nothing—for who knew the source of those tears, the secret reason for them?—Johnny had still felt bitterly sorry for her, and had found his attention continually and uneasily diverted from the road through the ruined land ahead to the locked and strangled grief he could feel beside him.

Seeing the girl now, Korvac smiled more fully and as if with relief, like a child who, brought into a room full of strange grown-ups, sees at last someone he knows to be kind to children.

"C'est Mademoiselle Bouliard, n'est-ce pas?" he asked, a kind of happiness in his voice.

The girl's hand dropped from her face inertly, as though its weight were suddenly impossible to sustain. For a moment Johnny thought he had discovered full panic in her eyes; then they closed, and when at length they opened again the thin, brown face was without expression. Korvac looked uncertainly at the captain, who leaned over and whispered something to the interpreter. Hudson emitted a quick geyser of French. Korvac sat down in the chair that awaited him, cocked his head to listen, and then replied eagerly.

"He says he knows it is she because he saw her photograph many times in Paris; Bloch carried it. He could not be mistaken. Bloch showed it to him last a few hours before he left Paris on his mission."

Lieutenant Starr said loudly, "By the way, Captain, I'm sure you needn't whisper your questions. It's definite he doesn't understand any English."

Johnny again glanced at Thérèse. She looked faint and ill. She said in a low voice, "That could not be true, about the picture."

Korvac regarded her questioningly, the little boy no longer so certain of the kindness he would receive.

Johnny felt a lump rise in his throat, as of actual fear, though he did not know what there was to be afraid of. He turned so that he could not see the girl and stared carefully at a square of wooden paneling just to the left of Korvac's flat and sourly clad figure.

"I'll expect you to take part in this, by the way, Phillips," the captain's voice said coldly. "When I'm not following up some special point myself. Now then—Hudson, would you ask this man whether he knows why Bloch should have been carrying Thérèse Bouliard's picture around with him?"

The tone of Korvac's answer this time was somehow coy, almost raffish.

"He says Bloch was very fond of the girl—talked of her a great deal, and said he hoped to go back to her after the invasion had been defeated."

A groan escaped Thérèse Bouliard. "No," she said. "No, no, no."

"Where did Bloch get the photograph?" asked the captain smoothly.

A pause. "He does not know. Presumably from the girl herself. But perhaps from the father, who was also an intimate of Bloch's."

Captain Weiller leaned forward casually and offered Korvac a cigarette from his package; the man took one delicately, with many flutterings of gratitude. To Hudson the captain said, "What does Monsieur—Korvac understand to have been the precise relationship between the Bouliards and Bloch?"

Korvac accepted a light and leaned back, puffing with exaggerated force like a man who smokes only occasionally, as a social obligation. He listened to the repetition of the question and then sat for a moment pondering, considering, weighing. Before he had replied Lieutenant Starr broke in, his voice hushed but somehow freighted with importance.

"Captain—I take it the girl understands English?"

Weiller answered impatiently, "Yes."

"I suppose you've thought of the fact that she's in a rather favorable position here—she hears the question before Korvac does, and gets his answer before you—uh—before we do. You understand, it gives her extra time to think. If you're trying to take her by surprise."

In the moment's silence that followed, Johnny imagined the captain surveying Starr with glacial dignity, but he did not turn to look. Then Weiller said in a voice surprisingly casual, "I've planned this fairly carefully. Insofar as the point matters, I think you'll find that I shall take advantage of it later on."

171

"Of course, sir," said Starr formally, but without conviction. "Excuse me."

Korvac had been looking humbly from one to the other. Now, haltingly, he began to speak; and as he paused, from time to time, Hudson would take the words from his mouth and deliver them to Weiller in neat little packages.

"This is a difficult question to answer. He wants you to understand that he, of course, only worked for the Germans for a short time, and then only because he wished to gather such information for the Allies as he could to help them when they landed. So all he can say for certain is that he met Bouliard once in Paris early in the spring of this year, when the man had come in for some sort of training, or conference, and that he heard of one or two more visits. He does not know whether the daughter ever accompanied the father, but he thinks not. He tried always to get such information, for the reasons stated before, but up until the invasion he was merely a technician in the radio school in Paris where agents were taught how to send and receive messages—a technician, not an instructor— and usually the Germans tried to keep him from learning who the agents were. But in May, Bloch, a man new to him, came in to the Paris headquarters, and he was not so reserved as some of the others. Bloch—"

Here Hudson said something rapidly to Korvac in French, received an answer and went on. "Bloch did not become a regular official of the Paris station, Korvac thinks, until after the invasion. Then he began to interest himself in the Paris agents. He was a friendly man, not entirely discreet, and Korvac insinuated himself into his good graces. But in Paris there was, from this time, little but confusion; Korvac could not learn much about the agents—he has already given what information he had—and he thinks that most of them were never dispatched. Finally Korvac himself was told by the head of the station— but in a friendly way, it was certain he had not suspected Korvac's intentions—that his services could no longer be used unless he wished to retreat with the rest of the station personnel to Germany. Korvac made his excuses, because in Germany he knew that he could do nothing to aid the Allies. It was after this that Bloch approached him to see whether he would take on the job of servicing some of the agents already in place on the coast, and perhaps become an agent himself; and Korvac, seeing the opportunity not only of learning more about the enemy's activities, but of putting his information quickly into the hands of the Americans, agreed. At once he received instructions. It was then that he first heard where the Bouliards were, and got a somewhat connected story about them."

It was more or less what was in the Korvac report, Johnny remembered; but there it had not seemed so specious, so unpleasant, somehow, as it seemed now, with Korvac sitting opposite him, fluttering his hands and smiling an eager, confidential little smile that was belied by the raw blood in his cheeks. Johnny averted his face, and caught sight of the expression on Thérèse's face—a look of numb horror and disgust and fascination. What could it mean? Oh, God, he thought, the captain must be right and she is guilty; surely she could not let Korvac go on in that obscene way if she weren't. He felt a surge of resentment against her, and at the same time an inexplicable sorrow; and what he felt made him realize that somehow or other —perhaps only because she had wept in the jeep coming down? —he had again swung around to thinking her innocent. He had no right to an opinion, on anything, he thought. Again he turned and stared deliberately at the paneled wall behind Korvac's chair, so lost in self-accusation that he hardly heard the interpreter's voice when it took up the story again.

"When Korvac accepted the mission to Cherbourg," Hudson was saying, "naturally he got as much background as he could about the Bouliards. But Bloch became more discreet, and as though crafty, then. He admitted that the picture of his—lady friend in Cherbourg, which he had shown Korvac before, was Thérèse Bouliard, one of the spies involved; and he admitted that Thérèse's father had been supposed to cover Cherbourg for the Germans, and so far had not come up on the air; but still Korvac could get no very comprehensive story from him. He gathered that Bouliard had been an associate of Bloch's for many, many years in Cherbourg, and that Bloch was surprised at not having heard from him following the invasion. He kept saying, apparently very upset, that he had done a great deal for Bouliard, and could not believe that he was not to be repaid.

Of course something might have gone wrong with Bouliard's transmitter; but it had been very carefully tested, and had always worked perfectly while Bloch was in Cherbourg. If it had gone wrong, Bloch admitted that Bouliard might not know enough to repair it himself, though he had been a very apt pupil. That was why Bloch approached Korvac, a radio technician, to make the contact. But it was obvious that Bloch feared he was being betrayed. At first when he would talk to Korvac about the Bouliards he would be very cheerful, his usual self, and then he would start arguing with himself about what must have happened, and soon he would become angry, so that by the end he would be very violent and abusive, and even more unpleasant therefore than one usually finds the Germans."

Hudson's voice was so composed as he relayed this story with its irritating final statement that Johnny looked at him quickly to see whether he were showing in any way the distaste he must feel. But he was not; and perhaps it was important, Johnny thought, that he should not. But how could anyone take this man's testimony seriously? His own motives and actions—surely it was impossible that they could have been what he now said they were. And he sounded increasingly happy and so confiding, so almost gay, at the prospect of getting Thérèse in trouble—wasn't it obvious that he couldn't be trusted? The captain's face at last showed nothing but interest. Johnny looked indignantly down at his hands, lying still in his lap.

Captain Weiller said, "And the girl Thérèse—did he appear to be angry with her also?"

As the question was put to Korvac, he burst into voluble disclaimers. Johnny was becoming accustomed now to the curious slow-motion effect of double question, double answer; indeed it seemed in a way consoling, since whatever disagreeable emotions Korvac's tone suggested, they were reduced in Hudson's clipped speech to impersonality. But how must it seem to Thérèse? Guilty or innocent, she must find the repetition of the questions like the merciless probing of a knife, and the answers, as they traveled through their double form, must seem to embroider senselessly upon the fundamental pain of the situation. Involuntarily his eyes were drawn toward her.

Hudson said, "No, Bloch appeared to have absolute confidence in Thérèse. He had trained her himself, and spent much time with her; she was, he said, expert at getting information and unmistakably eager to work. But of course she had no means of communication if it turned out that her father lost his nerve. That was why Bloch was willing to send Korvac, untrained in anything but radio, to Cherbourg; even if Bouliard himself had proved untrustworthy, Thérèse was sufficient to make a success of the new team." For the first time Hudson turned and looked at the girl. "She would have been willing to do so out of personal loyalty to Bloch, if for no other reason," he finished.

The captain too looked at Thérèse, delightedly. Slowly, as though drawn out of her chair by giant fingers, the girl rose to her feet, her lips working, her face full of disdain. Then her expression melted into a gray vacancy and she fell awkwardly back against her chair and slipped to the floor.

Almost before anyone had realized what was happening she was clambering doggedly to her feet again, pushing aside the hands of Hudson, who had darted over to help her. As she sat down in the chair she had occupied before, a dull color flooded back into her face, washed away, and reappeared again.

The captain said, "Mademoiselle is not enjoying the occasion? Perhaps she is not well?"

Thérèse said painfully, "No, m'sieur, I do not enjoy it. But I am all right, I am not ill."

"At least you would prefer that we go on with this another time."

"M'sieur," she said rapidly, "it is very much too hot in here. And I am fatigued. I am sorry for this. But at any time he will be able to tell lies, this man, and therefore it is no advantage to wait. Let him say all he can." Her voice, at the last, was low and firm.

"Mademoiselle," said the captain, "you are very kind to indulge us. But he has said enough for the present. I am interested, naturally, in what you have to say, also. You do not deny your acquaintance with Bloch?"

"Deny it, no. Only it was not as this man has said."

"Listen to me carefully," said Weiller, in a cold, terrible voice. "You have seen the letter Bloch sent you through Korvac. You must know that we have all the evidence we need to prove you guilty, and more than we need. I have been trying to impress this upon you so that we might all be saved time. If you will put an end to these senseless protests there may still be some mercy for you; a few more lies, and there will be none. Do you not understand your danger? Or see your position?"

She met his eyes, dejection and fear growing in her own expression. "Yes, m'sieur," she said. "I see that you will prove me guilty by the lies of strangers. But—I could not if I would tell the same lies this man tells, being unprepared. And so I see nothing to do but go on telling the truth. I have told you, this M'sieur Bloch wished vengeance on me. And if for you this does not account for the letter, for the entire tale, then I do not know what to say further."

The captain's voice was savage with annoyance. "I suppose, at least, you do not deny that Bloch was an officer of the German Intelligence Service? I assure you he was, and it makes no difference whether you admit the fact or not. Now, do you ask us to believe that his appearance in your home in Cherbourg was accidental? For this, remember, we have not only this man's evidence, but your own. You have admitted that your father, who seldom brought anyone to your home, brought Bloch there, not once but several times. Why? Are we to believe that this was accident, and that there was no relationship?"

"Perhaps," she said fearfully, "perhaps—my father did not know what Bloch did; perhaps Bloch did many things . . . ?"

"Doubtless," said Weiller, with heavy irony. "It appears that your father too did—many things. And even you . . . ?"

The girl covered her face with her hands.

"When," said the captain loudly, "during this last spring, did your father travel to Paris?"

"He did not do so," Thérèse answered, her voice trembling. "He—he went once or twice to—to see my aunt and uncle at Sartilly."

"When?"

"I do not—remember exactly. Once in March. And a month later, also. Perhaps once earlier—in February."

"Regularly once a month, in fact." The captain smiled ironically. "Seems odd, doesn't it? How long did he stay each time?"

"About a week, m'sieur."

"Did you not ask yourself why, after all the years in Cherbourg, he should suddenly have elected to spend one week out of every month, regularly, in Sartilly?"

"No, m'sieur. I have said that—he did not work, always. He grew more and more restive. They were our only relatives. There were—affairs to discuss, he said—business affairs. This seemed—enough reason."

"Ah, yes, of course," the captain said. "Business affairs. Is that why you did not go with him on his trips?"

"No. I did not like to go."

"Why not?"

"I do not like them," she burst out, "they are not kind to me!"

It was the first thing Johnny had heard her say that recalled to him the fact that she was young.

Captain Weiller regarded her without sympathy. "Your father, however, was fond of the Corrails?"

She hung her head. "No, m'sieur," she said.

"And still you did not question his visits to them? But of course, there were the business affairs." There was a pause. "You realize, do you not," he said acidly, "that we'll have no difficulty finding out whether or not your father went to Sartilly this spring at the times you tell us he did."

"I suppose that you will not—have trouble," she said.

"And if we find that he did not go to Sartilly at those times, what will you have to say?"

She was looking at him vacantly as though she did not quite hear, her lips slightly parted, her throat working. After a moment she closed her lips stubbornly and looked down at the floor, shaking her head once or twice, slowly.

"What will you have to say?" he repeated.

"M'sieur, what should I say? He told me then that he went to Sartilly. If he did not do so I—I do not know what he did instead." Her voice, Johnny thought, was barely controlled.

"Where was your father's transmitter installed in Cherbourg?" Weiller asked abruptly.

"I do not know—I—"

"You what?"

"I am sure there was no transmitter!" she blazed. "Anyone who knew my father would tell you this could be nothing but lies! He could do nothing with mechanical things, he could not even make little repairs in the house, it is ridiculous! He was a teacher; he had not learned such things!"

"Though there were several years when he was not being a teacher and might have learned—some new profession," the captain said thoughtfully.

Thérèse Bouliard shrugged. "We have spoken of this," she answered dully.

"Tell me," said Weiller. "When your father was away from the house so much, working as a laborer, or in the German offices. What did you find to do with your time?"

She stared at him in confusion. "M'sieur? I—worked about the house. I cleaned, and cooked, and did such things. We were—poor, m'sieur."

"But surely this did not take all your time? Perhaps you visited friends?"

"Occasionally Mademoiselle Vaugiron, yes, as I have said. But you do not realize, perhaps, that the care of a large house, with the shopping—when it is difficult to buy—all this takes the time, m'sieur."

"So you never read a book, never took a walk—"

"Of course, m'sieur," she broke in, "I did these things. Anyone does."

"Where did you like to walk?"

"Why—" She looked at him uncertainly. "There is a park, the Park Emmanuel Liais. And—I love the ocean, m'sieur; sometimes I would go out toward Tourlaville or, to the west, Querqueville. And there is some pleasant country to the south of Cherbourg."

"The hills," murmured Captain Weiller.

"Yes," she said softly, "the hills—that look over the city and the water. There are fine walks up there—among the trees, and the small fields."

Johnny looked at her uneasily. He did not know what was coming, but obviously something was, and for the moment she seemed unwary, soothed and charmed by a pleasant memory until it seemed that she must fall into any trap that might be laid.

"You liked those walks best?" asked the captain.

She shrugged. "To get high above yourself," she said in a far-off voice, "to look down at other people like dolls, and the buildings and the ships like toys—and then your worries, that make you unhappy, become such little things also. . . ."

"You can see the whole harbor from the hills up there, can't you?"

"Yes, m'sieur," she said. Her voice was still gentle, but there was the sound in it of uncertainty, of watchfulness being re-born—as though, thought Johnny, the expression on her face had acknowledged, fleetingly, a sound heard far away, or as though a sleeper had stirred at a footstep in the room where he lay, hearing the sound from the depths of his dream, and trying at once to rise to it, and not to rise.

"You can see ships entering and leaving the harbor, and tell whether they're fishing vessels or—"

"These waters were forbidden to fishermen during the war, m'sieur," she said gravely. "And for this reason many went hungry."

"Cargo vessels, then," said the captain negligently. "And warships."

She gazed at him silently, and then said in a voice that was no more than an escape of breath, "Yes, m'sieur."

"You can recognize the various warships—cruisers, destroyers, battleships?"

"Some of them, m'sieur," she answered.

The captain smiled. "Bloch's training did you some good, then."

Surprisingly, the girl's reply was calm; it was as though she had been taken out of herself and given strength and perspective by the memories through which she had been moving. She even smiled a little. "No, m'sieur; you cannot make me say I was trained by Bloch, for I was not. When one lives on the sea, he learns a little of ships—even someone like me, who comes late, learns a little. But I know, I should think, less than most people. And I did not walk on the hills above Cherbourg to spy on the ships entering or leaving the harbor; surely, m'sieur, the Germans knew what ships entered or left without my help!"

The captain said, "It was in the recognition of British and American warships, of course, that you were chiefly trained. And in the recognition of planes. And in the recognition of tanks and other military vehicles, with the signs they carry to identify the units to which they belong. This training you received, and we know that you received it. You could, of course, tell us more; what contacts you had to get more secret information, for example. And what form that information was to take when it was sent to the Germans. And whether you had anything to do with the phrasing and the enciphering of the messages, or whether this was all done by your father. But you will tell us these things; and I think soon."

Thérèse Bouliard did not reply.

"For now," said the captain, with a little wave of the hand at Korvac, "we must mend our conduct toward this gentleman, who has been so patient." Korvac leaned forward in his chair, his eyes wide, the ingratiating smile returning to his face. "There are some few questions that remain to be asked of him; and since they're rather—personal, I'd hoped not to have to ask them. But it seems we must do so. I've been thinking, however—perhaps it would be less embarrassing to you if you now served as our interpreter yourself. Mr. Green here"—he nodded at Hudson—"must of course remain to see that your interpretations are just. But otherwise— Well. I assume you're willing?"

Slowly the girl nodded, her eyes dark with doubt.

The captain took a handkerchief from his pocket and carefully, fastidiously, blotted his forehead. "First," he said, "will you please ask for a description of the clothing which your father wore when this gentleman saw him in Paris?"

As the girl saw the import of the question, her expression suddenly grew tense and still with fear. She translated the question slowly, avoiding Korvac's eager gaze. He cocked his head on one side, judicially; then, in little short bursts of speech, his answer began to come. The color slowly drained from the girl's face and she sat perfectly quietly, her head bowed.

"There's no need to tell us what he says," Captain Weiller said coolly. "Perhaps now you will not waste our time by keeping on denying your father's guilt. As for your own—will you please ask the gentleman to repeat to us, in detail, what Bloch told him in Paris about his personal and professional relations with you?"

Thérèse Bouliard raised her head and looked at the captain steadily, her eyes proud, her expression only a little clouded by pain. "M'sieur," she said, "I see now how this will end. And I must tell you that I do not care. You may declare me guilty of anything your laws will permit, and I shall not protest. Only I am not guilty. But I do not care, and I do not expect that you will care."

"Mademoiselle," said the captain in annoyance, "this is all very heroic. I have said to you, however, that we shall have the truth, and I am afraid that is all that interests us."

But though he kept the interrogation going for almost another hour, the girl could be persuaded to say no more.

After Korvac had been led back to his cell, his face a cringing, staring, bloody question—for God knows, Johnny thought, despising the man, how many times now he's offered to work for the Allies and had nothing to do but this, since of course anyone would know he's not to be trusted—Hudson took Thérèse out of the room, until the captain and Lieutenant Starr should have decided what was to be done with her. As soon as the door had closed behind them Weiller turned on Johnny.

"Well, Phillips," he said scathingly, "I must say you were quite a help. Those were brilliant questions you asked." His face was brick-red. If only, Johnny thought fleetingly, he could see how unbecoming the color was with the orange-red of his hair. But he could feel himself flushing with embarrassment and anger, and he did not know what to say. Lieutenant Starr had an avid expression on his face; clearly he would enjoy listening to a good fight.

Turning to Starr, Weiller said bitterly, "It was this young man who—unintentionally of course—closed the girl up in the first place. I've kept him on the case since to give him some experience, and a chance to make up for the way he muffed things before. But you can see the project isn't going very well. Looks as though maybe the damage can't be undone."

The lieutenant stared at Johnny, measured him, with open interest. Then he said to Weiller in his slightly overloud voice, "Too bad. She certainly is a stubborn little bitch."

Suddenly, and soundlessly, an explosion took place inside Johnny, and he realized that if Korvac was repugnant to him for one reason, he hated Weiller for another reason, and Starr for still another. Not one of them, he thought, had a trace of decency, a trace of humanity; both Korvac and Weiller, in their separate ways—but for reasons that were not so very unlike after all—were trying to sell Thérèse Bouliard down the river, and Starr would watch, and see it done, with pleasure.

And Thérèse was innocent. He'd been wishy-washy, he hadn't known what to think, he'd let any indication, any argument, sway him first one way, then another. But now he believed in the girl with as much certainty as though he had never doubted her. Weiller's talk about the letter that Korvac had carried—it was just words, complicated and meaningless, and he no longer had the least memory of what those words had said. Only if Korvac had been a spy, Thérèse had not. It was as simple as that.

He knew it sounded stupid, infantile, like most of the conclusions he'd reached in this case. But he felt deeply that this time, simplicity meant truth. These people were too used to complexity; and furthermore they liked it, they buried themselves in it, they let it trickle through their fingers and between their toes. And inevitably, and almost he thought purposely, they lost the human meaning of every fact they dealt with. Weiller could cross off the dignity, the sincerity of Thérèse Bouliard as acting, if he liked; he could ignore the girl's grief, or exploit it. Obviously he did not even know what had struck Thérèse at the last: it was the first time that she had permitted herself to believe that her father had been guilty of the crime of which she herself was now accused; and now that she believed, she cared for nothing more, since she had loved her father, and admired him. I know, Johnny said to himself; Thérèse, I know. And whatever your father did, I know you did nothing wrong. And I'm going to help you, I'm going to protect you from this—this wolf pack, these murderers with the high moral tone. I don't know how. But somehow I'll help you.

He realized suddenly that he'd never acted a part in his life, and that from now on he would be forced to act—would have to dissemble his belief in the girl, would have to seem to believe what the captain said, above all would have to bow to the captain's furious whims with no appearance of resentment. And what do I say first? he wondered. Hudson had left the door open when he had left, and a window had now been opened, but even the air outside was dead and the room was still oppressively hot. Starr was watching him again, after another exchange with the captain that Johnny had missed. Johnny took a handkerchief from his pocket and mopped at his face.

"Sir," he said, after a moment. The captain turned and looked at him, his features closed somehow, and as though swollen with the rage he could not quite contain. "Captain," said Johnny, "I'm sorry I wasn't of any help. I got mixed up, I guess—the photograph of the girl you were talking about, that Bloch had showed Korvac, and that business about what her father was wearing when he went to Paris, that was all new to me, and it just threw me off somehow."

Weiller said, "I suppose now you think I was holding out on you. For Christ's sake; what good would that do? No, that stuff, of course, wasn't any of it true."

"Not true?" asked Johnny numbly. "I don't—understand."

Captain Weiller took a little square of paper from his pocket and tossed it over to Johnny. "Here's the photograph," he said. "I found it in the breast pocket of a suit of old man Bouliard's when we were searching their erstwhile home a couple of weeks ago. Remember, when we first learned that Bouliard was our man? I told you."

"But—I don't see what it has to do with Korvac," Johnny said dazedly.

"Why, I had a little talk with him before this show was put on, of course," said the captain. "I showed him the photograph; naturally he'd never seen it, or the girl either. And he'd forgotten what Bouliard had worn in Paris, so I described to him the suit I remembered. And I worked up a good story for him on Bloch and Thérèse. I got the idea on the way down; I'd kept the photograph on me, for no special reason, after Tochyk gave it back, and suddenly realized what I could do with it."

"Say, that was damned clever, Captain," said Starr. "I thought you were up to something, but of course I didn't have any way of knowing what it was."

The captain shrugged. "It was just to make things a little more—concrete, shall we say? To convince her that we had the goods on her. Worked partly, too. But it's a hell of a case; she's been denying everything for so long now that I bet she wouldn't be able to say 'Yes' if we asked her, for a change, if she was innocent. And we haven't got anything on her except the testimony of Korvac, and that letter he carried. Of course we're morally certain of her guilt; but I'm not sure the letter would be enough for a conviction in the eyes of a court, without supporting evidence." He sighed. "So we've been trying to round up more evidence, without a damned bit of luck; and failing that to surprise her into a confession, only of course she's getting used to surprises. You can be damned glad if you never get a sticky case like this." He swung around and looked sharply at Johnny. "Well. Have you figured it out yet?"

"Yes, sir," said Johnny. You bastard, he was thinking, you brutal, unfeeling bastard. If there were any doubt of the father's guilt— But there wasn't; there was too much evidence there, and from unconnected sources. It wasn't a railroad job. But the poor kid, having to listen to that slimy Korvac talk about Bloch's intimacies with her—intimacies that could never have taken place, no matter what lush descriptions Weiller had put into Korvac's mouth. What had been the point of that? Deliberately to humiliate her, he supposed. Then, for the first time that day, he remembered the literal wording of the letter Korvac had carried; to which Weiller, it was apparent, literally and steadfastly adhered. That letter. How in God's name could it be explained?

"Well," said the captain, "we've got one surprise left for her."

Johnny looked at him questioningly.

"A chat with the home folks at Sartilly," said Weiller ironically. "I've still got an idea or two; I'm not easily licked."

"No, sir," said Johnny. And then, after a pause, "Does this mean we won't be driving back up tonight?"

"That's what it means." The captain turned to Starr. "By the way, when I asked if you could put us up, I wasn't thinking about the girl. But I suppose you can handle her too?" He smiled agreeably. "I'd be much obliged."

"Well," said Starr, "I'll be glad to, of course, Captain, but—" He frowned importantly. "You don't trust her a bit, do you?"

"Naturally not," said the captain stiffly.

"You'll understand, I'm sure, when I say I don't trust Korvac, either. And I've only got the one block of rooms I can use for cells. We've found the prisoners can communicate, right down one side of the hall and up the other, no matter what precautions we take. I suppose, in this case, you don't want that any more than I do."

Weiller said dryly, "No."

"I've got an idea," said Starr. "Come on with me into the outer office, would you?"

They walked out into the large room adjoining. Hudson and Thérèse Bouliard were in the far corner, Hudson looking out into the cobbled street, across which could be seen the low, open blocks of rubble, still baking hot and unshadowed, though the sun was far down in the west. Thérèse was sitting in a black upholstered chair, her small body lost in its huge and shabby depths; she seemed totally inert, abandoned to its comfort, and though she looked up when Weiller and Starr and Johnny entered the room, she closed her eyes again without changing expression.

Starr walked over to the desk in the opposite corner of the room, picked up the telephone, and after a few moments' struggle with the military switchboard, was bawling into the mouthpiece a kind of raucous French that was offensive even to Johnny's ears.

He put down the receiver at last with satisfaction. "That's all right," he said. "I have an arrangement with the *gendarmerie* here; sometimes they'll take care of a body for me overnight if they have room, and this time they have. You wouldn't have any objection to that, would you? Nobody's at all likely to know the girl here, I gather, so there'd be no breach of security. And the gendarmes won't ask any questions, they'll just take her in and release her again when you request it."

"That's all right, I guess," said Weiller. "Fine."

"Do you want Hudson to handle it for you, then?" Starr asked.

"No, no. You shouldn't be put to that trouble." The captain turned to Johnny, the ghost of a sardonic smile on his face. "Just give directions to my man Phillips, here, if you would. He'll take care of it."

Johnny and Thérèse followed the blue-uniformed gendarme in silence down the long, covered stone-walled corridor that led into the tiny prison yard. In his pudgy right hand the gendarme held the note Lieutenant Starr had written; occasionally he consulted it with interest and looked back curiously at the girl. She walked without animation, and her expression was lifeless.

Out in the open, in the middle of the right-hand cell block, the gendarme stopped, took a massive key from the bunch hanging at his waist, and unlocked the thick slab door of one of the cells. Johnny peered inside. It was a double cell; on each side of the stone partition that stood just opposite the door, a wide shelf of evil-smelling straw was fixed to the front, side, and back walls, about two feet above the earthen floor. In a cramped U around the partition was left space for a narrow walkway connecting the two cells.

As Johnny peered with disgust and horror into the almost complete darkness, a fat, sour-smelling woman, half undressed, swung from the shelf of the left-hand cell and waddled toward Johnny, staring at him, her wet red lips working and fluttering as she mumbled to herself.

Johnny stepped back quickly. "My God," he said to Thérèse sharply, "he can't put you in there!"

The gendarme stood looking at him, his eyes round with innocent incomprehension. Thérèse was staring fixedly at the ground.

"Tell him," said Johnny. "You—you have to have a cell by yourself."

186

As the girl translated slowly, the gendarme burst into expostulation. The prisoner watched, her eyes traveling from her jailer to Thérèse with a kind of bright, festive malice. She said one guttural sentence which Johnny could not understand.

Thérèse looked wearily at Johnny. As though in spite of herself, she had reddened at the gendarme's remarks; now she said without expression, "Do you wish to know what he says?"

"No," said Johnny. "No." He stood for a moment, growing more and more angry. Then he burst out, "Tell him you are to have a cell to yourself!"

Again Thérèse relayed the message, listlessly. In sullen silence, his lips compressed, the gendarme swung the heavy door closed and led them to a smaller door at the far end of the left-hand cell block. There was no aperture for light in this door, as there had been in the other; it was made of solid, heavy wood, and the rusty iron hinges extended all the way across to bear the prodigious weight. As the door was opened now, disclosing the low, single shelf of straw, the hinges squawked gratingly.

Again Johnny stepped toward the cell and peered inside. The odor of the damp, verminous straw, sour with filth and decay, ammoniacal with urine, was almost more than he could bear. He looked helplessly at Thérèse. For a moment her eyes met his in a look of misery and shame; then her face became stony and she dropped her gaze to the packed ground of the prison yard.

It wasn't human! The girl was clean, and decent, and unoffending; he could not leave her here. And yet he knew he could do nothing else. And he knew that he would not protest. He could visualize all too clearly what would happen if he should go back to the captain now saying that the cells at the *gendarmerie* were too dirty, that Thérèse Bouliard could not be expected to stay there.

The gendarme was waiting in surly impatience, looking from one to the other, his huge key poised in his stubby fingers. Abruptly Johnny said to Thérèse, "Tell him to give me the key. I will lock you in."

She looked at him in stolid, incurious acceptance as she translated the command. The gendarme, with a shrug, thrust the key into Johnny's hands and strode off across the courtyard. Thérèse dropped her eyes again and walked quietly into the cell.

Johnny thought, Like a bird into a stone cage. Or a brown seed floating, lodging at last in the mire. He put a hand on her arm. "Thérèse," he said.

She looked up.

"I'm sorry," he went on, in a low, miserable voice. "I'm sorry they're putting you here. I wouldn't do it if I could help it, but I'd only get you in worse trouble if I tried to do anything about it now. But I want you to know before you go into this —this damned hole that I think you're innocent. And that I'm going to do what I can to get you free."

Again he had the sense that he was watching someone rise, by successive stages, from the depths of a heavy sleep. Her eyes clung to his incredulously as she whispered, "You believe me?"

"Yes," he said. "I do. I have from the beginning, really."

Suddenly tears came into her eyes and she sank to the edge of the straw weeping soundlessly, the tears pouring down her cheeks.

"Don't," he pleaded. "Don't cry. It's awful, but please don't; I'll come and get you in the morning as soon as I can, and somehow we'll find a way to stop him. I don't know how, but we will. Honestly, you mustn't cry."

"It is all right," she said. "It is not this; the cell is nothing. In my mind there have been worse places. When I thought— that no one believed me, or ever would. And I did not know where my friend was. And everyone looked at me with hatred. I was so alone then—I—I—" She paused, gasping. "Once or twice I began to think I was mad, and to hate myself, for if everyone hated me how could I be—good? But if you believe me—" She seized his hand, and held it against her wet cheek. Then, quickly, she dropped it. "Forgive me. I—it is so good, to be touched—kindly—"

He was himself so close to tears that for a moment he could not speak. Clumsily he leaned over her and patted her on the shoulder. She put her arms around him and buried her face

188

in the folds of his uniform. After a moment he disengaged himself, and bent down and kissed her awkwardly on the forehead. Then he turned and stepped from the cell, swung the heavy door closed behind him, locked it, and stumbled blindly off across the courtyard, in his heart such hatred, and such pity, as he had not known existed in the world.

XII.

LIEUTENANT STARR'S mess was excellent. But then, reflected Captain Weiller, there was no reason why it should not be; Korvac was the only important case Starr had had so far, and the way the war was going, probably the only important one he would have. He'd had plenty of spare time to dig himself in. Squirming with sudden irritation, Weiller thought: Why hadn't they taken Starr's men to send to Le Mans, instead of his?

Well, Starr had had that one good case, if through no fault of his own; and he'd sewed it up. . . . The captain squirmed again. But Korvac had been meant to go to Cherbourg. . . . He couldn't kick, not right now, but if he were in a position to, later, he'd have to think about asking London to pull the La Haye-du-Puits team back and combine it with the Cherbourg team; then the two together could really get to work. Damned near the whole peninsula could be serviced from Cherbourg, he was sure of it.

Not that he was so nuts about Starr that *he'd* want him around all the time; and presumably Murchison wouldn't either. Anyway, Starr would outrank Murchison, and that wouldn't be so good. . . . Wasn't Starr somebody's nephew, or something? Weiller seemed to remember hearing that he'd got into the organization through pull. And if so, that was the end of it. Starr could stay in La Haye-du-Puits, building empires and eating soufflés. La Haye-du-Puits. Hooey da Pooey, the GI's called it. Hooey da Pooey.

"Enjoying your dinner, Captain?" Starr asked.

"Huh?—Oh, say, you bet I am," Weiller said heartily.

"Regular GI rations," Starr said modestly, "except for some

things, of course. But you'd never recognize 'em after Mignonne gets through with 'em."

"Mignonne?"

Lieutenant Starr giggled. "She's built like an automatic washer. Sure can cook, though. Matter of fact, she does all our work around here—cleaning, everything." He cast a guarded glance at the captain. "Naturally we've had her thoroughly checked; and she doesn't clean the offices except when someone's around. But she's O.K. Husband's dead; and she's got a couple of kids to take care of. We give her her food."

"Yeah." Absently Weiller looked over at the table where the men sat eating, Phillips among them, his face lowered and almost painfully without expression. Abruptly the captain turned back to face Starr, reached for his wineglass and took a careful sip. "Wine, too. Say, that's pretty good stuff. How'd you get hold of it?"

Lieutenant Starr winked and grinned. "Oh, one of my boys is pretty talented. I kind of give him a free hand—you know, don't ask him too many questions—"

Good food, thought the captain, and good wine, but the conversation? Jesus. He felt, suddenly, more kindly toward Johnny Phillips than he had felt in a long time. He'd have a talk with the boy after chow. Tomorrow was going to be tough; and after all Phillips had said he wanted to help, and his help would be needed. Maybe he was inexperienced; but he was serious, he wasn't by any means dumb, and in the end that would tell.

"How's it going?" the captain asked as Johnny Phillips entered the room. The boy gave him a look almost of incredulity, then arranged his features in a smile. Oh, great, Weiller thought, we're going to be friends. All I need is a friend. But he said gently, "Sit down. Get the girl stowed away all right?"

"Yes," Johnny said.

"Fine. Look, I thought we might talk about tomorrow for awhile—if you aren't too tired, that is."

"Sure," said Johnny. "I mean—no, I'm not. Only I haven't had much chance—I haven't thought much about it."

"Look," said the captain, "let's forget all this hogwash. It's not you I'm after, whatever you may think. I've just got a job to do." Hearing the sound of his own voice, hearing what he had said, he thought, Goddam. I wonder how often I've said that, how many other poor dumb bastards have said that, just about the time— Who the hell am I making excuses to, anyway? He rapped his knuckles hard on the table, gritted his teeth, and went on.

"I'd like to have your help. I said that to you before. Don't get me wrong; I know you haven't had much experience, and I shouldn't expect too much of you at first. Maybe I have been, a little. But—" He looked up, suddenly glaring with resentment, not of Johnny, but of traps, of pressures that came too quickly, and were too acute, and unnecessary anyway. "I'm not going to cry, and I'm not going to apologize," he said loudly, and then, seeing the stirrings of fear on the boy's face, he thought what he must look like, and laughed. "Sorry," he said, reaching across and shaking Johnny's shoulder lightly. "I'll try not to get so worked up. All I mean is there isn't enough time. I'd like to explain a lot of things to you. Like that business with the photograph this afternoon. As I told you, I didn't get the idea for that till on the way down; naturally I couldn't talk to you about it with her in the jeep, and once we got here I was too busy fixing things up, the confrontation, and then that special deal with Korvac. You understood, didn't you?"

"Sure," said Johnny.

Weiller looked up sharply; but the boy was smiling a little.

Reassured, the captain went on, "That's the stuff. Just hang on, the best way you can. You'll learn fast. If you don't understand what I'm doing, just give me the benefit of the doubt— I mean, I can make mistakes, like anybody, but I've been at this game a long time now, and—" He shrugged. "Hell, I didn't mean to give you a lecture. Let's get cracking on this deal tomorrow. O.K.?"

"O.K., sir. But—I really—"

The captain waved him silent. "I know. This stuff moves too fast. I haven't got it all figured out myself, don't worry. But just talking it over helps; you may give me just the idea I need."

"Captain," Johnny Phillips burst out in a despairing voice, "wouldn't Lieutenant Starr be more use to you than . . . ?"

"I could discuss it with him, sure," the captain said slowly. "But I'd rather not. This is our case, Mr. Phillips—yours and mine. It's a Cherbourg case. See what I mean?"

The boy nodded, his head inclined forward; Weiller could not see the expression on his face. The poor bastard, thought the captain—he's scared. Scared of the case, scared of the girl, even scared of me still. Typhoid Weiller. Bloody Weiller. Dirty old man Weiller. Hasn't he got any spunk? Oh, the hell with it. Abruptly he said, "How d'you think we ought to introduce ourselves to the girl's aunt and uncle tomorrow?"

"Why—"

"There'll be four of us," the captain interrupted. "Hudson's coming along; Starr said he could spare him, and while I could handle the French if I had to, I'll be under enough strain trying to figure out what kind of a setup we've got down there. So there we'll be—the three of us in uniform, and the girl. Any ideas?"

"Ought we—I mean, didn't you say you figured the aunt and uncle might be in on this? If there's a chance that they are, do we want to scare them? Or would it be better to—pretend we just gave the girl a lift, say—and chat with them awhile, and then suddenly whip out some question about—where Bouliard's set is, and take them by surprise?"

The captain sat back in his chair, considering. Already, he realized, his nerves had tensed a little, but pleasurably, as they always did when he was working on some case. What a strange game it was; but exciting, there was no denying it.

After a moment he said, "Maybe we'd better work backward for a minute. Where do we want to be when we get through? Quite apart from the girl, we want to clear up her old man's story—strictly for the files, maybe, but as I told you, that's always important. So we want to know whether Bouliard made those visits down there in the spring that the girl thinks he did—or says he did. My hunch is not; nobody'd have been likely to check his cover—"

"Except—" Johnny broke out.

"Except what?" The captain looked up, puzzled.

The boy's face reflected some kind of struggle. Finally he said, "Nothing. I thought for a minute I had an idea, but—I guess I haven't."

The captain waited a moment, then said, "Well, skip it for now. We'll find out about those visits if there were any, and definitely about the visit in May—provided, by the way, there was a visit in May. Had you thought there might not have been?"

Johnny looked up, astonishment on his face. "No, I—" He paused, considering. "Captain, I'd be certain there was one. The girl would know enough, after all, not to lie about anything we could check up on so easily, wouldn't she? But I don't see why she'd lie anyway—"

The captain felt the blood rising to his face. He said in careful tones, "I know this is all new to you, Mr. Phillips. And harder than it will be later on. But I hope you'll take my word for it that this evening I'm not trying to prove anything—I'm just thinking out loud, trying to cover every possible alternative, so I won't be taken by surprise later on. I'd do the same if this girl was Saint Genevieve. Forget you ever talked to her; forget everything but what's on paper. Try to think of all the possibilities. *Why* might the girl have lied? Or anyone else in the circumstances?"

Almost inaudibly at first, the boy said, "Why—if she and her father had been hiding out, in Cherbourg, or in the country somewhere, during that time in May—"

"Hiding from Bloch?" The captain shoved his hands in his pockets and looked up for a moment at the ceiling. "I don't see who else; and if Bloch, she'd have nothing to fear now from us—why wouldn't she have told us exactly where they did hide out? Nope. Try again—still supposing she's lying about the visit to Sartilly, remember."

"Well—if she and her father'd gone somewhere else she didn't want us to know about, I suppose."

"Like where?"

The boy, looking away with creased forehead, slowly shook his head.

"Well," said the captain ironically, "say Paris. After all, if the father could go there, so could the girl. And for the same reasons."

The boy leaned forward. "But wouldn't Korvac have known?" he asked eagerly.

"You can't be sure. He said, remember, that the girl had never gone to Paris with the father *so far as he knew,* but then he was only a radio technician at first, he didn't have Bloch's full confidence till after the invasion. And when Bloch gave him the mission to Cherbourg—well, recall that Bloch claimed to have trained the girl. Didn't say where, apparently; but it could have been Paris just as easily as Cherbourg, even if the girl wasn't meant to transmit. And maybe, after all, she was. Still, Korvac can be asked about that again." Weiller took from the pocket of his uniform blouse a thin pad of paper and a stub of pencil, and made a note. "I don't know if it'd be much use, though; Korvac's on the hook, and the only way his kind can figure to get off is to get somebody else properly on. You can bet that if he'd even heard she'd been to Paris—"

He looked up to see Johnny Phillips staring at him—was it sarcastically? With all his might he fought the giddiness of the anger he felt rising in him. Phillips said hastily, "You could have put that into his mouth, couldn't you, Captain? I mean— Korvac could have said she'd been in, and then we could have seen how she took it."

"I didn't think of it." The boy would miss the irony of that. Weiller thought suddenly, irrationally, of his wife Kate, looking at him with pride and tenderness; of the kids; of his boss —people who admired him, trusted him to do a good job, or the best job he could. . . . His mouth tightened. He would not slip into self-pity. Carl too had hated him, perhaps hated him still; but he could work with Carl. He would be able to work with Phillips.

The boy said, "If she was in Paris in May, and told us she'd gone down with her father to Sartilly, that means the Corrails are pretty likely in on the whole thing, and prepared to cover up. But they don't know how much we know. Maybe we could trip them up."

Heavily the captain said, "Maybe. But if they're in on it, you can depend that the girl talked it all out with them before she left for Cherbourg this last time, just in case something like this should happen, and their story'll be the same as hers."

"Then what would we do? Talk to the neighbors?"

The captain shrugged. "The Corrails' farm is pretty big, the girl said. If the neighbors *had* seen the girl and her father, why fine, but you couldn't expect them to remember exact dates. If they hadn't—well, it wouldn't prove anything." He paused. "Look, Phillips," he said after a moment. "This is what I think. I think the girl and her father *were* visiting down below in May. The whole business of Bloch and his *chère Thérèse* aside for the moment, we know the father was guilty. Don't we?"

"Why—yes," Johnny said. "I guess so."

"You *guess* so!" the captain burst out. "See here, my little trick on the girl didn't *prove* anything maybe, to us that is, but it didn't disprove what we already knew, for Christ's sake!"

"No, sir," said Johnny. "I—I didn't mean anything."

The captain drew a deep breath. "Well, let's not worry for the moment about whether Bouliard got sore at Bloch for propositioning his daughter, or whether that was all a phony. The point now is, we didn't find Bouliard's set in Cherbourg. We talked about this once before, remember? Before you interrogated the girl. Do you recall what the alternatives about the set were?"

"I was supposed to find out where they'd hid it," the boy said, flushing.

"I'm not rubbing your nose in that now." Weiller hoped that his voice sounded as kindly as he meant it to. "You couldn't expect her to say, 'There's no set, and it's buried back of the barn'—and she certainly wasn't prepared to admit there was a set, not right then. But—"

"What if it's buried back in Cherbourg?" Johnny asked. "I mean, didn't I read that the Germans gave them waterproof bags . . . ?"

"Yes. He could have. But really the bags were for use in case a spy's home town was about to be overrun; then later, when things quieted down and it looked safe, the set could be dug up and put to use. But Bouliard was killed before the invasion ever took place; so if he'd already buried the set he'd done it for some other reason. I'm assuming he wasn't expecting to be killed."

"I suppose he could have thought the set might be injured by bombings."

"That would mean, wouldn't it, that if he buried the set in or around Cherbourg, he didn't do it until he and Thérèse got back from—Sartilly, or wherever?"

"Why, sir?" The boy lifted puzzled eyes to his.

"Well, look. Bloch was, apparently, still around when Bouliard and Thérèse left Cherbourg."

"Not necessarily, if you don't believe Thérèse's story about Bloch, and about why she and her father left for Sartilly."

Weiller shrugged. "Korvac said that Bloch came in to the Paris station, as a new man, in May. Thérèse says she and her father left Cherbourg for Sartilly in late April or early May, and we can check that."

"Y-yes."

"Well, all I mean is—I'm not sure, but I don't recall that the danger from bombings in late April or early May in Cherbourg was especially great. Anyway, Bouliard wasn't likely to have buried his set *for that reason* while Bloch was still in Cherbourg unless Bloch told him to. And if Bloch did, and Bouliard never came on the air again, then I should think Bloch would have told Korvac about the set's having been buried, and we'd have heard about it. Instead, Bloch told Korvac that Bouliard's set had been very carefully tested, and had always worked perfectly while Bloch was in Cherbourg. Again, of course, we can check with Korvac, ask whether he ever heard that Bouliard's set had been buried." The captain made another scribbled note. "On the other hand, when the Bouliards got back to Cherbourg there was increasing danger from bombing, and Bloch was no longer there to tell Bouliard to bury his set or not to, either one. See what I mean?"

"Yes, sir."

"The only thing that's left is to try to figure out, under this explanation, where the set was while the Bouliards were in Sartilly—or wherever they were. I shouldn't have thought Bouliard would have felt quite easy about leaving it lying around the Cherbourg house—in case someone did some exploring while he was gone, or the invasion took place while he was away, or something; but he couldn't have felt too comfortable carrying it with him wherever he went, either. So—"

"Captain Weiller," said the boy. "All this just makes me positive that Bouliard was trying to get out from under—trying to get away from Bloch somehow. If he was on good terms with Bloch when he left Cherbourg, and was expecting to come back and use the set, why wouldn't he just have left it with Bloch for safekeeping?"

"Now wait a minute. I'm not through. If the set *is* buried in Cherbourg, Bouliard probably took a chance and hid it while he was gone, then, and buried it when he got back; or took a chance and carried it back and forth on his trip, and then buried it. But we didn't find a trace of it in the house; and we examined the backyard—it's damned small—and saw no signs of any digging or anything. Furthermore, the yard's not really private; he might have been seen burying something, and that wouldn't have been healthy. If he buried the set somewhere else —well, it's not impossible, but again he'd have been running an awful risk of being noticed. I don't know. I just have a strong hunch that the set isn't in Cherbourg at all. And if it isn't, where is it?"

The boy said, "We—we hope it's at the farm in Sartilly, sir."

Slowly the captain leaned back in his chair, smiling. The kid had said, "We hope." *We.* "What would that mean?" he asked.

"I—well, like I said, *if* it's there, I don't see what it could mean except that Bouliard was trying to ditch. Otherwise the set would have stayed in Cherbourg, or would have been taken back."

"I think that's right," said Weiller.

"But, Captain," Johnny said. "Why wouldn't he just have pitched the set out somewhere along the way—thrown it into a hedge or something? Unless he didn't want his daughter to see him; unless she didn't know what he'd been doing, and he had to wait until he could dispose of the set in private."

So that's it, Weiller thought bleakly. Well, I should have known, I guess. "Two things," he said. "In the first place, if he'd chucked the set out and it had been found by the Germans,

198

or by German sympathizers, it would have been turned in and could have been traced back to him. In the second place, right up to the minute he died Bouliard must have expected that he might have to account for the set, to Bloch or someone else. Spies don't just resign, you know. If he knew exactly where the set was, and could at a pinch get it again, or take his bosses to it, he might have a chance to wiggle out somehow, with an excuse which they couldn't disprove at least, though they might have their suspicions. But otherwise—" He made the throat-slitting gesture.

"Yes, I see that," the boy said, his voice unwilling.

Suddenly the captain felt very tired. Looking at Johnny Phillips, the young face closed and absorbed, a trace of sulkiness around the lips, he recalled his emotions of—was it only a few minutes before?—the exhilaration, the excitement of bending his mind to materials like these, the hope of striking sparks off another mind until everything should be illuminated, the possibilities of what was to come displayed in perfect order and logic, with nothing important left out and nothing false or negligible remaining to becloud the issues. Now they had scarcely begun, and Johnny's prejudgments were blocking him at every turn. What had he done wrong? Well, he'd got mad. You weren't supposed to get mad when somebody did something stupid; you were supposed to be patient and agreeable. Papa Weiller's Nursery School. Creative play in counterespionage. Real cases will help your toddlers grow. . . . He shouldn't have made Phillips take the girl to the jug; she'd have had to go there anyway, but Phillips shouldn't have taken her. How old do you have to be before you can take the facts of life? . . . But he shouldn't have got mad.

"Well, where are we now?" he asked quietly. "Bouliard and the girl are at Sartilly; Bouliard's got the set; maybe the girl knows it, maybe she doesn't; maybe the aunt and uncle know what's up, maybe they don't. It's possible Bouliard's trying to get out from under. How's he going to eat if he does? I don't know. Maybe he doesn't know. Maybe he's just got his fingers crossed, hoping the Allies will invade or something, and he'll be saved—or at least have a chance of being saved. The girl—"

"Captain," Phillips said. "I—I want to apologize."

The captain turned to him in surprise. But Phillips was not looking at him; he was staring at his hands, clenched on the table in front of him.

"There's no use pretending I didn't get off on the wrong foot in this case; I did. I'm trying to—take a different attitude. But maybe it's some use to have me take a definite side, for now, and have you pick holes in it—I mean, show where it breaks down, and what the other possibilities are. Just now I was thinking—supposing the girl was in on this with the father, and the father was trying to ditch, doesn't that sound as if the girl was, too?"

"I don't know," the captain said. "The letter Bloch sent her through Korvac doesn't sound as if *he* thought she'd pull out, anyway."

"Not if you take the letter straight, no. But Bloch was probably pretty desperate by that time, don't you suppose? After all, according to Korvac, Bloch didn't *think* Bouliard would betray him, either, but we've just decided that's what Bouliard was trying to do."

"We haven't *decided*, Phillips," said the captain. "It's one theory."

"Yes, sir," the boy said. "But if he'd really intended to work, wouldn't he have stayed in Cherbourg? Or got back there sooner, if he'd had to leave?"

Again the captain said, "I don't know. It looks like it. But there are a lot of loose ends, and a single new piece of information could change everything." He paused. "What are you getting at?"

"I—I just wondered if that would make you feel any different," the boy said. "If they'd been trapped, and were trying to get out of the trap."

"Feel any different?" Weiller almost shouted. "What does it matter how I feel? I'm not a judge, for Christ's sake. And I'm not posterity. I'm just trying to figure out what happened."

Johnny reddened. "All right," he burst out. "It seems to me she told me what happened. It seems to me it's in the report. She didn't know her father was a spy, so that's not there; but the rest is, and what isn't you can read between the lines. Bloch tried to—seduce the girl, maybe as a way of getting her involved in the case, maybe just for the pleasure of it, maybe both, and the Bouliards couldn't take it and lit out for Sartilly, and the father got rid of his set. Period. Why couldn't it be as simple as that?"

Don't get sore, the captain said to himself, his heart pounding furiously in his throat. Don't get sore. "I never said it *couldn't* be as simple as that," he said quietly.

"Only you just don't think it is. Because for some damned reason you want the girl to be in trouble. As if she hadn't had enough trouble already."

"Phillips," the captain warned, "I've had nearly as much as I can take. Remember I'm your commanding officer. A little more of this and I'll send you back to Cherbourg, and you'll be in trouble yourself, and I mean trouble."

The boy leaped to his feet and began pacing the room, then flung himself down at the table again and buried his head in his arms. When he looked up he said, his voice shaking, "I'm sorry, Captain. I really am. This—this business isn't easy to get into, and the last couple of days have been—rough on me, I guess. I guess I'm stuck somehow, I can't seem to think through it. When I think of the Bouliards going to Sartilly, for example, and staying—when they *hated* the Corrails. Why would they have gone, except for the reason the girl gave? And the logical conclusion from that, that Bouliard was trying to walk out on the German Intelligence Service?"

Slowly Captain Weiller relaxed. "I told you, I think maybe he was trying to walk out. Of course we haven't even considered the possibility that Bloch told them to leave Cherbourg, with the transmitter—the Germans thought the invasion might come in May, you know, though they didn't expect it to come where it did. I take it there wasn't much of any place the Bouliards could have gone except Sartilly. Then when nothing happened, and without further instructions, they'd have straggled back to Cherbourg, finally, with or without the set—and either way the reasons could have been either creditable, relatively, or discreditable. But wipe all that out for now. You can't seem to understand why Bouliard would want to quit being a spy except because his daughter's honor was threatened, is that it? Well, what if he was just a plain coward? What if they were both cowards, and played the game as long as it meant money in the bank, but backed out when it looked like they'd soon be playing for real?"

On the boy's face was the smile the captain had seen there when the interview had begun—the smile that seemed to convey nothing but the intention to smile. "Yes, I see. I should have thought of that," he said. "You sure know the angles in this stuff, Captain."

I know why you didn't think of it, the captain said slowly to himself, dismayed. You didn't think of it because you weren't capable of thinking of it, weren't capable of imagining that anything might be wrong with the girl at all. Jesus Christ. What a guy to be saddled with in a business like this. And at a time like this.

But something worse was wrong, and Captain Weiller knew it. What was Phillips acting so damned odd for? Buttering him up, saying things he obviously didn't mean? In a way it was more comfortable to have the kid getting mad, because then at least there was no question of what he was thinking. Now if he was going to turn into a sniveling yes man—well, there'd be no more spark-striking. And no sense in going on with this conversation. Weiller grunted sardonically. A fat lot of use it had been anyway.

He thought to rise, to dismiss the boy, but again suddenly he felt very tired, and as he struggled with himself he was conscious of something else, a wariness, a meaning so far overlooked. Why *was* the boy suddenly pretending to be on his side? Just to keep him from getting mad? He'd threatened—to send Phillips back to Cherbourg, to get him in trouble; but anyone would know that couldn't amount to much, an official reprimand, being taken off the case, maybe at worst being transferred to another unit, or back to London. . . . Maybe Phillips didn't want to be taken off the case. But why not? He'd had nothing but grief out of it so far, you'd think he'd be glad to get out, do something else. Yet here he was, hamming away. . . . Maybe he was up to something, some trick, to protect that fool girl, a German spy, for God's sake, or as near it as no matter. . . .

He realized that he was sweating. He raised his arm, shaking, and wiped his forehead with his sleeve, oblivious of the dark stain it made. He had to break this case, and break it fast! Thury—ready to move at any moment, he was sure of it—he *couldn't* lose control of Cherbourg, he *couldn't*—the colonel was no help, he never had a positive suggestion, but he'd be quick enough with a scalping knife, if he had to save his own reputation—and then Cherbourg would be wide open, with troops about to come in in strength, and nobody knew how many months, or years, of war left. He was alone. He had to break this case tomorrow; break the girl, break the Corrails, and—now—watch Phillips, to make sure he didn't do anything to queer the pitch. He couldn't even leave Phillips behind the next day, he didn't want him running around loose. . . . Kate, he said to himself, Kate, Kate, Kate, how long does this go on?

A beetle, some summer insect, struck at the light bulb over their heads, then buzzed and rattled frighteningly. Captain Weiller jumped in his chair, looked up, then looked across at the boy. The smile had stiffened, like one of those curls on the top of a gelatin pudding; but under the captain's gaze it re-vivified, a flower grateful for the rain.

There was a knock on the door and Lieutenant Starr stuck his head in. "Say," he said, "it was so quiet in here, I thought maybe you two had left, or something. Am I interrupting you?"

"No," said Weiller.

"Captain, I'd meant to ask you before—are you married?"

"Yes."

"Oh." Starr seemed crestfallen. Then he said, "I'd just thought maybe you and I ought to have a little—entertainment tonight. The town's not much for sights, I guess you know that all right, but I've got a bottle, and I know a couple of nice friendly girls—" He winked. "No field-grade officers in town right now, I think I can guarantee you—"

The captain got to his feet. He could not stand this room any longer; he could not stand his own thoughts. The idea of—well, you didn't even have to call it love—of someone to admire him, if only for an hour, if only because he was an American captain, in the absence of a major—someone to touch him tenderly, meaning nothing really, but meaning nothing else, disguising nothing. . . .

At the door he turned. The boy's face was fixed in an expression of disdain, of revulsion.

God damn you for a son of a bitch, the captain exploded soundlessly. Go play with yourself. Go jump off a cliff. I don't give a shit whether you understand or not. Kate would understand.

He said, "We don't seem to be getting anywhere, Phillips. And we won't have time to talk in the morning. I'd suggest that tomorrow you just watch what I do, try to figure it out, follow along the best way you can. Don't take part in the questioning unless you really want to, unless—well, maybe if you think of questions you'd better check with me, so you won't accidentally mess up anything I'm trying to do. Once we've got it started I don't think we'll have much trouble."

Johnny Phillips nodded. "I suppose it's safe enough to assume that if the girl didn't care much for her aunt and uncle, they didn't like her either. They'll probably be willing enough to talk about her." If there was bitterness in the words, it did not appear.

In his turn, the captain nodded. "Well, so long. Better turn in soon."

"Good night, sir," the boy said.

When they had got well down the corridor, Lieutenant Starr turned to Weiller and said curiously, "How's it going? Funny kid, isn't he? It must be hard to work with—"

The captain said coldly, "It's going all right. He gave me a damned good idea just then."

XIII.

JOHNNY waited, his head buried in his arms, until it seemed that Weiller and Lieutenant Starr must have left the building; then he switched off the hanging bulb in the room where he had been sitting and went out into the hall. At first the ground floor of Starr's headquarters seemed deserted. But as he groped his way toward the back stairs, Johnny saw an upright bar of light coming from a partly open door across from the stairs.

He peered into the room. Hudson was sitting alone at the kitchen table, eating a sandwich. There was a letter spread out on the table beside him, but he did not seem to be reading. Johnny knocked tentatively, and when there was no answer, knocked again. At Hudson's "Come in!" he pushed through the door into the room. It was cool in the kitchen; there was a faint mushroom dampness in the air.

"Hi," said Hudson. "You need anything?"

"Why—no."

"Forgotten where your sack is?"

"I don't think so," Johnny answered. "It's in the big room at the head of the stairs, isn't it?"

"The back stairs," said Hudson. "Yeah. We're all in there, except the lieutenant." There was a pause. Hudson said, "Want a sandwich?"

"No thanks."

Now that he was in the room Johnny did not know what he had expected to do here. He stepped forward awkwardly, pulled a chair back from the table and sat down. Actually he did know what he wanted to do, but how could he go about it? Seeing Hudson through the crack in the door, he had thought: That guy was the only decent one there this afternoon, or maybe he's decent, he must have seen what they were doing to Thérèse. . . . Now he was wondering: Do I dare talk to him about it, would he help?

Trying to decide what to say, or whether he could say anything, Johnny was looking, not at Hudson, but down at the table where the letter lay. Hudson picked up the letter, folded it, put it back in its envelope and stuffed it into his hip pocket. His movements were casual, but Johnny raised his eyes, hot with embarrassment.

"I wasn't looking at it," he said.

"Of course not. Anyway it doesn't matter. Just another installment of the International News. I expect you get it too." Hudson's civilized voice turned unexpectedly sharp. "Item: Danny's been exposed to measles, but Mother says if the house is going to be quarantined she can't have it, because that big party she's been planning for so long is all set for the third of September. Item: Rationing is getting worse and worse, I suppose all the good stuff goes to you men in the Army, I'm certain Ann is suffering from malnutrition, and I'm tired all the time. Item: The handsomest Marine major is visiting next door, he was badly wounded on Guadalcanal and has been invalided out, he seems so lonely, poor dear, and I think he'd like to have a date with me, but I don't think I ought to, but I don't know, what would you think, after all I didn't ask to be left alone here, I hate just being a child again in my mother's house. . . ." Abruptly the rush stopped. "Sound familiar?"

Johnny said apologetically, "I just came over from England a day or so ago. I don't suppose I'll be getting any mail for awhile."

"Lucky you." Hudson got up from the table. "Well, I'm going to sack out. Sweet dreams."

Hurriedly Johnny said, "The captain told me you were going to come down with us tomorrow. Is that so?"

Hudson shrugged. "First I've heard of it. But whither the lieutenant sendeth me, there will I also go, you can bet your boots."

"What—" Johnny cleared his throat. "What did you think of the case?"

Hudson stared at him in mock surprise. "Remember me? I'm an interpreter. I translate. I do not have opinions."

"No, but—"

"Oh, all right." Hudson yawned. "It's sticky. He's sticky. She's sticky. They're all sticky. Sounds like I'm conjugating verbs, doesn't it?"

Johnny said in a low voice, "Seems to me she's getting kind of a raw deal."

"So?" Hudson yawned again. "Well, don't worry, she'll pass it along to someone else. That, my boy, is what life is for. I just found out." He walked around the end of the table toward the door, singing "The same old STO-ry. It's as old as the stars above." At the door he stopped. "You through in here? Turn the light off when you go, will you?"

"Yeah," Johnny said.

There was a poker game going on just inside the door of the room at the head of the stairs; the players were sitting cross-legged on the floor, and Johnny had to step over them to get through. "Excuse me," he said. "Sorry."

"It's O.K." A tall, freckled boy straightened up after Johnny's passage and called after him, "You want to take a hand? It's a good game—you can lose your shirt."

Turning, Johnny tried to smile. "No thanks," he said.

Walking back toward the cot in the far left-hand corner where his gear was, Johnny passed Hudson, who was sitting with his head down. He was rereading his letter; he did not look up as Johnny went by. The poor guy, Johnny thought. And for a minute back there I was almost sore at him, too.

Johnny stripped to his underclothes and laid his uniform, neatly folded, on the chair beside his cot. Then he unrolled his sleeping bag and lay down on top of it, wadding it together a little under his head to make a pillow. He was still too hot; he'd have liked to sleep naked, only of course he couldn't, not here. The sleeping bag was soft and clinging. It made his legs itch, and under his back a pool of sweat began to form, spreading between his shoulder blades, soaking through his undershirt. He wriggled uncomfortably. . . . What the hell am I complaining about? he asked himself. I'm a damn sight more comfortable than she is.

But as he recalled the airless cell into which he had locked Thérèse, as his senses evoked the sour filth, the smell of urine, Johnny recognized the presence of danger and tried to turn his mind to something else. Two people bound on the same rack could not help one another. If Johnny thought about where Thérèse was now he could only fall into helpless rage and sorrow; and neither would help him next day, they would not help her. Perhaps the best thing would be if he could get a good sleep so that he would be rested in the morning, so that he would be alert and keen.

He closed his eyes and kept them closed, lay rigidly still against the urge to writhe and toss in the hot stickiness of his bed. But a torrent of unhappy thoughts, of painful images, assailed his mind, and he could not sleep. He remembered a trick his father had once taught him: you pretended that your mind was a blackboard, that every word, every thought that came to you was written down on the board, and you erased, faster and faster, until not even whole words could be formed, and finally the mind was wholly dark and blank, and you were asleep. He tried it now. But a voice from the other end of the room drawled, "Son of a bitch, I got one king, and nothin's wild, how come you got four?" and there was an outbreak of quarreling, of shouted laughter. Johnny whirled on his bed, lay face down, and tried to bury his head in the sleeping bag so that he could not hear. But at once his whole face tingled with sweat. He turned on his back again.

A cold, angry voice said, "Seven-card high-low."

"Ah, Jeez, that's a lousy game!"

From nearer Johnny, Hudson's voice said crossly, "Hey, knock it off, you guys. Some of us have got to work tomorrow."

The dealer said, "Fuck you, Jack."

Sure, Johnny thought morosely, everybody fuck everybody, that's what life is for. Well, he was finding out pretty fast himself. But did you have to accept it as fact, did you have to give in, do your bit?

For all the sleep he was getting, he might as well have joined the poker game.

But it wasn't because he wanted to sleep that he'd refused, he knew. If he'd thought anything at the time, he'd thought only that he didn't know how to play poker; he'd played only once, and hadn't especially got the hang of it. But he hadn't wanted to get the hang of it; he'd despised the game, a vulgar contest for money and power, he'd thought it stupid. And now he saw that he had an automatic contempt for the players at the door, assumed that their surface coarseness went deep, assumed them to be thoughtless, negligent, empty-headed. . . . What did I expect? he asked himself sharply. One of them to say "We're talking about early Picasso, would you care to join our discussion?" What's so bad about what they're doing? And you're not so damned sensitive to other people yourself; you barged in on Hudson without noticing that he wanted to be by himself, without even trying to find out.

Ought he know how to play poker? Johnny wondered. Maybe it wasn't so stupid a game after all, maybe that kind of limited struggle for power, for superiority, taught you something, and was fun at the same time; and surely it was better than Weiller's straight assumption of power, surely it was less damaging to others. He himself was alone too much, deliberately separate, acting humble, but secretly thinking himself superior. . . . Now he was condemning Weiller.

He tossed on his bed. But that wasn't automatic, he'd thought about that. What he had to do now was to think what he could do about it, if anything. . . . "If anything" was right; Weiller held all the cards. . . . Poker again. This is no game, or if it is, for any of us, then I've got to make it stop being one.

I don't know what to do, Johnny thought, bewildered, I just don't know what to do. His attempt to play-act had been a wretched failure so far; Weiller must have caught him at it, must have figured out what it meant. Yet he couldn't abandon it, for to show Weiller what he really felt would be suicide.

Would it? What could the captain do to him? You can't court-martial somebody for disagreeing with you. . . . No, Johnny recognized swiftly, but Weiller could send him back to England, or even simply take him off this case, and that would leave Thérèse unprotected, open to any kind of attack. Johnny had to stay on the case and try somehow to outsmart the captain, try to keep him from springing traps like the one of that afternoon. But Johnny hadn't seen that one coming; and how could he have? I don't know what to do, Johnny thought again.

Maybe he'd already spoiled his chances of doing any good. If he'd been able to play a part successfully, to convince Weiller that he too was on the attack, he might be able to stick to the captain now— If I was sticking to the captain now I'd probably find myself in a whorehouse, Johnny thought angrily.

No, that wasn't fair. Anyway, if he hadn't given himself away Weiller might really talk to him now, might let him know exactly what he was thinking about Thérèse, and Johnny might even be able to affect his decisions at times. As it was, Weiller would never trust him very far; he'd as much as said that Johnny was to keep hands off down in Sartilly, was only to watch and see what happened.

And if he tried to do anything more, secretly, what would it be? How could he help the girl escape Weiller's— Escape. Johnny sat up on the cot, then flopped back again. If things got too bad could he actually spirit her away, perhaps, get her into the hands of friends who would hide her . . . ?

But so far as he knew there was only one person, besides himself, who would help Thérèse, and that was Mlle. Vaugiron. And the captain knew as much about her as he did—maybe more. So that wouldn't work. Anyway, Mlle. Vaugiron was a teacher, an unworldly sort of person. . . .

Look who's talking, Johnny said to himself bitterly. He had known all along, perhaps, that he was unworldly, but the thought had never troubled him till now. But now— I've got a fight ahead of me, he thought with distress, a fight with somebody who knows how, who knows what you do when you want something in this world, and I'm so dumb I'm not even sure I know how to climb into the ring.

But then he steadied himself. If Thérèse was innocent—as of course she was; but even if there were only a strong chance of her being innocent—then she had to be protected. That was idealism, sure. But if you sacrificed ideals, especially in a business like this, what did you have left?

And anyway what was moving Johnny was more than idealism. He knew Thérèse, he'd talked to her for a long time and watched her, she was honest and good. And she was incredibly brave; how could she have held up the way she had, with her father dead and no one left to care about her or help her, and then this nightmare, this horror, settling down around her? No, the faith he had in her was real, it was based on what she really was. So was he so unworldly, after all?

It's just that I haven't been here very long, he thought; that's why I don't know what to do. But I can learn. Maybe if I knew as much about the world as the captain does I'd know right now what to do to help Thérèse.

But maybe if I were as worldly as the captain is I wouldn't want to help her.

He turned again, restlessly, on his bed. Yet why should that be? What got into a man like the captain, to make him do the things he was doing? Weiller had been a businessman before he'd got into the Army; a junior executive for an import-export firm, someone had said, supposed to have some insight into the Mind of the Foreigner. Was he showing his insight on Thérèse now? Or was he just treating her the way he'd treat a business rival? Or did being out in the world, knowing a lot of people, make you stop caring about people, caring about them as human beings, that is? Or was it something else still—if your job was to catch spies, did you get so, after awhile, that you just had to catch spies, whether there were any real ones around to be caught or not?

It wasn't, any of it, the way he had thought it was going to be, Johnny thought in discouragement. If he could truly hate Weiller he'd be better off; but he could do that only sometimes. For Weiller did not seem to be an evil person, exactly; nor was he unintelligent; nor was he, exactly, irresponsible. Unfeeling, perhaps—yet earlier that evening, when Johnny had made such an odd spectacle of himself, Weiller had been on the whole very patient, almost gentle at times. Only where Thérèse was concerned was he obdurate. It was as though he and Johnny were working from two different sets of facts.

Did Weiller know something he hadn't yet mentioned? It was possible, everything had gone so fast. . . . Johnny hardened. He remembered Weiller's voice shouting: "I'm not a judge, for Christ's sake, and I'm not posterity. I'm just trying to figure out what happened"—when only that afternoon, in the confrontation between Thérèse and Korvac, he had falsified what had happened and obviously half believed in his own falsification. If he and Johnny were working from two different sets of facts, Johnny thought grimly, it was because Weiller had made up half of his to suit.

So Weiller was, simply, out to win. And why? It must be because he wanted the new account; because he wanted to make good in the eyes of the boss. Sure, Johnny thought sardonically, that Paris job; he's bucking for major. And that might account for his patience with Johnny, too, if patience was what it was —one of the things Weiller would have to do to impress his superiors would be to develop a harmonious team that worked hard, and worked together well, under Weiller's dynamic leadership. . . . Johnny groaned. It wasn't fair, and he knew it. There was more to Weiller than that. He couldn't like the man (how *could* he have gone out with that phony Starr, for example? for some squalid adventure in the back streets), and he was afraid of him, but— He couldn't despise him, not if he thought about him. Weiller believed in something. Even if what he did was wrong, he couldn't have done it, have done so much, unless he believed in something. What is it? Johnny asked himself, almost in panic. What have I left out? Even his going out this evening—am I right about that? just because I wouldn't do it —just because I've never done it, and don't know? Is this just me again—inexperienced, smug, a damned fool? Which makes you more callous, experience or inexperience? He buried his head in his arms, struggling with doubt and dislike of himself. I'm a fine mess, he thought. No wonder the captain gets sore at me.

But something, some uncertainty or solicitude, still hovered at the back of his mind, and all at once, with relief, he recognized what it was. Possibly he was a fool; and doubtless Weiller, too, was infected in some way, with coldness, with a slightly inhuman zeal. But it was not Johnny who mattered. And it was not Weiller. It was the girl. It was Thérèse, who was innocent.

And if she's innocent, Johnny thought, what can happen to her? Tomorrow, or any other day? If she's innocent Weiller can't prove her guilty. He can't make her confess having done something she hasn't done. So what can he do? . . . In Johnny's ears the voice of Thérèse said, as it had said that afternoon, and in the same lifeless tone, "I see now how this will end. And I must tell you that I do not care." That was what Weiller could do; with whatever motives, he might be able to break Thérèse's will. And what could Johnny do to prevent it?

The answer was obvious. He could convince her that she still had something to live for. He could make her care.

Johnny's heart began to pound. With extraordinary clarity the scene at the *gendarmerie* rose before his mind, before all his senses. Thérèse clutching his hand against her thin, soft cheek, her cheek wet with tears. Thérèse with her arms around him, her face buried against his uniform jacket. Himself leaning over, kissing her on the forehead, saying—had he said it?—"I don't know what we'll do, but we'll do something. . . ." What could she live for, now that her father was dead and damned, except—another person? Except him, Johnny? How could he make her care again, except for—himself?

But I don't even know, Johnny thought wildly, I don't know anything about— He steadied himself. If Thérèse were to fall in love with him—but perhaps she loved him already, perhaps—

Half of him said: No.

The other half said: But why not? Why not?

Maybe he was in love with Thérèse, too. Why else would he feel so deeply about her, about her predicament? That was easy, Johnny thought; simple justice— No. No, it's more than that. Can it happen so fast? The books say so, but I've never believed it.

Why not? a voice inside him said. *What else?*

With wonder he thought: She's pretty. Kind of homely, but kind of pretty too. If only she didn't look so unhappy all the time, if only she didn't have to. . . .

But so far as she's concerned I'm only someone who's helped her, Johnny thought matter-of-factly. That's all. I'm the one who's been kind to her.

Yes, kind, the voice said. *Not merely just. Justice is disinterested. But you're not disinterested. And neither is she.*

Why can't I get to sleep? Johnny thought, terrified and aggrieved. This isn't the time to try to figure out an important thing like that, when you're trying to sleep. But maybe that was just when you did think about such things. . . . Anyway I can't *do* anything about it, Johnny said to himself, not now, what would I do, go up to the captain tomorrow and say, "Sir, I wish to marry your daughter, I mean your victim?" . . . The poor kid. Thérèse, Johnny said to himself; Thérèse. A tendril of something delicate and sweet poked up out of a shrouded corner of his mind. He thought hastily: But tomorrow is important, what will happen tomorrow?

If Weiller couldn't find the set he could do very little, surely. He could discover, perhaps, that Bouliard had not been in Sartilly at those times during the early spring when he had told Thérèse he had been there. But increasing the evidence of the father's guilt would rather heighten the girl's pain than incriminate her. And monstrous as it was, Thérèse was obviously due for more pain anyway.

If the set were found, then Weiller could try to hound the girl into confessing that she'd helped some way in its use. But she could deny that, and if she did, what could Weiller do but bully her? Could he play any trick? Involving the aunt and uncle, perhaps? But though Thérèse had said they didn't like her, nor she them, surely they wouldn't be willing to railroad her. Unless the captain could get something on them. . . . Would they exchange a faked accusation of Thérèse for their own immunity? But no, the captain wouldn't actually frame the girl. . . . But I don't know, Johnny said to himself. I don't know. All I can do is wait and see. All I can do is hang on. And show Thérèse, when the captain isn't looking, that I—

But if he were to help Thérèse he had to get to sleep! The noise from the poker game seemed to have died down; maybe the game was over. He wondered what time it was; late, anyway. He'd try the blackboard stunt again. This time it ought to work.

In the darkness his mother's voice said, cool and amused, "But Johnny, don't you see? You didn't take Sally to the prom; I'm afraid that—in the language of your generation—she took you! Oh, I don't blame you for thinking she's pretty. But you know she's going with Rodney, he's the only boy around here she really thinks anything of. Only she'd had a little squabble with him; so she thought she'd show him— And, darling, you know you wear your heart on your sleeve—" Too late, Johnny wielded the eraser.

His mother's voice, deeper this time, less amused, said, "Oh, no! Not Amy Stebbins! Johnny, you really *don't* know very much about girls, do you? Of *course* she's got an attractive figure, but have you ever stopped to think how many boys it must have attracted before now? Why, her mother and father are beside themselves, they're *wild* to get her married before—" The eraser.

Just above Johnny's cot, a real voice in the real world, a male voice, said, so close that Johnny almost jumped, "Hey Hudson, who's the Sleeping Beauty here? This guy on the end cot?" Johnny's closed eyelids went stiff with self-consciousness.

Another voice was saying, "Hudson's asleep, don't wake him. That's—I don't know what his name is, but he's from Cherbourg, he came down with Captain Weiller and that girl."

"A girl? What girl?"

"Dunno. She's a new case they got."

"God damn it," the first voice said, "some people have all the luck. And look at this kid. He don't look like he even shaved yet. Wish I could get my hands on a real live female spy—hey, you ever hear about that one they put in the jug over in Caen? They say she was doin' it standin' up, for anybody. So first the boys got her all cured up, and then—"

"Ah, give it a rest, Muggsy," the second voice said. "Can't you think about anything but tail?"

"Well, what makes you so high and mighty? Go screw yourself."

"Don't think he wouldn't," a third voice said, giggling. "Only he found out it don't reach."

"*Shut* up."

The giggling voice said, "But this girl, hey. Is she worth a little trouble?"

In Johnny's mind, the blackboard cracked across.

Wednesday,
August 30, 1944

XIV.

And Thérèse in prison! It was sweet, it was sweet— the self-righteous Thérèse, so superior, on the surface all goodness, all virtue, and underneath it more corrupt than the worst. . . . Estelle de Sombais, alone at her breakfast table, smiled with satisfaction and stubbed her cigarette out on her plate. She took a long, slow sip of the black liquid in her cup. It was cold.

"Blanchette!" she called angrily.

The maid Blanchette, ugly, black-mustached, pushed open the door from the kitchen and stood negligently in the doorway.

"The drink is vile!" Estelle said, and slammed her cup down into the saucer.

Blanchette stared at her with an expressionless glitter in her eyes. "The Germans are gone," she said. "No more coffee."

"I did not say it was not coffee," Estelle retorted. "I said it was vile. It is cold."

Blanchette shrugged. "The gas is off," she said. "What do you expect?"

Well, so the day was begun. Insolent pig! Fool! Estelle wanted to say, but would not, it was a practical matter, Blanchette must stay. She herself had other concerns than housework, and her mother, the Paris beauty, the incomparable hostess, had not left her shuttered room since the Americans had occupied Cherbourg.

Abruptly Estelle rose from the table and turned away. In any case one could not think of the frail, fashionable Mme. de Sombais with a broom or an oily dustcloth in her hand. Estelle smiled with a brief, wry affection, an affection that had become, she was aware, something of an effort since her mother's defection. Defection? More nearly, perhaps, it was a failure to adjust; and this was pitiable and a little shocking, but it was also instructive. Those who allowed themselves to be wholly committed could not easily change; not, that is, if they were no longer young. And since one could not help growing older, it was as well to avoid total commitment.

Blanchette had not stirred from the kitchen doorway. She said now, "Since I myself have had coffee it is—let me see, how many years? Though in this house you had enough—"

Estelle swung around and met her direct gaze with distaste, then, without answering, turned again and left the room. From the hall she heard the maid's dry snicker, then the clatter of china, the harsh scrape of a chair on the uncarpeted floor of the dining room. Fair enough, she thought, trying to brush the anger from her mind; the despicable must of course despise, and at least the woman goes to her task. And suddenly she realized: but Blanchette stays so that she may despise us boldly. For years she has been waiting just for this. I could call her a pig and she would feel only delight; for in the evening she could tell her family what I had said, and tell them who is really the pig, and why. . . .

For a moment weariness touched her, and something like sorrow, or despair; almost she could have left the house, unready as she was, just to be away, to be gone. But with her hand already on the doorknob she steadied herself, or was steadied, by an equal emotion, a fear of the street which she had not yet, this morning, admitted to her conscious thoughts. Auguste—Captain Thury—would not call for her today, she would walk to the office alone. . . . But of course she was alone; of course she was exposed. Only cowards, and people of no importance, no position, were not exposed. Now she was not ready to leave the house. She would go only when she was ready, when she had completed her toilette. And on the way to the office she would liven her spirits by thinking of the gratifications to come: of the first interrogation report on Thérèse Bouliard, for example, which must surely be brought over to Thury soon. . . .

Holding herself defiantly erect she turned and began to ascend the stairs. Yet on the stairway she made as little sound as her shoes, high-heeled and wooden-soled, would permit her to make. It would be better, today, if her mother were to think she had left without saying goodbye. She did not wish to hear, from behind the closed door in the upper hall, the sharp, thin "Estelle?"—and have then to go in and give the gray, daintily robed figure love and reassurance for the day. As one gives a portion of broth, she thought grimly, to an invalid. But one visits the sickroom only when one is oneself strong, and can resist the presence there, to all the senses, of weakness, of decay—

At the top of the stairs she paused, unable not to pause, and with her eyes closed heard, as though she were not hearing it, the muffled, questioning call. Deliberately she entered her own room and closed the door behind her.

Even with the bed unmade, the beauty of her room, its luxuriousness, the continuity it suggested with an aristocratic and stable past, gave her strength. She picked up her handbag from the bedside table and turned, with the stirrings of pleasure, toward her wardrobe mirror. *Et voilà*, she said to herself, surveying her slim waist, her superb breasts, her only less good legs and ankles. And her face, all beauty and pride beneath the silken blond hair. Taking a small gold case from her handbag, she began, with devoted care, to apply her lipstick. My friend, she said silently to her own likeness. You are my friend. And we choose, you and I, what we will do, and whether or not we will be alone.

She knew that she was proud; and she knew that if she were not proud she would be nothing. Her magnificence was something she had made, in only a few years, because she had intended to make it; as her father had made a fortune, by calculation, by intelligent and unsentimental business methods, under the German occupation. Her father, it was true, was now in flight, or in hiding. But she—she would not hide.

Out in the street she began to walk rapidly, her head held self-consciously high. But in the hard morning light, her mirror far behind her, she felt her confidence draining away, felt strangely and mercilessly assailed, so that almost at once her step faltered. She looked around. Was not the street unnaturally empty? Where was Javot, with his tools and his barrow? Where was the thick coarse-featured old woman in black who should now be scrubbing the steps of the house on the corner?

Yesterday morning when she had passed the corner the woman had looked up and grinned, showing a mouthful of rotten teeth, and had squatted back on her buttocks and said, "Eh, such lovely hair. And not yet shaved off, how is that?" Estelle had been startled, and must have showed it, though she had looked away at once and had hurried on. The woman had called after her, "Wait! Wait, till I get my scissors!" and then had laughed, loud, hateful peals of laughter. Others in the street had heard and had stared, with a curiosity that had seemed to eddy around Estelle and settle like soot. But no one had moved to touch her. . . .

Auguste should still be fetching her, taking her back each morning to the building which housed his office and his apartment and the rooms where, so carelessly, he held his few prisoners. Estelle had said as much to him yesterday. But he had replied only, "My dear, we are too busy, there is no longer time for such things. And there is no need." Then she had told him about the old woman. He had shrugged and said, "Ah, they will make jokes perhaps, cruel jokes. But they will do nothing. In France all that is over now."

She would not beg, nor even seem to be frightened. But she had said, "And if they should do something?"

Thury had answered heartily, "You forget that we are important. You are important! The police, above all, are in our debt."

The police! She knew the Cherbourg police as Thury, who came from Lyon and who had in any case been in England during most of the Occupation, did not. Many had tried, cravenly, to serve two masters, and had served nothing and no one. Now all were self-styled martyrs and heroes of the Resistance, hot to secure their own reputations by attacking others. Besides, of what use would it be to appeal to them *after*—

Tangled in these thoughts, Estelle de Sombais had reached the corner unmindful, for the moment, of where she was. Now swiftly an acute unease swept over her, and she looked up to see the old woman in black standing in the recess of her doorway, staring down with a cold sneer on her face. Estelle stopped, frozen. The old woman spat full upon her.

Estelle dropped her handbag, then stooped clutching for it

as she gazed in disgust and horror at the gobbet of phlegm and saliva beginning to run on her bare arm. Hysterically she screamed "Bitch!" and groped for her handkerchief, found it, a tiny square of fine cambric and Italian lace, blotted the ugly mess on her arm, gazed nauseated at the handkerchief for a moment, then hurled it into the street and tottered off around the corner. She expected something more. But no shouted words followed her. And no laughter.

Her thoughts torrent with rage and revulsion, she did not know how she reached the office, nor come to herself until she stood in the dark downstairs lavatory of Thury's headquarters scrubbing an angry red patch on her arm. But nothing made her feel clean. She stumbled back down the corridor, opened the door of Thury's office without knocking and plunged in. The room was empty. "Auguste!" she cried. "Auguste!"

Thury appeared in the far doorway that led to his apartment. He was erect, jaunty in his uniform, and his expression was smiling and crisp. "Yes, Estelle?" he said. "Good morning. I am working—"

"Auguste! She spat at me!" The words themselves poured out like vomit.

Auguste Thury stared at her. "What are you saying? Who—"

"The woman. The old woman I told you about yesterday. As I passed the corner she—"

Thury made an impatient gesture, then looked at her again and walked toward her across the room, his gait odd, with a slight bounce in it. "My poor Estelle. I am sorry," he said, but she knew his voice, unbelievably, he did not greatly care, he was not concerned. She dropped her eyes, then raised them again incredulously as he stood before her.

"My dear," he said, "sit down. Rest. You have had a shock, you are trembling." He took her arm and tried to propel her toward the deep leather chair in the corner of the room, but she would not move, and he dropped her arm and half turned away.

"What are you going to do?" she said.

"Do?" He turned back toward her. "Why—we must talk of this. Soon. But now you must calm yourself. Later you will tell me exactly what happened, and we will—there will be something—" He broke off with a gesture.

"What are you going to do?"

"Estelle," he said. Was his voice patronizing, pompous? Could it be? "I am very sorry for this, believe me. But if I must say it —I am also very busy, at this moment I can do nothing. You have forgotten that Cécile Aubanne sets out on her mission this morning. In less than two hours. I have yet some things to think of, and I must speak with her once more."

"I see," she said dully, and hearing the defeat in her own voice became enraged again and felt herself flushing red. She began to turn away, but felt his hands on her shoulders, turning her back. She stiffened. Then, as he pulled her toward him, she permitted her head to fall forward woodenly against his shoulder.

"My proud Estelle," his voice said. Did he see at last? His right hand dropped, brushed past her breast, rose again and settled there, moving minutely, tentatively. She was all raw nerve ends; the touch confused her. She closed her eyes. Then she felt his body move slightly away from her, though his shoulder remained firm against her bowed head. She opened her eyes again and found herself staring, empty of thought, at the expanse of carpeted floor between them. Slowly, lightly, his hands left her body and dropped down into the range of her vision; as though with stealth the right hand crossed over and tugged the sleeve back from the other wrist, baring the watch. He was looking at his watch. There was a moment in which she could hear her own breathing, and his. Then, with a positive movement, his hand returned to her breast, and with his other arm he turned her and began to guide her across the floor of the room.

Suddenly she understood. He was taking her to his apartment, he would make love to her, there was, perhaps, just time. And it was this that was to assuage her feelings, reassure her, keep her, for the present, quiet. She wrenched away from him, stepped back and struck him hard across the face.

As she stared at him, his hand stole up mechanically to his blotched cheek. Then he turned, walked through the open door of his apartment and closed it behind him. Estelle sank to the floor and burst into a storm of exhausted weeping.

She did not weep long; the fact that she had been driven to weep at all was so humiliating to her that her tears soon dried of themselves. She got up and walked over to her secretary's desk by the window, sat down and rested her head in her hands. So this was how it was. As with Blanchette. I am glad I know, she said to herself defiantly. It is always better to know.

Again she took the small gold case from her handbag, opened it and looked at herself in her tiny mirror. Then she rose, left the room, walked down the corridor to the lavatory and patted cold water onto her eyes. She dried her face and carefully reapplied her makeup. She felt calmer now, able at last to think what she would do. She returned to the office and sat down once more at her desk.

Love, she thought coldly, for most men a performance, a bedroom charade. How had she not known that Auguste was one of the empty ones? Then sickly she realized: But I knew. I have known for days now, perhaps for weeks. Thury is nothing, frivolous, self-important, not truly serious. In his work he is heedless, neither artist nor artisan, a ringmaster, a politician, interested only in theatrical secrecy, or in shallow display; and if in his work he is this, how could he be more as a man?

Eckhardt had taught her what a real man was; or had confirmed for her something she had already known. A real man is an important man; cannot help being important. Her father had begun it for her, perhaps. How many times, in how many ways, had he said: It means nothing to be the friend of the weak, it is self-aggrandizement, self-deception; men do it to compliment themselves, to seem kind and strong, without having to be so. Or: Never give; exchange. Or again: It is as easy to like an important person as a nobody. (That had been, she recalled, when she had offered her friendship to Thérèse Bouliard; but Thérèse might, after all, have been important, at that stage at least: the daughter of a professor, of one of her own professors at that. She could not have known that in the end Thérèse would accuse her of cheating—for nothing, for an innocent question or two she had asked. . . .) Estelle shook her head. Finally, over and over, her father had said: Stand by the side of the strong. It is they who are real, who do the work of the world.

Well, Auguste, too, might have been important, might have been strong; in the confusion of the past two months how could one have known that words would not become deeds? With Eckhardt there had been no question; but then he had been long established as Gestapo chief in Cherbourg when she had met him, the situation had been different. But what a man he had been—noble in bearing, stern with devotion to his work, and then in love magnificent, everywhere a whole man, with all the force of greatness. If the invasion had not taken place he would have risen, would have gone on to Paris, and she with him, perhaps. But he could not himself, of course, defeat whole armies; and when the Americans and the British and the runaway French had come, he had had to accept interruption, had had to leave.

"Come with me," he had said.

But she had seen the oceans of ships, and had been impressed. She had said, out of an instant certainty and a strength she had known he would understand, "No. I must—stay to protect my parents."

He had shrugged, and smiled. "We do not agree. But if you will stay, then protect yourself. Take the files."

She had gasped. "But—"

"Everything important is in my head. And how can *they* use them? Only against us; and since in the end we shall win, how can they use them against us? Take the paper; unless"—he had laughed—"you wish to be a martyr?"

This was greatness above goodness, and it had robbed her, for a moment, of the ability to think clearly, without emotion. "To whom shall I take the files?" she had asked at last.

He had lifted her chin with his hand and smiled humorously into her eyes. "My little patriot," he had said. "To the glorious French army, of course, returning in triumph to its own land. Later—well, that will arrange itself. Live in the present. Do not be afraid."

"I am not afraid," she had said.

And she had not been. She had found Thury within hours of his arrival in Cherbourg; and had continued with him. She had thought of him at first, perhaps, as Eckhardt's opposite number, and then had ceased to think of Eckhardt, who would not, it was soon apparent, return after all. Auguste had of course desired her; and that too had seemed fitting. With him she had been spared the early annoyances others had encountered—those attacks from the mob, from the spiteful nonentities who had done nothing, had "remained loyal"—as if, she thought, one "remained" anything, as if one did not either act and grow or cringe back and shrivel away. And to think that after all she had been mistaken in Thury, that, even ranged by his side, she must endure humiliation at the hands of the cowardly, the mindless—the old women, the goody-goodies like Thérèse—

She would not soon forget that day when, walking down the street with Eckhardt, she had met Thérèse and, willing to forget how their friendship had ended, had spoken to her. Thérèse had stared at Estelle, at Eckhardt, and then, in pretended horror, with a smug dislike written on her face, had turned away without answering. And others had seen.

Eckhardt, smiling, had put his arm around her. "Ah," he had said lightly, "she does not approve of you, the homely one." They had gone on.

Now Thérèse was behind bars. But she—

She beat her clenched fists softly against the desk, suffused again with the red dye of her shame, her anger. That she was vulnerable—not, as before, merely exposed, but *vulnerable*—was itself a bitter fact; but that she was so because she herself had made a mistake, in overestimating Thury, was hardly to be borne. And she could see now that she had made error after error. He had professed to love her; and she had permitted his love, even counted on it, thinking only, if she had thought about it at all, that Eckhardt had been more, not that Thury was less. Thury had complained of the officiousness of the Americans, of their intervention in matters which ought to be the province of the French; and she had accepted this, not till now perceiving, or confessing to herself, that if Thury were stronger, more able, he would not need to complain of Captain Weiller. And when Thury had begun to frame a case of his own, keeping it secret from Weiller, she had gone along with this, even helped, mistaking for strength in Thury, a gallant defense of principle, what was only, if one had eyes to see, pettiness and outraged vanity. For it was a bad case, ill-prepared, dangerous, probably in the end meaningless. And if it broke badly, if Weiller found out about it—

Suddenly she sat bolt upright in her chair. *If Weiller found out about it—* But of course. She was not without defense, after all. And though she had made one mistake, the gods were on her side; they had given her, as they always gave the strong, another chance.

She went out into the street this time without fear, even without thinking that she might have cause for fear. She ought, perhaps, to have considered more carefully what she would do; but time was running short, Cécile Aubanne would set out now in little more than an hour, and after all the matter was not complicated. One thing was certain; she would have to see Captain Weiller himself. The men who worked with him she did not quite trust, she had caught on their faces, at one time or another, rude looks of dislike or sniggering desire. But this was to be expected: they were nobodies, they could neither understand nor appreciate, if they had real worth they would themselves be officers, in the captain's position or a position like it. Weiller was another matter. He had been always correct, polite to her, even deferential. And once or twice—she had not failed to see nor, agreeably stirred, to know the whole meaning of what she had seen—he had looked at her as a true man looks at a woman.

She had seen, and yet she had been blind. For of course it was Weiller, not Thury, who was Eckhardt's opposite number. Having thrown in her lot with Thury she had continued with him through inertia, no doubt, as much as anything: nothing, till now, had occurred to disprove the logic of her choice; till now there had been nothing to test the value Thury placed upon her. Weiller had looked at her, and deep within she had responded; but ever since she could remember men had desired her, and why should they not? Now, suddenly, everything fell together. She belonged at Weiller's side. His worth would recognize her own; his strength, added to hers, would hold at arm's length the offered menaces of the spiteful and the stupid. Perhaps even his strength alone might do so: it would be good, for a time, to be only a woman, to be protected as a woman. . . .

She crossed a busy street and paused for a moment on the far sidewalk. Of course, she recognized, she could not actually leave Thury, or leave his office; it was not likely that Weiller could employ her formally, and she must have some formal place. Technically, then, she would remain where she was; and in secret she would serve as a link—a far stronger link than now existed—between the two operations. It was absurd that they were not more closely linked already; but it was Thury's vanity that had prevented this. Indeed, what was it but his vanity that kept him in Cherbourg at all? And that was a soap bubble, it might be pricked at any moment. Why had she not seen that Thury, accomplishing so little, might go, but that the Americans would stay? For a long time. For years, assuredly. They had the power; why should they not stay as long as they liked? Thury —she might be free of him sooner even than she had been willing, a moment ago, to hope. . . .

Someone, a workman, suddenly stood across her path, and she looked up with surprise and with a hateful, unwanted catch of fear at her throat. The man grinned at her. He said nothing; but as she lowered her eyes and moved to pass him he too moved and once more blocked her way. He stood so close that she could smell the odor of sweat from his filthy clothes, his unwashed body. She stepped back in sharp disgust. "What do you want?" she said. "Let me alone!"

But again he stepped toward her, and she looked around wildly. She could run, but would not unless she had to. The other workmen—there were perhaps a half dozen, squat, weathered, alien-looking men—had stopped their work and were watching with impassive faces, their shovels and picks held slack in their hands. They would not help. She could hardly distinguish them from the one who— Now he was touching her! He had reached out and taken the stuff of her sleeve between thumb and stubby fingers, and was rubbing it sensuously, as though it were her flesh. She was transfixed with loathing and fear.

Suddenly he spoke, a scramble of gutturals she could not understand, could not even recognize as language. She stared at him, then shook her head sharply and wrenched free. He looked down for a moment at his brown, empty hand, then a cunning smile appeared on his face and he thrust his hand deep into his side pocket, fumbling for something there. His expression changed to one of puzzlement. His tongue, a wild-rose pink against the brown of his face, protruded a little between his dry lips. Then he looked elated, and his hand came out of his pocket clutching a torn, dirty bit of paper. It was a twenty-franc note. He held it out to her, then nodded meaningfully, first at her, then at the door in the wall, a door standing closed in its frame, the house behind it bombed out, open to the sky, the wall open to the street, weeds growing and flowering in the sunlight among the rubble and earth that covered what must once have been a floor. With a moan Estelle raised her clenched fists to her forehead; then she threw back her head and screamed.

She heard a pounding of footsteps and opened her eyes to see an American soldier, a corporal or a sergeant, rounding the corner. "Son of a bitch!" he yelled at the workman. "You! What the hell you doing? Get away from her. Get back to work!"

The workman shrugged and turned away, thrusting the money back in his pocket and stooping slowly to pick up a trowel that lay on the sidewalk. The soldier gave him a shove as he went past, and cursed him. Then he walked up to Estelle.

"Sorry, lady," he said. "They been away from home too long. In fact"—he giggled—"they ain't got no home. You O.K.?"

She nodded wearily, without speaking. The soldier took her by the elbow and guided her through the group of workmen, who stared at them and moved indolently to resume their task.

"Say," said the soldier in a low voice. "You oughtn't to walk around by yourself, you're too good-lookin', an' dressed like that too, somp' might happen." He was holding her arm tightly. "Where you goin'? You want me to walk with you?" He smiled as with a happy foreknowledge of her compliance. "I'll take good care of you."

They had reached the corner. Estelle said, "Thank you. I have only a little way more. I will be all right." The soldier did not let go of her arm. She pulled it free savagely, and turned and walked rapidly away.

Behind her the soldier said, "Well, how d'ya like that?"

She was tired to the point of exhaustion. And she felt defiled. Too much had happened, and would happen. Captain Weiller —he would help her, she was certain of it, but she could not hide from herself, now, the knowledge that she might be subjected to some monstrous, irreparable indignity before he could move to defend her. And if she were—

Suddenly she was angry again, more angry than she had been when the old woman had spat on her, or when Thury had taken her humiliation so lightly, so indifferently. If anything were done to her, someone would pay. Thury—Thury, yes, but it was not enough, what would happen to Thury must already happen, it seemed, and besides, how could Thury be made to suffer as she had suffered? For years she had had to stand alone, to choose, to decide, strong, but paying out of herself all the price of strength; it had not been easy, it is not easy even to be right in the face of disapproval, to endure cruel slights—

Thérèse.

Perhaps, like Thury, Thérèse would in any event pay, now, for what she had done. But I know her, Estelle thought furiously, the innocent one, innocent-seeming; and it is not that the Americans are not competent, but could any man see through her as I do, could anyone who was not in France during these last years? And soon I will have Captain Weiller's support. . . .

Well; all in good time. Wait, Estelle said to herself; wait. But she knew with a cold certainty at last that, strong or not, she had suffered too much for too long. The account would have to be paid. And Thérèse, in one way or another, would pay it.

"Look at that," Carl Dolin growled. "Just *look* at it." He was sprawled in his chair behind the lobby desk, glaring listlessly at the clutter of papers surrounding his typewriter: three or four plump folders, unsteady piles of single sheets, yellow, white and pale blue, and on top of everything a thick wad of crumpled pages evidently retrieved from the wastebasket. The windows on the street shone like clear water with reflected morning light; but where Carl sat there would have been shadow if a floor lamp had not been turned on, trained blazing on the memoranda and reports waiting to be typed. "God damn it," Carl said, "I've even got to retype the kid's interrogation of Thérèse Bouliard—just because old fat-ass got sore and messed it up. Hell, maybe it isn't perfect. But it's the only report we got. Talk about *woman's* work never being done!"

Jim Murchison yawned and stretched, then smiled suddenly, reached across and pinched Carl's cheek. "Why, Carl!" he said. "You know, I never thought about you that way before, but I can see you could be a pretty good-looking secretary if you'd just fix yourself up a little. Harlequin glasses—a bit of lipstick —a touch of rouge on those sallow cheeks—"

"Watch it!" Carl roared. "Take your—" He straightened up violently in his chair, his knee hitting the desk; a pile of papers slid off and scattered, rustling, across the floor. "God damn it to hell! Now look what you made me do!"

"Excuse me," a soft voice said. Carl and Murchison looked up, startled. In the doorway stood Estelle de Sombais. "I knocked," she said, "but you did not hear me. So I came in."

"Yeah, you did, didn't you?" Carl muttered. He gathered the last of the papers from the floor, stacked them on the desk, and went back and sat down.

Murchison, still standing as he had been, smiled formally. "Good morning, Mademoiselle de Sombais," he said. "Can we help you?"

"I—thank you," she said, and then in a rush, "I must see the captain."

"He's not here."

"Not here?" The news seemed to agitate her extraordinarily. Then her face calmed a little. She said, "But I suppose he will be back soon. In a few minutes?"

Murchison shot a guarded glance at Carl. "Well, no," he said. "I don't think he'll be back today—not till late, anyway."

"May I sit down?" Estelle de Sombais asked in a weak voice. She groped to a chair by the door and settled in it, bending forward, not looking at them.

"Of course. I'm sorry. Are you—are you ill, mademoiselle?"

"No, no. I must think." She sighed heavily. "I had something —something important to tell the captain."

"We can do anything he can, lady," Carl said in a loud voice. Murchison made a fierce silencing gesture at him.

Estelle de Sombais looked up doubtfully from one to the other, then looked away. "I—I do not know," she said.

Murchison said, "Mademoiselle, you look tired. Wouldn't you

like a cup of coffee? Carl, there's a pot on the gas ring. Get us all some, will you?"

"Hey, look!" Carl said belligerently. Again Murchison gestured at him. "O.K., O.K.," Carl said, and got up sulkily and left the room. When he was gone Murchison turned again to face Estelle de Sombais.

"Mademoiselle," he said, and there seemed no eagerness in his voice, "it's too bad the captain isn't here. But we're in charge while he's gone, and as Carl said, we'll be very glad indeed to help you. I'm sure we'll be able to."

She did not reply.

"Unless it's something strictly personal?" Murchison went on. "Otherwise—well, you know as well as I do how organizations like this work. The captain does the planning, but he hasn't time to do much about the actual operations, and normally we'd be in on it almost at once, if it's anything like that."

She did not acknowledge what he had said. While minutes passed she sat there silent, bowed forward, her head in her hands. Carl brought in the coffeepot and cups, poured the coffee and set a steaming cup on the floor beside her. At last she picked it up, took a sip, another sip, and then looked up at the two men, her face composed.

"Very well," she said. "But I warn you that there must be the utmost secrecy about what I shall tell you. It must never be known to anyone but you and Captain Weiller that I told. You will understand my position; this is very difficult for me, a terrible thing. But I do it—to protect the American Army."

On Carl's face there was an open, incredulous sneer; but Estelle de Sombais was looking at Murchison now, and he was leaning toward her, his face tense with excitement.

"You may depend upon us, mademoiselle," he breathed. "Go on."

"Cécile Aubanne," she said, "has made wireless contact with the Germans. You were not to know it, but she was an agent of the Sicherheitsdienst. She was to send out political information principally; but now they want other things as well, military identifications, everything. And it was for this reason I came to you. If it was to be a political case only—" She spread her hands in a helpless gesture. "Who am I to judge? But if military information is to be sent—then—then I think—you must know."

Carl said, "Why, that low-down bastard."

Murchison looked at him vaguely, then looked back at Estelle de Sombais. "We are deeply grateful to you, mademoiselle," he said, in a shaken, exultant voice. "But—if we were not to be told —what do you suggest we do?"

"That is why it was important that you know of this today," Estelle said. "Another agent is being sent through the lines to bring Mademoiselle Aubanne money and wireless parts. We expect him this morning. Just before eleven Mademoiselle Aubanne will go to the Parc Emmanuel Liais; unless something has gone wrong, the man will meet her there. She will give him some information, presumably there is too much to transmit, she would dare be on the air only briefly at first, and he will take it, leave her the money and equipment, and go on back through the lines."

Carl said, "But my God, why should he show up this morning? That's quite a trip by now, he might get in all sorts of trouble, even if he finally should make it—"

Estelle smiled thinly. "They say they are sending a very trustworthy man. And if he does not come this morning, Mademoiselle Aubanne will go back tomorrow morning, and the next."

Murchison said thoughtfully, "If he gets here, he'd better not go back."

"That was not how Captain Thury had planned it," Estelle said.

"I see," said Murchison. "Well, if we pick him up, we'll do it quietly, so that Mademoiselle Aubanne doesn't know."

"*We'll* do it," Carl said acridly. "*You'll* do it, I suppose. Or Tochyk. Or even Barker."

Murchison turned to him, smiling. "Want to take it on, Carl?" he asked.

"*Do* I?" said Carl. "D'ya mean it? My God, I'd—"

"Messieurs," Estelle de Sombais said. "Please—be careful. This is out of my hands now. And I must go home. When Captain Weiller returns I will contrive to see him, and to tell him

234

all I know of this. Meanwhile, I am very tired, ill almost—
would one of you escort me? Not all the way, but—"

"Of course," Murchison said. "Look, Carl, I'll run her home
in the closed jeep. You've never seen Aubanne, but you've probably seen the picture of her in the files, look it up again while
I'm gone. Then when I get back you can take off for the park.
You know where it is?"

"Sure," said Carl.

"O.K. Now look. Take it easy, will you? I'll send Tochyk
over a little behind you, with the closed jeep again, and tell him
to follow you at a distance when you leave. He's good at that,
he won't get in the way. You get as careful a look at Aubanne
and the guy who meets her, if he does, as you can without showing yourself. There's a lot of cover in the park, shrubs and stuff,
benches all over, and usually as many GI's in the park as towns-
people. Whatever you do don't scare the guy off; and don't lose
him. When he leaves the park stick to him like invisible glue.
Don't—"

"What if he heads right out of town?" Carl asked.

"Well, you'll have to do what you can about that. Flag
Tochyk maybe, and offer the guy a ride, all innocent-like, and
then haul him back here. Hold a gun on him if you have to.
If he doesn't stick to the roads I don't know what you'll do; but
you'll have to think of something. Don't worry. Most likely he'll
hole up somewhere, and you'll be able to nab him and bring
him in easy. Anyway don't attract attention, or not any more
than you can—"

"Messieurs," said Estelle de Sombais. "Please. Please, take me
home."

"Right," said Murchison. "I'm sorry, mademoiselle. But don't
worry—"

"I do not worry," she said as she rose.

XV.

THE morning colored everything with its brightness. Hedgerows were beaded with cornflowers like cut-out disks of sky, and where there was shadow the dew clung late, breathing freshness into the air. The sun climbed slowly in the east, a cool gold too far away for heat, and in the west a low white bank of retreating fog was a reminder of ocean, of tides too far away for sound.

Even driving the jeep, over roads sometimes cratered and broken, Johnny was singularly at peace. He had slept late; no one had waked him, and though this was perhaps only because Captain Weiller too had slept late, and though the reason for that, if it were true, was obvious, Johnny felt too light of heart to frame in his mind, once more, the implicit reproach. The captain's moral problems could remain his own. And as for the problems they shared—somehow the morning was a comment on those, a profound reassurance that goodness and decency would prevail.

Johnny had had breakfast with Weiller, in a silence that was curiously like the silence of mutual accord, the silence of contentment. When Johnny had asked, at the end of the meal, whether he should go pick up Thérèse, the captain had said that Hudson had already done so, and that the jeep was gassed up and ready to go. As they left the dining room, Weiller laid his hand for a moment on Johnny's shoulder. It seemed to Johnny a gesture less of affection than of absolution. Does he see that we've really split apart? he wondered. Is he telling me that he understands, that he doesn't blame me? But as they stepped out under the bright pallor of the sky, the meaning of the question was broken into by a bird's dipping flight, erased by the smell of earth from a neighboring garden.

They had set out with no further discussion of what was to come at Sartilly. But once, when Weiller's back was turned, Johnny had managed to catch Thérèse's eye, had smiled at her warmly, protectively; and she had responded with a smile so full of dignity and courage that Johnny's last traces of uneasiness had been dispelled. A surprising thought had occurred to him then. Was it possible that in the end he would like both Thérèse and Weiller? Or love Thérèse, take her side, yet understand the captain, learn to suspend judgment of him? It was strange how a fresh morning could cleanse and heighten the spirit. For Johnny himself the weak, chaotic thoughts of the night before were as though they had never been. And Thérèse too, strengthened doubtless by the acknowledgment of what lay between them, had survived the degradation of her night in that filthy cell to face the new day assured, resolved, without fear.

And she's beautiful, Johnny thought with tranquil wonder, stealing a glance at her profile as they drove along. Whatever the night had given her, and this morning, it was all she had needed to make her beautiful. *But you know what's happened to her,* the voice inside him said, and among the fresh and opening fields he found no disquiet in the thought. *You know what's happened to her. It's happened to you too.* It's happening to me too, he said to himself, and felt a stillness and ease of faith enveloping them, isolating them from the two who sat wordless, jammed together on the back seat of the clattering jeep.

Lessay, Coutances, Bréhal, the towns and cities south of La Haye-du-Puits appeared and fell behind them as though on long, deepening waves of golden light. The appearances of war rose on a different pulse, harsher, more rapid and erratic, but even these could not destroy the suspended calm of the morning. An occasional broken building, a caved-in bridge, seemed nothing among the green and tawny fields; a tank overturned in a ditch seemed to carry less meaning than the dusty tiger lilies that straggled up around its ruined bulk. The German sign MINEN lettered in red at the corner of a field surrounded with rolls of barbed wire seemed, almost, a guidepost to a mythical country.

At the fishing port of Granville they touched the coast briefly. Granville, almost undamaged, seemed already to have forgotten the war. They maneuvered through the busy streets and turned inland.

At the far outskirts of the city the road forked. Johnny slowed down and looked questioningly at Thérèse, but she was staring quietly ahead. He braked to a stop and turned in his seat. "Which way here, sir?" he asked.

Weiller said to Hudson, "What's the pitch? You been down here before?"

"Doesn't too much matter," Hudson answered. "The right-hand road swings around to the coast again, and down a way you can see Mont-Saint-Michel, if you're interested. Then we could cut back in to Sartilly."

"Which way's shorter?"

"Well, the other road's direct."

"Take the left," Weiller said.

Johnny obeyed.

When they were on their way again Weiller said, "I'd like to see that Mont-Saint-Michel sometime, though. Maybe when the war's over." Suddenly he chuckled. "Or this afternoon on our way back. Part of the war'll be over then. Mademoiselle Bouliard?" He leaned over and spoke to Thérèse in a loud voice. "You'll have to direct us when we get close."

The girl nodded calmly, without looking around. But as he drove on Johnny felt a tenseness in her which had not been there before, and his own confidence, already attacked by Weiller's callous words, began precipitately to ebb. The peace of the morning had been an illusion, after all. In only a little while now the ordeal would begin again. Thérèse's ordeal. . . . Poor kid. But perhaps today would end it; and not as the captain supposed. If Thérèse survived— She must survive. With his help, she would. But Weiller's composure, his earlier placidity —why had Johnny ever trusted it? What would the man do? What had he planned before Johnny woke, what had he planned as Johnny drove through the still summer morning? What was he thinking now?

"Turn left here," Thérèse said, in a voice so low that Johnny could scarcely hear her.

The road had been good, and Johnny, lost in uneasy reverie, had been bowling along more rapidly than he had intended.

Now he braked hard and, with tires protesting, swung left into a narrow dirt lane bordered with high hedgerows. A team of horses coming toward him shied violently, backed, then bolted through an opening in the hedge, half dragging the shouting, cursing man who held the reins.

"Say, take it easy, son," Weiller remarked mildly. To Thérèse he said, "D'you know that man? Who was it?"

"That—was my uncle," she said. "M'sieur Corrail."

"Did he see you?"

"I do not know."

"Well, I guess it doesn't matter," the captain said. "If he did he'll probably come high-tailing it to the house. But we can take care of him. Naturally I'll want to talk to your aunt and uncle separately. Where do we go now?"

"The farm buildings are less than half a kilometer along this road, m'sieur, on the right."

There was no more time. Johnny, driving now as slowly as he dared, tried to will strength into Thérèse, tried to tell her without speaking that she could count on him, that she had nothing to fear. But he knew deeply that the unspoken words did not carry; that they were cut off by his own increasing fear. Weiller, quite evidently, had it all figured out.

In a few moments the hedgerows disappeared, and fields and pastures, high and rolling, opened out at either side of the road. There was a steep knoll ahead, crowned with dwarf oaks. As they passed it Thérèse said tonelessly, "Here."

Johnny pulled into the dirt courtyard before a shallow, U-shaped stone building. A flock of chickens scattered, squawking, in front of the jeep, and continued to squawk and to dash frantically about the enclosure for what seemed minutes after the jeep had stopped. The dead air smelled of feathers, of dust and manure. For the first time that day the sun's rays, reflected from the stone of the buildings, beat heavily upon them. Johnny felt sweat beginning to moisten his forehead.

"Well, I guess this is it," Captain Weiller said contentedly, and climbed down out of the jeep.

As the captain approached the farmhouse door it opened, and a woman stood in the entry. She was short and dark, solidly built;

her black hair, streaked with gray, was drawn back tightly from her broad face and gathered in a hard knot at the back of her head. She seemed at once to be staring at Weiller, at the occupants of the jeep, and at nothing; and though she must have seen Thérèse, her features betrayed no sign of recognition. At the doorstep the captain paused. The woman neither moved nor spoke; only once her eyes dropped to the holster at the captain's belt, then returned, expressionless, to his face.

Weiller called back over his shoulder, "Well, what are you waiting for? Come ahead."

The girl swung her legs over the side of the jeep and dropped to the ground. Johnny followed, and Hudson brought up the rear. They walked slowly; it was as though, Johnny thought, they were all guilty children expecting punishment. He squared his shoulders and looked up to see the captain watching him, grinning at him without humor.

When they had gathered at the door Weiller said sharply to the woman, "Madame Corrail? We wish to come in, please."

Still she stood without moving. She was staring now at Thérèse, and as she stared her features settled into an expression of indignation. Thérèse said, "Tante Rose—"

The captain turned on her. "One thing I should have made clear, Mademoiselle Bouliard. You are not to speak, down here, unless I tell you to speak. Unless *I* tell you—not my assistants, and not your aunt. Do you understand?"

The girl nodded and turned away.

Weiller said, "Green, will you get us into this dump? We're wasting time."

Hudson spoke to Mme. Corrail. After a moment she stood heavily aside, and the four filed past her into the dark interior of the house.

"We'd better go somewhere where we can sit down for a minute," the captain said.

When the message had been relayed to her, the woman hesitated a moment, then led them into a shuttered room, a parlor evidently little used. The captain strode across the room and folded back the shutters of one window, exposing an interior furnished so ponderously, in such dark and ugly masses, that the light admitted seemed more threatened by shadow than the

others. They sold nothing on the black market; everyone in Sartilly would vouch for their strict honesty—though of course they were very poor, and when the burden of supporting lazy and ungrateful relatives had been thrown upon them, life had become difficult. . . .

The spate of words unsettled Johnny. Wanting, indignantly, to defend Thérèse, yet knowing that even if he had known how, this was not the place to do so, Johnny found himself torn, undecided, unable to think in advance of new questions; found himself instead waiting rigidly for Mme. Corrail's reaction to the last question, listening in repelled fascination to the grating of her voice. The now-familiar routine of double question, double answer, which should have afforded him some respite, gave him none.

Hudson was saying, in an impersonal voice, "A girl who thought herself too fine to work in the barnyard, how would she know . . . ?"

It was all wrong, Johnny thought in revulsion; and it was all useless—wounding, and useless.

Or perhaps not quite useless.

It was true that new facts were not appearing, except for that information about the mortgage; and what did that prove? And doubtless no relevant facts could appear as long as Johnny went on—well, provoking Mme. Corrail. He couldn't do much else, with as little tangible information about her as he had. But he had thought at least, in questioning the aunt, to spare Thérèse. Sparing her in one way, however, he had exposed her in another. And perhaps the captain had known that that would happen. Perhaps he had so maneuvered it that Johnny could not avoid seeming to attack Thérèse, directly or indirectly.

Johnny glanced at the girl in dread. She was staring at him with an expression of embarrassment and fear on her face.

Neat, neat, Johnny admitted savagely to himself. He was in the trap all right, more inextricably caught than he had imagined. Weiller hadn't been able to shake Johnny's faith in the girl, so he was solving the problem from the other end, by making Thérèse feel that Johnny had gone back on her.

And of course that was "the trick." Doubtless it was the only trick there was—which would account, too, for the captain's not being willing to tell Johnny about it. Even now perhaps Weiller was standing outside the door; and when he felt that Thérèse was completely demoralized, thoroughly convinced that even Johnny was against her (since why else would he systematically expose her to her aunt's vengeful tirades?), Weiller would simply come in and take over the interrogation, hoping that Thérèse would no longer care enough to resist, would confess anything just to have the torment over with.

Would the trick succeed?

The room had been in silence for long minutes. Hudson must realize that Johnny had lost his way; Mme. Corrail must think she had won; Thérèse must think—

But how could he help it? What could he do?

Change to the other kind of questioning, the specific kind which he had so far—to protect Thérèse!—avoided.

Or could he risk bawling out Mme. Corrail, to show Thérèse that he hadn't wanted the answers he'd been getting, that he was still on her side? Even if the captain was in the hall; even if he might hear—

Johnny turned in angry decision to the farm woman. "Madame Corrail," he said icily, "like all your kind, you've been trying to—to shift blame away from yourself by accusing others. Now I want no more of it. If I wish to question Mademoiselle Bouliard I can do so. Until I wish to do so I will ask you to answer my questions without making irrelevant charges, against her or against anyone else. Do you understand?"

Once more Hudson looked at Johnny in surprise. But before he could translate the outburst there was a sharp movement from Thérèse's chair. The two men turned to look at her. She was gazing at Johnny firmly, her eyes dark.

"M'sieur," she said, "may I speak?"

"Why—why yes," Johnny said.

"Why is it that you accuse my aunt? So that of course she believes that I must have accused her first; what else could she think? And yet I told you nothing against her—" Thérèse's voice broke. "Not like this; not that she had done anything to harm your country, or her own. And you could know nothing about her except what you learned from me. What is it that you want? Have you nothing to do, any of you, but sow bitterness, nothing to do but hunt out and destroy those who have not harmed you, who cannot protect themselves against you . . . ?"

Johnny looked at her appalled. Didn't she understand? Didn't she see that he was, precisely, trying to protect her?

But there was no way to explain; not unless he could speak to her alone, and he could not. The captain had won. Thérèse no longer trusted him.

But surely she could have given him, a little, the benefit of the doubt, he had tried so hard to help her, in every way he could think of.

He began, his voice gruff, "Mademoiselle—" But nothing followed. He would not reprove her. He felt as though there were a heavy weight upon him, pressing him back, back, into his chair. Why didn't the captain come in and take his lousy victory?

But there was no sound at the door, no movement in the room. Johnny glanced around wearily. The heavy clumps of furniture, the shadowed faces, questioning, angry, bored, seemed to be closing in on him. It was still up to him to speak; his part in the incomprehensible scene had not ended, perhaps would never end. . . .

There was one definite question, at any rate, that was to be asked, and he remembered it, plucked it out of the churning chaos of his thoughts, almost without recalling why, or to whom, it was important. "Madame Corrail," Johnny said, "Monsieur Bouliard visited you and your husband this spring —how many times?"

Hudson translated the question, and Mme. Corrail answered it contemptuously. Hudson said in a smooth voice, "You would not have needed to come to Sartilly to find that out. The girl could have told you. He came only once, in May. She came with him. She returned again, alone, after the invasion."

Johnny remembered now what the question meant and he knew that he should look at Thérèse, but he could not, did not want to, it did not matter. . . . He said, "What did they do here during their visit in May?"

Again Hudson translated the question.

But before it could be answered the door was flung open and Captain Weiller walked into the room. Johnny stared at him dully. He was looking as he always did—big, brisk, efficient, neatly uniformed. He was carrying what seemed to be a narrow black leatherette suitcase.

Johnny turned to look at Mme. Corrail. The aunt's face betrayed nothing but curiosity. But Thérèse was rising slowly from her chair.

"I—I did not think anyone could find it," she whispered.

In the captain's smile there was relief, and then triumph, a vast and growing delight. "I daresay you were right," he said. "This is the extra transmitter Korvac was supposed to take through the lines to your father. I brought it along from La Haye-du-Puits. The one you hid—" He laughed out loud. "Well, suppose you show us, now, where it is."

"No," Thérèse said.

And then, "Yes. If you wish."

XVI.

STANDING in the north entrance to the walled park, Carl Dolin joyfully patted his forty-five, which had slept in its holster almost since the day it had been issued to him. Then he looked around with exaggerated nonchalance and began to stroll down the dirt path, partly bordered with evergreens, that encircled the lawn, the flower beds, and the central pond.

He wasn't the only GI here; good. He could see a few others lying here and there on the grass, one or two sitting on benches. An old woman with a basket was standing near one group, trying to sell the guys something, it looked like. Over under a big tree a man and a woman were stretched out, necking for all they were worth. Jesus, would they be the ones he was looking for? Carl wondered, and then thought, giggling to himself, Well, no. Aubanne and her imported stooge were probably pretty hard up, but it would take them a few minutes, at least, to get to know each other that well.

He wandered idly for a time, seeming to examine with pleasure the late midsummer flowers, to revel in the peace of the park. Then, behind a thin screen of branches, he caught sight of a woman sitting alone, on a bench at a little distance from the path, with no trees or bushes nearby. She was a big woman with a heavy, white face, a face foreshortened and empty. Aubanne, all right. He drew in his breath excitedly. Jesus, what a game—to be here, knowing what was happening, when to most everybody else around it was just an ordinary day, with ordinary people— He looked behind him swiftly, saw no one, and breathed a sigh of relief. He'd better walk along; the guy might come in at any time, look the situation over, see him rubbering, and just plain get out.

Christ, what a fool Thury must be. Here Aubanne had lived in this city for years, Thury'd had her in the jug for anyway a month; and now he'd started letting her out to prowl around town as if nothing had happened, had let her come to this public place to meet another German spy, when anyone she bumped into might know who she was and start asking questions, might notify the police or even the Germans, if there was any way of doing it. Cherbourg must still be lousy with German sympathizers, some of them in too deep to pull out, or even to want to pull out.

Of course, the really dumb thing had been to keep Aubanne locked up and then put her on the air, when everyone in town must know what had happened to her. Suppose the Germans had another agent around, reporting on everything, including people like Aubanne? What a neat job that would be—to be working two agents in the same area, one uncontrolled and one you knew was controlled, so you could compare the stuff they sent you. You could learn a hell of a lot that way—unless, of course, the controlled case was so stupidly handled that no sense could be made out of it at all. A case of Thury's might work out like that, all right, especially when he was trying to run it secretly, without getting his messages cleared. The jerk. Couldn't he see the damage he might do?

Well, maybe the Germans *didn't* know that Aubanne was controlled; would they risk sending another agent through to her, if they knew they were sending him into a trap? Could be; they probably didn't give a goddam about anyone they sent out, or else would risk anything at this point—and anyway they might figure that in a controlled case a linecrosser would have an extra good chance of getting through, would be treated like royalty in disguise, just to build up the case, and so maybe get them to send a lot more bodies through, if it was as easy as all that. . . . Pretty complicated. And a hell of a lot of fun, by God. Though he didn't know but what all these bastards oughtn't to be machine-gunned, what good did it do to play around with them?

The path swept in a wide semicircle around the bench where Cécile Aubanne sat; Carl followed it, and found no place where he could conceal himself to listen in, in case she should start talking to somebody. Well, Thury might be dumb, but she was smart enough, he'd have to give her that. He'd sneaked a look at her once or twice, and had seen that she was pretending to take a nap there on the bench, lying back in the sunlight. How was the linecrosser supposed to recognize her? he wondered. Some way she was dressed? Or by this asleep gag? Still anyone, anyone who had the time to go to a park in the first place, might fall asleep on a bench.

He settled down on the grass under a funny-looking tree where, through a flower bed, through the tall stalks of lilies gone to seed, he could just see Aubanne, but not especially be noticed himself. He pulled a stalk of grass, started chewing the soft end, and looked around. Let's put the show on the road, he said to himself impatiently. This is better than typing that damn report over, but it could get real dull. Then he groaned, remembering: the guy might not even show up today. Or to-morrow. Carl might have to come back here day after day, he might be sending his grandchildren—

There was a man lying on the grass over by the pond. Carl had noticed him before, but had paid no attention; he'd looked like a GI. Now Carl could see that the uniform was mismatched, something was funny about it, color or something—the pants were British, that was it. With half the local population wearing army castoffs you couldn't tell who the hell was who these days till you got real close. The man was sprawled out on his belly; there was a thin sheet of newspaper under his head, and under the newspaper—well, there must be something, because the man's head was raised as if he had a pillow.

Slowly, as Carl watched, the man lifted himself up, pulled his knees under him and squatted back, shaking his head and yawning. Then he folded up the newspaper and stuffed it in his pocket. On the grass where the paper had been lay a package wrapped in butcher's paper and heavily tied. Two packages, a big one and a little one. The man picked them up, got to his feet, and as though aimlessly wandered over to the bench where Aubanne was sitting. He put the big package between them, sat down, opened the smaller package, took out a sandwich and began eating.

Carl's heart was pounding. Well, I'll be god damned, he said to himself. This is it. It's really happening. If this was the wrong guy she'd get up and go, wouldn't she? 'Course she wouldn't necessarily know, herself, not right away. She hadn't moved since the man had sat down; she seemed still to be asleep. The man continued to eat, looking around vaguely as though unaware of her or anyone or anything else. Still he could be pretending to eat, couldn't he, and really be talking instead? He was being slow enough getting through the sandwich; that was for sure. He was a young guy, hard-faced, but very good-looking—handsomer than most of these Frenchmen. Well, what the hell did I expect, Carl asked himself—Dracula?

Lying still, his chin on his hands, his eyes half closed, he watched the two closely, covertly, for any sign of communication, any telltale movement. But there was none. Gradually he became aware that he was uncomfortable, lying too stiffly, that a twig was pressing sharply into his wrist, an ant or something crawling on his neck. He wanted to shift position, to brush the insect off—or was there one there at all, was it a drop of sweat? the sun was pretty hot—but if he moved they might notice him. Shit. Probably the guy wasn't anyone at all, just some local yokel. But the package? Hell, anyone could carry a package, at least he supposed they could. Not a damn thing was happening; nothing was going to happen. He might as well have stayed home and tried to figure out some way to make de Sombais. Carl thought about de Sombais for awhile, then shifted at last, cautiously and uncomfortably. Now, *there* was a good-looking piece—if it wasn't reserved for officers, which it probably was, like everything else in this goddam town.

The man took out a second sandwich, opened it, took out the meat, or cheese, or whatever was in it, and stuffed it into his mouth. Then he looked at the two pieces of bread in his hand and looked around as if trying to find some place to throw them. He put them down on the bench for a moment, then fumblingly picked them up, put them together carefully and dropped them back into his paper parcel. Cécile Aubanne groaned, as though in sleep, and rolled away from the man, sitting with her back to him now, her head resting on her right arm. The man folded up his food parcel, shoved it into his side pocket and rose to his feet. Without looking back at the woman he strolled away. But he had left the big package on the bench beside her.

Without thinking Carl leaped to his feet. Then realization struck him and he dropped to his knees again, cursing himself silently and praying that Aubanne had not seen him. He stole a furtive glance at her. She was still turned away, her head pillowed on her arm. God! He might have blown the whole thing then. For of course she did not know that she was being watched any more than the man did. And must not know, or she would tell Thury, and if Thury suspected—

Well, anyway it was O.K. Carl gazed with longing curiosity at the package. A goddam shame he couldn't just pick it up. What was in it? Money? Radio parts? What Weiller wouldn't give to get his hands on that stuff! But they'd have to wait till Thury turned it over to them of his own accord—*if* he did, the sneaky bastard.

Now where was Dracula—Adonis, rather? Regretfully, Carl turned back to look for the linecrosser. He was nowhere to be seen.

His heart in his throat, Carl got to his feet again and walked as casually as he could across the grass and through the screen of trees to the path that encircled the park. Then, trying not to run, he headed for the north entrance. If the guy was hiding somewhere, watching him— But there was no reason why he should suspect anything. More likely he was just getting the hell out, heading for the tall timber. And now he had a head start. But of course he'd have had to be given one anyway. And he wouldn't dare go too fast; he'd be trying not to attract attention.

A bunch of GI's was blocking the narrow entry to the park. Carl came up short against them. He stood impatiently for a moment, expecting that they would let him through, but they were bent in absorption over a tiny photograph and did not move. Carl caught a glimpse of a nude figure on the print. The boy looking over the shoulder of the GI who was holding the photograph said in a soft, hushed drawl, "Christ amighty, that's a *nigra.* An' you see what he's doin'? Mean to say in this fuckin' country they'd let a *nigra* do that to a—"

For the fraction of a second curiosity almost got the better of Carl. But time was passing, and where was the linecrosser now? "One side, fellas," Carl said. "No kidding, I'm in a hurry." He pushed through.

"Hey, watch it," one of them called after him in an injured voice. "You got no respect for art?"

"Mus' be a No'thener," the soft-voiced boy said. "They got no sense, nothin'."

Some other time, boy, Carl said to himself. I'll fight the Civil War with you, and by God I'll win, too. Just now you couldn't be righter. I got no sense. Where the hell *is* that guy? If I've lost him—

If he'd lost him, it was all over, there'd never be another chance. And it wouldn't make any difference what his excuse was. Outside the park walls he stood squinting into the harsh sunlight. The green of the park had muted the sun a little; here it beat down intolerably on sidewalk and street, as metallic almost as the stream of jeep and truck traffic that poured on past, or slowed at the corner of the Aviation Maritime opposite to turn on up, with a grinding of gears, to the waterfront. The sidewalks were crowded, but the suntans of the Navy, present in strength in this part of town, he did not even need to look at, and the civilians dressed as civilians he could ignore also. Among the khaki-clad figures he searched for one with no cap, and with dark, wavy hair. But as far as he could see, west, north and east, there was no one who could be the linecrosser.

A dismay, a sickness of failure, was washing through him when suddenly, across and a little way down the street, he caught sight of the closed jeep. Thank God. That would be Tochyk, old Antie. Antie would have been watching; anyone who'd come out of the park he would have seen, and he'd know what direction they'd gone off in. Carl turned to sprint to the crosswalk and bumped head on into a man wheeling a bicycle out of the entrance to the park. It was the linecrosser.

Oh Jesus, Carl thought as he went down, sprawling across the bicycle, oh Jesus, a fine way to keep out of sight, a fine way to follow somebody. The man had managed to let go of the bicycle, to step aside as it went down, and Carl, tangled in wheels and pedals and handlebars, his skinned hands raw and smarting on the cement, his shins and body aching, could see, as he slowly raised his head, the man's feet and lower legs a few inches from his eyes. With difficulty he restrained an impulse to reach out and grab the guy, and yell for help—no, get into an argument with him, pretend he was going to lead him off to the cops, or the MP's—no, for God's sake, there'd be a fuss about that, he could see other people stopping already, and maybe Aubanne would come out of the park and see him, if she didn't know who he was now she'd likely know sooner or later, he had to let the guy get away quick—but a *bicycle*, it was the thing they hadn't thought of, how could he follow, on foot, a man who had a bicycle? Could he wreck it now without being noticed, had he, pray God, wrecked it somehow when he'd fallen on it? He felt arms around his chest, someone lifting him, and in a moment was standing up on the sidewalk again, facing the linecrosser.

"I'm sorry," he mumbled. *"Pardon."*

Someone behind Carl put a hand on his shoulder and said, "Say, you hurt, buddy?" but Carl shook his head and shrugged off the hand. He wanted to turn away, to get the hell out, but that was not natural either, and he did not know what to do. The linecrosser was staring at him closely, without expression, as though cataloguing and memorizing details.

Carl said, with a feeble attempt at anger, "What the . . . ?"

The man dropped his gaze then, and stooped and picked up his bicycle. Straightening up, he rolled it backward and forward a little on its wheels. It was undamaged. He looked up at Carl once more, and said in a cold, rusty voice, *"C'est ma faute."* Then, quickly, he wheeled the bicycle to the curb, mounted it and rode off down the street. At the first corner he turned south, and at once disappeared from sight.

The voice behind Carl breathed, "Well, I'll be god damned. The lousy Frogs. You'd think they—"

"Think they owned the place, wouldn't you?" another voice said, and laughed.

"Ah, shut up," the first voice said.

Suddenly Carl moved into action. Watching for a slight break in the traffic, he darted across the street, ran to the closed jeep and jerked the door open. "Move over, Antie," he said.

"My name's Anton," Tochyk said in a sulky voice. He slid over to the other seat, and Carl climbed in behind the wheel and started the motor.

"Listen," he said breathlessly. "That was him, the guy on the bike, did you see him? Anyway I can't follow him on foot. He went down that street there, it's a long son of a bitch, and 'course I don't know whether he's going to turn off or not. But—" He saw his chance, slewed around in a U-turn, and pulled off onto the Rue Emmanuel Liais. As he straightened the wheel he said, "I'll take her as long as we're safe to follow like this. Then if he looks like stopping, or if he gets off onto a side street where there's no other traffic, so he'd see us following him, I'll get out and do the best I can to tail him on foot, and you'll just have to keep track of me the best way you can without getting in the way till I need you. Got it?"

Tochyk snorted. "Sure I got it. You think I never done nothing like this before?"

"Don't get sore, Antie." Carl grinned. "I forgot you was Perry Mason in private life."

But talking about getting sore reminded him of his barked shins and the bruises on his chest; the grin faded from his face. He *was* sore, damn it; he was sore all over. His hands ached on the wheel. And he felt as if he might start getting stiff pretty soon. He hoped this chase didn't go on too long, and that there didn't have to be any rough stuff at the end of it; he might not be in too good shape for that.

He peered anxiously down the street ahead. There was not as much military traffic here as on the Rue de l'Abbaye, but still enough to be confusing. He could see only two or three cyclists. The one farthest— No; none of them was his man. Jesus. That was one way not to have too long a chase—to lose the guy you were following.

In discouragement he slowed a little; and suddenly, pulled in beyond a jeep parked at the curb, he saw the linecrosser. The man was standing at the edge of the sidewalk, staring back in the direction from which he had come. Christ, does he know he's being followed? Carl thought. As the closed jeep came abreast, the man's eyes swung around to look at it. He can't see us in here, he can't, Carl said to himself, but on an impulse, to seem to have other business, he swung left into the next side street. There was a scream of brakes behind him, followed by a shout of rage; he'd pulled right across the path of a six-by-six. Oh, great, Carl thought, shaking; the least noticeable guy in Cherbourg, that's me. To Tochyk he said nervously, "We're kind of stuck. There isn't another jeep on the street that looks like this one."

"You keep on driving the way you are," Tochyk said moodily, "and the jeep won't look this way long."

As he drove Carl watched, in the rearview mirror, the street off which he had just turned. But he saw no sign of the man he was supposed to be following. And he dared not park; if by a miracle he had escaped identification as the man's pursuer, or possible pursuer, to stop in the side street now would give him dead away. He kept on driving, feeling a growing tension that was almost fear, as though a cord were stretched out behind him, pulling tighter and tighter until suddenly it would snap, leaving him loose, aimless, and a failure.

"Where you goin'?" Tochyk asked. "That was him, wasn't it?"

"Yeah. He didn't look like he wanted an escort, though."

Now what, Carl asked himself; now what? He was coming to the end of the block; should he turn right or left? He turned left. He had to get back to the Rue Emmanuel Liais. This way he'd have a chance of seeing the guy if he'd doubled back; if he'd gone ahead they could speed up and probably catch sight of him again. And let him catch sight of us, Carl thought miserably. How the hell do people do this kind of thing when they know how?

Suddenly Carl made a decision. The hell with whether the linecrosser knew he was being followed or not. If he knew, he'd be more watchful, and maybe more dangerous (did he have a gun? Carl wondered)—but he had to go somewhere, and he wouldn't be wanting to call attention to himself, he probably wouldn't dare ask anybody for help, and if they got right on his tail and stayed there maybe he'd lose his nerve, maybe they could herd him into a quiet back street and pick him up right off the sidewalk. If anybody saw the arrest—well, it would be crummy security, but they could always *tell* Weiller that nobody'd been around, and hope for the best. Would Tochyk go along with him on that? he wondered. Christ, maybe it was a lousy idea; but what the hell else was he supposed to do, play it so cozy that the guy got away?

He swung left again at the next corner, speeded up, and in a moment was back at the Rue Emmanuel Liais. Quickly he scanned the street. A girl on a bicycle was pedaling slowly in the direction of the harbor, the direction from which they had come; there was no one else. Looking south, Carl could see the parked jeep, but the linecrosser seemed to be gone. O.K., Carl said to himself. He pulled out into the street again and drove along rapidly, peering ahead to look for the bicycle and its rider. One good thing; the shops and houses along here were all built out flush with the sidewalk, and were joined to one another. A guy on foot might hide for a minute or so in an entryway, but a guy with a bicycle could only get away down a side street. I haven't lost you yet, brother, Carl said to himself.

At each successive intersection Carl pulled up for a moment and scanned the angled cross streets rapidly. It was the noon hour by now, fortunately, and not many people were around. At the end of the Rue Emmanuel Liais Carl hesitated, glanced briefly down the Rue Guillaume Fouace and, to the left, down the broad, almost deserted Rue Gambetta, then on an impulse crossed the square and turned half-right down the Rue Émile Zola. The Rue Gambetta would have taken the linecrosser over to the quais, and to the main artery of traffic leaving Cherbourg; but would the guy know that? He must have come in from this other direction, Carl thought; if he's trying to get out he may try the same way. Otherwise—well, if he really knows this town he probably knows it better than I do, and I'm sunk anyway. I'll just have to take a chance.

"Hey, look," Tochyk said.

Hastily Carl focused again on the street in front of him. There at the curb was a bicycle. And in the doorway of a small, dingy café across the sidewalk from it stood the linecrosser. He was looking at the jeep with a still, unreadable stare. Then he turned, entered the café and closed the door behind him.

As he drove past, Carl caught a quick glimpse of a dirty, fly-specked window with the legend CAFÉ-BUVETTE arched across it in white enameled letters, and a peeling advertisement for Byrrh stuck over at one side. Momentum carried him to the end of the block. He rounded the corner with a faint squealing of tires, pulled the jeep in to the curb and stopped.

Again, he thought heavily. By God, he's done it again, he's bitched me up. How does he always know how to do that, to do what I don't expect him to? Turning to Tochyk, Carl said in a voice he could not keep from sounding angry, sarcastic, "O.K., Bright Eyes. It's your ball."

"How do you mean?" Tochyk asked warily.

"Well, what the hell do we do now, sit here and wait for him to come out and ask us for a lift back to headquarters? We can't go in there after him."

"Why not?"

"Because we're not supposed to arrest him in front of anybody, that's why not. How do we know who he is? He may be their long-lost son or somebody. Maybe they got a direct wire to Berlin to tell Adolf how his curly-headed spy is doing. Anyhow they might talk all over town about how somebody got arrested in their place, and the wrong person might hear about it and put two and two together. I don't know. Hell. With Weiller gone we don't even know what we're supposed to be doing, for Christ's sake." Carl sighed wearily. "So I was just asking you. You got any good ideas? I sure haven't."

Tochyk considered for a moment. "I might have an idea," he said.

"Well, spill it, will you? Wait." Carl opened the door of the jeep, climbed out and walked cautiously back to the corner, with Tochyk following. "Bicycle's still there. I thought he might just have been trying to ditch us, he might have walked in there and walked right out again." Carl sighed again, nervously. "Jesus. I can't even figure out if he knows we're after him. Well anyway. What's your idea?"

Tochyk shook his head sadly. "I guess it ain't any good. He seen you back there, pretty close, he'd figure somp'm was up if he seen you again."

Carl said, "I decided I don't care if he knows I'm after him, just so nobody else knows. What you got on your mind?"

Tochyk brightened visibly. "Well, why don't we just go in there ourselves? You know, like we wanted a drink. We could order a bottle of Calvados, and just sit there and wait him out."

"Places like that are off limits to us, you know that." Carl considered. "Everybody would think it was funny we were in there. They might not even serve us, and then we'd have to leave anyway. All we'd do is just warn the guy—if he isn't suspicious already."

"Aw, they'd serve us," Tochyk protested. "I been in lots of places with Josie, and they figure it's your own funeral if you get caught."

"They could get closed up."

"Look, you can see as well as I can. There ain't no MP's around. Why don't we just go on in?" Tochyk paused. "I'm kind of thirsty," he said shamefacedly. "It's hot."

Carl said, "Suppose there's more than one way out of that joint. You think there could be?"

Tochyk frowned. "Well, yeah, I guess," he said. "Usually there's a can out back, or in a little dump like this maybe only a wall to pee on, back of the house."

"So he could pretend to have to take a leak, and get out into the backyard, and just take off from there."

"He could *really* have to take a leak," Tochyk objected.

Carl looked at him incredulously, then burst out laughing. "Perry Mason!" he gasped when he was able to speak again.

"No, but look," Tochyk said, in an injured voice. "Supposing he was just going to go out there, and come back. We'd look pretty funny, wouldn't we, following a guy to the can and back?"

Carl giggled. "You could go," he said. "You could tell him how much you love Josie, back there, so he wouldn't get the wrong idea about you."

Tochyk reddened. "You shut up," he said. "You ain't funny."

"We're wasting time," Carl said. "Look. I've got it now. He hasn't seen you, so you go on in the place like you said. Order a drink. Wait him out. If he leaves by the front way you give him a half a minute and then leave too, and follow him in the jeep. If he goes out back you go too, and crowd him—give him the idea you're after him so he'll take off. I'll go around to the other side of the block and wait for him; I got a hunch he'll try to get away that way anyway. If you can start him running, go on back through the front of the place, so's the others won't get suspicious, and come on around and join me. The other way, if you have to follow him again in the jeep, I'll hear the motor starting and come running and pile in with you. I'll be close enough for that, I hope. You got it all O.K.? I got a feeling we're going to get him this time." He clapped Tochyk on the shoulder.

"I'm all set," Tochyk said. "See you." He ambled off toward the café.

Left alone, Carl began to walk on down, past the jeep, toward the far corner of the block. For a moment he was conscious only of satisfaction. Then suddenly he felt the slow crawling in his guts, the tightening, and it almost made him stop. What the hell, he thought, am I scared?— You're damned right I am. And why not?

Only a few hundred yards separated him, now, from a man who knew, or would know within a minute or so, that his enemies were closing in on him. A French Nazi. A dangerous man, probably half crazy too, a guy who'd probably like nothing better than to knock off a few Americans if only he could get away with it. And Carl was alone. There was nobody on the street back here, that was the way it was supposed to be, but it didn't make it any better. Security. Whose security, for God's sake? Carl was alone, and somewhere behind these walls, perhaps coming toward him now, was a man who'd kill him sooner than not.

And what am I in it for? Carl asked himself angrily. So Weiller can take the credit for it, so he can play funny games with Thury. I'm a fine sap. Weiller, what's he doing? He's off tooting around France in a jeep, trying to pin something on a poor dame who couldn't and wouldn't hurt anyone, and here I am fixing to get myself shot to put him in good with G-2. No, no, *he* doesn't want me to get shot; I won't be so much use that way. All he'd want is for me to truss this guy up like a Thanksgiving turkey—real easy, no strain at all—and cart him back to headquarters safe and sound, nobody hurt, especially not the spy, *he's* too valuable, he's got to be asked a lot of questions— At the thought that he himself had asked Murchison for this assignment Carl could have vomited. A fine sap I am, he said to himself again. Sure I was bored sitting at that goddam typewriter. But I'd rather be bored than dead.

As he neared the corner Carl heard the clear sound of running footsteps, and stopped, his heart in his mouth. Is he coming this way? he asked himself. He edged over to the wall and flattened himself against it. The sound of footsteps had died away. Hardly breathing, he inched along the wall until he got to the corner. As soon as he could summon up his courage to do so he peered around it. The stone-paved street, high-walled on both sides, was empty.

It was a long block, Carl saw; whoever had been running could not have reached the other end. The guy must just have run across, then. In the wall opposite, about halfway down the block, there was a brick archway, and in the opening, white-washed like the wall but only waist high, stood a gate. Carl gazed at it in fascination. It would be easy to get through there, he thought; it was the only place he could see where it would be easy. I bet you're in there, you son of a bitch. And I bet you don't know where I am.

Should he wait for Tochyk? But God only knew how long it would take Tochyk to get there, and meanwhile the guy might climb another wall, and another, they'd lose him for sure. Carl was ashamed, now, of his fear of a moment before. I can handle you, you bastard, he said to himself. I'm as big as you are, and if you got a gun, by God, you're not the only one.

Swiftly and quietly he crossed the street and turned down toward the low gateway. He'd be better off here than on the other side of the street; if the guy was watching over the wall he'd see him quicker over there. Of course here he could pour boiling oil on me, Carl thought, grinning to himself; but I bet he hasn't got any on him.

Just before he reached the gate he looked up and saw the roof of a shed poking up over the wall. The guy's probably watching the gate, Carl thought suddenly; if I climbed over this side of the shed I might get some cover. By standing on tiptoe Carl could barely hook his fingers over the top of the wall. But when he tried to pull himself up the rawness of his hands sent a throb of pain down his arms, and his stretched body, bruised and stiff, ached savagely. He dropped back to the sidewalk, landing with a thump. Silently he cursed himself. Could the guy have heard that?

Aware now of the intransigence of his body, he felt fear again, and with fear returned anger. Raging inside, he edged the last few feet to the gateway and cautiously peered in. He was looking into what once had been a lawn and garden; but the windows at the back of the house beyond were boarded up, and the yard was choked with grass and nettles. There was no one in sight. Damn, he thought; the son of a bitch isn't here. But then where is he? The shed. But it sure doesn't look as if anybody's been through here. I better check the shed. And then I better get the hell back to the jeep and find Tochyk, and see if we can't run this bastard down. Oh, hell. If I get all the way in here could I get back to the jeep in time if I heard Tochyk starting it?

He tried the latch; the gate was locked. He put a hand on top of the gate and vaulted clumsily over, wincing with pain. Damn it; he was just wasting time, the guy wasn't in here. That could have been anybody, there in the street before; a kid, maybe. The linecrosser was probably back in the café, swilling down Calvados. Worse yet, he probably wasn't a spy at all; just some poor bastard who'd left a box with some new shoes in it on a park bench by mistake, and as a result was being tailed like he was Dillinger.

Carl rounded the corner of the shed. A tremendous blow caught him on the shoulder; he reeled to the grass, a sob of pain and surprise and sheer terror choking in his throat. He looked up. The linecrosser stood there, his face frenzied, a garden rake held high over his head. As Carl watched, the steel teeth plunged down toward him. He rolled to one side, grabbing frantically for his pistol. The rake head landed with a loud clang on the hard ground beside him. Oh, you bastard, you son-of-a-bitching bastard, he thought, or said, and his pistol was in his hand, the safety off, and he jerked the trigger. There was a deafening report, and the linecrosser sagged forward against the rake handle, trembled a moment on its point and then slipped sideways to the ground.

The walled garden still echoed with the sound of the shot; the air was sharp with the smell of burnt gunpowder. In a daze of horror Carl got to his feet and stood, shaking, over the man lying there. The man's hand rose to grope feebly, aimlessly, at his lapel, below which, from the wound in the right side of his chest, dark blood was soaking into the khaki jacket. Carl, gagging, readied his pistol again. But the linecrosser was not looking at him. The man's hand, as though by its own volition, crept to an inside pocket, came out with a photograph, lifted it partway into the air, and dropped. The photograph fluttered to the ground. Carl turned it over. It was a photograph of a woman and a little boy; across the bottom of it, written in faint ink, were a name and an address.

A sound came from the man's throat, but it was not distinguishable. Simultaneously, from the street outside, Carl heard Tochyk calling his name, softly, anxiously.

"In here," he said.

The linecrosser's head was lying in a clump of nettles. His eyes stared up, at once aware and empty, into the emptiness of the sky. As Carl watched he tried to speak again, and the blood began to come from his mouth, in thin bubbles that broke as soon as they were formed.

Tochyk came around the corner of the shed and stopped abruptly as he saw the man lying on the ground. "Jesus," he breathed.

Carl said, "God damn it, he jumped me! He was trying to kill me!"

Tochyk looked at the rake. "Sure," he said uneasily.

"Well, how the hell would you like to have those teeth coming down at your skull?"

"I didn't say nothing, Carl," Tochyk said mildly. "It—it must have been awful. I was just wondering what Weiller would say." He looked away. "I better go get the jeep," he said.

"Fuck Weiller!" Carl screamed at him.

268

Tochyk was walking away toward the gate. He did not turn. "Antie!" Carl called after him. Tochyk stopped.

"Antie—he wouldn't necessarily die, would he? Shot like that?"

"I don't know, Carl," Tochyk said humbly, and was out of sight.

XVII.

"NOW I am glad," Thérèse said.

The captain gazed at her ironically. "Splendid. That makes two of us. But—why are *you* glad, may I ask?"

Thérèse's eyes were heavy, and her face was white, but the expression on it was serene. "Is it not clear?" she replied. "Now the worst that could happen has happened. Now there is nothing more to hide, no more that you can find out."

Captain Weiller was sprawled at ease in a black horsehair chair that should not, it seemed, have permitted ease.

"Do you know why I'm glad?" he asked, conversational, cold. "I'm glad because the worst that could have happened didn't happen—because two spies whose work might have cost the lives of thousands of Allied soldiers did not succeed in working. I'm glad"—he hesitated, but only briefly—"because one of the spies is now dead, and the other has been proved guilty."

Thérèse did not answer. Slowly she closed her eyes, her features twisting with a grief which she made no attempt to conceal. Then her head sank forward.

"You think I'm brutal," the captain said. "That's because you're thinking that it's *your* father who's dead, and you feel you've got a right to remember him as your father, to remember a ribbon he once gave you, tenderness he showed, the good things he did, the trouble he had. But I'm going to say to you something you've apparently never thought of. On the day he contracted with the Germans to spy for them, to commit treason for them, for the money they would pay him, on that day he lost the right to be considered by the world as a human being. Whether he thought about what he was doing or not. Whether or not he thought what the consequences to others might be. If he didn't he should have. I could say, of course, that *you* can remember him as you like; that it doesn't matter. But I don't believe even that. I believe that you must think of him as I do, as all the rest of the world will now think of him. And, mademoiselle—"

The captain leaned forward and stared intensely at the girl, who had now raised her head and was looking at him in sick horror. "You must look upon yourself in the same way. For on the day you undertook to help your father, or acquiesced in what he was doing, for pay, or out of what you thought loyalty, or for whatever reason, on that day you too forfeited all but a negligible part of your humanity. I say this to you not wantonly, to cause you pain; because whether you feel pain or not is now meaningless, it could not concern me. I say it because I want you to face what you have never faced. I want you finally to understand. I want you to see before your eyes the blood you would have shed, hear the human screams of the torn and the mangled and the dying—and then I want you to tell me without pity for yourself all that you have done, all that was done by anyone else you knew engaged in the same —trade, so that we may know, take every possible precaution, make or prepare for other arrests, do everything we can to cut out this cancer which, if you now fail, must continue to work, and kill, and kill, and kill!" At the end he was shouting.

The girl wept, quietly at first, then more and more loudly, deep sobs wrenching her body to and fro in her chair, the sound convulsive, uncontrollable, though she pressed her hands tightly over her mouth, like a small child who has been punished once for weeping. In the narrow room the sound was almost unbearably harsh.

The captain watched Thérèse for a time, his face without emotion. Then he turned to Hudson. "Would you do something?" he asked composedly. "Go and ask Madame Corrail if she can give us lunch. It doesn't matter what; and we'll pay her. I brought some K rations along, but I'd just as soon not have to eat 'em."

Hudson nodded and went out.

Johnny settled deeper into his chair and looked around the room, his mind numb, as empty of thought as he could make it. With the passage of noon a lozenge of light had appeared inside the unshuttered window at the far end of the room, and a trapped wasp snarled against the pane there, skated endlessly up and down the glass in a hostile blur of sound and of sun. The white veins in a marble-topped table stood out as though in relief; on the table stood a lamp, grotesquely ornamented, and from the wall over its round-shouldered glass-and-metal shade a picture leaned, a cheap colored print of a plump, bepetti-coated child sitting in a chimney corner, with a curled-up kitten in her lap. Johnny thought of Mme. Corrail's hard face and looked away.

The weeping had lessened now, but it had not ceased. On the floor at Thérèse's feet lay the two transmitter cases, identical in appearance except for the dust that had gathered on Bou-liard's where it had lain in a hayloft in the Corrails' barn. Korvac's transmitter was still closed; the other case lay open on the rug, exposing the beautifully made, beautifully fitted contents.

Johnny stared at it once again in nameless dread. It was close, and implacably real. The brass key centered in the forefront of the case seemed to tremble under his gaze; the sound of the wasp became its sound, an angry, alive buzzing that tried to but could not pierce the glass, the miles of air that separated them from the murderous Germans.

Hudson walked back into the room. "She isn't nuts about the idea," he said, "but she will. She can give us soup and bread anyway. She'll call us when it's on the table."

Weiller nodded. "Has Corrail come back yet?"

"He's out there with her. D'you want to speak to him?"

The captain considered. "Maybe. I honestly don't know yet. Depends a good deal on how we get along here." He turned to Thérèse. "Mademoiselle," he said, "are you ready to talk to us now?"

She looked up at him, her face streaked with tears. "You—make me wish," she said in a husky voice, "that I could tell you—a great deal. But you are still mistaken in me. I am not a spy. I do not know the things a spy would know. And if I may say so—" Her eyes glistened again, and she turned away. "There are also things that you do not know."

Abruptly the captain sat up in his chair. "What I don't know

272

already I intend to know soon," he said angrily. "Look. What's that on the rug in front of you?"

"A radio transmitter, m'sieur," Thérèse said.

"Who just showed us where it was hidden?"

"I did, m'sieur."

"Who had put it there?"

The girl hesitated. "I had."

"Who told me, in La Haye-du-Puits—and told me, oh, very indignantly and self-righteously—'I'm sure there was no transmitter'?"

"I, m'sieur." She looked up at Weiller firmly. "And in saying that I—I lied, it is true. Therefore you mistrust me, and I understand that you must. But, m'sieur—I lied because your purposes were intolerable to me, because I had—a great need of my own, and—"

"You had a great need, all right," the captain interrupted savagely. "You were trying to save your damn neck."

She lifted her hand toward him as he spoke. "No. Now I think—I will try to save my—damn neck. But then I was trying to save my father."

"Your father was dead," said Weiller.

"Do you think I do not know that?" she blazed. "He *is* dead, *is* dead, and there is not a man of you in this room his equal for honor, for worth. He is dead, but he is still something to me, and a name in the world that was not to be dishonored—in France—" She hesitated. "In Cherbourg—" She dropped her head, and covered her eyes with her hand. "If only—within me."

The captain said, wearily, "Mademoiselle Bouliard—recall, please, that we knew about your father before ever we knew that you existed. You could not have saved him from dishonor because he did not save himself from dishonor. And you could have saved yourself only by dissociating yourself from him—however painful that must have been. Because it would have been painful—let's say, at least, that that was the reason—you did not do it. But let me remind you that personal pain does not weigh against the lives of the innocent. Holding this in your mind, will you now say that you were right to become a German spy out of—loyalty to your father?"

Thérèse raised her head. "M'sieur," she said, "sometimes I

wish we were all—animals in the fields. Not, as you may suppose, because no one accuses an animal of treason. But because then we would not have words with which to deceive, and confuse, and misunderstand one another. I no longer know why you think I have become a German spy. I do not believe that I ever became one. But you are sure that I have done wrong, and perhaps I have—though I thought only to—to cancel a wrong, I was certain I would hurt no one—"

"I told you," the captain said, "that by telling us everything you know, you may still be able to cancel a part of the wrong, may still be able to save a great many people from harm."

"No," she said in a flat voice. "No. I can save no one—except perhaps myself."

"Oh, for God's sake!" the captain shouted. He rose to his feet.

"I will tell you!" she said hastily. "All the story, all I know. At once. Only—"

Mme. Corrail appeared in the doorway. The captain turned toward her, and she nodded at him.

He turned again to face Thérèse. "We're going to eat now," he said. "Then we'll take your story. But I wish you'd get it into your head that you're through. Saving the skin of Thérèse Bouliard is no longer of any importance; and it won't even be possible unless you cooperate with me now." His voice grated. "Get ready to turn yourself inside out. And don't think"— he glared at her—"don't think I won't help you." He turned and stalked out of the room.

It was as though Johnny's mind were an ocean, its surface spun out across unending miles under sun, rain, and wind, vast seas of calm upon it balanced haphazardly by scattered enclaves of storm. If storm and calm were connected, the ocean could not know; simply, it contained both at once, responded to both, but as from a distance, from a depth.

In the kitchen now, Johnny could not eat. Obediently, when it came his turn, he ladled soup into his bowl and took a chunk of heavy bread from the board, but both remained untasted before him. When he moved, it was as though some other intelligence directed his body; when he looked around, it was as though he saw with eyes that were not his own. He was aware of hunger, but it did not concern him.

Weiller was sitting hunched over at the head of the table, composed, eating with a good appetite, talking occasionally in low tones to Hudson. Once he looked up at Johnny and said in an encouraging voice, "It's good soup. Better eat some." Johnny nodded and picked up his spoon. "Needs salt," the captain said, and Johnny salted his soup, but still did not eat. The captain watched him for a moment, then shrugged and turned back to Hudson.

For the wraith of an instant then Johnny was conscious of himself as he must seem, the young man dazed, so stunned by a tragic blow, by realization of the world's deceitfulness, that, anguished and alone, he could not touch his food. *"How it must have hurt him!"*—and to his shame, a brief, melancholy pleasure in this scene brushed his mind before he rebelled against its spuriousness. The captain would not have thought that; thank God. I'm a fool, Johnny thought, and remembered—as he had not for years—the night on which his mother had come to his room, had crept into bed with him and taken him into her arms, holding him close, telling him in a broken voice that his father had just had a serious accident, might die in the hospital. He had wept unrestrainedly, half out of real grief, half out of the realization of the drama of his situation: he was a grief-stricken child, a boy whose father was perhaps even now dead: soon they would telephone from the hospital, and next day in school the others would look at him with silent respect, and women, friends of his mother, would pass him in the street and touch their handkerchiefs to their eyes, saying "Poor little fatherless thing!" . . . His father had not died, but for weeks he had felt himself an outcast, ashamed and terrified of his own falseness, until at last—he did not remember how, or when—he had been able to draw a curtain between himself and the incident, close it out of his mind. Almost forever. . . .

In the stillness he raised his head a little and looked across at Thérèse, who also had failed. She was able to eat, apparently. But why not? Why should he have supposed that the blow (which, after all, she had in a way dealt) should have affected her as it had him? As for the blow which she herself had received, she must always have known that it might some day come. And yet it was clear that she was not disposed to accept it as final; evidently she would still fight, with whatever weapons she could find, with lies, and the knowledge she must have of what could be proved against her and what, on the other hand, could never be proved.

It was incomprehensible to him, but there was no reason why he should comprehend; this was not the Thérèse he had thought he had known, the Thérèse he had made up in his own mind, but another girl entirely. She was, perhaps, the girl of whom the captain had spoken so many days ago (was it only day before yesterday?): "The girl's only a little thing, it's true. And she has big, brown, frightened eyes. And if you didn't have the story you might think there was never anyone so foully wronged. . . ." The Thérèse Bouliard of the paper case had been, then, more real than the Thérèse who had presented herself to him in the flesh, the Thérèse he had come to think he loved. . . .

As though she felt his gaze, she looked up at him, but surprisingly he did not even have to look away (it was another girl), and presently her eyes clouded and dropped. "So young, and so untender" or something, "So young, my lord, and true!" and suddenly he wished he could break the table, the dishes, the house, the world, but the feeling passed as swiftly as it had come. Anyway what he felt no longer mattered; he had, and properly, been washed to one side.

When the captain had brought in the transmitter he had not known what it was; when Thérèse had said "I did not think anyone could find it" he had not known what her words meant. Then as the truth had come in upon him he had wished, simply, that he could die. She had lied to him. . . . And in her behalf he had fought the captain, or tried to. . . . But so weakly; he could almost have thanked God for being ineffectual. . . . For a few moments he had been wildly angry, at Thérèse, at the captain for not telling him in advance that he was going to play a trick using Korvac's set—but why should the captain have told him anything, when he had tried at every turn to undo the captain's work?

276

As for Thérèse, he had soon told himself that of course she had lied, and of course she had tried to enlist his—anyone's—help: would he not himself, in her place, have tried to save himself? No matter who got hurt in the process?

Maybe it was only his good luck that he was not in her place. But that changed nothing. All that was changed was—not even Thérèse herself, but his image of her. As they had climbed to the loft, as, in the pungent half-dark, they had dug down, throwing aside the dozens and hundreds of small tied-up bundles of hay that had been piled on Bouliard's transmitter where it lay hidden deep in the farthest corner, that image had shifted, shifted in his mind until by the time they had reached the house again, bearing their trophy, the Thérèse who walked beside him had become someone he knew less than he had known her when he first saw her, imprisoned in her room, on his first morning in Cherbourg.

And when he realized this the chaos of emotion he had felt resolved itself. He might have blamed himself, bitterly, if the captain had seemed disposed to blame him; but with a tact for which his delight in his triumph certainly did not fully account, Weiller had said nothing to remind him of his earlier fatuousness. Johnny had been able to realize, simply, that the defenseless, persecuted Thérèse was gone, had in fact never existed; and with the real Thérèse he had no relationship.

There would be questions, but they were not for him to ask. If he were to blame himself, it would be later. Until it was time to drive back to La Haye-du-Puits, or Cherbourg, he would have no further function, almost no further existence. He had felt many things today, and how much more there would be to feel he could not tell; but now, for a time, there would be a respite, he could feel relief, his own irrelevance. He could feel, if he would, as empty as a shell of the sea.

Thérèse looked up at him again, with an expression on her face that seemed to want to be taken as bewilderment. She's trying to tell me, he thought impersonally, that she's the same Thérèse, that there's only one. . . . Did she know what she sounded like, there in the other room, when she said she could save no one but herself? Well, it's her affair. . . . The funny thing is, he told himself, that it doesn't even hurt any more. It doesn't matter that she lied to me. What matters is that she lied. *And what about you?* the voice said. *You believed her.*

The captain pushed back his chair and got to his feet. "We've finished," he said to Johnny. "If you're not going to eat any more, should we go back in the other room? There's a lot to do."

Johnny nodded and rose from the table. At the captain's gesture, the girl rose too, and preceded them through the door to the hall.

Back in the parlor, Captain Weiller threw open the shutters of the two front windows, took his pad and pencil from his pocket and sat down in the horsehair-covered chair. The others seated themselves as they had been. "Now," said the captain. "Mademoiselle Bouliard, when was your father first contacted by a member of the German Intelligence Service?"

"Contacted, I do not know that word," the girl said in a humble voice.

"Approached, then. When did they first try to get him to work for them?"

"I am sorry. I do not know."

The captain sighed and kept silence for a time, sitting immobile, gazing around the room over the heads of its other occupants. "All right," he said finally. "Seems you've got some reason for wanting to tell the story in your own way. It's not unusual with spies." He looked down at her, his eyes veiled. "Go ahead. But I warn you, you won't get off any easier this way."

She returned his gaze without flinching. "I do not expect it to be easy. And if I could have answered I would."

"Go ahead I said."

"Well then—" Thérèse sank back into her chair and fixed her eyes on nothing, on some point in the room that lay between Johnny and Weiller. "I have lied to you only about one thing; about the transmitter, about knowing that my father possessed it. I learned of these things in May, two or three weeks, perhaps, before my father died. Otherwise it was as I told you. During the years after he was discharged from his teaching position he told me—almost nothing of what he was doing. When he visited—"

278

"*Almost* nothing?" the captain broke in. "What does 'almost' mean?"

The girl shrugged. "Nothing, then. But I spoke once to you of his decision to register for work at the Kommandantur—"

"When was that?"

"Perhaps—late in 1942, or early in 1943."

"I want to know exactly," the captain said.

Thérèse's brow furrowed. "The time of those years—is not clear to me," she said, "it is all the same. But I will try. Only now—I do not think I can do better."

"Go on."

"I told you, too, I think, of asking my father once whether he had work or was merely looking for work. And of his reply, that because he knew languages the Germans at the Kommandantur had sometimes small tasks for him, which he would accept or not as he thought them honorable or dishonorable—"

"Apparently he thought spying honorable," the captain said icily.

The girl's shoulders bowed.

"Well, go on," Weiller said. "You were talking about visiting. I'd like to hear more about your father's social calendar."

"Please?" Thérèse looked doubtful. When the captain said nothing more she went on. "It was of the visits to Sartilly I meant to speak."

"The visits to German Intelligence Headquarters in Paris," the captain said.

Thérèse's expression was sad. "Since my aunt says that he did not come here, and that man in La Haye-du-Puits says—"

"Korvac," said Weiller. "I don't mind your knowing his name; you won't be able to do any more harm with what you find out from us."

She bit her lip. "Since M'sieur Korvac says my father was in Paris on various occasions during the spring, I can only say that of myself, I do not know. It is true that he said little about his trips, and never urged me to accompany him; but thinking that he was coming here I did not in any event wish to do so, and supposed that—the talk would all be of the debt, of why we did not pay—"

"Why did you not tell us that the Corrails held the mortgage on the house in Cherbourg?"

"Why—I did not see that our money troubles—concerned you. That they would have interest for you," she amended hastily.

"Believe me, mademoiselle," the captain said. "Any troubles of yours are troubles of ours. Go on."

"M'sieur, you confuse me so, I do not know where I am." She closed her eyes. "Oh. I did not, then, question my father's —absences from Cherbourg, and so had no reason to think much about them, except that they must cost him pain. As everything, in those days, did. Finally—I told you of M'sieur Bloch's visits to us in April; and in this also, I—did not lie."

"Well, somebody lied," Weiller said. "You heard Korvac say that Bloch had known your father for years, had done a great deal for him—"

"Yes, and of what Bloch did for my father I learned something at last!" Thérèse burst out. "It was through him, at the very beginning, that my father lost his teaching post."

"Ah, ah," said the captain. "Now you begin to interest me. How do you know this?"

"My father—did not know," said Thérèse uncertainly. "But it seemed that that was how it must be. For when he went to the Kommandantur at last it was at Bloch's suggestion—"

"Then he had met Bloch before that."

"Only—weeks before, m'sieur. When he had lost his last job, for no reason that he could understand, since there was more to do, and he had worked well. This man Bloch was there when he came out, in despair—it was from a laboring job of some kind—and spoke to him, seemed sympathetic, and drew my father's story from him. He then suggested that my father apply at the Kommandantur; and when my father said that he would not, that he would seek other work, Bloch implied in a manner so strange that my father did not understand at the time, that he would find no other work. And this was true. At last, in desperation, my father went to the Kommandantur, and was at once shown into the office of—M'sieur Bloch. Bloch interviewed him, and my father told me that the man knew more about his past—about what work he had done, what jobs he had lost—than he himself had told him. Or so it seemed; but in such a matter it was possible to be mistaken, and my father was very anxious for work, since our savings were by then gone, and there was need of money even to buy food. It was only later that he really became suspicious of Bloch."

"Alas, the villain unmasked himself too late," Weiller said amiably. "But, mademoiselle—you know a great deal about Bloch, for someone whose father never told her anything."

"He told me this in May, m'sieur," Thérèse said.

"What a strong man he must have been, to keep all his harrowing experiences from you when they occurred," Captain Weiller observed.

Thérèse said proudly, "He was strong, m'sieur."

"And what a lot I'm learning. I would have said that all spies are weak."

"Then you do not know," she said, and went on hastily, "But my father—was not a spy."

"Oh, come now, mademoiselle," said the captain. "With all that training—it's a shame to belittle him."

The girl looked at him wanly. "Am I to tell the story, m'sieur?"

"By all means. And first I want to know why your father found it necessary to tell you all about Bloch in May, when, according to what you said earlier, you had already fled Bloch, put him behind you—though through all the years before, when Bloch was apparently exerting constant pressure, your father was able to tell you nothing at all."

"It is very simple, m'sieur," said Thérèse. "In May I found the transmitter."

"In the hayfields?" said the captain.

"No. In the wardrobe in my father's room, upstairs here."

"Extraordinary," said the captain musingly. "You had never seen it in the house in Cherbourg; you had not seen it when your father assembled the luggage for the trip; you did not see it during the trip; you did not see it on your arrival here. How do you account for this? Mademoiselle, how did you and your father travel to Sartilly in May? Blindfolded, in the back of a German van?"

"No, m'sieur. When my father determined to go, he made

inquiries among our neighbors in Cherbourg, and one of them knew a man, M'sieur Coulet, who was about to drive to Avranches, having permitted business there. My father called upon this M'sieur Coulet and made the financial arrangements necessary for us to go with him to Sartilly. On the day of the trip we left very early, and the cases were all in the car before I left the house, since my father had called me as late as possible."

"Considerate of him. And when you arrived at Sartilly?"

"Then I saw the case and, it is true, did not recognize it, but of course said nothing."

"Of course."

"But later, when I wished to wash our soiled clothing—"

"Yes, yes. Mademoiselle—how does it happen that you had not seen the set in Cherbourg? When you were cleaning the house, say, as it seems you did so lovingly and so constantly? I take it the set must have been in the house; if it had been with Bloch at the Kommandantur, I can't quite imagine your father going up to him—if, that is, relations were as you say at that time—and announcing: I'm leaving town, give me my transmitter."

"There was a part of the house which I did not enter, m'sieur. My father's study, on what is I think to you the second floor. Doubtless the transmitter was kept there."

"You felt no curiosity, and no anxiety, about the existence of this—this Bluebeard's closet of your father's?"

"M'sieur?"

"Didn't you wonder about it when your father suddenly announced to you that you weren't to go into his study?"

"It was not suddenly, m'sieur. It had always been so. Ever since I can remember, my father's study had been—private to him."

"Perhaps he'd been a spy all that time, too," the captain said sourly. "All right. So you found the transmitter in his wardrobe down here, and went to him and said, 'Why, Daddy, what are you doing with the finest type of transmitter made for the German Intelligence Service in your wardrobe?' "

Thérèse said in a low voice, "I thought I knew—what it was, but I did not at all suspect where it had first come from. As I regarded it my father came into the room and found me; he was

282

then about to—hide it more securely, I think. At first he was terribly angry with me; and then very sad; and then he told me —about M'sieur Bloch."

The captain kept silence for some minutes. At last he said flatly, "You know, of course, that I don't believe any of this. I can see a dozen glaring flaws in your story already. But go right ahead and hang yourself. What did your father say about Bloch? Besides what you've already told us? You'd just said, as I recall, that Bloch had got your father fired from his teaching job and every legitimate job he held after that, but that your father didn't become suspicious of him till later."

A wry, weary smile curved the girl's lips. "I did not say quite that, m'sieur. But since I am sure you know what I did say, I shall not repeat it. My father did not become truly suspicious of Bloch until Bloch told him who he was."

"And how was that?" the captain asked.

A distant look appeared on Thérèse's face. "My father told me that Bloch used him as a translator," she said. "At first only now and then, so that—not much money came in, and we were hungry—" Her voice rose steadily as she said, "But I do not say this to ask for your pity, m'sieur! Only my father explained to me that he kept asking Bloch for more work, anything he could do, and Bloch would think and at last produce some document that my father—could not translate, it would seem to be—in some way against France, he could not tell, but he would refuse, and then Bloch would shrug, and again there would be no money for a time, no work, though my father would go every day and wait. . . . It was like this for perhaps six months, and at last my father determined to leave Cherbourg, with me, and seek work elsewhere, and he went a last time to Bloch to try to earn—a small sum to help with the journey, and then Bloch told him."

"Told him what?" said the captain.

"That we would not be permitted to leave Cherbourg, and that if we tried to do so secretly we would be found, and I would be—killed, or maimed, taken prisoner, and my father would be required to—go back to work. That for many months already he had been working under Bloch for the German Intelligence Service, and that this was on record with the Germans, and would be told the French, or communicated somehow to the Allies, if ever he tried to—stop working. That he would never be able to convince anyone that what he had done was innocent, or done in ignorance. That he would never get any other job as long as the Germans were on the soil of France, and that at the very least he would starve, and I would starve, if he did not go on. But if he would accept his position realistically, a ·bright future was in store for him. His abilities were so specialized that he might never have to do anything that would offend his own scruples. He would be paid very well indeed. He would be safe; I would be safe. And no one in Cherbourg, in France, in all the world, except for the German Intelligence Service itself, would know what he was doing—" The girl broke off, and bowed her head stiffly.

"Your father agreed to this?" asked the captain.

"M'sieur, what would you have done?" Thérèse said passionately. "He had seen me starving, or almost starving—"

"Your friends would not have helped you? Mademoiselle Vaugiron—your father's colleagues at the Lycée?"

"Do you suppose we would have asked them, would have admitted that we were—unable to care for ourselves . . . ?"

"A noble pride," said the captain. "Much more valuable than loyalty to one's country."

"M'sieur," said Thérèse, "no one we knew had more than— just enough for himself. And there was the hope that my father would not have to be disloyal."

Weiller said, "Quite a hope. But let's get back to the other point. How about the Corrails? Had they no more than just enough for themselves?"

The girl said dully, "We could not have come here."

"Why not?"

"Because my father told me he had already asked them!" she cried out. "Some time before! And they had said that they could not keep us. We would have worked, done anything, but they did not want work; they wanted the debt repaid, wanted my father to get a job, get money, so he could pay them back—"

"Yet they were willing to keep you after your father died."

"They were not—'willing,' m'sieur. But my father had repaid them, a little—"

"From his German salary," the captain said.

"Yes." The girl shivered. "And with my father's death they thought—that they would have the house itself, and the land, when this could be arranged by law—" She straightened up in her chair. "They may have it," she said bitterly.

"Who else?" Weiller said. Then his voice hardened. "Now, mademoiselle. When, precisely, was it that your father formally accepted employment with the German Intelligence Service?"

With a slow, weak gesture Thérèse brushed her forehead with the back of her hand. At last she said, "Precisely, that I do not know, m'sieur. Recall that—when the incident occurred I was told nothing; and in May—well, m'sieur, then I was not—interrogating my father. I would say that he learned—sometime in the last year, in 1943."

"And do you know whether the nature of his work changed at once, with the change in his position?"

"No, m'sieur, I do not know. My father told me only that in spite of Bloch's promises, the work became more and more impossible; that he protested, and was threatened; that when he saw his position he resisted where he could do so without seeming to resist, made excuses, postponed—but could not avoid receiving some training, some equipment. He was told only at the beginning of this year that his final assignment was to be— to remain in Cherbourg after it was occupied, and transmit information about the invading troops to the Germans. This he intended never to do. Instead, from the moment he learned that Bloch and his organization expected an invasion, and a successful invasion, my father longed for this, for the time when Bloch would be gone, and he could destroy the transmitter and begin slowly to take the way back toward his old life."

"Very touching," said the captain. "And now the invasion is history, and the transmitter—is not destroyed."

Thérèse said distantly, "It was my father who was destroyed, m'sieur. And it was he who would have—broken the transmitter, got rid of it—"

Captain Weiller leaned forward. "Precisely, mademoiselle," he said softly.

"No, no!" she cried. "You cannot—I did not mean that I would not have done so—"

"Then why didn't you?"

"M'sieur, surely you can understand this! We left Cherbourg, fleeing Bloch; my father told me that he would have killed Bloch and taken his own life instead, except that the invasion did not occur, and did not occur, and he feared that vengeance would always follow me. Even in Sartilly he did not expect that we would be spared; but he had to think what to do, gain time somehow. Bloch had at first promised him that I, at all events, would be safe; if I was not to be safe after all, if Bloch himself threatened me, then my father decided that whatever the consequences, he would no longer work. But—"

"But what?"

She pressed her hand to her brow. "I am fatigued, m'sieur, I cannot think."

"It's rough going," said the captain in sympathetic tones. "Let me help you. Your father had decided not to work any more, so instead of destroying the set he hid it—*you* hid it rather, that's odd; oh, well—and instead of staying in Sartilly, or trying to find some other place to hide out, you went back to Cherbourg, where you thought Bloch was looking for you."

Color came and went in Thérèse's cheeks. "M'sieur—we could not, in fact, stay in Sartilly. We had been able to come with the excuse of bringing the Corrails some money; after that my father pretended—and it was not all pretense—to be ill, but of course my aunt did not like this. After he recovered, then we could not at once arrange transportation back to Cherbourg. But it was to Cherbourg we went finally because"—she made a helpless gesture—"that was where we lived, m'sieur. We thought if we attempted to—hide in the fields, in the woods, we would have been discovered all the sooner, not knowing how to do such things, my father being—almost old; and wearied out. So I persuaded him that he must be brave, play a part, a little longer; and I would help him.

"We would tell Bloch that we had gone to Sartilly to take money; that could be proved. I had accompanied my father because Bloch's treatment had upset me nervously. The transmitter had been taken along because my father had not dared leave it in an empty house in Cherbourg; in Sartilly he had concealed it so that my aunt and uncle would not learn of its existence, and then, when the time of departure had come, he had not been able to go to the place of concealment without being seen, and so had been forced to leave it. He would beg Bloch, the Germans, to take him back secretly to pick it up.

"This is why we could not destroy it, m'sieur. If Bloch would take him back, at least we would have gained a few more days; and if Bloch could not, then we might have gained a great deal. If Blòch tried further to—molest me, I would say that I knew now of my father's work, and would help him with it, but only on condition that I be left alone. If the condition were not accepted—" She shrugged. "We were hoping for the invasion to save us both, m'sieur."

"Well, is that all you have to say?" said the captain.

She looked at him questioningly. "Almost, m'sieur. When we returned to Cherbourg, Bloch was not there. At the Kommandantur no one could, or would, tell my father where he was, or when or whether he would return, or whether someone else would take his place. All seemed—confused, m'sieur; and this gave us great hope. And then my father was killed."

The captain stared at Thérèse somberly. "Why was it you who hid the set, and not your father?" he asked.

"He was—after he had told me the story, m'sieur, it was as though he had lost all strength for a time. He had had to be strong for too many months, and years. So it was I who hid the set, who made the plan."

Again the captain leaned forward. "But you returned to Sartilly after the invasion. Why did you not destroy the set then?"

"Why should I, m'sieur?"

"Well—so that your aunt and uncle might not find it, for one thing. Unless, of course, they already knew about it?"

She smiled a sad smile. "No, m'sieur, they did not know. And I did not think they would learn. I had gone down to the very boards of the loft to hide the set; and usually there is a little hay left from one year to the next. It was not likely that the set would be uncovered. If, at the end of some winter, it should be—" She closed her eyes. "I hoped that I would be long gone by that time; that nothing would be understood. I—did not wish to touch the set again, can you not understand that?"

"Mademoiselle Bouliard," said the captain, "where are the papers that should accompany this transmitter?"

She opened her eyes wide. "The papers?"

"Yes. The rules for encipherment, your father's instructions, and so on."

"I—do not know, I—"

Weiller got to his feet. "You know, mademoiselle," he said in a terrible voice.

There was a long silence. At last Thérèse whispered, "I—I destroyed them, m'sieur."

"Why?"

"If my aunt and uncle should have found the set the papers would have—told them the story, m'sieur."

"But you hid the set in May, and you say you did not go back to it again! In May it was not your aunt and uncle you were thinking of; they would not find the set, if they found it at all, until 'at the end of some winter.' On the other hand there *was* a likelihood that Bloch would bring your father back to get the set. The papers would have betrayed nothing to Bloch—but their absence might have betrayed a great deal. Why did you destroy the papers *in May*, mademoiselle?"

"I thought—perhaps to create more difficulty, cause more delay—if the papers were gone, if they had to be replaced—before my father could be made to—work again."

"But surely, as a matter of fact, your father knew his instructions by then, knew his cipher by heart!"

"I did not think so, m'sieur. I did not know then that he could use the transmitter, I thought he had not been trained—"

"Even in May, you mean, your father did not tell you about his trips to Paris?" Weiller asked sardonically. "What had he to gain by hiding them?"

"I suppose," she said in a low voice, "that even then he did not wish me to know how far it had gone, how low they had brought him—thinking that perhaps if I knew I might no longer believe in him." She raised her head. "I would always have believed in him!" she said.

"Very filial," said the captain. "But you still haven't explained why you destroyed the papers. Or rather you've given me two reasons, neither of which fits the other, and neither of which holds water. What have you got to say about that?"

She made a frightened gesture. "I—I wanted to destroy something, and the papers I could destroy, if not the set—"

"Three reasons, mademoiselle."

"I am tired!" Thérèse cried out. "I have had almost no sleep, for many nights, and you give me no peace, I cannot think—"

"I. can think, mademoiselle," the captain said. "And I'll tell you what I think. I think that either you did not destroy the papers; or that if you did so, you destroyed them because the cipher, and the instructions, were for the use not of one spy, but of two."

"Oh, no!" Thérèse cried.

As though she had said nothing, the captain went on. "I think more. I think you destroyed the papers, if you destroyed them, after your father died, and the invasion took place, and you came back to Sartilly alone."

"Then why, why did I not destroy the transmitter also?" the girl asked.

"It does seem curious, doesn't it? Perhaps you did what you did because if the Americans discovered the set, the papers would not be there to incriminate you; but if the Germans sent someone through the lines to you, you could show that the set was intact, could say that you had always intended to go to work once it was safe to do so." The captain paused. "That argues, of course, that the papers are still in existence, hidden separately from the transmitter."

"No," said Thérèse. "No, no, no." She sat heavily silent, her eyes closed. At length she looked up. "M'sieur?" she said timidly. "Even Bloch's letter—even that shows that I could not use a transmitter."

Weiller raised his eyebrows swiftly. "Ah? You're willing to accept the Bloch letter now?"

"No," she said.

The captain smiled at her calmly. "Let me tell you the rest of what I think," he said. "Since you're still—confused. I think there's a great deal of truth in what you've told us this afternoon —but that the story is false wherever your own part in it is concerned. I think you've known Bloch from very nearly the day your father learned that he was working for the German Intelligence Service; and that you have been working for that service also, in very close relationship with Bloch. I think—"

"Why then should we have come down here in May, my father and I?" the girl asked, terror in her voice. "If not to flee Bloch, if not—"

"Of course, to flee Bloch," the captain said. "You were trying to run out on your contract. But it didn't take Bloch's lovemaking to make you decide to do that, to make you lose your nerve."

Thérèse was shaking her head dazedly from side to side. "M'sieur," she said, "is there—another Thérèse Bouliard? Because I am here as in a bad dream, I do not recognize myself in —anything you say."

"If you're such a good, clean, honorable kid," the captain said harshly, "why didn't you tell us this whole story before? Why didn't you come to the authorities with it without waiting to be arrested? If you had to wait, why didn't you tell us during your first interrogation?"

"My father had done nothing wrong," she moaned. "You saw. He had transmitted no message, betrayed nothing. And I thought—no one knew of him but the Germans, and they, thank God, were gone."

"But then you discovered that we knew," the captain said.

"I thought you could prove nothing!" she cried out. "And I knew nothing, nothing but grief, nothing to help. Why should the grief not die, I thought, as my father died? I loved my father, he called himself a failure and I knew that he was not, his only sin was to have been tried past—any man's endurance—" She stopped. "I believe that still," she said fiercely. "And why then should I have helped you to make him—a name hated in the streets, a name of loathing, spat on, condemned . . . ?"

"It was not for you to decide whether or not what you knew could help us, mademoiselle," the captain said. "And I do not mean—help us by bringing to justice the name of your dead father. I mean help us in our urgent and dangerous battle against the German Intelligence Service. You knew, remember, a good deal about Bloch."

"But you also . . . !"

"Ah, but you did not know that. Not for a long time. And incidentally we now know much more in fact than we did before you talked to us today."

She hung her head. "Perhaps I was wrong," she said. "But it is hard to conclude that—one's father's whole life, his agony, his despair, his name forever, mean less than—a few notes in a notebook—"

"And even harder," the captain said, "when you're a spy yourself, and your own skin is at stake. Really hard then, eh?"

"No, m'sieur!" she said. "I am not a spy!"

"Mademoiselle Bouliard," said the captain menacingly. "You've done very well. But not well enough. There are still questions you have not answered satisfactorily. There is still the Bloch note. There is still Korvac's mission. What have you to say of these things?"

"Nothing. Because I know nothing."

"You are throwing away your last chance for mercy."

She looked up at him proudly. "Let it go, then," she said.

The captain got to his feet and turned away, thrusting his hands deep into his pockets. When he turned back he looked, not at Thérèse, but at Hudson and Johnny. "I'm tired," he said. "And I'm sick of this. She knows she's through, and Korvac can finish up the job. But time's getting on, and we're not going to do any more good here. Let's hit the road, O.K.?"

"It's all right with me, Captain," Hudson said.

"I've got to go pay Madame Corrail for lunch," Weiller said.

He strode out the door and back to the kitchen, where he laid some bills on the table. Mme. Corrail picked them up, counted them and nodded with grudging satisfaction. Weiller walked back into the hall, where the others were waiting for him.

In the kitchen doorway behind him appeared a short, gray man, carrying a bottle in one hand, glasses in the other. He coughed. Weiller spun around. Monsieur Corrail, making a vague gesture with the bottle, put on a smile of comradeship, of alliance. *"Avant de partir?"* he said. *"Un petit peu . . . ?"*

291

Weiller swung sharply back to Hudson. "Tell him to shove it up his ass!" he roared, and walked down the hall and out the front door. After a moment he poked his head back in. "Sorry," he said, his expression unchanged. "Tell him 'No thank you.' "

They drove back the way they had come, and without conversation. At the *gendarmerie* in La Haye-du-Puits they dropped Thérèse, Hudson taking her in, and a few minutes later drove into the bare lot behind Starr's headquarters. Hudson excused himself and went in; but Captain Weiller made no move to get out of the jeep, and Johnny, watching him uncertainly, remained also.

Finally Weiller looked up at him. "Well, what do you make of it now?" he asked somberly.

Not to have to answer . . . And how could he, what could he say? The storms of ocean rocked, mounted, in the corners of Johnny's mind; the calms, still vast, were empty, without clarity. A phrase he had heard came back to him, and he brought it out. "It's sticky, sir," he said.

But it was he who had made it sticky. "I'm sorry—"

"You don't have to be," Weiller said. "I guess that's what I waited out here to say. I know I bawled you out at the beginning, for closing her up and all that, but it doesn't look now as if she'd needed any help. She's pretty tough; and she's got herself quite a story. Sometimes I'm almost tempted to—"

"What, sir?"

"Turn her over to Thury. For free. And the hell with it." The captain looked sadly at Johnny, and after a moment went on. "You know, it's almost funny what big ideas I came down here with. Or anyway they were in the back of my mind. I thought—well, first of all that this case would crack, that the girl would see that we had the goods on her and would tell us the whole story. Just that in itself would have taken—I can't tell you how much heat off me. But with her story and Korvac's complete we could have done more, maybe. I'd have had to get permission from London, and Starr might have kicked, but— I figured we could take Korvac to Cherbourg and get a really good American radioman to study his transmitting style there.

Since Korvac had been an instructor, hadn't been intended to have an actual mission until the very last minute, it seemed likely that the Germans might not be too closely familiar with his own radio style, so that a reasonable similarity might have been enough. Then we could have held Korvac himself, and Thérèse, under close guard, put the American radioman on the air as Émile, and made contact with the Germans. We'd have pretended that 'Émile' had completed his mission successfully, but of course had found that Bouliard was dead, and at first hadn't been able to locate Thérèse. Now, however, he had his transmitter all set up and Thérèse at his side, and the two of them were ready to go. We'd have let Korvac himself phrase a lot of messages which we wouldn't actually have sent, just to learn his general way of handling the language in radio traffic; then we'd have been off and away. Thury could have been in on the whole deal; that would have made *him* happy—" The captain broke off and shook his head despondently.

Johnny looked at him in wonderment. "But, Captain, why couldn't you do that right now?" he asked.

"Why—on account of the girl, of course."

"I don't see—"

The captain yawned. "Korvac is a stranger to Cherbourg, and supposing he'd got there, he'd have had to lie low, for quite awhile at least. He couldn't have been expected to get much information himself."

"But how would the Germans know that Thérèse wasn't getting it for him, if you told them she was? Then if you weren't *actually* using her you wouldn't have to worry about whether she'd—broken all the way or not, you could just go ahead and—"

"No, Phillips." Weiller shook his head. "I should think you of all people would be able to see why that wouldn't be possible —or why it would be too dangerous, anyway."

"I don't, though."

The captain looked at him curiously. "Well, I guess I should take that as a compliment. If I've convinced you, maybe I can still convince her."

"Of—what, sir?"

"That she was in that business up to her neck."

Johnny stared at him in alarm.

"Look, Phillips," Weiller said. "Suppose we set it up the way I said, made contact and sent out information supposedly collected by Thérèse Bouliard."

"Yes, sir?"

"Well. Do you think *you* know exactly how Thérèse's mind works?"

Johnny looked away, and shook his head.

"All right. Suppose Bloch does."

"But—" Johnny was puzzled; in a moment he said, "The information sent would be going through 'Émile.' If it sounded enough like him it wouldn't have to sound like her, would it?"

"I guess I haven't made myself clear," Weiller said. "Suppose Bloch knew that Thérèse wouldn't have collected any information?"

It was something Johnny himself had suggested, a long time before. "But—the Bloch note?" he said.

"I know, I know. I've been convinced she's guilty, as guilty as her father. And maybe she is. But I haven't proved it yet, have I? In something like this you've got to know. And I mean you've got to know everything. If you don't, your case is blown from the beginning. And if we put this case on the air and blow it, we lose more than just the case; we let the Germans know that we're trying to double their agents, and so make them automatically distrustful of every future case we might try to run under control. Don't you see that? We wouldn't dare put this case on the air unless we *knew* every last damned thing there was to know about Korvac *and* Thérèse Bouliard."

He sighed, wearily. "Well," he said, "we're not licked yet. Not quite. We've got one final chance to break her, with Korvac, tomorrow."

But Johnny had not really heard the captain past the fourth sentence. "I haven't proved it, have I?" I thought you had, Johnny said to himself. He felt a sickness rising inside him. After all the hours of pain—it had been terrible, he had never known anything like it, but he had, at last, reached a kind of resolution. And now it was all to do over again.

Lieutenant Starr appeared in the doorway of the building. "Say, Captain," he said, "aren't you coming inside? Hudson told me you'd stashed the girl, so I figured—"

"Coming in now," Weiller said.

The tone of his voice did not encourage conversation, but Starr said genially, "Your boys in Cherbourg seem to be lost without you, Captain. They've been trying to get in touch with you all afternoon. Wanted you to call as soon as you got back."

Weiller looked up sharply. "What is it about, do you know?"

Starr said, "I haven't the foggiest."

In the front room, the captain lifted the receiver of the military phone and held it away from his ear until it stopped crackling. Then he bawled into the mouthpiece, "Barley, please." There was another spitting and crackling, then a faint voice. "Barley, Blue Flame, please," the captain shouted.

Suddenly the connection cleared and Johnny, across the room from Weiller, could hear a voice saying "Hello? Hello?"

"Murch!" said the captain and pressed the receiver to his ear. "What's the trouble?" He turned and shifted himself up onto the desk, sitting there with his heavy legs dangling. "Careful what you say over the phone. . . . Yeah, I get you. . . . Yeah." There was a long silence. Suddenly Weiller burst out, *"No shit!"* A giant smile slowly overspread his face. Then it faded. "Well did you, uh, cage this exotic bird? . . . Oh, *no!* That goddam fool. . . . Not—dead? . . . Oh, brother. . . . Sure. Sure, we'll be right up, or however long it takes; you know. Just hold on. . . . Sure. Thanks a hell of a lot, Murch." He replaced the receiver and looked around, smiling again, but uneasily and as though to himself. *"Jesus, what luck!"* he said.

"Captain, is one of our men hurt?" Johnny asked.

"No," said Weiller brusquely. He slid down from the desk. "But we've got to get up there. Gas up and let's go, huh?"

"All right, Captain." Johnny could feel excitement and curiosity rising in him. "But what about Korvac, weren't you going to . . . ?"

"That can wait," Weiller said. "Come on. We'll pick up the girl—"

Starr broke in. "Captain, you've already put her away for the night, haven't you?" His voice was injured and overloud. "I'm certainly sorry. But I have to be careful of my relations with the French. I wouldn't want to disturb the people at the *gendarmerie* again this evening."

The captain gave him a look of disgust and turned away. Over his shoulder he said impatiently, "Could Hudson or somebody drive Phillips and the girl up in one of your jeeps in the morning, then?"

Starr said, "I'm afraid I need Hudson tomorrow. The jeeps too." His brow furrowed thoughtfully. "Now let me see. What's the best way to handle this? . . . Tell you what," he said at length. "If you're ready to go now, Captain, I have a man Porter who can take you up, in one of my jeeps, and still get back tonight; and then Phillips can take the girl up in your jeep tomorrow. How's that?"

Weiller swung around. "O.K. Fine. Thanks." He darted a sudden, speculative glance at Johnny. "You know, Phillips," he said, "this isn't too bad. If you wanted to, you could put on the show between Korvac and Thérèse yourself in the morning, before you left. If Lieutenant Starr could spare Hudson for just a half hour or so."

In a panic-stricken voice Johnny said, "Captain, I—do I have to . . . ?"

The captain stared at him. "No, of course you don't have to." He paused. "Maybe better not, as a matter of fact, since we won't have time to plan it. Just bring her on up. If you can get anything more out of her on the trip, why, that'll be good enough."

Johnny glanced in embarrassment at Starr; then he hung his head. "I don't feel as if I could—even talk to her right now, sir," he said.

Starr looked at the captain, and then back at Johnny. "Say, what happened today, anyway?" he burst out curiously.

Weiller ignored him. "Hell, boy," he said to Johnny. "Don't worry. Just bring her up, then. You can do that, can't you? She won't—eat you, for Christ's sake."

Starr laughed.

The captain glared at him. "Thanks for all your understanding, Lieutenant," he said. "Now if you'll send Porter out, I've got to get cracking." He turned a last time to Johnny. "Just take it from me, kid," he said. "Relax. We can afford to, a little." He smiled and winked at Johnny, and left the room.

Thursday,
August 31, 1944

XVIII.

If he was to be a child again—but if he was it was his own fault, wasn't it? "Boy," the captain had called him, and "kid." Meaning nothing, probably; or nothing but kindness. But that it should have seemed kind to call him that! And Starr, of course, had taken it all in. The lieutenant treated him condescendingly for the rest of the evening, when he wasn't trying to pump him, and Johnny felt himself squirming under the patronizing glances, the smirks of contempt.

It was some satisfaction that Weiller hadn't told Starr what the new development in Cherbourg was. But then, Johnny said to himself uncertainly, he didn't tell me either.

He excused himself early and went upstairs. Hudson was nowhere to be found. But the poker game was in session again, and this time Johnny played, until he lost what money he had with him. He didn't care about the money; it even seemed rather appropriate to lose it, somehow. The queer thing was that the other players appeared to know how he felt and to be vaguely disappointed, as though winning the money weren't enough, as though he'd cheated them out of something else that they'd expected, but couldn't complain about not getting.

Well, and maybe I did, Johnny thought disconsolately, lying awake later in the dark. It was the initiation into the ways of the world, the today-you-are-a-man ritual, or the best version of it they know about, and I didn't measure up because I didn't care. You've got to care. You've got to lose, and it's got to hurt, and you've got to pretend it doesn't, but not so successfully that they can't tell. You're supposed to be a good sport, but if it really *doesn't* hurt, then the whole thing's no use, they've got to figure out something else.

In Africa they smash your front teeth in with a rock.

301

Of course the poker players didn't know that the captain had got in ahead of them. No, Johnny said to himself, not the captain, Life. This is Life.

But the captain helped.

Then why did he call me "boy"? He ought to know if anybody does—

Maybe he's just sorry for me. Maybe it was a little more thorough than even he would have planned it. When he calls me "kid" it's as much as to say "Let's pretend it didn't happen —not for long, of course, up and at 'em again tomorrow—but relax for a minute now, we can afford it, take a little breather—"

Or maybe it's just a convention. Maybe you're technically a boy till you stop bleeding.

And even Thérèse had taken an interest. . . .

Let's not get conceited, Johnny said to himself. Thérèse had had other concerns; she had had, as she had put it, "a great need of her own."

Waiting outside the *gendarmerie* the next morning, Johnny knew that his most agonizing trial was about to come. It was fine for Weiller to say he could relax; the trip would have held no terrors for Weiller. But Johnny had not seen Thérèse alone since evening before last, when they had parted, only a few steps away from here, on so tender a note. And if she tried to resume, now, on the same note . . .

She would not; she, at all events, was not a child. And if he had been one then, Johnny told himself, he would not be one now. . . .

Her very appearance was a trap. As she walked toward the jeep in the crisp morning light he could not help observing the slowness, the stiffness of her movements, the dead, disheveled look of her hair, the staring whiteness of her face. Her dress hung splotched and shapeless on her body. Her eyes were half closed against the brightness of daylight, and the gendarme led her roughly, as though she were feigning blindness, or were refusing to come.

Johnny's heart contracted in a spasm of pain. But it doesn't mean she's innocent, he said to himself harshly, and the answer, *It doesn't mean she's guilty, either,* flooded over him so swiftly that he could think only, All right, then it doesn't mean anything. . . . He nodded curtly to the gendarme, in dismissal, and as the man turned Johnny wondered suddenly, Am I supposed to tip him? No, you don't tip an official doing his job. "*Merci*," he called out. The gendarme shrugged and walked away without answering.

Thérèse stood silent beside the jeep. A sudden movement of the air brought Johnny the odor of her garments, an odor so sickening that he twisted in his seat, half turning away. Almost he would have asked her to sit in the back seat, but she could not sit there, he could not guard her there. Of course she didn't need to be guarded. But didn't she?

He motioned abruptly at the seat beside him. "Get in," he said.

She climbed wearily into the front seat and arranged herself as far away from him as she could. Her expression was vacant; only when her fingers touched her dress revulsion showed for a moment on her face.

"You all set?" he asked.

She nodded.

He started the jeep motor, made sure he had it in low, and with a jerk pulled out into the deserted street.

He had reached the northern outskirts of La Haye-du-Puits before Thérèse said, "We do not visit M'sieur Korvac, then?"

"Not today," Johnny said.

"Oh, please—" She turned toward him. "It is not that I—wish ever, ever again to see this man, but—all night I said to myself, Let it be ended, and m'sieur, now I am prepared—"

He would have given anything not to talk, not to think of her falseness, above all not to expose himself again to the destroying doubts. He too had said to himself, Let it be ended. It was, it should always have been, Weiller's case alone; the captain, after all, could keep an emotional distance, as he, it seemed, could not, and it was Weiller who had said 'I haven't proved it, have I?' so he would not be unjust—doubtless had always been more just than Johnny—

But the girl had said 'I am prepared.' And that must mean something. It had to be followed up, he supposed, and there was no one else to do it. Just because he didn't want to know what the answer was, or feared what it might be, that didn't excuse him from doing his duty. What should he say?

The answer was clear. It was Weiller's case. What would Weiller say?

Johnny looked straight ahead at the road he was following. "Mademoiselle," he said, carefully and perhaps too loudly because the voice with which he was speaking was unfamiliar, it was not his own, "if you are prepared—to confess your guilt, then Korvac's presence will not be necessary."

With a sudden effort he turned to look at her, saw her eyes widen before she turned away. "Do you—wish me to confess guilt, m'sieur?" she asked.

So she had managed to turn it, again, to a personal matter, between them. Which was just what it must not be. Why did she do it? he asked himself in a rage of sadness, and the answer came to him: Because she knows she can, of course, because it's worked for her before. . . . He said coldly, "What I wish is of no consequence, mademoiselle."

"But to me it is!" she said. "Only I had not thought you wished—that."

In spite of himself, tears formed in his eyes. Damn you, damn you, he said without speaking. His foot pressed down on the accelerator and the jeep leaped ahead so that, rounding a curve, he swung out dangerously over the center of the road.

She did not seem to wonder that he had not replied. She said, "It was a way I thought of, you know? In the night, late. I thought—the heart says my father was not guilty; and I am not; but—the law, it seems, says there was guilt, and I know that the law and the heart cannot be the same. If even through no fault of his own, then, my father left—debts he could not pay, must not I, his daughter, pay those debts? To the law as well as to my aunt and uncle? It is not—as though I have something else to do with my life." There was a brief silence. "Only," she said in a small voice, "I do not know why it is, but I do not wish to die."

Johnny said furiously, "Mademoiselle, please—I do not know this road very well—"

"I also," she said softly, at once, and it was as though there was nothing he could say that would not touch some flow of thought in her and release it to speech, "I also do not know—this road." She sighed. "But perhaps it is the road that knows, m'sieur. You will see that yours will take you to Cherbourg, there will be little chance to stray, and if you should do so it would only—put off your arrival a little. I have been thinking that my road also will take me where I am to go; and if I do not know where that is, perhaps it is enough that the road knows."

Johnny said stiffly, "More than once you could have changed your road, mademoiselle."

"No," she said. "One tells oneself that, and I have thought it, but—now I know I could not. On one's own road, at a place where one could—go straight ahead, or another way, no one else puts signs to say 'A mile ahead the bridge is gone,' or 'This road is forbidden.' One goes ahead, and then he finds out; and then the people standing around block the way back and say, 'You should have known that, anyone would have known,' or 'If you had been a good girl the bridge would not be gone, now what are you going to do, if it is the wrong thing again you will be punished.' I am who I am, child of my father—" She paused. "I suppose you are thinking," she said, "the bad child of a bad father."

Johnny said harshly, "You cannot say, mademoiselle, that the captain did not tell you what roads were forbidden. And besides one can look ahead—"

As she turned toward him he could hear wonder in her voice. "Are you so strong, m'sieur?" she asked.

Johnny did not answer.

"And the captain," she said. "My enemy, he showed me that in the beginning. If I had seen then that I was—bad, m'sieur, that what I wished must therefore be bad also, then perhaps I could have thought my enemy good, even in his cruelty. Like the surgeon who hurts to help. But when one has been—in desperation for years, doing all one can, then it is not easy to say, 'I am bad, my soul is sick, this man must be good if only because he like all the others wishes to hurt me,' one sees only —the hard face, the great, unclean knife, and one hears the lies with the advice, and—goes on as he can."

It was so like what he himself had thought of her for so long, or of the captain rather, that Johnny felt himself being stirred, drawn toward her again in spite of himself, the young girl alone, set upon in experienced fury by a man who had behind him in anything he chose to do the weight of an army, of an entire nation— And only yesterday Johnny had moved finally away from Thérèse, had set himself in ice away from her, had locked himself against further change, and if he were to move now would not bend, but would break, would splinter. . . .

The threat was itself like physical pain, and he thought, I can't, I can't—it all sounds so fine, it always sounded so fine, and there was something wrong with it before, what's wrong with it now? She'd accused the captain of lying, and he had, but so had she. But that wasn't it, she'd say that of course she'd had to lie— What had she left out, what had she hidden under all that fancy metaphor . . . ?

"M'sieur," she said, and touched his arm with her hand.

He jumped, and the jeep swerved. "Be—careful," he said sharply.

"I am sorry!" She was silent for a moment, and then went on with a timid stubbornness in her voice. "But—it was to say something. To say that as all this goes on I know less and less who I am, or what I do, or even what I have done, and why. And I fear that I will forget some things, or let them go because they seem already gone, already lost, it will even seem—right to forget, m'sieur. So will you—let me say one thing again? About my father."

"No, wait," he said. They were rounding a curve, coming into —was it Valognes?—along a walled street which he did not think he remembered. He kept an eye out for an MP, but there was none in sight, no soldier even. Well, he thought, half annoyed and half relieved, here's that slight delay she spoke of, and was about to ask her if she recalled the way when the turn around the ruined church presented itself unmistakably. In a few moments they were on the main road north again. Her father . . . Suddenly, reluctantly, he was alert. Was it this that was wrong? "All right," he said. "Go ahead."

"Your captain told me that my father was not human," she said in a sad voice. "You heard this. And that I must no longer remember him as a human being. But, m'sieur—if I do not—

who will? And though the captain's eloquence, and his anger, stopped my tongue, I know that my father will not be accounted for if it is forgotten that he was human. He tried to be more than human, m'sieur; but who could be that for long? And so—"

"I think," said Johnny dryly, "that the captain meant only that it was not his function to 'understand,' or to judge or to forgive your father, either one."

"You do not call that judging?" she flared. "To say that he was not human?"

"Mademoiselle—"

"No, please, you said I might speak, now let me," she said urgently. "Consider, m'sieur, a lonely man, proud, hurt by many misfortunes, very poor, who comes to a strange city where at last he believes that his life will change. And for a time this seems possible. But in little more than a year the German conquerors come also to that city. And they seek a man with just the knowledge—and the loneliness, the bitterness—of this man. And they find him; and he is everything they wish, he has even —a child, only one, the only person he trusts and loves, through whom they can hope to enslave him if he will not work for them willingly, out of his own dissatisfaction with the world. He is not as weak as they had hoped; but they have time. And so they pursue him, m'sieur, month after month, year after year, but from the shadows, so that he does not even know he is pursued, until at last they have cut off his work, his bread, every path of escape, and the trap closes upon him, and they have him. And they are many, they are everywhere, and he is only one; to his child most of all he cannot say what has happened to him. M'sieur—no doubt he should have loved a France that no longer existed, a world sealed off by neglect and ignorance and pain, more than he loved his child, but—can you not see that he could not? Could you, m'sieur? Could your captain? Can you not imagine that life could put a weight upon you greater than your strength could bear? And, m'sieur—since in the end he did you no harm, as in the moment of greatest despair he had sworn he would not—can you not let him go?" She was weeping. "Ah, let him go!"

"Mademoiselle," Johnny said in a shaking voice, "you speak

of him as though he were alive! You make us keep saying to you that he's dead! How can we—let him go, or hurt him, either one? It is you, mademoiselle—"

"I, yes, I!" she cried. "It was I for whom he did it, without me there could have been no trap! Why will you not let me make his peace for him now, let his name live nobly, without shame—" She pounded her small fist on her knee. "M'sieur, can you not see that this is—everything to me? Once I thought—once you seemed—kind—"

Not this way, Johnny thought bitterly. He rapped out, "Once I was kind. Once I fought for you, every way I knew how, I went way out on a limb for you with the captain, and then I found out—you'd lied to me."

She looked at him wide-eyed. "But, m'sieur, it was not to you I lied—"

"Wasn't it?"

"It was not to hurt you—"

"Well, it did hurt me," he said.

"I am sorry." She was silent for a moment; then she said in a strained voice, "What else could I have done? You and the captain were the same—"

He had known that he'd been a fool to think she loved him. But this he could not bear. He looked at her in horror, then turned his face away.

"Not as persons! I thought you—kind, as I said, and he—is not. But you were both of the American Army, which sought to prove that my father—"

"Yes," he interrupted. "Forget it. But I'm trying to say to you —same as the captain again—that I can't do anything about your father. Because whyever he did what he did, he did it. And all we can do is put it down on paper and pass it along."

"M'sieur," she cried, "can you not destroy your papers? I told you, I will confess. To anything. That it was I who worked for Bloch, and only I. That the transmitter was mine, all. The—crime—would not have been but for me, then let me—"

"Don't be a fool," Johnny said. "How can I destroy the papers? Do you think the captain would, if I would? Anyway—" He looked at her bleakly. "How could I take your confession about something you didn't do when you haven't even told us what you did do yet?"

"But I have, m'sieur," she said quietly.

"Oh have you? What about the papers that were with the transmitter then—speaking of destroying papers. Why did you do that?"

"It was—as I said. What my father had told me—hurt me very much, it enraged me against Bloch, if Bloch had been there I think I would have tried to kill him, m'sieur. But he was not. And the power was still his for a time. If I destroyed the transmitter I might destroy my father. And so—I damaged what I could, m'sieur, I tore up the papers and burned them in my aunt's kitchen fire. It was—a release, of no other importance." She looked away. "And it was not enough."

Why hadn't he left it alone? Johnny thought, shaken. Because again, it could be true. . . . But she was the one who hadn't left it alone. "All right," Johnny said. He drew a deep breath. "What about the Bloch note?"

There was a pause before she answered. "I have told you, m'sieur, many times. I do not know, any more than you. But surely it is not surprising that such a man—might wish revenge—"

Suddenly a thought that had been suspended forever, it seemed, in Johnny's mind, struck him with avalanche force. He slammed on the brakes. Thérèse cried out, but if she was afraid he did not care, she ought to be, and now until this was cleared up he dared not go on driving. He pulled the jeep over to the side of the road and turned off the motor. Without looking at Thérèse he said, his voice sharp with accusation, "You're lying again."

"M'sieur—"

He turned toward her. "The captain said it didn't make sense, and it doesn't. The letter wouldn't have got revenge for Bloch unless Korvac were caught, and Bloch *couldn't* have wanted him caught, Korvac knew too much about the Paris station, about the coastal network—about him, if it comes to that. Even if Bloch thought the Germans were through, he wouldn't have handed us everything on a silver platter like that, wouldn't have led us back to himself, for God's sake, just to get even with you for snubbing him!"

"Perhaps—it would not lead back to him," she said, "perhaps Bloch—is a false name—"

Johnny ignored her. "Why, hell—if you were innocent, and he knew you were innocent, he'd have known he couldn't *get* even with you with that letter, only get you in a little trouble maybe—"

"And has he not got me in trouble?" Thérèse said in a low voice. "And not only a little—"

Johnny shook his head savagely. "There's got to be a straight reason why Bloch wrote that letter," he said. "He must have believed what he was saying, must have believed that it would work." Johnny was staring at her directly, fiercely, now. "And if that's so *you* must have given him some reason to believe that it would work."

Thérèse covered her face with her hands. Johnny reached across and yanked them away. She permitted them to drop to her lap and lie there inert. Staring straight ahead of her, she said at last, in a whisper, "Very well, m'sieur—"

"This time don't lie!" Johnny shouted.

"I will not lie again, m'sieur," she said. "Only—one day I hope you will ask yourself what questions you have a right to ask and what you have not."

"Tell me," he said.

She made a still gesture with her hands. "On that day when Bloch told me that he could do my father much good, or much harm," she said. "And tried to—make love to me. At first I fought, as I have told you. But then I thought of my father, of his despair if this last work should be taken away from him. And I was—still young, there was much I did not know. And I let Bloch—have me." She turned away. "I tried even to pretend that I had fought him only out of coquetry, that I also desired him, though—this would not have deceived him if he had in fact cared about—me, a response from me." There was a pause. "After he left I was very ill, shocked, I could not help it, and when my father returned I could not hide from him what had happened, as I had intended to do. And so when my father

310

could make arrangements we—left for Sartilly, m'sieur, and did not see Bloch again."

For a long time Johnny sat silent, bowed over the wheel of the jeep. At last he looked up at Thérèse, defiled within, defiled without, and thought, Whose marks on her go deepest? He said, "It hadn't happened before, you'd done nothing else . . . ?"

"I swear it, m'sieur," she said, and then bitterly, "Are you content now, do you know more about spies, more that will help you . . . ?"

He started the jeep again and swung out into the road. For a long time he did not answer. Then he said, his voice rigidly controlled, "No. No I don't. I don't know a damned thing about you, and I never did, and I guess I never will."

"M'sieur?" she said faintly.

"Suppose I take this story to the captain now," he said, "and tell him that this is it, this is absolutely all, and it clears you —what'll happen? He'll just get sore again, and get something else out of you tomorrow—"

"No, m'sieur. I said that I would not lie again, and—I have not."

"Sure," he said. "And what's to prevent that from being a lie? You lied to me about the transmitter, and when the captain caught you on that you went on lying about Bloch till I—made you say some more. Why should I think you've stopped lying? It doesn't matter to me, it's nothing personal, I'm just asking you—if you want me to believe you, what makes you think you've fixed it so I can, how am I supposed to know . . . ?"

She said, "There are many things one does not—know, m'sieur. But one can—believe—"

He turned on her. "Are you so strong, mademoiselle?"

She was gazing at him sadly, her eyes wide and dark, her cheeks still damp with tears shed—how long ago?

Then she lifted her chin and turned away. "If you do not know, m'sieur, then—no doubt the road knows."

The girl's just a little thing, the captain had said. *And she has big, brown eyes. And if you didn't have the story—*

Johnny's mother said, *You really* don't *know very much about girls, do you—*

"Shut up!" he cried. "Shut up, shut up, shut up!"

XIX.

"*MON CAPITAINE,*" said Thury, bowing.

"*Mon capitaine,*" said Weiller, bowing even lower.

Thury straightened and looked at Weiller with an odd glint in his eye. "You honor me with an early visit."

You bet I do, bud, Weiller said to himself. But if it was five this afternoon it'd still be too early for you, considering what I'm about to put you through. He said blandly, "I hope it isn't inconvenient."

"Not at all!" Thury poked his head quickly inside the door of his office, then swung the door wide open. "Come in!" he said. "Here we can talk undisturbed."

Weiller walked in and looked around curiously as Thury closed the door behind them. There was the safe, which Thury usually left open all day. It was closed now, Weiller noted with amusement; inside it, ten to one, was the package Cécile Aubanne had got from LeMaire.

If LeMaire was his name; it was the name on the photograph, but the woman might be his mistress or a married sister. And the child didn't look like him—not that you could tell much from the face of a dying man, still less from the face of a stiff.

Thury said nervously, "Will you be seated? I will call Estelle, and ask her to brew us some coffee. Or—" His lifted his hands palm upward, apologetically. "What we French are forced to call coffee. Estelle!"

"Don't you get American coffee?" Weiller asked.

"A—a bit," Thury said. "But it is so useful in gaining entrée, in making needed friends—" He shrugged. "Yet I had not wanted to ask—"

"Well, of course," Weiller said heartily. "You should certainly have all you want. I'll tell Colonel Engstrom, and I'm sure he'll see to it you get fixed up."

"Believe me, I should be most grateful!" Thury bowed again and swung around toward the back of the house. *"Estelle!"*

There was no reply.

"Doesn't seem to be here," Weiller said. "Say, Captain, maybe it's just as well, at that. I've got something pretty important to tell you, and—" He shook his head gravely. "Maybe you'll want to tell her and maybe you won't. It's up to you, of course—"

Thury, seated now behind his desk, was looking across at Weiller with thinly disguised alarm. "What has occurred?" he asked. "Does it . . . ?" He sighed. "Yes, of course. It concerns Mademoiselle Bouliard?"

"I'm afraid not," said Weiller with luxurious regret. "No. I'm afraid not." He paused. "But let me tell you the story," he suggested.

"Please," said Thury. His face, Weiller thought, looked slightly green. Like a big quince.

"Yesterday—" said Weiller and then interrupted himself. "You understand I myself wasn't here yesterday; I was out of town, on business relating to Mademoiselle Bouliard. That's become a very perplexing case, by the way. You'll be surprised to know that—"

"Yes, yes," said Thury. "I shall want very much to hear about it. But you were saying that yesterday—"

"While I was out of town," Weiller confirmed. "My men Murchison and Dolin were here, but it was some time before they themselves learned what had happened, of course. And by then—" He turned his head and stared sadly out the window. O.K., he said to himself, that's about enough of the thumb-screws. Now brace yourself, you bastard.

"A man, a Frenchman, was stopped by the MP's," he said. "As he was leaving Cherbourg, I think. On a bicycle. They just asked him for his *permis de circuler,* and it turned out he didn't have one."

Thury's pallor had sunk to gray, but his expression was attentive, unemotional.

"I don't see why he didn't just say he was a native of Cherbourg, going out into the country to get some wood, or something," Weiller went on, "but luckily for us he didn't have that much presence of mind. It wasn't lucky for him, though. He tried to run for it, the MP's yelled at him to stop, he didn't, and—he got shot."

"Is he dead?" Thury asked in a rush.

"He is now, yes," Weiller said. "But he didn't die right away."

It was a good story, Weiller thought complacently: tailor-made. But—something was funny about it, all the same. What was it? And then he realized—oh, Christ, the way he had it the guy would have been shot from behind, presumably at some distance, while he was trying to run away; and actually LeMaire had been shot at close quarters, from in front. But the doctor had bandaged him—and Thury might not notice, and if he did, of course, he probably wouldn't dare say anything.

"Go on, *mon capitaine*," said Thury.

"Yes. Well, the MP's took him back to headquarters and called an army doctor, then they went through his clothes. Didn't find much at first; just the usual personal stuff, comb and so on, and a picture of a woman and a boy. But—the picture had a name and an address written on it, Denise LeMaire I think, and the address was somewhere in Nancy. One of the MP's was pretty bright; he figured why would you write an address on a photograph unless—"

"Unless you wished the person notified of something, yes," Thury said forlornly. "Of—accident, or death, for example."

Weiller nodded. "And why would an ordinary traveler think he might be killed? So they looked through his stuff again. They'd found a food parcel before; all that was in it was a hard roll, sliced in half and buttered, or anyway there was some kind of fat on it. And—"

"Of course, of course," said Thury. "He was intelligent, this MP. The sandwich is not usual with the French."

"So they pulled it apart, and there was a piece of paper inside—all greasy, but *very* interesting. There were a lot of notes on it, that looked like the sort of information a spy would collect." Weiller paused. "Only if this guy was a spy, he hadn't collected the information himself. Because the note was typed."

Thury sighed heavily.

Go ahead, squirm, Weiller said to himself, hardly able to keep from laughing. For a guy who's in training to be a son of a bitch you didn't do so well, did you? And what are you going to say now?

"Alas, always more work for us, eh?" was what Thury said. "But we must not be despondent, *mon vieux; this is why we are here. Et alors?* At this point the MP's called your men. Or the bicyclist died; which first?"

"Oh—the MP's called G-2. Colonel Engstrom's office. The colonel went on over himself; and when he saw the paper he telephoned—me, but of course I wasn't there. Murchison went in my place. The doctor had arrived and had treated LeMaire—we might as well call him that—cleaned his wound, given him a couple of shots, and so on. But LeMaire was completely out, and there wasn't much hope. The doc, of course, wanted the guy transferred to hospital; but if he was a spy, and should come to, he'd have to be questioned right away, and Murchison figured he himself couldn't go to hospital too, and take the cot next to LeMaire's, just to control that situation. Anyway, if it turned out we could use LeMaire, Murchison knew we didn't want him seen any more than he had been. So Murch talked to the colonel, and the colonel suggested that LeMaire be transferred to our place if possible. The doctor didn't like it, but he finally agreed, and went along to make the guy as comfortable as he could. It was a cinch LeMaire couldn't stay where he was."

Thury shook his head somberly. "Most dangerous," he said. "Most unwise, to move a wounded man in this way. If not to the hospital, of course. He—died en route?"

"No," said Weiller.

Thury looked at him helplessly.

"Wait a minute, I was talking about the note, wasn't I?" Weiller said, reaching into his pocket and pulling out a greasy, folded sheet of paper. "Captain, you really ought to see the information this man had been given." He got up from his chair, walked across the room and handed the paper to Thury.

Resignedly Thury picked his spectacles up from the desk and put them on. The wide, black horn rims changed his appearance entirely, Weiller thought; it was as though a pair of glasses were wearing a man.

Thury read, or appeared to read, with absorption, occasionally pursing his lips or cocking his head on one side. Weiller watched him closely. At last Thury looked up—and if anyone could look innocent with those glasses on, Weiller thought in amusement, Thury looked innocent. "I do not think this is true, any of it, is that not so?" Thury said. "Not that I am informed on these matters. But though it seems we have an undiscovered enemy, I should doubt that—fantasies like this could injure us."

.Weiller reached across the desk, took the paper, walked back to his chair and sat down. "That's not how I look at it," he said coldly. "Take this fifth item. Remember it?"

Thury shook his head.

"'I have been talking with a young American soldier,'" Weiller translated. "'After we had become friendly he asked me if I had any relatives in Brest to whom I would like to send personal messages.'"

"*Et alors?*" said Thury. "The young man's unit is not identified— This is of no use to the Germans, surely."

"Maybe not," Weiller said. "But what I wonder is—what *is* going to be done about Brest? I grant you that whoever wrote this probably just made it up. But suppose, by coincidence, a big surprise attack on Brest *is* being planned?" ·

"The Americans do not commit suicide!" objected Thury. "It would be ridiculous!"

Weiller folded the paper and dropped it in his lap. "Well, after all, you and I don't have to argue about it, do we?" he said amiably. "One man isn't a division, either. All I meant was—*we* don't know, and the person who sent that doesn't know, what the Army's plans are; and that being so, a completely false message could cause a lot of trouble, if only by accident. But I've got off my story. I was telling you that the boys took LeMaire back to our place—"

Thury removed his spectacles, his face wrinkling momentarily, showing weariness. But he said nothing.

"They tried to telephone me at our headquarters in La Haye-du-Puits, but I hadn't got back there yet. So they kept on trying, in between times seeing if they could revive LeMaire." Weiller looked mournfully at Thury. "But what could those kids do, you know, the guy was in shock, in coma—"

Thury shook his head sympathetically. "A pity," he said.

I wouldn't even have needed to come in here, Johnny thought acidly. Of course he wouldn't be *here*. But where is he?

He could feel the tension in his back, his shoulder muscles, and forced himself to relax. Who cares where Weiller is? he said to himself. You're here, aren't you? And she's—taken care of. With slow, almost indolent steps he walked back to the outer office and sat down at the desk.

If there were something, anything, to do while he waited. . . . There was. Carl's typewriter sat in front of him. He could rewrite, and complete, the report on Thérèse Bouliard. He got up from the desk and began to pace the lobby, looking for a magazine, a pack of cards— To his relief, the lobby door opened, and Carl and Tochyk walked in.

"Well, hi," Carl said. "Got back O.K., I see. No bones broken? No prisoners escaped? No illusions shattered?"

Johnny turned away. "Everything's fine," he said. "Lay off."

"Hell, I'm not pickin' on you," said Carl. "Why should I? After all I'm as happy as a lark, as fresh as a daisy—I got to rest up from Weiller almost two whole days, didn't I? Only you know what he's got us doing now?"

"What?" said Johnny.

"Peddling corpses."

"Peddling—"

"*A* corpse," Tochyk said mildly. "One."

"That's right, Antie," Carl said. "In this business we got to be strictly accurate, we got to be—"

"Murch!" Captain Weiller's voice boomed out in the back passage. "Hurry along, will you? We've got a lot to do."

"Watch it," Carl said. "Here comes Little Caesar. Big Caesar, I mean. He's grown."

Weiller burst into the lobby and looked around with satisfaction. "Good," he said. "You're all here. Where's Barker?"

"I sent him upstairs with Thérèse Bouliard, Captain," Johnny said. "Do you want me to . . . ?"

"No, no," said Weiller. "That's fine. Only—" He paused a moment. "Tochyk, would you take the desk for awhile? I want to get a report from Phillips, and there are some plans to be made about this new case."

"Sure, Captain," Tochyk said. He looked at the clutter on

Thury stopped pacing, his back still to Weiller. "There is more?" he asked.

"Here." Weiller took from his pocket another piece of paper, unfolded it, and laid it beside the first. Thury whirled around, strode over and picked them up. "That second sheet is a page from a report sent us from this office," Weiller said apologetically. "Do you see the broken 'h' and the nick out of the bar of the 'e'? Both those were typed on the same typewriter."

Thury hurled the sheets of paper to the floor. "Traitress!" he shouted.

"I'm very, very sorry," Weiller said. And seeing the expression of terror, of loss, on Thury's face, he added to himself, It's funny, but I really am sorry.

But by the time Thury had begun to regain his composure, Weiller's purpose was firm again. It's rough, old man, he thought, watching the figure bowed over the desk, head in hands. But you didn't worry about what was going to happen to me in all this, did you? And we haven't finished yet, either. There's still a lot of ground to cover, and it's going to be hard on baby's little feet. So—shall we get on with it?

At last Thury looked up from his desk and said, his voice trembling, "It is true, as you know, that I have upon occasion permitted Mademoiselle Aubanne to leave her room, to take a little promenade—for her health, you understand, and to attend the doctor, she was not altogether well, and—she assured me that she would not attempt to escape, that she needed the sun—" He looked down at his hands, with which he was shredding a corner of the blotting paper. "I did not tell you details of this, because it seemed unimportant, one does not discuss all one's arrangements—"

"Naturally," said Weiller.

"And I am not always in this office, nor is Estelle—Mademoiselle de Sombais—" Thury flushed, glanced quickly at the door that led to his apartment and looked away again. "Each of us has much other work to do," he said peremptorily.

"Quite," said Weiller.

"Thus perhaps the use of the typewriter—" Thury paused and glared at Weiller, his face stiffening. "But no, *mon capi-*

taine. Even so it is not possible. You are sure you are not playing a joke on me, an American prank . . . ?"

Weiller gazed at him evenly. "I wouldn't do that," he said.

Thury made a futile gesture with his hands. "Then I do not understand," he said. He rose from the desk and began once more to pace the room. "Do you not see the impossibility?" he asked insistently, pausing in front of Weiller. "Consider. All other difficulties apart, Mademoiselle Aubanne would have had to have an appointment with this—M'sieur LeMaire. How could she have received word of the appointment here? No, no, m'sieur." His expression became indignant. "It is very nearly as though I myself were accused of—having dealings with the enemy."

"That certainly would be ridiculous," Weiller said contentedly.

"Or—" Thury's eyes widened. "Mademoiselle de Sombais—"

Whoops! thought Weiller. I didn't see that one coming. Let's get out of here. "Now, Captain," he said swiftly, "I'm sure that neither you nor Mademoiselle de Sombais is at fault. You yourself have convinced me of her loyalty, and—I need not speak of the high esteem in which you are held, among all of us. This new occurrence is unfortunate, but no doubt it could have happened to me as easily as to you, and after all, it only goes to prove that spies are spies, doesn't it? Actually it may turn out to be very lucky—as long as we've found out about it, that is."

"Yes," said Thury weakly. "Yes." He sat down at his desk again, swung his chair around and stared out the window.

"I've thought of something," Weiller said. "That appointment yesterday—she could have had that since before she was arrested, couldn't she? So that her problem was only to convince us that she was changed, loyal to us now, and relatively harmless—I know we both felt that way about her—and then perhaps she could get a little freedom, and—go back to her old work even though she was technically under arrest."

"Unbelievable," Thury muttered.

You bet it's unbelievable, Weiller said to himself. He felt vaguely disappointed because he had had to change his tack; it had been fun needling Thury, getting him out on one limb after another just to see what he'd do. But he certainly didn't want Thury suspecting de Sombais, not right now, not till there was a chance to talk to the girl and figure out what was going on there. And after all, he owed her a lot; overnight he had regained control of Cherbourg, his worries were at an end, and he had no one to thank for it but her.

And there was more to it than that even. Sad as it was, Thury had to be permitted to save his own face. Because I've got to go on working with him, Weiller thought. If I go all the way with this now, make him eat all the dirt he ought to eat, he'll just hate me for it, and I'll never know from now on whether he's playing straight with me or not. . . . Weiller sighed. Well, he could still have a little fun with the double-crossing bastard.

"On the other hand," he said, "maybe that isn't the explanation. Maybe Mademoiselle Aubanne has another contact, a go-between, here in town. You know, it seems to me that there's only one way really to find out how her rendezvous with LeMaire was arranged."

Fearfully Thury said, "And how is that, *mon capitaine?*"

Weiller sat up in his chair. "Let's go ask her," he said brightly.

"I—I am afraid—" Thury almost stuttered in his agitation. "That will not be possible. As it happens, Mademoiselle Aubanne is at this very moment taking a little walk. For her health, you understand. I do not—" He took a deep breath. "I do not know when she will return."

Weiller raised his eyebrows. "Really," he said. "Well, you can understand that I do want to get this cleared up; perhaps I'll be able to wait." He studied his watch and then settled back in his chair, putting on a thoughtful look, a look of concentration. Suddenly he sat upright again. "I've got it!" he said enthusiastically. "While she's gone let's go back to her room and search for that package LeMaire said he gave her—the one containing money and equipment! I certainly would like to know what the equipment could be. A spyglass, do you suppose? Or an invisible ink outfit?"

A little moan escaped Thury's lips. He cleared his throat loudly, as though to account for the sound, as though he would now speak, but he seemed unable to find words.

Weiller got to his feet and walked toward the door. "Tell

320

you what," he said gently. "I've got to go to the can. When I'm through let's go back there and look, shall we?" He smiled at Thury, opened the door and walked out into the corridor.

In the lavatory, with the door shut, Weiller permitted himself to grin, to dance up and down for a moment, silently, to strike his fists lightly against his thighs out of sheer exuberance, out of an amusement that he could no longer contain. But after a moment he felt silly, and leaned up against the washbasin to think. In the quiet of his body he heard Thury scuttling softly past the lavatory door, his steps unsteady; he's carrying the package, Weiller thought, grinning to himself again, and it can't be exactly light. Now, let me see. He's got to tell Aubanne what's happened—no he doesn't, he can do that later, he's just got to get her the hell out of her room and into a place where I won't stumble onto her, and then he's got to hide the package. But I better not give him too much time, or he'll get rid of the batteries. . . . Weiller looked at his watch again, waited while the second hand went around once, flushed the toilet, opened the lavatory door and walked out.

He knew which room Aubanne occupied and he went to it at once. The door was unlocked; he threw it open. Thury was standing in the middle of the floor, looking helpless.

"Oh, you here already, Captain?" Weiller said pleasantly. "Now then; where shall we begin?"

"Perhaps the *garde-robe*—" Thury said, looking at the bed.

Weiller strode over to the wardrobe and pulled open the doors, one after another. A few dresses hung there on cheap wooden hangers; on the shelves there were a few pieces of underclothing. There was no package. Weiller closed the wardrobe again and turned around, his expression thoughtful. "Nothing there," he said.

Thury was kneeling by the bed, peering into the darkness underneath. "I think—it is there," he said.

Together they moved the bed out of the corner. The package, opened at one end, lay on the floor. Involuntarily Weiller, stooping over, drew his finger across the paper and looked at it. There was no dust on it, though the floor under the bed was deep in accumulated dust. A faint, clean trail on the varnished boards showed where the package had been sent skating across into the corner.

But the trail *is* faint, Weiller thought. The package must be light. He picked it up. It weighed almost nothing.

He turned to Thury and dumped the contents of the package into his arms, which rose at the last possible moment to receive their burden. Bundles of crisp new notes poured out, overflowed onto the floor. "Say, that looks like quite a lot," Weiller said enthusiastically. "You'll have to count it. But—" His brow furrowed. "Where's the equipment?"

Thury shrugged nervously, spilling one or two more bundles of bank notes to the floor. "I—do not know," he said. "Perhaps there is none, perhaps you misheard—"

"No, no," said Weiller. "Anyway, look at the package: it's big, there was obviously more in there than just the dough." His eyes roved speculatively around the room. Get your explanations ready, mister, he said to himself. Because I'm going to find those batteries if I have to look in your safe.

Thury said, "We should count the money, do you not think? And then later I will search again and see what can be found—"

Suddenly Weiller took hold of a corner of the puff that covered the bed and twitched it off onto the floor. The batteries lay exposed, black and shining against the white of the sheet.

"Ah-h-h!" said Thury, on an expiring note.

Weiller turned to stare at him, wonder in his eyes. "Radio batteries!" he said. "Captain, I certainly didn't expect this, did you? I didn't know that Aubanne had a transmitter!"

"Nor I!" Thury cried.

"But this is wonderful!" Weiller sat down on the edge of the bed. "Say, Captain, where did Aubanne live before we arrested her, anyway? I've forgotten."

"She had—rooms here in Cherbourg," Thury said haltingly.

"You searched them, of course?"

"But of course!"

"Anyone living there now?"

"No—I—I do not know, I should have to find out—"

"Say, you find out," Weiller said. "Because I bet she just had her radio set so well hidden that it couldn't be found." He smiled at Thury in delight. "But she'll tell you where it is now, you can bet. There isn't a thing she'll be able to hold out on you after today."

"No. Nothing," Thury said.

Weiller rose from the bed and clapped his hand on Thury's shoulder, dislodging one or two more bundles of notes. He stooped over and picked up all that had fallen, and crammed them back into Thury's arms. "Well, I've got to go in a minute," he said. "I've got a million things to do, and I expect you have too. Let's go back to the office for a sec, shall we?"

In the office Thury let the packets of bank notes slide from his arms to the desk, and sat down in the chair he had occupied before. His face was gray, but composed.

Weiller remained standing. "Look, don't feel too bad about all this," he said. "I know how you must feel—being tricked like that, being double-crossed. Hell, nobody likes being double-crossed; I don't myself. But it's over now. And from now on—why, there's no limit to what we can do! This case is only beginning!"

Thury looked up wanly. "Beginning?"

"Don't you understand?" Weiller said with enthusiasm. "The Germans sent Aubanne batteries, they must expect her to come up on the air! She's undoubtedly got a cipher, complete instructions, everything! And she'll tell us what they are now. So we'll talk with her, prepare the case carefully, and try to make contact as soon as possible. I'll notify the colonel, and he'll set up the channels through which we can get our messages cleared by the military authorities. I'll get started on that right away. You get the set and so on out of Aubanne, and call me up when you're ready to start working out details—"

"*Mon capitaine,*" Thury said heavily, "this will not be a success."

"Why not?" said Weiller.

"Because—LeMaire was killed. *Voyez.* The Germans send someone to provision their spy, and the someone does not return. So—he has been captured, doubtless, and doubtless has talked, and the spy is therefore also probably under arrest. If the spy sends wireless messages thereafter, must it not be, almost certainly, under control?"

Weiller said, "I know, that isn't easy. But it wouldn't have been any easier to let him go back. How do we know Aubanne didn't tell him she'd been arrested? And wouldn't he have told the Germans? These things are never simon-pure. My hunch is we'll just have to pretend the guy never got here. We'll work it out. And working together on it, carefully—" Weiller smiled. "You'll see. It'll be a hell of a good case. Bold, imaginative—" He paused for a moment. Then he said, "Even if it isn't, I'd a damn sight rather have it be just an ordinary case, or even fold up, than have Aubanne running her own operation, wouldn't you?"

"Of course!" said Thury. "But I think perhaps—if we simply closed the case—"

Weiller shook his head. "I don't think the colonel will want that, Captain Thury," he said.

Thury rose to his feet. *"Eh bien,"* he said.

"Just one last thing," said Weiller. "What do you think we ought to do with LeMaire? I'm not exactly equipped to dispose of dead bodies."

Thury considered for a moment. "I can take care of this," he said. "Have one of your men bring the body to me."

"What will you do with it?" Weiller asked curiously.

"Never fear. It will be buried somewhere." Thury smiled wryly. "The French too have their—channels," he said.

"Thanks," said Weiller.

There was a slight pause. Then, "Thank you, *mon capitaine,"* Thury said, and bowed.

Whistling loudly, Weiller walked out to his jeep, jumped in, started the motor and was off with a tremendous, heartening roar. Thankgodthankgodthankgod, he caroled to himself, it's all over, the heat's off, I've got it back— He rushed the corner, and turned it with so magnificent a screaming of tires that he almost did not hear Estelle de Sombais's cry.

"Captain!" she shouted again, and he half turned in his seat, saw her, wrenched the wheel sharply and pulled the jeep in to the curb.

She walked up to him slowly. A damn nice piece of work, he

thought approvingly—that figure, the black dress, the high heels, the silk turban—

"Captain, I must speak with you," she said in a low voice. "Not here—" She turned and looked behind her. But there was no one in the street.

"Well, hop in," the captain said. "I'll take you over to my place. Say—" He lowered his voice, but after all he was a good block from Thury's headquarters now, he could be neither seen nor heard. "I want to thank you—"

"Not now!"

Her voice was so agitated that he looked at her in surprise. "What's the matter?" he asked.

"I—I cannot tell you—"

Great, the captain thought. She's got to talk to me but she can't talk to me. He climbed out of the jeep and stood beside her. "Let me—" He looked down at her benignly, wondering what to offer.

Suddenly, and with enormous difficulty, he suppressed a bellow of laughter. Two strands of the silk turban had slid apart, revealing what Estelle de Sombais's problem was. Her head had been shaved. She was, in the words of a phrase that had long ago impressed itself indelibly upon Weiller, as bald as a baby's ass.

XX.

GLID BARKER was sitting at the desk in the lobby when Johnny and Thérèse walked into Weiller's Cherbourg headquarters.

"Where's the captain?" Johnny asked him.

Barker looked up, his face blank and moony. "Dunno," he said.

"Where are the others, then? Jim, and Carl?"

"Dunno that either."

Johnny made an impatient gesture. Finally he said, "I've got to find the captain. Take Mademoiselle Bouliard on up, will you?"

"I'm s'posed to stay at the desk," Barker objected.

"I can watch it. I'll be close enough," Johnny said in annoyance. He started toward the door of Weiller's office.

"Oh—O.K." Barker got up from his chair and stretched.

"And by the way—" Johnny's voice carried no emotion. "See that she gets a chance to wash, and gets her clean clothes from the room back there."

"Now look here!" Barker said crossly. "The captain never said to do nothing like that!"

"Then do it because I said to!" Johnny paused at the office door, swung around and glared at Barker. "After all she's a human being, isn't she?" he shouted.

Thérèse's face turned toward him. But he did not meet her eyes.

Captain Weiller's office was neat and empty, the desk bare of papers; a hush transfixed the air. In the corner the slant box of light shone dimly, like a jewel that has been thrown away by accident, to lie forgotten in its molding case.

326

I wouldn't even have needed to come in here, Johnny thought acidly. Of course he wouldn't be *here*. But where is he?

He could feel the tension in his back, his shoulder muscles, and forced himself to relax. Who cares where Weiller is? he said to himself. You're here, aren't you? And she's—taken care of. With slow, almost indolent steps he walked back to the outer office and sat down at the desk.

If there were something, anything, to do while he waited. . . . There was. Carl's typewriter sat in front of him. He could rewrite, and complete, the report on Thérèse Bouliard. He got up from the desk and began to pace the lobby, looking for a magazine, a pack of cards— To his relief, the lobby door opened, and Carl and Tochyk walked in.

"Well, hi," Carl said. "Got back O.K., I see. No bones broken? No prisoners escaped? No illusions shattered?"

Johnny turned away. "Everything's fine," he said. "Lay off."

"Hell, I'm not pickin' on you," said Carl. "Why should I? After all I'm as happy as a lark, as fresh as a daisy—I got to rest up from Weiller almost two whole days, didn't I? Only you know what he's got us doing now?"

"What?" said Johnny.

"Peddling corpses."

"Peddling—"

"*A* corpse," Tochyk said mildly. "One."

"That's right, Antie," Carl said. "In this business we got to be strictly accurate, we got to be—"

"Murch!" Captain Weiller's voice boomed out in the back passage. "Hurry along, will you? We've got a lot to do."

"Watch it," Carl said. "Here comes Little Caesar. Big Caesar, I mean. He's grown."

Weiller burst into the lobby and looked around with satisfaction. "Good," he said. "You're all here. Where's Barker?"

"I sent him upstairs with Thérèse Bouliard, Captain," Johnny said. "Do you want me to . . . ?"

"No, no," said Weiller. "That's fine. Only—" He paused a moment. "Tochyk, would you take the desk for awhile? I want to get a report from Phillips, and there are some plans to be made about this new case."

"Sure, Captain," Tochyk said. He looked at the clutter on

Carl's desk and then, diffidently, back at Weiller. "But do I have to sit right there? I mean—"

"Sit anywhere you want to," Weiller said. "Just stay in this room is all I meant. Answer the phone if it rings, take care of anybody who comes to the door—*you* know."

"O.K." Tochyk walked over to the bench nearest the window, glanced back once apologetically at the others, and took a pack of cards out of his pocket. Then he sat down and began to lay out a game of solitaire.

Weiller grinned. "Let's go into my office," he said to Carl and Johnny. As they were leaving the room he called back, "Send Murch in when he gets here, will you?"

"Red eight," murmured Tochyk in absorption. He looked up. "Oh—yes, sir," he said.

"And see that we're not disturbed, Antie."

Tochyk mumbled something in an indignant voice.

"What?" Weiller said.

"Nothin'," said Tochyk.

When they had assembled in the inner office, Weiller sat down in his desk chair, leaned forward, surveyed his audience and grinned magisterially. "Well, men," he said, "it's going. It's really going. We're on our way. Murch and I just got back from seeing the colonel—" The captain stopped and looked at Johnny. "But I forgot," he said. "I'll bet Phillips here is pretty mixed up about all this. That so, fella?"

Johnny winced and looked swiftly at the others. Jim Murchison seemed to be paying no attention, but Carl caught his eye and smiled broadly. Johnny felt his cheeks burning.

"Captain," Carl said, "maybe you'd like to have me quick fill him in before we go ahead."

Weiller looked at Carl with a glint of amusement in his eyes. "You can quick fill him in for hours later, Carl, if you want to. Right now—" He looked at his watch. "I'm in a hurry, I've got an appointment for lunch." He turned to Johnny again. "Let's just say this. You may know I've had an impression for a long time that Thury was trying to pull something on us, trying to run a case behind our backs. He isn't supposed to; *everything* like that has to be cleared through Supreme Headquarters, and G-2 CI here's been expecting me to keep tabs on Thury. Anyway, while you and I were down below the cat got out of the bag. Turned out that Thury's prisoner Cécile Aubanne was an SD agent with a transmitter—England hadn't had any information about her of any kind, and when Thury found out who she was he never told us—and he'd actually put her on the air and made contact with her German bosses. Completely without authorization. Could have been a mess, but I think it's going to work out all right.—You got it straight so far?"

Johnny nodded.

It was easier to nod than to tell the truth. Johnny had all but lost the captain's first words as he tried to control his resentment. Then, when Weiller had gone on talking busily, incisively, Johnny's mind had strayed back to the morning when the captain had outlined the Bouliard case for him. Even with Jim and Carl here now—but silent, of course—it seemed all one occasion; Johnny had been thinking: I'll have to remember this, he'll hold me responsible. But his mind had refused to register all but a few scattered phrases.

Carl said something and was answered; the captain was speaking again. "The first thing Thury had Aubanne do after they'd made contact was to yell for more money. That's taking a big chance, but apparently the Germans are so desperate that it worked. They sent a linecrosser through, with money and radio parts. He arrived yesterday morning, and—" Weiller looked expressionlessly at Carl. "Dolin shot him for us."

"Well, jeez, Captain—" Carl protested.

"I know, I know," Weiller interrupted. "He pulled a rake on you." The captain turned again to Johnny. "Anyway he's dead. Died in the night without recovering consciousness, so we didn't learn a goddam thing from him. But—" He threw up his hands and smiled. "If things could be better, they sure as hell could be worse. There's a controlled agent case running in Cherbourg, the first in France since the invasion; apparently the Germans believe in it; and—" Again the captain grinned. "For all practical purposes it'll soon be our case, because we've got Thury right by the balls."

"You sure will get a lot of credit for this up the line, won't you, Captain?" Carl said heavily.

"I suppose I will." Weiller looked at him with narrowed eyes. "Only if you're suggesting that that's why I'm interested in the case—"

"Oh, no, Captain!" Carl said.

"As a matter of fact I'm beginning to be pretty proud of this team of mine, on the whole," Weiller said grimly. "And I'm a man who gives credit where credit is due. Right now of course I'm laboring under difficulties. I've got to keep my mouth shut about Estelle de Sombais—"

"She's the one who gave Thury away," Murchison said to Johnny. "She told us where and when Aubanne and the line-crosser were to meet."

Johnny nodded.

"She deserves most of the credit for this, if you don't mind my saying so," Weiller observed coldly, "but I don't want that fact to leak back to Thury, of course, and I don't trust the colonel, so—mum's the word. For now. She'll have to be paid back some other way. Jim and you"—Weiller looked directly at Carl—"deserve a lot of credit, and you'll get it, don't worry. You, of course, would look a little better to the higher-ups if you hadn't killed that son of a bitch, but—" The captain shrugged. "Anyway, I suggest we get on with the case, and wait to divide the bouquets till later."

"You got me wrong, Captain," Carl said. He was red in the face. "I was only—"

Murchison said quietly, "What did you say to Thury this morning, Captain? We've been so busy since you got back that—" He stopped, and began again. "Apparently he admitted the whole thing, is that right? Thank heaven—"

"Nope," said Weiller, his face clearing. "Thank me. I doubt if heaven is in on Thury's gyrations." He smiled. "But he didn't admit anything to me, actually, because I fixed it so he didn't have to."

"You *did?*" Carl said. "For the—I mean—why, Captain?"

"You ought to be able to figure it out, Carl," Weiller said. "If I'd rubbed his nose in it, he'd hate me, and he'd double-cross me again. Right now he knows that I could have put him

330

in a lot worse spot than he's in, and believe me, he's grateful. He'd give me triple my weight in German spies, if he had any more around."

Carl shook his head dubiously. "Me, I'd'a put it right on the line," he said. "You been nice to him all along, haven't you? And look what he did. That guy's about as square as a golf ball."

There was a heavy silence. "Well, Carl," Weiller said, "granted that your way of dealing with the French *is* more— direct than mine, still you've had your turn, is it O.K. if I take over for awhile now?"

Carl laughed, then reddened again. " 'Scuse me, sir," he mumbled. After a moment he said, "But if you didn't make him admit anything—"

"I told him LeMaire had talked a bit before he died," Weiller said with satisfaction. "And had implicated Aubanne. And I let Thury feel that *I* believed that Aubanne had done all the double-crossing herself, with no help from him."

"But if she's on the air—" Carl said. "She couldn't have managed that by herself, could she, Captain?"

"No. So Thury's going to 'look for the set,' and then, according to the plan I've maneuvered him into, we're going to *put* her on the air—theoretically for the first time."

"I've been worrying about that, Captain," Murchison said. "Ever since you talked to the colonel about it. I'm sure you're right, and this is the way to handle it from our point of view; but it's going to look funny to the Germans, isn't it, having the same case started on them twice?"

Weiller leaned across the desk and grinned at him genially. "It would," he said, "if we let it happen that way. But we won't. I'll just tell Thury I'm all tied up for the time being, and for him to go ahead without me and try to make contact. I'll tell him to use his own judgment about the introductory messages. That takes the heat off him, you see; he can fake along for a few days, and then we'll move in after he reports that he's got the thing 'started.' Meanwhile we'll be collecting real informa- tion and getting it processed, and—when we do move in, we'll move in to stay."

Murchison nodded. "I guess that ought to do it, all right," he said, and then paused a moment, looking doubtful again.

"But we may find ourselves in a kind of funny position about the first messages we propose to send. We'll get them officially cleared in one form; but we'll have to let Thury work them over, so that they won't contradict messages he's already sent, and by the time he gets through with them—well, it might be bad security to send them, isn't that possible?"

"Trust your Uncle Bruce," said Weiller. "At lunchtime a certain young lady is going to bring me copies of the messages Thury's had Aubanne send out so far. So we'll know what's been done, and what we've got to do next. I'm hoping, of course, that no serious mistakes have been made. If they have we'll have to find a way of correcting them without seeming to; and for the rest, we can just see to it that the new stuff we prepare doesn't get in the way of what's already been sent out." He smiled. "Sure, we'll be walking a tightrope for a week or so. But hell, the damn thing's only about two feet off the ground. If you want to feel sorry for somebody—which I don't—you can feel sorry for Thury. He's the one who's got the acrobatics ahead of him. And for nothing. Just so he can hand us the case he thought he was going to have all to himself." Weiller chuckled.

So Thury had lost, Johnny thought. And Weiller had won. Goody. And someone had been killed, but that, apparently, wasn't worth talking about. He looked across the room at Carl, whose face was calm.

"Now, then," Weiller said firmly. "Plans. Murch, I don't know how long I'm going to be tied up over lunch, and after that I've got to see the colonel again and get him cracking on this business of clearance for messages. Thury's got to have peace and quiet for today, because theoretically he's searching for the set, and actually he's telling Aubanne what's happened and getting her lined up and letter perfect in her new part. After today I'm going to send you over to talk to her, get details of the cipher and so on, because for obvious reasons you're the one who ought to sit in on the transmissions. For the rest of today, though—well, this afternoon will you take on the job of seeing Mowbray in Army Signals, and telling him not to get upset about anything funny he and his men find on the air around here during the next few days? We're damned lucky they haven't put the D-F equipment on that fool Thury already. Maybe they have. Anyway find out the situation, and tell him we'll give him exact information on the wavelength used in this new case, times of transmission and so on, as soon as we can. *Don't* tell him any more. If he gets curious, refer him to the colonel."

"Who'll spill his guts over morning coffee any day," Carl muttered.

"I think I can assure you he won't," Weiller said, his voice icy. "Now. You got all that, Murch?"

"Yes, sir," Murchison said.

"Good. Now about the information we'll be sending out. One of you's going to have a full-time job for awhile making like a spy—going around town, seeing what you can see and where you can see it from, figuring out what a Frenchman, or woman rather, a private citizen, could find out just by looking, talking to GI's, and so on. Tochyk's a possibility—" The captain paused and considered. Finally he shook his head. "You don't have to tell him I said this, but the job's got to be done imaginatively—"

Carl said eagerly, "How about me, Captain?"

There was a dead silence in the room as Weiller surveyed Carl, his face expressionless. "I could consider it," he said at last. "Though after yesterday, it does look as though you're just too valuable on the desk, Carl."

"That's a dirty crack!" Carl burst out. "I—you don't—ah, hell!"

"I'll talk to you about it sometime, Carl," Weiller said smoothly. "If you're sure you really want to talk about it." He turned to Johnny. "I guess that leaves you," he said.

Johnny sat up straight in his chair. His thoughts had been wandering; he had given the captain only half his attention. He had heard, vaguely, the discussion of the new assignment, but it had not occurred to him that the assignment might be given to him.

"Captain," he said. "What about Thérèse Bouliard?"

"What about who?"

"Thérèse Bouliard." Johnny paused, then said uncertainly, "Will you be . . . ?"

"Will I be what, for Christ's sake?"

"Taking over her case?"

"Her case?" Weiller said impatiently. "There's nothing left of her case. D'you think I've got time to mess around with her, with all this new stuff on my mind?"

"I—guess not, sir." Johnny looked at Weiller with dazed wonder. *It's his case,* he kept saying to himself, but even as he said it he knew that Weiller had not even thought about it from the moment he had left La Haye-du-Puits the evening before, and that when Johnny had mentioned it just now Weiller had at first hardly remembered who Thérèse Bouliard was.

Weiller snapped his fingers. "But by God I almost forgot," he said. "I'm glad you reminded me. Nothing happened on the way up, I suppose?"

Johnny looked down at the floor. He could feel the eyes of the others on him. "She—admitted she'd slept with Bloch," he said. "Just once, or that's what she claimed. The time in late April when, according to her earlier story, Bloch had just tried to—make her."

"Yes, well, that could be," the captain said. "It would give some kind of color for the Bloch note, and it doesn't upset the rest of her story, she could still be in the clear."

Johnny looked up wildly.

"What I was going to tell you was this," Weiller said. "For some reason or other Estelle de Sombais seems to have her claws sharpened for the Bouliard girl. Wants her turned over to them —to Thury and her. In lots of ways it would be a good move; it might make Thury feel a little happier about losing control of the Aubanne case, and as I said, de Sombais really seems to want Thérèse Bouliard bad, and God knows I owe her something, and this would help pay *that* debt. But—"

Johnny's heart was pounding in his chest. "But—what, Captain?" he said.

Weiller shrugged. "Well, I just thought, when she asked me, about how you'd—felt about the case, and I decided you could keep it if you wanted to. So I told her I didn't know, we'd have to see where we were."

Johnny's throat tasted bitter as gall. You son of a bitch, he thought, *you* couldn't care less, you've got new toys to play with, but you're the one who got her where she is now, and I'm supposed to pick up the pieces, I can have her if I want her—

"Well?" said the captain impatiently.

"I—I don't see what there is left to do, Captain, I—we've asked her all the questions, over and over again—"

"All the questions!" Weiller snorted. "You must have found some new ones to ask, to get this additional information out of her. And we were going to take her down to see Korvac again; remember? And there's Durand, the head of the Lycée, to be asked about the father; and Mademoiselle Vaugiron could be asked a lot more questions about him too; and you could maybe find out which other Cherbourgeois were working at the Kommandantur, and talk to them about the Bouliards, and about Bloch; and you could go to work on the Bouliards' neighbors; and—" He paused. "I don't doubt you could get a lot more out of the girl herself," he said.

I could, *I* could, *I* could, Johnny thought desperately—why can't *you?* You're assigning all the jobs on this new case to the rest of us, you'll have a few minutes here and there, and god damn it you've got a responsibility—

"Look, kid," Weiller said heavily. "Don't you get it? I'm giving you a chance to prove Thérèse Bouliard innocent. Wasn't that what you wanted? For your information, Estelle de Sombais didn't look to me as if she was interested in proving the girl's innocence. Now do you catch? Me, I'd just as soon use you on this new job; there's a lot to be done, a lot of really productive work. But—" He shrugged.

I can prove her innocent, Johnny thought, *I* can—or if I can't I can spend hours and days tearing myself to pieces. Or no, we'll have that cozy little mattress in that cozy little room, we can sit there talking about how hard life is when one is alone, and then I can inflict my virginity on her— She slept with Bloch, after all, maybe many times, it ought to work out handily enough.

Of course it was unlikely that Bloch had been a virgin.

Oh, so? "It is not possible that you have abandoned me, your Rudolph." Just the language a recent virgin might use.

Suddenly Johnny wanted to vomit. "Captain," he said, "what happens if—I can't prove anything?"

Weiller's face reddened, and he half rose behind the desk.

"No, I mean it, seriously," Johnny said hastily. "If I find out all I can, and it still isn't—conclusive, what's the next step?"

Slowly Weiller settled back in his chair. "Why, then we write up our report and turn the girl over to the French, I guess."

"And then what would happen?"

"They'd—work on her. And when they were through, if they thought there was any doubt of her innocence, she'd go up for trial."

"Are the French executing spies?"

Weiller made an impatient gesture. "If she could make her present story stick, I doubt she'd even be sentenced. But there's the Bloch letter. I don't know. If they decided she'd worked for Bloch for awhile, under the pressures she described—they might give her, oh, five, ten years in the jug." He paused. "We're wasting time," he said. "Do you want to take the case on, or don't you?"

Johnny closed his eyes. "I—don't," he said.

Weiller stared at him in silence. "All right," he said, after a moment. "This afternoon make up a final report on it, will you? Here are my notes on the interrogations down below." He unbuttoned his breast pocket, took out a dog-eared pad of paper and threw it on the desk. "This evening, if you're through, I'll talk to you some more about what I want you to do tomorrow—about getting material for the radio traffic in this new case."

"All right, Captain," Johnny said in a low voice.

There was a knock at the door, and Tochyk stuck his head in. " 'Scuse me, Captain," he said. "But that dame's here."

As though with difficulty Captain Weiller, still staring at Johnny, looked away, looked at Tochyk. "What'd you say?"

"That dame's here. She wants you."

There was a long silence. Then the captain attempted a smile. "Well—you don't have to go telling everybody, do you?" he said.

The others turned toward him.

"Uh—did you say you had a lunch date with her, Captain?" Murchison said awkwardly. "Shouldn't someone tell them back in the kitchen to lay an extra plate?"

"No," Weiller said. "We're going to her place." He stood up and stared at the others defiantly. Then his expression changed, became confused, as though somehow he wanted to laugh and yet was angry, or sad. "Liaison," he said.

Johnny looked up at him bitterly.

"A human sacrifice, that's me," the captain said. He picked up his overseas cap from the desk and walked to the door. "Well, I know my duty when I see it. Don't wait up for me." With a flourish he saluted, and was gone.

Carl broke the silence. " 'A human sacrifice,' " he mimicked. "*He's* human."

Jim Murchison stirred in his chair. "Maybe that's just the trouble," he said. "Maybe if he weren't you couldn't get at him so easily. But what do you expect? Why do you needle him all the time, Carl? Of course he gets sore at you, and then things like this happen."

"What am I supposed to do, lick his boots?" Carl said fiercely. "He always gives me the dirty jobs anyway. Like carting the stiff over to Thury."

Murchison nodded. "I know," he said. "But we had the—the body. We couldn't let it rot here."

"God damn Weiller!" Carl exploded venomously. "Ever notice how when something goes wrong it's always somebody else's fault? He'll never let me forget now that that guy died. But the way it happened, it was either shoot him or get killed myself, or crippled for life, one, and then the guy would've got away. And if he had, where would Weiller be, I'd like to know? I'd like to have seen him do any better with it than I did, by God. Only *he* wasn't here, of course."

"Don't blame him, Carl," Murchison said, his voice troubled. "I guess it was my fault really, I—" He stopped.

Carl turned on him. "Go on," he said silkily.

"Well, all I meant was, if Weiller *had* been here, he'd probably have planned it better than I did—I mean more thoroughly—"

"Thanks!" Carl's voice was loud with sarcasm. "I been wondering if you were going to say something like that. You think I bitched it up too, huh? So you'll be big and take the blame.

'Sorry, Captain, I should never have let that jerk loose on anything important—' "

"You know I didn't mean that, Carl," Murchison said.

Johnny listened, and watched, as from a great distance. It didn't matter who was right—if anybody was. Murchison had been trying to pacify Carl, but Carl wanted to blow up, and why not let him? Let him blow himself right off the team, if that's what he wanted to do. "The team." Carl and Weiller were a team, all right. Both "human." And what was so good about that?

Suddenly he remembered what he had said about Thérèse Bouliard: "She's a human being, isn't she?"

Why had he said it? He sat up in his chair, glimpsing something— Being human was supposed to be quite a thing, better than being an animal, for instance. But it didn't always work out that way. And you didn't look at other people with pride and say, There goes a human being. If you used the phrase at all you usually meant—just barely human. You were usually commiserating with them, or excusing their weaknesses. Like Murchison, apologizing for the captain.

And with the justification of being human, Weiller went right on stomping around, hurting other people, taking mean revenges, hiding his moral failures under any convenient cover, outside pressure, or loneliness, or—duty. But that didn't mean they weren't failures. The only people Johnny knew who hadn't felt the backlash of Weiller's "humanity" were Murchison— and that was part of the reason, perhaps, why Murchison was so ready to defend him—and Thury. Thury, who deserved, apparently, the treatment Weiller had been giving everybody else. But in the name of "duty"—or politics—Weiller was being humane to Thury.

And Carl. A sorehead, never willing to deny himself the pleasure of blasting off at other people, but furious if he had to take the consequences—

"Well, *kid?*" Carl said scathingly, and Johnny realized that something else had been said before, something he hadn't caught. "Aren't you talking to us poor white trash, now that the great man's taken you under his wing?"

"Don't, Carl," Murchison said as Johnny said ominously, "I was thinking about something, Carl."

"Your rosy future, no doubt," Carl said. "While I type your shining reports, and de Sombais skins Thérèse Bouliard alive."

Johnny was trembling with anger. "What are you talking about, Carl?" he said.

"What am I talking about? Do you think they're going to let her go, or put her up for trial, either one? If you do you're kidding yourself. Why do you suppose they want her? Thury's lost control of the Aubanne case, he must be sore as a boil, and that hot bitch de Sombais's always sore, maybe Thury can't satisfy her, I don't know, anyway she sure queered him, and do you suppose she's just after Bouliard so she can treat her like her little sister?"

"Carl, lay off!" Murchison said and turned quickly to Johnny. "Don't mind Carl," he said. "He's upset, you can see why. But—"

"But what?" Johnny said.

Murchison shrugged helplessly. "I wouldn't put it the same way, but—I've been wishing too that you'd reconsider about Thérèse Bouliard. I don't know why you decided not to go on with her, I'm sure it wasn't just to get in on this new case—"

"You're very understanding," Johnny said.

Murchison continued stubbornly. "But anyway—the captain told us when he got back that the girl hadn't broken all the way; that it was not even impossible that she was innocent, legally at least; and . . ." His voice trailed off.

"Go on," said Johnny coldly.

"I'm coming to realize that this is an inhuman game we're in on," Murchison said in a low voice. "It's got to be in some ways, I guess, it's not our job to worry about people's feelings, and if it were we haven't got much time. But—now the captain's given you the chance, offered you the time—" He stopped again. "Believe me, Johnny," he said, "even if she's guilty, you'd be doing her a favor if you proved it to the hilt, got her all set up for trial, before you turned her over to that headquarters."

Half weary, half frozen with anger, Johnny thought: There it is again. *I* can do it, *I* can prove her this or that. And how neatly it all ties in: I can do it in the name of humanity. Weiller's human, Carl's human, and now Murchison, the great apologist for the human, is giving me my chance.

Murchison was looking at him steadily. "Carl," he said after a moment, "would you mind—could I talk to Johnny alone, please?"

"Hell yes!" Carl said. "Don't think I'd want to horn in on anything. Anyway I s'pose *I'm* needed on the goddam desk." He slammed out of the room.

Johnny half rose.

"No, wait—please." Murchison's voice was strained, but he was not, now, looking at Johnny. "This— You aren't convinced. And I don't know what to say," he said. "I wasn't going to say anything, this isn't a prepared speech. Please anyway realize that if it sounds ever as if I'm criticizing you, I'm not; I'm criticizing myself."

Like he was criticizing himself for sending Carl out to deal with the linecrosser? Johnny thought wintrily, but he sat down again, saying nothing.

"You don't know me, and I haven't seen enough of you to make it easy for me to—talk about myself to you, but I did some damage once, Johnny. To my wife. I don't know how much. I don't know if I ever will know, she—" He stopped.

You'd better be careful, a savage voice inside Johnny said. *I've had too many talkings-to—*

"It's not the same, I know that, but it's not what anybody's done I'm talking about. It's the chances they've got. I didn't use mine, Johnny. I made some assumptions about—Louise, probably they weren't true, but then by the time I'd really made them I don't think I even wanted to find out, I guess I could have, but—the pleasure was already gone out of my marriage, I'd spoiled it for myself. And suddenly I had this position, you see, I was an injured husband, and I didn't know it then but I think I actually enjoyed thinking that, it was clearer and more dramatic than—"

Sharply, with revulsion, Johnny broke in, "You said it wasn't the same. It isn't."

"Please, Johnny," Murchison said patiently. "Did you ever—

have something to say, and think it was the right thing to say, and know that you weren't the one who had a right to say it? But I've got to—go ahead anyway."

"Go ahead then," Johnny said after a moment. "If you have to."

"I'll try to put it a different way. I know it's hard not to be sure of the real truth about another person, but—it's hard for them too. Forgetting any relationship. Even if there isn't one. Innocent or guilty, or somewhere in between, a person under suspicion—however he got that way, it's as though he were— being eaten away by some kind of hidden infection. As though only a doctor could help him. And first a diagnostician."

A pre-med with two years of college French Weiller's voice said, sardonically, in Johnny's ears. Had Weiller told Murchison . . . ? Well, why not, after all?

Murchison's eyes had been lowered; now he looked directly at Johnny. In a quiet voice he said, "A doctor does not think about—" And then, *"In my own case, I wasn't thinking about the—patient, I was thinking about myself.* And that wasn't the point."

Johnny got to his feet abruptly. "Doctors have to call in specialists sometimes."

His head bowed, Murchison said, "What kind of specialist is Estelle de Sombais, do you know?"

Johnny looked at him in horror.

"No, I didn't mean that, it isn't fair. But—sure, you can fail. Doctors can. Only—it's so natural to think mostly about one's own part in things, about *I;* and to get out from under that is such a release, it lets you see—"

It isn't the same! Johnny wanted to shout, or *All right, I'm a lousy doctor, I was never trained, doesn't it make sense that I'd like to know what I'm doing for a change?* but he heard the *I* and fell to pacing the room. He was supposed to think think think about Thérèse. After Murchison tiptoed away he was supposed to sit around and take a beating from his conscience, he was supposed to soak in the hard-won wisdom, the selflessness of—God's only grandson, and after a suitable interval burst out of the office crying in an exalted voice, "I'll do it! I'll do it!"

Think about Thérèse. . . . But he'd done nothing else for days, and where had it got him? All he knew now, that he hadn't known at the beginning, told him how little there was he could be sure of. Of course he didn't want Thérèse mistreated, or anybody, he never had, but—

Murchison's wife. His *wife.* He'd have had a *responsibility* toward her even if he hadn't done the damage himself, which he admitted he had. But for Thérèse, why was the sole responsibility Johnny's? Simply because Weiller had ditched it? Simply because Thury and Estelle de Sombais . . . ? Suddenly Johnny grinned furiously. No doubt they were "human" too. But did that mean they could not be expected to behave responsibly? Couldn't Carl? Or Murchison?

Had Thérèse herself no responsibility?

All at once Johnny remembered something he had thought long ago, down in Sartilly—that Thérèse's best defense lay, and must lie, in herself.

By God it did all tie in. Thérèse's plea for her father—on what grounds had it been made, after all, except that Bouliard had been—human? Which, translated, meant—weak. Sure he'd been put in a hell of a spot. It happened to people sometimes. But he'd ended up a German spy, and you couldn't laugh that off. Thérèse—she was in trouble exactly to the extent that she'd condoned weakness, participated in it, and lied about it afterward. Whatever extent that was. But I don't know, Johnny said to himself, and I don't think I can find out, and I don't see why I should have to. People looked at you with big eyes and said, "Help me, I'm only human"—or Help So-and-so, *he's* only human, or *she's* only human. Let's treat everybody as human beings. Sure. Exactly. In the end, people had to pay the penalty for their own weakness. In the end, they had to take responsibility for themselves.

"Chances to help—don't keep on coming," Murchison said. And then, urgently, "Keep the case, Johnny."

Across the room, Johnny stood still, turned and looked at him. *Just because you screwed up . . . ?* When he spoke, his voice was colder than he knew how to make it. "Is that an order?" he said.

A look of puzzlement came over Murchison's face. "An order, of course not, I—"

"Carl tells me you're about to be put in charge here."

"That may never happen, it's—"

"Until it happens, then, if you'll excuse me, I've been given a job to do—" He gestured toward the door. "I'm sorry. You heard what I said to the captain. The decision has nothing to do with—your wife."

Slowly Murchison rose to his feet. His voice even, he said, "I didn't mean to offend you, Johnny."

Johnny turned away.

"But let me say this. If I *were* in charge, yes, I think I would —not order you, but—"

"But since it's only a suggestion, suppose you make it to Carl?" Johnny said hotly. "After all he's not too loaded down with spies right now." He paused. "If he's—called in on the case you'd better, of course, take the forty-five out of his black bag."

There was a heavy silence. Finally Murchison said, "I've been given a job to do too, Johnny. And like you I'm about to go do it. But—if I do get the command of this unit—get it soon enough—I'm also going to try to do something about Thérèse Bouliard. Only there isn't—" He looked at Johnny, then down at the floor, shaking his head as though in bewilderment.

Johnny closed his eyes. When he opened them again Murchison was walking, almost aimlessly, toward the door. He said something which Johnny could not make out.

"What was that?"

"Nothing." Murchison turned back, fatigue and sadness in his face. "I was just reminding—" Again he shook his head. "It wasn't anything you'd understand."

For a moment Johnny almost felt sorry for the things he had said. But he too was tired; worn out, nearly. And it was at him that the pressure was directed, not at Murchison. If it came to that, he had his own painful memories. His mood hardened once more.

"I understand very little, I know. But I like to hear what's said to me."

When Murchison answered, it was as though he were quoting something, in a voice so quiet still as to be almost inaudible. *"You do not get there all at once,"* he said, and turned again, and left the room.

Friday,
September 1, 1944

XXI.

In the night Johnny had waked, and had lain awake for a long time, his mind sick with doubts. But that was what night was for, he thought now, as he walked out into the cool early-morning city. Night was the time of weakness, the time when the human being suffered most from being human. With the light, strength returned, if there was strength to return.

And there was. In the night Johnny had thought: I can still change my mind. For the evening before, he had heard Weiller on the telephone making the arrangements, and he knew that Thury would not come for Thérèse Bouliard before midmorning. True, Thury had been promised— But now it did not matter about the promise, and still Johnny knew that he would not change his mind, was certain he should not. There would be pain, but that was irrelevant, and it was, besides, the penalty exacted from him by his own humanity.

The blue that trailed its ribbon above the narrow street was blue or perhaps gray, so early it was. The buildings, squares of shadow, did not sleep, but drowned, with no one to say at what moment it would be too late even if the sun were then to burst out above them. The air was damp. On the stone at Johnny's side drops of water collected their heaviness and ran downward, leaving trails like the trails of rain on window glass.

Or tears. The world weeping itself to water.

But he was through with tears, Johnny thought, the tears that said I cannot, I cannot; through with his own and others'. For what he had to do he would do, and what others did they must do, and take what followed as he would take for himself the consequences of what he was and would be.

And suddenly the waters, many drops and many rivers, flowed together, and he became certain of what it was that had happened to him in these last days. He had learned the secret of living in the world. He had grown up. And not because of Weiller or anyone else, but in spite of them all.

His mother had always known how to keep him a child, how to swamp him in his own emotions, how to dig for his raw nerves and tie him to her by them. For the first time now he could strike off those bonds, whatever the hurt to himself, because he knew now what they were and what they meant. And Weiller, Murchison, Carl—Thérèse—not one of them again, nor anyone like them, would successfully seek an emotional hold on him, telling him to be a man and at the same time (whether they realized it or not) trying to undo his manliness, trying to revenge upon him, and involve him in, their own failures. Johnny thought: I don't care what he said, you have to protect yourself. And again, looking at the empty street ahead of him: I'm all alone. But now I know who I am. I've got rid of them. They can't hurt me any more.

He almost ran across the Place de la République, suddenly delighted with the sound his heavy shoes made on the stone, knowing that no one would hear besides himself. A private sound, in his private city. . . .

He wished that he could be above the city at this hour. When he had flown in, the water of the Channel, far below, had been gray and wrinkled as an elephant's hide, had crept minutely as he had gazed at it, had been netted occasionally with gold from the late afternoon sun. He had looked around at the other passengers in the plane, wishing he could tell them what he saw, how he felt about it. Not yet knowing why it was that he could not.

Now, in this early morning hour, the water would be, from the air, an inky blue-gray. . . . He could glimpse it from where he stood, and walked rapidly along past the food dump and out to the edge of the cement apron that bordered the harbor. A breeze off the water chilled him, but he lifted his head and breathed it in, swinging around to look at the full circle of what lay before him. It was beautiful, it was all beautiful. . . . A first ray of light broke from somewhere behind the transatlantic docks and, across the harbor, touched to dazzling whiteness the stone of some broken tower far out beyond the Arsenal. A gull, flying in from the sea, took the same light, then tilted its wings and slipped down into shadow. Johnny drew in his breath sharply, contentedly, then turned, his back to the water, to look at the dark buildings that were the city.

Soon to wake.

Tomorrow morning, perhaps, he could be, at this same hour, somewhere on the hills south of Cherbourg, looking back down. . . .

He remembered the first time he had ever gone on a trip with his mother and father—had it been to Utica, or Albany? No matter. But he had got up very early in the morning and crept to the hotel window, and stood watching for a long time while the low morning light washed in like a chill golden tide among the almost deserted streets, and while a few flights of pigeons wheeled among the buildings, sole possessors of the towering roofs and the ice-blue sky.

He had had an intuition then: that there was an hour at which any city was a work of nature, and not a work of man; when buildings stood like trees in a massive stone forest, lofty and remote, their existence hardly connected with the little, animal existences that touched them, perhaps made use of them, and then were gone. If you watched at that hour you were the instrument of a kind of magic that gave the city meaning and coherence; you could feel that you were at once the projector and the only spectator of something vast and imposing and silent, an iceberg, a mountain seen in its dawn colors.

A few hours later, under a more commonplace light, the impression would have vanished, the ice would be broken up and dispersed, the mountain blotted with cloud, the pattern gone. The city, in a jungle of noise and a haze of smoke, would have become dependent again on what was happening within it; the scurrying crowds would have involved the tallest buildings in the dimensions of their own concerns. But if, like a clumsy magician, you then saw the materials of your spell escaping from you, at least you were not discredited, having had no audience; and the next morning again you could call the towers up as brittle as glass from their lake of shadow, and see the city again in its own massive truth, apart from man.

Johnny stood for a long time spellbound with his own imaginings. When he stirred at last it was to recall that when he had first thought these things he had been, almost, a child; and now he was no longer a child.

But perhaps, if you recognized early enough that you were alone, manhood would return to you your most clear and private vision, the best that you had known before. Growing up did not need to be all loss.

And that this was true he felt the more surely as he looked, once more, out at the harbor, where a dozen or so ships, tankers, cargo vessels, a hospital ship painted white with a big red cross on it, lay at anchor. For as he looked the earlier vision did not die, but opened to embrace what he now saw before him, and this was of the very stuff of his new work. He was to pretend to be a spy, to see what a spy walking the streets of Cherbourg might see. . . . The ships were beautiful, like carven gray ice, the white ship like chalk on the slate of water. Alone on the strand Johnny began to count, fumbling as he did so for his notebook and pencil. No sound came from anywhere.

And so he would ride out the war, Johnny thought. Alone as he had not known he would be, but as, now, he wished. Working with others but bound to them in no other way. Reserving his emotion for—scenes like this.

Working with others. . . . Johnny remembered, suddenly, something that had passed through his mind a few mornings earlier, not far from this very spot. Ironically he said to himself: How right I was. Now that it's all shaken down. Now for the first time, really, I'm doing as I'm told.

But for Johnny there would be more pleasure in it than the boy working on the engine had showed. For Johnny's luck still held. He was in on something big. It would be a real satisfaction to double-cross the Germans.

When he got back to the hotel there was no one in the lobby. Carl's desk was strewn with papers. Johnny grinned.

He could hardly wait to find the captain. He'd seen something very interesting, a new kind of ship had come in. Could it be carrying troops? It was small, but—

Carl walked out of the back room wheeling a bicycle. When he saw Johnny he stopped.

"Where . . . ?" Johnny said.

"They came and got her."

Silence hung heavy over the narrow room.

Johnny said, "I meant—where's the captain?" Without waiting for an answer he turned and started into the inner office, hoping that this time he would not find it empty.

EPILOGUE

In the spring of 1943, a teaching fellow at Harvard, living in Cambridge with my wife and a new baby, I was awarded a Guggenheim Fellowship to write a long war poem. But already I knew that I must have the fellowship postponed, that I could not excuse myself from getting directly into the war. Things moved very rapidly. I was picked up by a secret intelligence organization and trained in secret camps outside Washington; I was commissioned in the U.S. Marine Corps and given officers' training at Camp Lejeune, North Carolina; I completed that course in mid-November and by December 3 was in London beginning another intensive period of training at the hands of British Secret Intelligence. I had an astonishing six months to look back on. The Commandant of the Marine Corps was, it came to be known, as astonished as I: 'This is the first time,' he is said to have snapped, 'that I have ever been asked to commission a god-damned poet in the Marine Corps.' Assuredly war was not what it had used to be.

My own greatest astonishment was, in retrospect, at what might have been called my graduation exercises from the last of the secret intelligence courses I had taken in America. To demonstrate to my superiors such skills as I had acquired I had been set loose in a vast industrial city with instructions to spend two days getting as much specific information as I could that would be of use to the enemy. I was, it might have been argued, testing the city's security. Naturally I could not use my own identity. I pretended to be a free-lance writer, down from New England, his identifying papers in his other suit, intent on collecting material for an article on the magnificent things being done by industry on behalf of the war effort: the article would be the last one I would write before, blazing with patriotism, I joined the army myself. ... The information I managed to pick up still makes me shudder when I think of it. I got with ease into numbers of top-secret places; I got photographs; I got figures; I learned – 'off the record' – things which in the hands of the enemy could have been used in a matter of hours to set back our war effort for months. Either my informants were very trusting – indeed, there is no question but that they were – or I was by that time the smoothest liar who ever came down the pike. It is a strange thing to learn about oneself. It is a strange thing to have wanted to become. It was strange, too, to learn that one had to betray in order to protect one's country against betrayal – really, that this was to be expected.

It was a lesson that was to be borne in on me again and again in the months that were to come. Those months took me up to, and through, the invasion of the Continent, and in July 1944 deposited me in Cherbourg. Ultimately in France I came to be involved with a Nazi agent whom we – my men and I – ran back against the Nazis as though he were working freely, as though he were not under our control. Of course we had to give the Nazis information: of course, though our ultimate purpose was deception (a lofty aim), some of the information we sent had to be verifiably true, and this meant that we had to betray our own forces, a little, in the interest of the greater good. Fortunately it was someone at Supreme Headquarters, not I, who had to decide how much betrayal, of whom, was acceptable on any given day. But in order to build up my double agent so that ultimately he would be able to deceive and damage the enemy as much as possible, I had of course to press constantly to give away as much good information about our own troops as could be thought, in balance, not too unsafe. ...

In the end we caught – did we not? – most of the spies the Germans had trained and left behind to work for them in France. Many of these I interrogated, or came to know in other ways. One of them all was, I think, an evil person; a few of them were morally empty, had become, somehow, human trash. Most of them were decent men and women – not strong, not heroic, but basically decent – whom the German Intelligence Service had manoeuvred into impossible situations, had subjected to impossible pressures. I kept thinking how lucky I was that I had not been they; for I was not sure, 'good' as I thought myself, or hoped myself, to be, that in their situations I could have done much better, or even as well.

One of the men I came to know was an old sailor with cancer of the vocal cords. He had had a beautiful young wife and a baby boy.

He had had to go into hospital for an operation. When he came out his house was empty. The Germans told him his wife had run off with a German officer. And yet, they implied, perhaps that was not quite it: and perhaps they might be able to help him find her, or at least find his child, if. ...

Another man had been a wireless operator aboard a fishing boat; when the Occupation commenced, and French vessels could no longer put out of harbour, he lost his job. Somehow, try though he would, he never found another. For a long time he did not understand why, did not understand that the Germans wanted him for their own purposes. His few family possessions melted away. Friends and neighbours helped as long as they could, but some of them began to think that he might have found work if he had really tried. His wife and daughter went hungry, then hungrier. He slipped away to Paris; the only work he was offered was with the Organization Todt, helping to build machine-gun emplacements against the Allies in the Atlantic Wall. He refused, and went back home. Things got worse. A German from the Kommandantur dropped by and asked him to do a little innocent radio work for them: they were shorthanded. He refused. In the next six months his family and he came close to actual starvation. At last the German came back and said mildly that they really *did* need help, and that all they wanted him to do was keep a radio contact in existence temporarily: he would have to send nothing but weather messages, in the clear; nothing enciphered, nothing that could offend his scruples. He would be paid at a decent rate, nothing out of the way. ... Finally he agreed. A few months of innocuous activity later, he was called in and told that he had been working, during the period just past, for the German Intelligence Service. He would never be able to convince anyone that he had not known that. If he tried to stop, his wife and daughter would be taken prisoner, tortured, possibly killed. If he tried to escape, his record would be got into the hands of the Allies. He would now accept training, thorough training, as a spy, or else. When and if the Allies overran his city, ultimately, he would have a W/T set, a cipher and a wave length, and he would send military information to the Germans, or else. ... When the Allies overran his city in fact, he broke up his W/T set, dropped the pieces down the town toilet, and prayed. After it became clear that he was not coming up on the air, the Germans identified him to one of their (our) working agents and asked that agent to find out what the trouble was. We arrested him. The French gave him ten years.

There were others; their stories differed little. And meanwhile, I saw myself and my skilled colleagues doing things – often having to do things – of which I was in human terms ashamed. But of course our side was in the right, and therefore anything we could do on its behalf, and on behalf of its ultimate victory – or anything we could even argue might work out that way – must also be in the right.

By the summer of 1946 I was back in America, back in California, finishing work on my second book of poems, and ready under by Guggenheim to go to work on – on what? At first I did not really know. But it would not be a long war poem. It would be fiction. Probably it would be a novel. What about? All the winter of 1946–47 I tried my hand at short stories, the first I had ever written, just to try to figure out what I was doing. And then I began a story called 'The Green Place', and I knew I had found my theme.

It was about a French war bride, a girl who, wrongly arrested for treason and later cleared, falls in love with the American soldier who establishes her innocence, and he with her. They marry: he brings her back to the United States, to his home. There his possessive mother cuts husband and wife apart, isolates the girl, and drives her to suicide. A story of betrayal, based perhaps on a rather obvious irony. I wrote three sections and discovered that I could not bring the story to conclusion; discovered that I had to know – and show – more of what I had earlier been prepared merely to assert had happened in France. You cannot drive a girl to suicide merely by wanting to; who *was* this girl?

At about the same time I read Rebecca West's *The Meaning of Treason*, and learned from Miss West what dirt traitors are, and how inhuman are the things they do. Something very deep, and very old, stirred in me, and I began to write *The Serpent Sleeping*. It was about the same girl and the same boy I had begun to write about, but they grew, and changed, and their situations, and the things that happened between them, made it clear that the novel might never get back to the United States at all, might never get back to the chapters already written. I applied for, and received, a renewal of my Guggenheim, and during the year of 1947–1948 wrote, in awkward first draft, the first half of the novel.

356

And then I had to put my own writing to one side, in order to finish the graduate studies I had not finished before the war. In 1950, Oxford doctorate in hand, I went to Pomona College to teach. I taught writing, but did not write – except for a poem now and then. In 1953 I received a fellowship from the Fund for the Advancement of Education, Ford Foundation, a fellowship for which I had applied so that I might complete the novel. But five years had passed since I had begun it; was it, in effect, dead?

Curiously enough, in my mind it seemed clearer than ever. Even the title had come to have, for me, an absolute existence. That title came – comes – from *Paradise Lost*, from words spoken by Satan in soliloquy: Satan inside the Garden wall, determined to seduce and betray Adam and Eve if he can, but afraid of the 'flaming Ministers' who protect them:

> Of these the vigilance
> I dread, and to elude, thus wrapt in mist
> Of midnight vapour glide obscure, and prie
> In every Bush and Brake, where hap may finde
> The Serpent sleeping, in whose mazie foulds
> To hide me, and the dark intent I bring.

Eden is gone now, the flaming Ministers are gone, Satan himself is gone. And still there is evil; which moves now openly, now obscurely, to find complication, confusion, in whose mazy folds to hide, awaiting – us, the clumsy and accessible guardians of the good that survives.

The second half of *The Serpent Sleeping*, then, was written in 1953–1954: so well did it go that toward the end I was writing as much as five thousand words a day, words that would never need rewriting. The new chapters were far better than anything in the first part of the book. Why? Why had I not forgotten? Perhaps it was just that I was older. Perhaps there is, after all, some use in growing older.

The remainder of the book's history is the triple tale of the need of the first half for adjustment to the second, of my need to find time for the rewriting involved, and of my need to find a publisher who would undertake to publish the novel if effective revision were made. In 1957–1958 my family and I spent a year in Holland, where I was Fulbright Lecturer at the University of Leiden; in the spring I travelled down to Cherbourg and spent a week there on the trail of certain facts I needed to know, about what had gone on in that city during the German Occupation – facts I had not learned when I had been stationed in Cherbourg so long before because I had not known, then, that I was going to write a novel. By this time my characters were as real to me as was my own family; I had to find out about them, not invent them.

And so I found out. And the new material went into *The Serpent Sleeping* that year, and the novel began to call on publishers. Most of them said they thought it was beautifully written; most of them said they thought they would lose money if they published it. In 1960 the then editor-in-chief at G. P. Putnam's Sons saw the novel, showed it to his readers, and wrote a long critique of it. We corresponded. The following year he gave me a contract. We talked at great length, and corresponded further, and though my editor made no requirements of me, and few specific suggestions, our talk enabled me to see things I had not seen before: it enabled me to cut, and add, and focus, and effect in my own way the final tuning of the manuscript. The novel was now as good, I thought and think, as I could make it. Still uneven, doubtless. But in any event truly marvellous: a real novel, that had already endured for fifteen years. A real spy novel. A serious novel of counterespionage. In September of 1962 *The Serpent Sleeping* was published. And, its hour come round at last, began losing money.

That is, as they say, another story. But the story of why someone (one person at least) writes, what leads to his writing poetry, and something of what is behind a change, or a widening out, to the writing of fiction – that story I hope I have told. Long ago I knew that if the girl in my novel was betrayed by the boy's mother, it would be through the boy himself. Long ago I knew that the boy had something to do with a special kind of American innocence, or confusion, and a righteousness that comes into play when that innocence is – as it almost must be – deceived. Long ago I knew that the boy was one of my selves.

But then all the characters in *The Serpent Sleeping*, French and American, young and old, good and evil, are, I suppose, among my selves. In John Peale Bishop's magnificent poem 'Ode' occur the lines

> I have been as many men, as many ghosts
> As there were days

and I have tried honestly to show here some of the ghosts, some of the days. I could have shown more. But to do that now I must write another novel, and more poems. For I have not exhausted my reflections in the earth. I have not yet said fully how beautiful I think life is; and I have not yet confessed all my sins against it. My sins which are yours and yours which are mine. Not different, in the end, at all. Our sins which we would not commit if we knew what else to do.

Classics of Espionage

Titles in the series include:

British Agent

John Whitwell

*Introduction by **Wesley K Wark**, University of Toronto*

> *'Espionage-addicts and -allergics alike will enjoy* British Agent. *The former as an antiseptic, the latter for the laughs'.*
> **Malcolm Muggeridge**

British Agent tells the story of a bygone age of espionage. This unique memoir vividly describes a time when a hard-pressed British spy service, with only a handful of agents in Europe, sought to keep track of a continent descending into war. With Nazi Germany increasing in strength the stakes were high, yet this was still the low technology age of the amateur agent. Even a radio transmitter was a rare item; while stationed in Riga, Whitwell had to build his own. John Whitwell, the pseudonym of senior British intelligence officer Leslie Nicholson, conducted his secret work in a succession of European capitals without diplomatic cover, and at times with the German Gestapo and Soviet NKVD perilously close. His story is not one of derring-do, or spectacular coups, but of underground work when every scrap of intelligence was hard-won, and when dark fantasy and uncomfortable fact were exceedingly difficult to distinguish. It is hoped that this tale of British secret service work in Prague, Riga and London, first published in 1966 and long out of print, will provide insight and pleasure to a new generation of readers curious about the still-secret history of espionage.

256 pages   1997
0 7146 4730 6 cloth
0 7146 4280 0 paper

Spies of the Kaiser
Plotting the Downfall of England

William Le Queux

*Introduction by **Nicholas Hiley**, Head of Information at the British Universities Film and Video Council*

'As Nicholas Hiley demonstrates in his fine introduction to Spies of the Kaiser, MI5 itself owed its inspiration to the fiction of William Le Queux. Here, it appears, we have art imitating life, which is itself imitating art (of a sort)'.
Keith Jeffery, *Times Literary Supplement*

'Le Queux's novel played a significant part in the founding of the modern British intelligence community and thus fully deserves its place in the new Frank Cass series, Classics of Espionage.'
Christopher Andrew, *The Daily Telegraph*

'Extraordinary!' I declared... 'But while you've wrested from Germany the secrets of some of our most important defences, you have, my dear Ray, temporarily lost the woman you love!' 'My first duty, Jack, is to my King and my country,' he declared, sitting on the edge of the table in the spies' photographic studio'

In these stirring terms John James Jacox and Ray Raymond, the heroes of William Le Queux's 1909 novel *Spies of the Kaiser*, dedicate themselves to defeating the army of German agents at work in Britain. Le Queux was the first and most prolific of all British spy writers, but *Spies of the Kaiser* was not just another tale of scheming foreigners and plucky British heroes, for this paranoid tale of German secret agents plotting the invasion of Britain played a major part in the formation of MI5, Britain's counter-espionage organisation. In his introduction, intelligence historian Nicholas Hiley explains how Le Queux's powerful blend of fact and fiction inspired a whole generation of British secret service officers, and led MI5 in a nation-wide hunt for a non-existent enemy.

256 pages   1996
0 7146 4728 4 cloth
0 7146 4278 9 paper

The House on Garibaldi Street

Isser Harel
Former Head of Mossad
Introduction by *Shlomo Shpiro*
University of Birmingham

The House on Garibaldi Street is the true story of one of this
century's most audacious intelligence operations - the kidnapping
of Adolf Eichmann in Argentina by the Mossad, Israel's secret
intelligence service. In a daring operation which shook the world,
a team of elite Mossad agents, under the personal command of the
legendary Mossad leader Isser Harel, kidnapped Eichmann and
smuggled him to Israel. Eichmann's trial received unparalleled
media coverage, and brought home to millions around the world
the horror of the Holocaust through its principal co-ordinator.
Eichmann was found guilty of genocide and was executed two
years later.

Harel's account was first published in 1975 and won world-wide
acclaim, being translated into more than 20 languages and selling
more than a million copies. This new edition has been completely
revised and updated. For the first time the real names and details
of all Mossad personnel are revealed, as are important diplomatic
contacts which shed new light on the political acceptability of the
kidnapping, the operation being officially sanctioned not only by
Israel, but also by West Germany. Shlomo Shpiro who worked
personally with Isser Harel on the preparation of this new edition
is an Israeli scholar specialising in intelligence and security issues.

The House on Garibaldi Street has all the suspense, action and drama
of a classic intelligence story – it is also an engrossing account to
rival the best spy fiction.

312 pages   1997
0 7146 4754 3 cloth
0 7146 4315 7 paper

The Dark Invader

Wartime Reminiscences of a German Naval Intelligence Officer

Captain Franz von Rintelen

*Introduction by **Reinhard Doerries**
University of Erlangen-Nuremberg*

The Dark Invader is indeed an intelligence classic – a first-hand report by a top German intelligence agent sent to the still neutral United States in the First World War. Official German records, captured by British and American forces at the end of the Second World War, clearly show the colourful memoirs of the German naval officer to be accurate. Von Rintelen's orders in Berlin had called for measures to prevent the shipment of American war material to Germany's enemies. In the US, this meant buying arms to keep them from being purchased by the Allies, but it could also mean placing bombs in the hulls of ships sailing for Europe and fomenting strikes among the labour-force of American ammunition manufacturers.

Captain Franz von Rintelen most likely would have kept his secrets to himself, had he been treated more tactfully when returning from years of British and American imprisonment. The memoirs, not entirely free of emotion, are therefore also an attempt to tell what Berlin stubbornly denied had happened. As might be expected, the German Foreign Office and powerful men in the Nazi government were able to quash publication in Germany, thereby forcing von Rintelen to seek a publisher abroad. Embroiled in a bitter legal dispute with his government over financial claims arising from his activities in the US, von Rintelen wisely left the country, probably just in time to avoid arrest by the National Socialists. The officer of the Imperial German Navy now moved to London. He befriended 'Blinker' Hall, his former captor in the First World War, and asked if he could don a British uniform and join the fight against Germany.

320 pages illus. 1998
0 7146 4792 6 cloth
0 7146 4347 5 paper

Studies in Intelligence

Nothing Sacred
Nazi Espionage Against the Vatican, 1939–1945

David Alvarez and Robert A Graham

Nothing Sacred is the first book to document the Nazi espionage campaign against the Vatican in the Second World War.

Nazi Germany considered the Catholic Church to be a serious threat to its domestic security and its international ambitions. In Germany, Hitler's agents recruited informants to provide intelligence on Church finances, and on the political views and activities of bishops, priests and lay Catholics. In Rome, however, German attempts to penetrate the Papacy were less successful, with the efforts of the local *Gestapo* office proving largely futile.

The German codebreaking operation on the other hand was highly successful: the Nazis systematically intercepted, decoded and read secret communications between the Pope and his representatives worldwide.

208 pages   1997
0 7146 4744 6 cloth • 0 7146 4302 5 **paper**

Intelligence Investigations
How Ultra Changed History

Ralph Bennett

Ralph Bennett, who worked for four years as a senior producer of the intelligence ('Ultra') derived from the Énigma decrypts at Bletchley Park, illustrates in this collection of reprinted essays some of the steps by which he and others developed the new type of information and in the process provides a candid glimpse of the workings of British intelligence both past and present.

216 pages   1996
0 7146 4742 X cloth • 0 7146 4300 9 **paper**

Dieppe Revisited
A Documentary Investigation

John P Campbell, *McMaster University, Ontario*

This book reappraises the ill-fated raid named operation *Jubilee*, focusing on aspects such as naval and air operations in the Channel, signals, radar intelligence, agents and deception.

262 pages illus.   1994
0 7146 3496 4 cloth

Espionage: Past, Present and Future?

Wesley K Wark (Ed), *University of Toronto*

Highlights of the volume include pioneering essays on the methodology of intelligence studies by Michael Fry and Miles Hochstein, and the future perils of the surveillance state by James Der Derian. Two leading authorities on the history of Soviet/Russian intelligence, Christopher Andrew and Oleg Gordievsky, contribute essays on the final days of the KGB.

166 pages   1994
0 7146 4515 X cloth • 0 7146 4099 9 paper

The Australian Security Intelligence Organization
An Unofficial History

Frank Cain, *University of New South Wales*

This book traces the history of Australia's highly-secret Intelligence Security Organization. Established in the early days of the Cold War, like most intelligence organisations working under covert conditions, it exceeded the vague powers entrusted to it.

302 pages illus.   1994
0 7146 3477 8 cloth • 0 7146 4124 3 paper

Policing Politics
Security Intelligence and the Liberal Democratic State

Peter Gill, *John Moores University*

Drawing on extensive foreign material and making use of the social science concepts of information, power and law, this book develops a framework for the comparative analysis of the domestic security intelligence agencies in the United Kingdom such as police special branches and MI5.

384 pages figs. tables   1994
0 7146 3490 5 cloth • 0 7146 4097 2 paper

For Product Safety Concerns and Information please contact our EU
representative GPSR@taylorandfrancis.com
Taylor & Francis Verlag GmbH, Kaufingerstraße 24, 80331 München, Germany